MADE FOR LOVE

Kathleen Winsor, author of the fabulous new bestseller, *Wanderers Eastward, Wanderers West*, explores the kinds of love that three women—driven by desire—find with the men of their choice.

Dark, voluptuous *Jacintha* goes on a madcap excursion to a wicked resort—and finds the kind of man she has been looking for all her life.

Sleek, red-headed *Amoret* delights in her fling with a romantic and gay adventurer—until she awakes to the shock of a lifetime.

Blonde, feline *Dulcie* leads on a susceptible doctor who is afraid of women—with astonishing results.

Here, in this unusual book, Kathleen Winsor, a born story-teller, exposes the innermost secrets, dreams, torments, and raptures of women in love.

Other SIGNET Novels by Kathleen Winsor

☐ **FOREVER AMBER.** The world-famous bestseller about Amber St. Clare who rose from the streets of London by her wits, charm, and beauty to become a favorite of Charles II of England.
(#Y2717—$1.25)

☐ **WANDERERS EASTWARD, WANDERERS WEST.** Ranging across the continent, this is a shocking novel of bold men and women, from the rugged mining camps of Montana to the ruthless business of Wall Street, the people who shaped America. (#Y2822—$1.25)

☐ **AMERICA WITH LOVE.** A bold look at small-town America through the eyes of an earthy and innocent young heroine. (#T2703—75¢)

☐ **STAR MONEY.** What happens when a small town girl writes a fabulous bestseller and suddenly finds herself surrounded by money . . . and men.
(#Q2708—95¢)

THE NEW AMERICAN LIBRARY, INC.,
P.O. Box 999, Bergenfield, New Jersey 07621

Please send me the SIGNET BOOKS I have checked above. I am enclosing $_____(check or money order—no currency or C.O.D.'s). Please include the list price plus 15¢ a copy to cover mailing costs.

Name_____

Address_____

City_____State_____Zip Code_____
Allow at least 3 weeks for delivery

THE LOVERS

by

KATHLEEN WINSOR

Ⓢ
A SIGNET BOOK from
NEW AMERICAN LIBRARY
TIMES MIRROR

Copyright, 1952, by Kathleen Winsor

All rights reserved. This book, or parts thereof,
must not be reproduced in any form without permission
of the publisher. For information address
Appleton-Century-Crofts, 440 Park Avenue South,
New York, New York 10017.

*This is an authorized reprint of a hardcover edition
published by Appleton-Century.*

ELEVENTH PRINTING

All names, characters, and events in this book
are fictional, and any resemblance which may seem
to exist to real persons is purely coincidental.

The four lines from "The Lovers" are reprinted
by permission from *Skylight One* by Conrad Aiken,
Oxford University Press, Inc.
Copyright 1949 by Conrad Aiken.

 SIGNET TRADEMARK REG. U.S. PAT. OFF. AND FOREIGN COUNTRIES
REGISTERED TRADEMARK—MARCA REGISTRADA
HECHO EN CHICAGO, U.S.A.

SIGNET, SIGNET CLASSICS, SIGNETTE, MENTOR AND PLUME BOOKS
*are published by The New American Library, Inc.,
1301 Avenue of the Americas, New York, New York 10019*

PRINTED IN THE UNITED STATES OF AMERICA

Contents

ON ROARING MOUNTAIN BY LEMONADE LAKE
page 7

THE SILENT LAND
page 209

IN ANOTHER COUNTRY
page 283

"agony of the senses, but compounded
of soul's dream, heart's wish, blood's will, all confounded
with hate, despair, distrust, the fear of each
for what the other brings of alien speech."

—"The Lovers,"
Conrad Aiken

ONE

On Roaring Mountain

By Lemonade Lake

JACINTHA HAD CALLED out several times to ask the driver to slow down, but apparently he did not hear, for they had dashed along recklessly ever since leaving the railroad station. She was not at all sure when that had been, but it seemed many hours ago.

Between bouncing up and down in the open-sided Concord coach, hanging onto its railing and clutching her hat, she had not had a chance to enjoy the country as she would have liked. For they had been passing through the most magnificent, and astonishing, landscape she had ever seen:

For a time they had followed a broad smooth-flowing river, meandering through yellow-green flowerless meadows set against pine-covered hills and, behind them, great rising mountains. They darted into a pine forest with a floor of tender green grasses and purple-blue flowers, still and cool and murky, as if they had sunk far beneath the sea—then emerged suddenly upon a desolated area of gray and white rocks, little yellow flowers, warped pine trees, and a vast terrace descending in broad steps over which poured steaming water, yellow and orange and rusty red. While she was still craning her neck, looking backward at that empty cruel scene, she discovered that they were now hurtling through fields thick with sweet-smelling white and pink clover. Nearby was a steaming pool, subtly colored as an opal.

"Good heavens," murmured Jacintha, marvelling. The coach bounded against a rock and her head struck the roof again.

There were acres of white floating steam across little and big pools. They passed beneath a black bear in a tree, draped casually over flexed branches, and she gave a shriek of alarm as, leaning eagerly out, she looked directly up into his face and small blinking eyes. A great gnarled knotted cone of white crusty matter—like a sore on the earth, a wicked painful boil of some kind—suddenly began to grumble and hiss and water shot out of it thirty or more feet straight into the air. Jacintha turned to look back, hoping to see it happen again, but her driver was rushing furiously on. She had heard about these western coachmen and that it was all your life was worth to drive with one of them.

"I never should have come," she told herself, for the tenth time. "God only knows how *this* will turn out."

The coach slowed down and came to a hard jolting stop. Even that happened so suddenly that she was flung forward off the seat and had to grab the one in front to save herself from sprawling on the floor. She heard the driver's voice from outside and above where he sat on his perch.

"You!" he bellowed. *"Out here!"*

Jacintha, adjusting the small bonnet which perched on top of her head, leaned forth and looked up at him, questioningly. "I'm not sure that I want to get out here," she said, after a moment. "Where are we?"

The driver jerked his head. "Roaring Mountain, by Lemonade Lake."

Jacintha moved to the other side of the coach and looked in the direction of his nod: Lemonade Lake, a small body of water to be called a lake, was directly before her. It was a strange yellowish green with many dead tree stumps sticking out of it at crazy angles and its shore was bordered with stunted unhealthy pines.

Behind and beyond the lake was Roaring Mountain and, as Jacintha looked at it, her face sobered, lost its eagerly expectant look, grew serious and troubled and reflective. There was nothing reassuring in the mountain's appearance; it was clearly an evil place of destiny and foreboding.

"I never should have come," she murmured again, her hand to her throat, then touching her lips with her fingers like a child to reassure herself.

The mountain was whitish, smoking and steaming everywhere, bare and rocky, with little wispy pines growing at random along the sides and top. Knotted gnarled tree roots lay strewn about. It looked as if it had been desolated by an enraged giant. After a moment Jacintha shook her head and settled back in the seat.

"Drive me somewhere else," she said.

"Get out!" shouted the driver. "You're expected!"

"I am?" she asked, tilting her head to one side. "How can that be? This is as much a surprise to me as anyone else. Well—" Apparently she must get out. She was not accustomed to being ordered about by anyone, much less a coachman, and yet she knew that he would insist and that, eventually, she would be forced to obey. He did not offer to help and she climbed down as gracefully as she could manage, with her long skirts and many petticoats. Then she stood beside the coach and unfurled her parasol. He was grinning at her, but his face was so ugly the grin seemed an unpleasant leer.

Jacintha bore the impertinence of his expression for a moment, wondering whatever had happened that she should find herself exposed to such insults. Then haughtily she raised her chin.

"I'm sorry I have nothing to give you," she said.

He was still grinning, and she would have liked to bash his head with the parasol. "Never mind," he retorted. "This is one of the few things in life you get free." Then he gave a roar of laughter.

Jacintha pretended to ignore him. "My baggage," she said. "You forgot it."

"It'll be along. Don't worry. In fact, you may as well stop worrying about everything." He swept down his whip with a flourish, the horses leaped forward, and the bright red coach with bright yellow wheels, went flying away. Jacintha watched it disappear, which it did almost instantly, then turned once more to survey the mountain.

"Oh," she whispered, finally, and chills crept over her,

ending in a shudder. Sorrowfully she shook her head. "Ugly, ugly," she murmured.

Jacintha was, herself, extremely beautiful.

She was rather tall and her body was both slender and voluptuous. Her gown was new and very fashionable, though it had not been designed for travelling in this kind of country, an inconvenience resulting from the unexpected haste with which she had undertaken the journey. Bustles had lately gone out of style and this dress was made in the new mode, fitting tight over her breasts and waist and hips, down to her thighs, with the skirt gathered up low in the back and garnished with ribbons and loops and fringe. It was made of stiff electric-blue taffeta with plum-colored ruffles around the skirt, plum-colored fringe and much passementerie. There was a pleated flounce which kicked out flirtatiously above her pointed toes as she now moved slowly toward the mountain, still frowning.

Her bonnet had a small stuffed blue bird on it and was tied beneath her chin with a plum satin ribbon. She wore plum kid gloves and small diamond earrings.

Her face was patrician, smooth and white-skinned, with hair that was almost black and dressed in the new fashion—swept up off her neck, but for a few curling tendrils, with a mass of careless curls upon her forehead. She was a lady and consequently wore no cosmetics but a touch of powder. Her eyes were large and dark brown, their expression seemed both soft and brilliant; something in them implied that she simultaneously sought love and gave it, and because of this look she had, men had adored her all her life. There was a delicate expectancy in her face, a hint of receptiveness. Every move or gesture was soft, fluid, gentle. She was a woman either gifted or practiced in every subtle art of pleasing and evoking responsive masculine admiration.

"How strange," she was saying softly, "that I should be in such a place as this at my time of life." Jacintha was twenty-five.

Still, here she was, and she had always been of a curious nature, eager as a child for investigation, retaining still the original capacity for honest wonder. She had always been ready for life and given it a warm welcome. She was not, and never had been, a coward, and that was probably the characteristic she most admired in herself.

Consequently, picking her way carefully over the uneven squashy white earth, she walked around the edge of Lemonade Lake and took a few steps up the mountain. All day she had been noticing numbers of great black dismal-voiced birds which soared and flapped about and, when she asked the driver, had been told that they were ravens, common in these parts. She found to her surprise that it was difficult to breathe. The altitude here, he had said, was almost eight thousand feet and she paused a moment to catch her breath. Depressed still by the morbid sight of Roaring Mountain, she turned her back on it and faced across Lemonade Lake to where, far beyond the meadow, stood a respectable pine-covered mountain.

Finally, when she could breathe easily again, she slowly turned around, lifting her skirts and glancing upward.

There stood a man, nearly naked, directly above her and not more than three feet away. She screamed and stumbled backward, almost toppling, turned and started down the mountainside as fast as she could go, her heart pounding, her high heels twisting in the rutted earth. She had taken only a few steps when she tripped and started to fall, her parasol flying out of her hands as she spread them frantically to catch herself.

At that instant he moved in front of her and she fell into his arms and against his chest where she remained for a second or two, afraid to look up. She had not actually seen him but had gained only a horrified impression of a naked gigantic man, looming above her.

Now, all at once, she began a furious struggle to free herself. She had taken him to be an Indian in the brief glimpse she had of him and was sure that she was about to be scalped.

"Let me go!" she cried and, to her astonishment, he did so.

"Certainly," he said politely.

Amazed to hear him speak English, she stepped back and looked up at him. He was not an Indian, after all. At least, he was probably not an Indian, or perhaps only a half-breed. It was difficult to be sure since she had never seen an Indian. He was very tall, six feet three or four, and as he stood above her on the slope he seemed gigantic. His body, naked, for he wore only a loincloth, had the color and shine and apparent hardness of polished mahogany. His chest was broad and imposing, swelling out magnificently to his shoulders, narrowing sharply to his flat muscled belly and symmetrical widespread legs. There was an awesome majesty about him as he stood, entirely unselfconscious, permitting her to look at him—Jacintha was unaware that now she was gaping, astounded by this overpowering and gorgeous creature.

Then, all at once, she realized that she had been staring and was horrified to imagine what he must think of her. She had never stared at a man like that in her life before. On the other hand, she had never seen one who looked as he did. That was no excuse, though. Her behavior had been shameful and she could feel her face and throat burning with embarrassment.

"What a way for you to dress!" she chided.

At that, he threw back his head and burst into hearty laughter. Jacintha was hurt by the laugh, by her own feeling of having made herself ridiculous, the insults she had endured from the rude coachman, and her tiredness from the difficult trip. She would have found it restful to cry. And yet he was so entirely fascinating to her that even now, as he laughed, she watched him with her dark eyes wide and shining and intent, marvelling.

For it was not merely the splendor of his body which astonished her; he was handsome, as well, in a manner so entirely reckless and virile that he created the instant impression of being resistless, incontestable. His eyes were black, his hair black, his teeth straight and startlingly white. He wore an Indian headdress of white and red feathers, spreading out enormously, falling down his back to the ground. The impression he created was of great extravagance. He was so much of everything—strength, power, arrogance—that he seemed an essence of the very concept of masculinity.

He is *beautiful,* she thought. My God, but he's beautiful. Where did he come from and what's he doing here?

What, as far as that goes, am *I* doing here?

"Did you come by way of Wraith Falls?" he inquired now, a kind of challenging smile on his face.

"I don't know. Some repulsive creature in a Concord coach drove me. I expected to have my neck broken."

He laughed again. "That must have been Grant. He always drives like a demon." He shrugged. "After all, why shouldn't he?" Now he was smiling at her and Jacintha smiled back, though she had no idea what was supposed to be amusing. She smiled to please him, in response to him.

To her surprise she found that she was no longer frightened, not even tired, but was enjoying herself. This was certainly as exciting an adventure as any she had ever had and this naked man, whoever he was, stimulated her interest and admiration as no other man had ever done: there was both danger and fascination in him. She felt, as she stood and looked up at him, as though her nerves had been strung taut and set gently vibrating. She was tremendously exhilarated.

He, she told herself, is the man every woman hopes she'll be raped by.

Jacintha!

She was horrified that such a thought had entered her mind. Where could it possibly have come from? There was something sinister about him, in addition to his potent magnetism, to have stimulated such an idea less than two minutes after she had first seen him.

All about and above them the whispering steam drifted and swirled. There was a strong unpleasant sulphurous odor in the air, which now and then blew across her face and caused her nostrils to flare with delicate resentment. The sky was unnaturally blue and full of thick white clouds.

"It's strange," she said, when they had stood looking at each other for several moments and she had begun to feel dizzy. "I know we've never met before—and yet you look familiar to me."

"Of course," he said, matter-of-factly. "You've known me all your life."

"I have?"

"Certainly. Each one draws his personal private picture of the Devil."

"Oh."

The dizziness turned to a sick sinking in her stomach. She had known where she was ever since she got off the train this morning and that nasty grinning man approached and offered to drive her in the coach. But she had continued to hope that she was having a nightmare and would presently awaken in her own bed at home.

I'm dead, then. My life is over. I shall never— She gave a sudden horrified gasp. *I will never see my children again!* She had two children, a boy and a girl, the boy four years old and the girl two. They were the prettiest children, and the sweetest, imaginable. She had cherished and adored them more than anything in the world—except, perhaps, Douglas.

And I will never see Douglas again, either.

Her gloved hand was against her mouth, her eyes staring. She did not see him, now—or even remember that he still stood there, watching her. She closed her eyes and shook her head and a slow heavy despair seemed to plunge through her body, emptying it of hope, leaving only a desperate despondency which rose swiftly, flooded her being and overpoured its boundaries, sweeping her away helpless into a bitter sea of grief and nostalgia.

For those things to be over—those parts of my life which I took so entirely for granted, as it seems now—

With her eyes still closed she looked inward, and back: There she discovered herself, with the two children, in their nursery at night. She spent a good deal of time with them, more than most women of her position did, and the happiest hour of the day came just before they went to bed. It was more precious to her than all others, she sometimes thought, because it must last her until they woke in the morning. Her husband would usually join them for a few minutes, but he was not disposed to be present for very long at a time. Jacintha did not mind this, understanding that men were likely to be more interested in the fact of a child's existence than in prolonged association with it. Actually, she was pleased that his interest in them was so entirely masculine and perfunctory. Had it been otherwise she might have resented an encroachment upon her exclusive possession of their babyhood. It was her joy and privilege to have them press against her, to kiss and fondle them, to watch them at their play and enter their games with them. Flesh of my flesh—she understood the phrase with passionate grateful intensity.

And yet, sometimes, sitting on the floor in her dressing gown, the lamps burning a low soft light, with one of them snuggled at either side while she read or told them a story, a strange premonition would rise, as if a silent figure had entered the room and beckoned her: This will end. She would draw them closer, telling herself that she must not be foolish and superstitious, that the premonition was nothing but her own reluctance to realize that they must someday grow up and leave her.

There, with her children, she was one woman.

With Douglas, she seemed quite another. The tenderness and devotion carried across to her feeling for him —but it seemed of a different nature, entirely.

She had been surprised at the discovery of an eager sensual appetite within herself. It had been in hiding, apparently, for most of her life—through the conception and birth of her two children, in fact—and then one day it had appeared. Once that had happened her life altered completely, as if, after years of observing her surroundings through a blur, she had suddenly been given a new vision which changed the shapes and colors of her entire environment.

"You'll never know," she had told him, the first time it happened, "what it is you have done for me."

She lived for the moments of their privacy, recalling them, evoking them; her memories were extraordinarily vivid. There seemed no possible satiation and she was always reluctant to leave him and go about her ordinary life. He engrossed her so completely that she had no moment of absolute freedom from him, nor did she want it. She clung to his image with a kind of desperation, as if she were not even yet entirely convinced of her good fortune. If their eyes met across a drawing room filled with polite people, Jacintha sensed an imminent collapse of the world, so powerful and tremendous their infatuation seemed.

Now—these things were gone.

She did not cry as she stood there on Roaring Mountain, her head bowed, her eyes closed. There were no tears, apparently, which had been made available for your own death. Tears belonged to hope; they could fall at pain or disappointment, releasing tensions, and thereby altering the specific gravity of your emotions. But nothing like that was possible now.

The Devil had stood watching her silently and, as she raised her head and looked at him once more, he was regarding her soberly, almost sympathetically.

"All newcomers feel as you do," he told her quietly. "There is a terrible moment when they realize that life is over. Whatever was sweet, becomes sweeter, of course."

Jacintha slowly shook her head. "I'll miss my children most of all."

"Perhaps I can console you a little. There's a saying you may have heard that there can't be any hell because in two weeks everyone would get used to it. Well— In a couple of weeks, or less, you'll be so taken up with what's going on here that you will scarcely remember your former life. All the people you knew then will seem vague and unreal, as if you had only imagined them."

Jacintha listened, but her expression was dubious. "Really?" she asked at last.

He smiled. "Really."

She looked around. All about them the glaring white mountain steamed and whispered. Here and there were smears of bright yellow sulphur. Shallow luke-warm streams trickled over white and greenish beds. Farther up the mountainside were many knoblike terraces, one above another, with reddish-brown rocks covering each knob; dead trees stuck up amid the red-brown ruin.

"I can't imagine anything at all going on here," she said dismally. "It's much too dreary and there isn't another soul in sight."

"This is only part of it, after all. You've come to a place which is infinite. In spite of the size, people will turn up, I assure you. Coincidence is the law—even here."

Jacintha was peculiarly aware that what he had predicted was, in a sense, beginning to happen already. The terrible despondent melancholy had begun to lessen and she was actually taking an almost lively interest in her surroundings and in this splendid indomitable man who confronted her.

Her interest in him was sufficiently acute that she found herself growing angry with him for standing there naked and beautiful, so constant a temptation that she longed to cover her eyes with her hands and demand that he put on something decent before she would trust herself to look at him again.

"What*ever* makes you go around like that?" she demanded suddenly, her voice irritable and anxious.

He smiled, understanding, apparently, why she asked. "It's the only sensible getup for this part of the country. After all, should I wear horns and a tail and cloven hoofs just because some nervous old maid thought that would do me for a costume?"

Jacintha burst into a sudden shocked little laugh, since that was a new slant on the subject to her.

"Why!" she cried. "You have a sense of humor!"

"That's one of my vices." He sat down then, spreading his legs wide apart and resting his elbows on his knees. He gestured for her to sit beside him, but Jacintha declined.

"No, thanks. I'm afraid I'd soil my gown."

He shrugged. "I've never yet seen a tourist who was suitably dressed. You all wear the goddamnedest rigs." His eyes were going over her slowly, amused, it seemed, by her beautiful and fashionable gown.

"How can we be suitably dressed when we come here at such short notice—and have no idea what we'll find when we arrive?" She was glancing around once more. "In fact, this looks like a caricature of what I expected Hell to be. This mountain does have a malevolent look to it, and certainly Lemonade Lake could be a pool of poison —but all around is the most innocent and delightful mountain scenery. It really isn't so very terrible, you know," she added, turning back once more as if to inform him of something he might not have realized.

He was watching her, his face speculative, his eyes roving over her body, so that she wondered if it was one of his attributes to see through a woman's clothing. Very likely it was. A proper Devil should be equipped with all the traits a man would like to have.

"No," he agreed after a moment. "But were you damned for anything very terrible?"

Jacintha opened her eyes wide. "Don't *you* know why I'm here? Aren't you the one who decides which of us is damned and which is saved?"

He laughed. "Of course not. It is your contemporaries who determine your fate. And, may I add, they keep me well supplied with companions of all kinds—some of them much too dull and respectable for my tastes, but apparently guilty in the eyes of their friends."

"Oh," murmured Jacintha, "I don't like this. I'd rather—"

"You'd rather I were the culprit?"

"Yes. Yes, I think I would. That's what I was always taught, at least."

"You will find, my dear young lady, that you were taught a great deal of rubbish. What is your name, by the way?"

"Jacintha. Jacintha Frost."

"Pretty—and very odd, too, isn't it? All you Victorians have exotic names."

"I have always liked it," said Jacintha proudly.

"I'm sure you do. Tell me how you happen to be here. I'm curious about you. You don't look a sinner to me at all."

"I am, though. I sinned grievously." As she said those words she heard her voice take on a solemn churchgoing tone. Then, with conscious effort, she reverted to her natural voice, which was soft and light and caressive, one of her greatest charms and a quality Douglas had never ceased praising. She drew a deep breath. "I am here because of a crime of passion—two, in fact: my passion for another man, and my husband's when he discovered me."

"Tsk, tsk." He shook his head. "Catch you in flagrante?" At that, he grinned maliciously, and Jacintha could see that he had a very clear picture in mind.

"Of course not!" she said sharply, rebuking him. "He found a letter Douglas had written me. I was a silly fool to have kept it—and yet, I thought he was an honorable man. I had no idea he would sneak through my possessions."

He laughed again. "My God, but you sound naïve! And what happened, then?"

"He shot me." Suddenly she stopped, frowning a little, with puzzlement rather than anger. She looked at him. "Did you hear what I said just then?"

He glanced up, squinting against the sun, smiling.

"Yes," he drawled. "I heard you. You said that he shot you." From somewhere or other he had taken a small pocketknife and now, picking up a piece of wood, he began to whittle at it, rapidly peeling and shaping it, turning it this way and that to study his handiwork and, with his leftover attention, glancing now and then at Jacintha. "Isn't that what you said?"

"Yes," she replied softly. "I did. But how is it possible?"

"He must have done *some*thing drastic—since here you are."

Jacintha looked at what he was whittling and was alarmed to see a cross, to which he was now adding a figure. He worked with such carelessness and precision that it was clear he was a practiced and extremely talented craftsman. She wanted to tell him to stop, that he was being blasphemous, but she did not dare. Instead, she looked down to where her fingers twisted the silk cords on her handbag.

"But the way I said it—so casually—as if it were nothing at all. As if I had forgotten already what it was like to have him come into the room and stand there staring at me without a word until my flesh began to crawl and I knew he had somehow found out— And then!—" She stopped, gave a low moan, and covered her face with her gloved hands. She stood shivering, overcome with reminiscent terror as slowly, once more, she turned and saw the look on her husband's face:

She felt as if she were in the midst of a nightmare, where every effort to save herself, to scream or run or force herself to waken, proved impossible. She seemed weighted by her guilt. She knew that her expression had betrayed her already and that she would, if he desired, betray herself even further. An inexorable force rushed her toward disaster.

"Good evening," he said.

Jacintha tried to answer, but found her lips paralyzed. She nodded, though even that required tremendous effort and was scarcely perceptible.

He was the distance of the room from her. Between them lay their rich and elegant bedroom, furnished in the fashionable *Louis Quatorze* style, with carved and gilded ceiling, walls of tufted red brocade, handsome sweeping velvet draperies, flowers and books and crystal lamps.

He did not come any nearer, but he continued to stare at her.

Jacintha stared back, scarcely able to see him, for her terror was so great that her vision had blurred, as though she crept about in deep water. He's going to kill me, she was thinking. I will never see Douglas or the children again. Nothing I can say or do will stop him. He is a man bent on murder. She had a swift vision of her two children in their charming Kate Greenaway clothes, running to greet her.

They continued facing each other, motionless, silent.

At last, he slowly lifted his hand and she watched while it moved toward the inner breast pocket of his coat. Jacintha gasped and, the next moment, heard herself scream. He drew forth an envelope, and now he was smiling. The smile horrified her more than the knowledge that he would kill her. How could she have imagined that this man with whom she had lived for five years, who had been, at least, a devoted, if not a tender husband, to whom she had borne two children, could be capable of such evil as his smile conveyed?

In another moment she realized that this smile had always been his potentiality, that, in a sense, he had been smiling at her in this way during all the years of their marriage and that she had hated him all along for knowing him capable of such cruelty. She also realized that she had fallen in love with Douglas partly, at least, because she hated her husband.

"Why did you scream?" he asked her, and he continued to smile. He was enjoying this moment, her terror and guilt, his power, far more than he had ever enjoyed an affectionate moment between them. "You thought, perhaps, that I was reaching for a gun and that I would shoot you. No— Not just now, at least. This, I believe, is an envelope you will recognize."

She felt an uncanny terror—produced, not by his revelation of the letter, but by her own understanding that it was his intention to torment her—to let her beg and plead for her life, while he wallowed in her degradation. Then, once she began to believe that he would let her live, he would kill her.

"I know you too well, Martin," she said slowly, "not to know exactly what thoughts and intentions your face is reflecting." Her chin was up now and she was panting, but with excitement and pride, not fear or remorse. She faced him squarely, her breasts raised high, her arms falling to her sides, and her voice spoke out in a strong clear ringing tone: "Of course I recognize the envelope! There were many others—I kept only that one, because I thought it the most beautiful!" The effect was instantaneous. His sense of power crumpled and he stood staring back at her with the sickly look of a caught criminal. "I do love Douglas—and I do not love you. If you don't kill me, I shall continue to see him, and nothing you can do will stop me. I knew a moment ago when I saw that smile that I haven't loved you for years—and that I actually never loved you at all—"

She had an exultant moment of triumph, a conviction that she had torn the power from him and forced him to act without any of the cruel pleasures he had expected to derive from her murder. She continued to face him proudly, as his hand reached once more to his breast pocket, brought forth the pistol and levelled it at her—

"And now I am here," she concluded, telling her story's ending to the Devil.

He gave a sigh, though she could not tell if it came from boredom or sympathy. Then he flipped the cross aside and stood up. Shutting one eye he took aim with his knife and shot it into a tree trunk several yards distant, where it stuck and quivered.

"It's a common enough story," he said. "You'd be surprised how many adulteresses turn up here." He smiled at her. "I like that word: adulteress. Quaint, isn't it?"

Jacintha haughtily raised her chin. "You may call it quaint. It cost *me* my life."

"And yet you must have known it would. After all, there are few things more aggravating to a husband than to have his wife in love with another man. And you did keep the letter. You've just told me how well you knew him, how you could read his thoughts from his expressions. If you knew him that well, then you knew that he would find it someday and, when he did, would kill you. I think you wanted to die."

"*What?*" Jacintha took a step or two backward and stared at him with an expression of outraged horror.

"How dare you say such a thing! How dare you accuse me of—"

"Now, now," he said softly. "It was not an accusation. Not unless you think so. Anyway, there's very little difference as to whether you are dead because you wished to be or because you could not help yourself. And, of course, I played my own part in your untimely demise, as you earthlings call it."

"You? You played a part? I beg your pardon. What part could you possibly have played?"

"Don't you know that when a woman commits adultery, it is the Devil who puts his penis into her—and that it emerges from her husband's head as two horns?"

Jacintha gasped, and felt her face turn scorching hot. She flared out her fan and began to flutter it nervously. She had never heard such shocking talk. It was disgraceful. She did not know what to do, where to look, what to reply. She should have pretended that she did not even know what he meant, but it was too late for that now.

He had watched her a moment. Now he threw back his head, planted his fists on his naked hips, and rocked and roared with laughter. "Oh!" he groaned. "Oh, my God!"

Jacintha stared, as if she could make him ashamed of himself, but, when he paid no attention to her stare, only continued his ribald laughter, she turned and began carefully making her way back down the slope of Roaring Mountain. She returned to the edge of Lemonade Lake and stood, her folded fan pressed thoughtfully against her chin, gazing into its opaque surface, trying to gather her wits and thoughts.

Too much had happened to her during the past few hours. She felt dizzy and bewildered, unsure of herself for the first time, helpless and lost.

But the worst thing of all was this—Devil—for she found it almost impossible to think of him as what he was and that, she knew, must be the result of some fatal trick he had. She must guard herself against him, as she had always been warned to do. She must not permit him to gain a victory over her. She must be more alert than ever, for he undoubtedly had formidable and mysterious magic at his command.

Even now, she could feel it working.

At this very moment, she longed to turn and look at

him. Had she merely wished to glance, to see where he was or what he was doing, she would have followed her inclination. But this feeling was neither so simple nor so normal. In a matter of seconds it had grown to be outrageous, persistent, tormenting and tantalizing her, until she had a sudden horrified glimpse into the sensations of gluttony. She felt herself to have been overwhelmed by some merciless hypnotic spell.

She was terrified, and violently excited.

She whirled suddenly and confronted him, only a few feet away, approaching her.

To her infinite dismay, she found the sight of him reassuring, quelling her anxiety. It was as if she had already become dependent upon him and had been convinced that he had deserted her and would not be there when she turned to find him. She smiled a little, timidly, with relief.

The rhythm of his body, walking slowly toward her, gave her a weird sensation of her veins being filled with quicksilver.

He was triumphantly male, elemental and spectacular beyond any dream she had ever had. She gazed at him now with the candid unashamed awe of a child. But only for a moment. Then she was embarrassed, both because of his nakedness and her own avid pleasure in his beauty. She began to twirl her ruffled parasol as fast as she could and to tap the pointed toe of her right shoe at a furious rate.

He was standing beside her again.

She waited, breathing faster, feeling both foolish and helpless, trying to think of something to say. She knew that he was teasing her, but found herself at an absolute loss as to how she should behave with him.

Then, with sudden recklessness, she threw back her head and looked up into his face, allowing him the full vision of her beauty: Her pink soft mouth was apart, so that the even edges of her teeth showed. Her head tilted so far back that her eyes were partly closed. Her skin, in the strong sunlight, was almost luminous. There was a lyric warm opulent quality to her face and manner which had been greatly disturbing to every man she had known. Now, still gazing up at him from between her black lashes, she let her nostrils flare slightly—Douglas had told her more than once that the miracle of a nice woman was where she learned the tricks she did.

She had intended, as she turned her face upward for him, that he should concentrate upon her beauty and thereby lose himself. Instead, she found that her own energy and interest drew slowly into focus and centered upon his mouth, which was full and sensual, yet sensitive as a work of the finest artist. She began to wonder how his mouth would feel upon her own and whether he would be as ruthless and as violent in love as everything about him seemed to indicate.

Moments passed. Gradually, his face blurred until she could see nothing but his mouth, slightly parted, slightly smiling. Her eyes felt heavy and weighted and her lids began to fall, and, though she seemed to struggle for a long while to keep them open, at last she gave up and they closed.

Very very slowly, as if she moved in a dream or under water, she felt herself begin to sway forward. It did not happen by intent. Her own volition was paralyzed. There seemed some compelling imperious force at work, subjecting her to a massive and alien will. She seemed to sway endlessly forward through space and then, after a long while, her body touched his, though he stood, in reality, only a few inches from her. She felt one arm go about her waist to hold her steady, and she waited for whatever was going to happen—relieved of all personal responsibility, since his power was incontestable. Passively, dreamily, as though she drifted on a vast surface of water, she waited.

Then, in an instant, she realized what had happened.

She had been tempted!

She shoved at him and he let her go. He was grinning again, she saw, watching her and grinning.

"Oh!" she cried. "For a moment I felt faint! I—I don't know what happened!"

She stared at him challengingly. He nodded, still watching her with a look of amusement disturbingly tinged with contempt.

"Of course you never fall in love," she said, and heard herself with surprise.

He laughed, a short laugh of mockery and disdain. "Of course not. I hope you're willing to permit me a few advantages in my dubious position. Why? What difference does it make to you?"

She had been scratching the earth with her toe, making a small semicircle. At his last question she glanced up in alarm. "Why, none!" she declared indignantly. "None at all, of course. I'd never heard about you ever being in love with anyone. I was curious, that's all." Her explanation sounded absurd. She was furious at herself.

What kind of woman can I be? I haven't been here an hour, when I have begun to wonder what it would be like if the Devil made love to me. Wonder? I was hoping he would take advantage of me—as one would most certainly expect him to do in this lonely place.

I *am* a sinner.

I belong here.

I've come to the right place.

And Douglas, at this very moment, is grieving and heartbroken. She had hung her head slightly, as if bowing beneath her self-castigation and now, as she shook her head from side to side, her eyes shifted unexpectedly and she glanced at him.

"You weren't sure I had one?" she heard him drawl.

The glance had been so swift, so covert—how had he even seen it? Angrily she looked up at him. "I don't know what you're talking about! I haven't been dead twenty-four hours and you're making fun of me! You're trying to put filthy notions into my mind already! I find you disgusting! You're—"

As she talked, her eyes flashing and her face lively and intense, he watched her, still smiling, wearing that same look of sardonic audacity. He made her feel as though she were an amusing inconsequential child, ornamental but entirely unimpressive. How strange and wicked it was for a man to lack respect toward women. It made her feel helpless, belittled and humiliated.

"You Victorians," he said, shaking his head. "Sometimes I think I'll be glad when there's a new age and a different kind of woman begins to show up around here. Of course," he added, "you are, at least, womanly women —in the sense of being totally without logic or any genuine human (that is to say, masculine) attributes."

"Oh!" cried Jacintha. "How dare you!" Before she realized what she was doing, she raised one fist and began pounding at his chest. "I won't permit you to talk to me like that!"

He caught hold of her wrist, and lightly twisted her arm to one side. She winced and gave a little cry of pain and horrified surprise. He had not even tried *not* to hurt her. And, as she looked up at him, shocked to realize that this was no gentleman into whose hands she had fallen finally, tears filled her eyes and ran down her cheeks. He turned away, flattened his lips against his teeth and gave a shrill piercing whistle.

Jacintha was sobbing softly, a mournful little sound that had instantly turned either Douglas or her husband to anxious apology.

"Keep quiet!" he said sharply. "What did you expect? That I would turn out to be like all the men you've known—considerate and tolerant of the whimsies of a creature clever enough to have herself treated like a goddess? You can consider that part of your life over along with the rest of it. Things go the way I like them here—I consider no one's wishes or preferences but my own."

"Well!"

At that moment she heard a sound almost like thunder and, while she stood listening, a great shining black horse came galloping toward them. He was not saddled, but only bridled. He came at a furious rate and Jacintha watched him with wonder and awe, for she had never seen so beautiful an animal. He slowed his pace abruptly as he approached and stopped beside them, his gleaming black sides heaving and quivering.

He jerked his head. "Climb on."

She gave him a look of alarm. What kind of place might he take her to? She was afraid of him now.

"I will not!" she cried, then instantly covered her mouth with her gloved hand and stared up at him with her eyes big and apprehensive.

Almost before she knew what was happening he had placed his big square-fingered hands about her narrow waist and hoisted her sideways onto the stallion's back. With a swift leap he was behind her, his arm passed about her body, drawing her close against him, and the horse was off at a gallop.

Jacintha hung onto her hat with one hand and her parasol and beaded bag and fan with the other. The horse went rushing along, moving with a swift tread which was strangely light for so great an animal. Jacintha, during the first few moments, was wholly occupied with this new sensation of height and bewildering speed, as though she had been lifted off the earth by some unseen force and was now being blown through space against her will. Suddenly she felt her hat snatched from under her clutching hand and looked frantically around to see it go sailing away. She gave a cry of protest as her bag and parasol and fan were wrenched from her other hand and flung into the distance.

"Stop!" she cried. "My hat! My—"

"Stop worrying about your damned trinkets, and enjoy the ride. Look around you. This is magnificent country. I designed it myself." He smiled. "Stop staring at me—and look at it."

Jacintha obeyed. He was the first man she had known who undoubtedly meant what he said.

The ride was exhilarating. The movement of the fleet swift flowing animal beneath them. The feeling of his body against her back, holding her against him, his spread hand upon her belly, warming and vitalizing.

Now that she knew this was his handiwork, she looked about her with even greater interest than on the ride from the railroad station. He pointed out a distant herd of grazing buffalo and two or three elk feeding chest-deep in succulent grasses. They sped through fields of pink and purple and blue flowers. There were numerous showy magpies, whose feathers appeared to be comically loose and floppy.

But amid all this natural innocent beauty rose weird and awful sights. Whichever way she looked, nature seemed out of kilter. That was his idea, no doubt, of a joke. They passed hot waterfalls, pouring over orange rock. The stallion plunged into a meadow and they found themselves splashing and floundering through hot shallow streams which went rushing by in all directions, enveloping them in sulphur-laden clouds. There were bubbling brilliant blue pools, surrounded by haloes of blue steam. There were dead trees, black at the top, white at the bottom—they looked like the petrified legs of giant horses from which the bodies had decayed and fallen away. There was a yellow terrace overrun with hot hissing water.

All at once, feeling suddenly gay and reckless, Jacintha turned her head and looked up at him. "It does like like hell!" she cried joyously, and they both burst into laughter. She started to turn back again but found herself caught, gazing at his mouth once more, her senses swirling and bemused by the feeling of his body, the pressure of his hand, the glittering light of his black eyes.

"Wake up!" she heard him say, a soft laugh behind the words. "We're here!"

She started, almost as if she actually had fallen asleep, and looked bewilderedly about. "Where? Where are we?"

"This is where I live."

The next moment he had alighted and was beneath her, holding forth his arms. She slid into them. He set her quickly onto the ground and turned to begin giving orders to the smartly uniformed lackeys who had appeared with almost magical promptness.

While he was occupied with them, Jacintha looked about.

They were at the entrance of what appeared to be an enormous mountain lodge or hotel—so tremendous that it seemingly might house whoever had been sent here from the beginning of sin to the present.

The building was made of dark rough weather-stained logs. It had great spreading porches and innumerable shining windows. Boxes filled with bright flowers stood along the porch walls, hung from overhead, and were attached beneath every window. Elk and deer horns projected high above the doors and at intervals along the veranda. Totem poles, blue and red and yellow, stood on either side of the doorway. The building was a very fine one, handsome to look at, well planned and executed. Its only peculiarity, so far as she could see, was that it was not yet finished. Various wings jutted out within her vision, and each was incomplete, a framework upon which workmen still labored.

Very likely he never would finish it, since new tenants were always turning up.

Having given several instructions, he turned, touched her elbow with one hand, and they walked into the lodge. More lackeys followed them, and Jacintha was disgusted by the extreme degree of their humbleness, their cringing snivelling desire to please the master. It seemed to annoy him, too, for he spoke to them rudely and, occasionally, gave one a kick that sent him sprawling.

The lobby was of such immensity that she could not see from one end to the other. It, too, was finished with crudely sawn logs. The ceiling must have been eighty feet high, with tiers of balconies running around all sides. Kerosene lamps dangled from varying heights. Shaggy black and brown bearhides were hung on the walls and flung across balcony railings. She could see one fireplace, big enough to burn a twenty-foot log, and there must have been several others to warm a hall of such stupendous magnitude.

Furthermore, it was crowded.

Jacintha gazed about in wondering awe. If she had found him impressive before, standing alone on Roaring Mountain, to see him now in his own palace—which must be what this place was—surrounded by men and women who were his subjects in every sense, made him soar suddenly, in her estimation, to a glorious invincibility.

How little I am, she thought, with almost thankful humbleness. And how great he is.

The next moment she was angry with herself for such prideless servility and gave herself warning to be on guard against his despotism, for his vigor threatened to lay waste anything of lesser intensity.

She glanced about and saw that the men and women who were strolling up and down, standing in groups of two or three or several, talking, sitting in chairs along the walls or examining articles apparently for sale in the small shops, were all dressed in clothes of the latest fashion. Furthermore, their clothes were extraordinarily beautiful and looked very expensive. She might have been at the Oriental Hotel in Manhattan Beach. Except, of course, that there were a number of Indians mingled among them, half-naked like him, painted with vermilion and yellow pigment and blue earth, or swathed in blankets. Some of the squaws, she saw to her horror, had had their noses cut off. She must remember to find out why.

To the right, as they entered the hall, was a very long desk with a straggling line of men and women, apparently waiting for their accommodations to be assigned. Bellboys ran frantically up and down, laden with baggage, and what appeared to be at least an acre of trunks and suitcases stood in the center of the hall.

From time to time, as she waited—now entirely ignored by him, for he was engaged in a dozen conversations at once—she discovered herself being stared at by various men. Each time she gave them a brief cold look and haughtily turned her head. They seemed unusually brazen, and she wondered if that was the kind of men the place attracted.

She was pleased to be standing at his side even if he was no longer paying attention to her. For his entrance had been like a signal to the others, who came swarming—the women flirting, the men asking favors or telling him jokes first and then asking favors. Sometimes he laughed. Other times he scowled and gestured the supplicant away. He looked, she could not help noticing, more magnificent than ever by contrast with the other men.

And yet, both men and women, they seemed an extraordinarily attractive group: the human race was obviously much more frail than she had realized. It was a young-looking crowd, too. Few were beyond middle age and many were as young or even younger than she. Who said the good die young?

At last, when she had waited a long while and he gave no evidence of any longer even remembering her presence, but talked above and around her to people on all sides, she grew impatient and angry. Jacintha did not recall that anyone had ever so flagrantly ignored her before. She touched his arm, timidly, quickly withdrawing her fingers. He did not respond and gave no indication he had even felt it.

She stepped up closer, put her hand on his forearm and lifted her voice to make it pierce the babble. "Please!"

He turned his head and glanced down, seemed puzzled for an instant, and then laughed. "Oh." He smiled. "I had forgotten about you." He snapped his fingers. "Boy!" A boy appeared instantly, scooting in among those who thronged about him, crouching slightly as if to dodge a blow. "Take this lady's baggage to Room 69,000. Quick!"

He did not speak to her or look at her again but, having given the order, turned instantly away and began to discuss buffalo hunting with two painted naked braves.

Jacintha gave him a glance of hurt dismay, but the bellboy was already scuffling over to the baggage and she ran after him. He began searching for hers and seemed almost hysterical as he went crawling among the hundreds or thousands of suitcases like a dog on a rabbit's scent. Jacintha strolled about to help him, and it was she who found them.

"Here!" she called. "Here they are!"

He gave her a quick grateful sheepish grin, came leaping and crawling, hastily shouldered the trunk, tucked one bag under his arm and picked up the other two. Then away he went. Jacintha was forced almost to run to keep up with him. They set off down a broad hallway. She followed as quickly as she could, but he was fast and cunning and sometimes he almost lost her.

Once he got two hundred feet or more away and she had to shout at him to wait. When she had almost caught up he went shuffling on again. Finally she came panting up behind him.

"Why are you in such a hurry?"

"I must get back. He may want me again."

"What if he does? What can he do to you? You're *here* now."

He gave her a roundabout glance and shuttled on. She took several more running steps. "You don't know him," he said, but refused to elaborate, though she coaxed him to tell her more.

It was incredible, how fast he went. He must have been doing this for years. A terrible thought entered her mind.

"How long have you been here?" she asked him. It was not, of course, the length of his stay which interested her but the possibile length of her own, to which she thought his answer might give a clue.

He kept scuttling ahead of her, the trunk across his shoulders and bent neck and head, the suitcases dangling from either arm. He seemed not to have heard.

"Please!" cried Jacintha, for now she was frightened. They kept rushing along those vast hallways, and had taken so many turns that she would never be able to find her way back. She ran up beside him, wringing her kid-gloved hands together, pleading. "I'm new here, as you must know! Tell me something! Answer my questions!"

He glanced at her, and even as he glanced his own momentum carried him ahead once more. "Why must you bother me? Why can't you learn for yourself? Can't you see how busy I am?"

"You're not busy!" she cried in anger and exasperation. "Aren't you ashamed of yourself! Rushing about as if you have no self-respect at all—terrified of that rascal out there!"

"Thank God! Here we are!"

He had stopped so suddenly that Jacintha almost ran on by him, but brought herself up sharply before a closed door with brass numerals on it reading 69,000.

In another moment the door was open, he grovellingly invited her to enter, and she sailed into her new quarters and began to look them over appraisingly—while he unloaded her baggage, set a match to the wood in the fireplace, asked if there was anything else he could do and, when she shook her head, was out the door.

She ran after him, calling, "Wait! I want to give you something!"

"Nothing, madame, thank you. The management won't permit it." He bowed low. He was already several yards away.

Jacintha surveyed him with contempt. "You disgust me. God knows what *your* sin must have been."

He bowed once more and, as he left, finally gave her a bit of information. "We were the cowards and hypocrites." He jerked his head in what she supposed was the general direction where the Devil might be expected at this moment. "He hates us worse than anything." With that, he was off again.

Jacintha watched a moment as he went bowling along the hallway. He was so entirely repulsive, everything about him suggested that he had carried with him here more his emotional than his physical characteristics.

At least, she reflected, as she turned and slowly closed the door—at least, I am not here for either of those sins. She felt somewhat pleased, almost smug, that her own vice had been, instead, the result of daring and recklessness.

I am here because—once I fell in love with Douglas—I was honest enough to act, rather than cowardly or hypocritical enough to retreat. Douglas was everything in the world to me— He was my— She paused, uncertainly, then stopped and closed her eyes and covered her face with her hands, trying to remember what Douglas had looked like. She shut her eyes hard, trying intensely and with mounting anxiety to recall his image.

Why can't I remember?

She flung out her arms in a sudden frantic despairing gesture and stared around the room, seeing nothing.

What has happened? I could always see him as clearly as if he were in the room—

"In a couple of weeks, or less, you'll be so taken up with what's going on here that you will scarcely remember your former life. All the people you knew then will seem vague and unreal, as if you had only imagined them."

Was that happening to her so soon? Was she forgetting Douglas, for whom she had died? The thought was incredible, sickening, terrifying. She must put her mind on other things—her quarters here, which she had not yet investigated.

The room was a large one, luxurious and impressive. As she stood near the door she faced two ceiling-high windows hung with fresh gold-stamped muslin curtains and extravagantly looped draperies of crimson damask. Between the windows stood a small tulipwood desk, elegantly carved and inlaid with mother-of-pearl.

The walls were covered with crimson flock paper, the texture of cut velvet. The Brussels carpet, reaching from wall to wall, had a flamboyant blue and red floral pattern. The white marble mantelpiece to her right was surmounted by a great gold-framed mirror and opposite that stood the bed with its carved ebony headboard six feet tall and its spread of pale-blue velvet edged with heavy black fringe.

There were wax flowers under a glass dome on a marble-topped table. There were thickly upholstered blue velvet chairs with lavish swags and cascades of fringe. There were many lamps edged with sparkling crystal beads.

The room, no doubt, was designed and furnished in

the most perfect rococo taste. She would have been pleased to have such a room in her own home and, in fact, had had several which were not very different. Its only fault was that, like a hotel room, it was entirely without the personal touches or warmth of an inhabitant.

Exploring further, she found large closets and an adjoining private bathroom with a tub almost big enough to swim in.

I like this, she thought. I could be very happy here. If it were any place but here, she added ruefully.

How easy it was to forget, momentarily at least, where she was and what had happened to her. How easy—and how treacherous.

Well, at least, if she was to be punished—though she was beginning to think that was a superstition believed in by fools—still, if she was to be punished, it evidently would not consist in the deprivation of any material comforts. These surroundings were as rich and handsome as her own had been and she even had with her many of her own clothes. Things could be very much worse.

Jacintha strolled to the window.

The sky was still bright blue and the clouds foaming white, as if they had been stirred up by a swizzle stick. Before her window in a great sweep lay a desolate scene of bare earth from which nothing stood erect but dead trees and yellow goldenrod. To one side was a boiling hot lake and in its center spouted a geyser, spraying and splashing from an apparent excess of energy. Steam coming from it whirled like a dancer, then drifted in slow desultory fashion, obscuring and revealing the landscape, behaving, it seemed, like a coquettish woman with a scarf or veil. Far in the distance, halfway up a pine-covered mountain, steam shot upward in a great cloud so that it appeared the mountain had blown open and was spending itself in ecstasy, or in anger.

Here, when she looked at his handiwork, it was not so easy to forget where she was.

She turned abruptly. I'll unpack. That will take my mind off thinking for awhile.

Her dress was dusty and wrinkled from the long trip and she got out of it, a feat which was not very easy to accomplish alone. When, at last, she had succeeded, she slipped on a dressing gown of sheer white nainsook with pink satin ribbons laced through it, a four-foot ruffle train that dragged about the room behind her, and pink roses tacked here and there upon the skirt. In this becoming costume she stepped before the tall mirror over the dressing table and moved slowly through a personal ballet which had produced, in private, some of her most effective public gestures.

She smiled and her face was suddenly radiant. She lifted her chin and gazed at herself from half-closed eyes. She turned and cast a quick winsome glance across her shoulder. She swept forward, gracious, serene, and proud. Her body seemed to melt with delicate seductiveness from one attitude to the next.

But though, in her previous life, she had been beautiful for herself as much as for anyone—even Douglas—now, she was interested only in what his response to her beauty would be. What expression, what look or tone or mannerism would please him most? She must try to remember when it was he had looked at her with the greatest interest, exactly how she had been standing and what she had been doing at that moment. And, next time she saw him, she must notice very carefully what pleased him and what he was indifferent to.

There, as those thoughts were in her mind, she paused, leaned forward, and looked at herself long and carefully.

What has he done to you? she demanded.

You were so scornful of that lackey. What about your own pride? He will despise you, as he despises him, if he ever sees you so eager for his approval.

She hung her head and turned away.

Something must be terribly terribly wrong with me. I don't even know him—and everything that I know about him is bad. He's the wickedest man who ever lived. So wicked that even God could not forgive him. And *I* stand here wondering how I can please him most!

She turned, went swiftly to her trunk and began to take things out of it, laying her gowns on chairs and across the bed, tossing her shoes into a heap on the floor, piling her fans and pincushions on a table top. She was so helpless, so untrained to do anything for herself, even to unpack a trunk and put her clothing away. The more things she unpacked, the more disordered and littered and confused the room got, the greater was her own distraction and anxiety. I'll never get this done! she told herself. Never?

Because I do, actually, have forever.

And suddenly, for the first time, she felt a dreadful empty loneliness and despair. Once these things are put away—what is there for me to do? She began to turn, glancing around the room. There were no books, and none had been included in her luggage. There was no needlework. There was no harp. There were no paints or sketchbooks. She could not talk to the cook or visit her friends or have a new gown fitted or drive in Central Park or play with the children or steal out to meet Douglas or plan her next dinner party or accompany her husband to the theater or opera. She could not do anything—but wait, and hope that he would send for her.

Frantically, her face drained white, her dark eyes big with terror, she began to dart about the room, lifting covers, shoving chairs aside, peering into corners, bending down to look under the bed. She had no idea what she was looking for, but her search became increasingly wild and excited.

There can't be nothing for me to do!

There *must* be something!

She was on her knees, surrounded by all the disarray of her garments and belongings, staring straight ahead with a look of pain and despair, when there was a light surprising rap at the door.

She rose instantly, afraid that she would be caught in that hysterical undignified attitude.

"Come in!" she called.

After a brief silence, the knob turned slowly, the door was pushed gently open, and there stood smiling at her a very beautiful young woman. "May I come in?" she asked, in a tone that was at once sweet, clear, compelling.

"Yes. Please do." Tremendously relieved at the mere fact of having a visitor, Jacintha moved forward, wondering what she wanted and why she had come and marvelling, as well, at the girl's beauty.

"I wonder—" said Jacintha's visitor, "if I might ask you to hook me up the back. It's my maid's afternoon off and I can't reach them myself."

"I'd be glad to," said Jacintha with eager graciousness.

The room felt warmer and friendlier to her already. Some of her terror was dissipating.

The girl turned and Jacintha began to hook up her dress. It was an evening gown of rich heavy black satin and fitted her body almost to her knees, as though it had been plastered onto her corset. The skirt, in front, was an intricate arrangement of diagonal folds, finished with two rows of pleated white ruffles. In back it had a five-foot train and the skirt was hung with masses of velvet loops caught by clusters of wisteria blossoms. The bodice was cut low and square to show her superbly shaped arms and shoulders and the full beginning rise of her breasts.

"What a beautiful gown!" cried Jacintha enthusiastically. It was one she would have enjoyed wearing herself.

She finished the last hook and her visitor turned, smiling, touching the back of her hair with delicate fingers. "Thank you. I think it is, too." She revolved slowly so that Jacintha could admire it from all angles, for a fashionable gown was meant to create a different, but equally lovely, portrait of its wearer at every turn of the body.

The girl was perhaps two or three inches shorter than Jacintha and seemed to have a somewhat more voluptuous figure. Her hair was a rich red-brown, drawn back off her ears, with the same mass of curls upon her forehead, while in back it fell into a luxuriant cascade of folds and twists and braids, arranged in almost as complicated a style as the back of her gown. Her eyes were dark, large, soft and brilliant, with long curling lashes.

Her manner was eager and artless and her beauty both so vivid and so ripe that she seemed almost literally to bewitch her surroundings. She was, furthermore, in no sense a spoiled beauty, but one who would minimize her loveliness with women and who would seek to please men as hopefully as if she were plain.

She and Jacintha stood silently a moment and looked at each other, and they smiled with honest friendship. Perhaps because they were essentially different kinds of women, they could admire each other objectively, each taking pleasure in the other's beauty and feeling, in some sense, drawn together by it, since beautiful women live a life very different from that of unfavored ones.

"Won't you sit down?" asked Jacintha. "I just arrived

—as you can see—" She gestured at her opened trunk and bags and the welter of gowns and petticoats and gloves and fans and pincushions lying everywhere about. She swept a heap of garments off one of the chairs and offered it to her guest.

"Thank you." Smiling, she seated herself delicately and gracefully, crossing her narrow pointed black satin slippers. "I may as well tell you the truth. My maid *was* there. But I had to have some excuse to come and visit. You don't mind, do you? It's lonely here. There are so many people and so much excitement and yet one is always lonely. Perhaps it's the lack of a goal, or perhaps it's just knowing that it's forever—"

Jacintha watched her as she talked, speaking with such sweetness and gaiety, without any complaint in her tone, and yet with an intense pathos. She watched her and listened, feeling only pity, as though she were herself a casual visitor, having no part in the afflictions of the permanent residents—until all at once she realized that this was her predicament, too. At that she felt a chill shock which went down her arms and back like a bucket of cold water, ending in an uncontrollable shudder.

Her visitor was chatting on, lightly still, as if they were only discussing the new fashions. "The millennia go fast enough, I'm told. It's the moments that drag."

Jacintha swallowed. Her throat felt dry and her breath was coming quickly but with difficulty. She wanted to ask how long she had been here, and yet it seemed such a tactless question. Worse than tactless—cruel, as well.

The other girl was looking at Jacintha, her head tilted to one side, slightly smiling. "You are here," she said, "because you committed adultery. Your husband was jealous and he killed you."

Jacintha's hand went to her face, which had turned white, and she took a step backward. "How did you know that?" she whispered.

She stood and came close to Jacintha, touching her hand with warm and tender fingers. "I'm sorry if I startled you. I simply felt it, that's all. It's the very reason why I am here—though my husband did not shoot me. He was subtle. He used poison and people thought I had died of consumption. The moment I entered the room I felt that we had some strong bond in common."

"You did?" asked Jacintha, wonderingly. "So did I. Isn't that strange?"

"Nothing is strange here. Look out that window. Everything would have been unbelievable, anywhere else. You probably want to know how long I've been here—it's been twenty years."

"But—you—"

"I know. I haven't changed at all. Neither will you. That's one consolation—you'll never get any older than you are. Age is the penalty you pay for staying alive." She made a little gesture, slightly shrugged, and smiled. Every move she made, every tone of her voice, every gesture, was at once spirited and oddly touching.

"Well," said Jacintha, "at least there is something."

"There are other things, too," said the visitor softly.

But, though Jacintha waited to hear what they were, she did not elaborate. She opened a beaded jet bag she carried and took out an enamelled fan-shaped mirror into which she glanced for a moment, touching a curly tendril beside her cheek, smiling in a friendly sort of way to herself. Then she slipped the mirror back into the bag, glanced at Jacintha, and smiled.

"Are you sorry?" she asked, after a moment. "Do you wish you had been cautious and respectable and—cowardly? And that you were still alive?"

Jacintha frowned, catching her lower lip with her teeth, looking down at the roses in the richly patterned carpet. She put one forefinger beside her mouth and thought carefully of what her visitor had asked. Finally she raised her head and they faced each other directly.

"No," she said. "I could not have done any differently from what I did. Once I met Douglas, everything else had to follow. I know it was wicked, at least according to the world, but it wasn't wicked to me—or, if it was, I preferred it to being moral. My life, I suppose, was quite gaudy—not at all suited to the times in which I lived." This last she added with just a touch of pride.

The other girl sighed, and lightly tapped her fan against the palm of her hand. "Yes—that's a thing which seems very difficult for women like us to learn. Whatever age you live in—you must live up to it and accept it, or you are damned. Perhaps because we are beautiful, we have so very much more temptation. It's so easy, haven't you noticed, for plain women to condemn beautiful ones?"

They smiled at each other, like two gently mannered conspirators.

"And yet," added Jacintha after a moment, "I had dignity. I was never coarse or common. My mother would not have been ashamed of me—if she had lived."

"I am *sure* she would not," said the other girl warmly, and reached out impulsively to touch her arm. "Come— let's be friends. We are already. Heavens—" She gave a light pretty gesture of mild distraction. "Everything is so strange here, so informal: I haven't even introduced myself. My name is Charity—though I have always been called Cherry. Cherry Anson."

Jacintha felt a plunging shock and yet, almost at the same instant, she realized that the shock was far less than it should have been.

"My name," she said quietly, after a moment, "is Jacintha Anson Frost."

The other girl drew a soft quick breath. "Why—then *you're* my child." Her face grew faintly sorrowful as she looked at Jacintha. "You died so young?"

Jacintha inclined her head. "The same age you were, Mother. Isn't it a strange coincidence?"

Cherry was still watching her, very carefully, with great interest and appraisal. "Coincidence?" she repeated. "I wonder."

"What do you mean by that?"

Cherry sighed a little. "Nothing, I suppose. Only here you get to thinking— Peculiar thoughts, most of them."

She smiled once more and then held out her arms. Jacintha hesitated a moment and suddenly, with the same throat-tearing agonizing love she had felt when she was five years old and had been summoned the last time to her mother's bedside, knowing in some fathomless way that her mother was dying and would never hold her in her arms again—she walked into them and they stood together, close and silent, until Jacintha began to cry.

"No, my darling," said Cherry softly, coaxingly. "No. There's nothing to cry for. I was sorry to leave you—but I was not honestly sorry to die. I don't believe anyone is, really. Do you?"

She stood back, her hands still holding Jacintha's shoulders and Jacintha faced her, tears streaming down her cheeks, little sobs breaking from her spasmodically. She had not felt her mother's death with this tormenting keenness since the day she had watched her coffin being lowered into the ground and begun to wail uncontrollably so that her father had picked her up and held her, trying to comfort her. The sobbing had continued, for two or three days, until she was sick and exhausted. After that, she had shut her mother's memory away and kept it as though in an airtight room, where it was preserved, dry and odorless and dehumanized. Her mother had then become a sweet and cherished but no longer agonizing memory, until this moment.

"*He* killed you!" cried Jacintha, her voice strangling and harsh. "He poisoned you!" She gave a long moan and, covering her face with her hands, sank to her knees.

Cherry knelt swiftly beside her, putting her arms about her, stroking her hair, as if she were, indeed, that five-year-old child she had last known her daughter to be.

"Don't cry, Jacintha. Don't cry, please. Here we are —together, after all. Why, it's as if a miracle had happened, that we even found each other here. Look, Jacintha—look at me—" She was smiling eagerly, though once she had to brush a tear from her own cheek and give her head a quick admonishing shake. She put her hand beneath Jacintha's chin and gently turned her face upward. "Look what's happened to us! Here we are—together—and both of us at the very best time of our lives!"

"The very best time of our lives," repeated Jacintha, twisting a ruffle, winding it round and round. "Except that we're dead."

The two women looked at each other suddenly, then rocked back on their heels and both of them started to laugh. They laughed as if at the greatest joke they had ever heard, rocking backward and forward, their voices pealing out, rippling one over the other like bells stuck in different steeples, laughing and laughing and laughing, until they had to fold their hands across their stomachs and bend double with the pain of laughing so hard.

"Oh!" they gasped every few moments. "Oh!"

Gradually the laughter dwindled and finally they sat, still facing each other, sober and solemn now, every trace of merriment gone, their faces absolutely serious.

"What a terrible thing it is," said Jacintha. "You—and me. We should have lived a long long time. We had every right to life and happiness and love! We're the kind of women who should not have died until—"

"Until we were old?" asked Cherry softly. "And had lost our beauty and grown bitter on the memories of it? I've thought about this a great deal. Jacintha—it's not a game which can be won by anyone, no matter how clever or how lucky. What do you suppose would have happened to you and Douglas, if you had lived?"

"We'd have gone on, of course, as we were. Being happy."

"You loved him?"

"I did. I loved him completely—as he loved me. I loved him the way—" She hesitated, searching for an expression.

"I know," said Cherry, and bowed her head. "The way I loved the man your father killed me for. But there's something more, Jacintha, which may not have occurred to you. It's this: In any perfect love there is a finality which is terrifying—because it is deathlike. A love of that kind is very rare, of course, but when it happens I think then it is time to die."

Jacintha shook her head. "Oh, I can't believe that. I *can't* believe that! I don't know what I think or believe—but not that. Love is the purpose and end of life!"

"Yes," agreed Cherry gently. "The end of life. When women die as we did, still young and beautiful and very much beloved—don't you think it's more suitable to us than if we had waited too long? We died the way a story should end—at its climax. At least—" she added, and gave a weary little shrug, and for the first time her vivacious light-struck face was full of sorrow and regret. "At least we may as well think so."

Jacintha looked at her as she got gracefully to her feet again and stood smoothing the folds of her gown, then walked to the mirror and touched the sides and back of her hair, holding up a hand mirror and turning to observe herself from other angles. She watched her with tender admiration, momentarily forgetting her own beauty. And then suddenly, determined to put out of her mind everything they had been talking about, she went to stand beside her.

"Your hair looks so beautiful. That's *such* a becoming style—would you show me how to do mine like it?" She sounded wistful and appealing, like a little girl, and Cherry turned to her with a quick impulsive smile.

"Of course I will. It would look wonderful on you. It's the newest thing, you know."

"I'm sure it is. Oh, Mother—" She had begun with a rush of eagerness, but, at that word, she stopped and frowned, a puzzled look on her face, and regarded them both in the mirror. "That sounds odd. I don't believe I can call you that—under the circumstances. May I call you—"

"Of course, darling. Call me by my name."

"Cherry. Such a lovely name. Do you know—at our home in the country I had Martin plant cherry trees. And every spring, when they bloomed, I would go out and bring in branches of them. I loved them more than any other flower—" She bowed her head again, and shut her eyes. "How much I missed you!"

"Hush, darling." Cherry touched her cheek. "Don't cry any more. Think of how lucky we are. Why—it seems more like Heaven, than Hell. And we're together now—for eternity."

"Yes. For eternity," repeated Jacintha, gazing across her mother's shoulder, out of the great window. "Though I still have no vaguest comprehension of it."

"They say you never do," said Cherry softly. "I've talked to people who've been here two or three or five thousand years. They all say exactly what you did. I believe it's best not to think about it," she finished crisply. "Now, darling—why don't you finish unpacking and get dressed and we'll go out and stroll in the lobby and talk to some people and then it'll be time for dinner."

"Yes! Let's do that!" She walked to her trunk and then turned back once more. "Will you stay with me?"

"Of course I will. Can I help?"

"No thank you. I don't want you to help. I want you to sit down and talk to me. You say they serve dinner? Things aren't so very different in the essentials, are they?"

"In the essentials—they are. For, while they serve every meal, wonderful food, too, you don't need it to sustain life, and consequently you don't enjoy it."

"Then why does anyone bother?"

"It's something to do. As I think of it, I don't believe I've been to dinner in a year or two—possibly longer."

"Really?" cried Jacintha. "Isn't that incredible!" She sounded almost pleased, as if this were an odd and interesting fragment of information given by her hostess about a place she was briefly visiting.

They continued chatting merrily along, like two schoolgirls spending the night together, exchanging confidences, asking opinions and advice, going over all the minute details of their lives and deaths.

While Jacintha moved about, hanging her gowns in the closet, setting her shoes in neat rows, arraying her hats along the top shelves, folding her dainty lace-trimmed petticoats and chemises, Cherry lounged on a sofa, playing with her fan. The sofa was curved up high at one end and dwindled to nothing at the other; it was covered with crimson velvet and made a strikingly effective background for her black satin gown and cream-colored skin. As the afternoon faded, Jacintha lighted the kerosene lamps which, reflecting off the crimson walls, filled the room with a delicate intimate rose-tinted glow.

"I always knew your father would be sorry that he killed me," said Cherry. "And I'm glad to hear that he was."

"I don't believe he had one happy moment, after you died. Of course, we all thought that it was because he had loved you so much. He was known for his great devotion to you and we visited the cemetery every Sunday with armloads of flowers. When the weather was nice, we spent the entire afternoon. Your grave really was beautiful—there was a fringed marble cushion on top and an inverted torch. We would sit—under the weeping willow he planted the day of your funeral—and he would stare at the stone and sigh. Your stone was very tenderly engraved, too, with a verse he composed himself. It read—"

Cherry, who had listened to this recital with a look of contemptuous amusement, now quickly raised her hand. "Please. I couldn't bear hearing it. Tell me—were you and your father close?"

"No. I never liked him. I don't quite know why, but I was afraid of him every moment after you died. He was kind to me—almost too kind, out of his own guilty feelings, I suppose. And yet—" She paused, holding several bonnets covered with flowers and ribbons and feathers in her arms. "And yet, in a way, I was fascinated by him."

Cherry laughed again, her happy rippling laugh, which sounded to Jacintha like a long-delayed echo, reaching her twenty years after it had first been scattered into the air.

"A man can generally be fascinating as a father even if he was never successfully fascinating as a husband. It's the greatest comfort most of them have, I imagine— poor dears."

"Oh!" cried Jacintha delightedly. "How witty you are! How wonderful it is to be with you again!"

"*Are*n't we fortunate? What are you going to wear tonight?" They strolled into the closet, Jacintha holding a kerosene lamp in one hand, and began to look through her wardrobe. "You must wear your most beautiful gown. He may be there and, if he is, I want you to make a good first impression."

Jacintha turned with a look of surprise. In all their eagerness to get reacquainted, she had not thought to mention her encounter with him. "But I've already made my first impression!"

"What? You've met him? Already? Where?"

"Why, I met him on Roaring Mountain by Lemonade Lake." As she spoke, it seemed she mentioned something which had happened long long ago, so long ago, in fact, that it might not have happened at all, but only been imagined. Even the sound of her voice as she said it, vague and soft and wondering, indicated that now she was doubtful. "This place," she said, and brushed one hand before her face. "It's like living in a mirage, isn't it?"

Cherry had been watching her, carefully, her expression showing concern and something more, a kind of hurt dismay, as well. "How did it happen?" asked Cherry finally, and then she gave a self-conscious little laugh. "Both of you on Roaring Mountain. That's a strange place for a meeting."

"His coachman—Grant, he called him—made me get out there. I didn't want to but he insisted. And there he was—the Devil, I mean. What a start he gave me! I turned around, not thinking there was a soul within miles and saw him standing there, looking at me. When I screamed, he laughed."

As she was speaking, the feelings he had roused in her returned, to rush through her body like the sudden flight of startled birds, leaving her stunned and bewildered. She experienced once more the profound shock of his fierce and dazzling beauty. She grew warm and restless inside upon memories of his vast, strangely menacing energy and vigor. Undoubtedly, he had enthralled her—by means of himself alone—without gallantry or flattery or any kind of obeisance. And that, in itself, was a frightening realization.

She glanced up at Cherry and they looked at each other for a long moment—Jacintha's face clearly puzzled and unhappy, Cherry's surprised, chagrined, but solicitous, as well. Quickly, briefly, she patted Jacintha's hand.

"He loves to do that," said Cherry reassuringly. "He loves to scare people, you know. Girls, especially." She turned then and started slowly out of the closet. "He must have been eager to meet you."

"Don't go!" cried Jacintha. "We haven't selected my gown!"

Cherry swung back, laughing, tilting her head so that the clear line of her throat and chin was displayed, and her laugh had a sound which made Jacintha think of coins flung into the air, tinkling together as they fell. "Of course! What was I dreaming of? Sometimes I'm absent-minded, darling. Forgive me." She touched Jacintha's arm and clasped it for a moment, smiling directly into her face, and her charm and warmth and beauty were so great that Jacintha marvelled she had ever arrived in Hell. Surely she could have softened the heart of any villain, even her father.

"Do you know," said Jacintha softly, "you're the first beautiful woman I've ever known that I wasn't furiously jealous of—down underneath, that is. Of course, I was clever enough not to show it."

"I know. I feel the same. I'm delighted to find you grew into such a beauty—but I knew you would. You were the loveliest child anyone ever saw. That's why we're not jealous of each other, I suppose. Being mother and daughter, our beauty seems a mutual possession—

yours belongs to me and mine to you, and we admire it in each other as we admire it in ourselves. It's a very comforting and rather mystical kind of love, isn't it?"

"This has been the happiest day of my life!" avowed Jacintha, and they both laughed. "Now—what shall I wear? You really think he'll be there?"

She paused a moment, carefully observing her. "Do you hope he will? Are you looking forward to seeing him again?"

Jacintha frowned. "I suppose I am. After all, he's the only man of any consequence around here."

"How did he impress you?"

But at that question, her confusion grew almost tumultuous; she turned her back and pretended to be looking at her dresses. She would have been ashamed to have her mother know how he had impressed her.

"Why—" she said, after a few seconds, "he's rather attractive, I suppose—in a crude sort of way. Certainly, he's no gentleman." Of all the absurd things to say!

"No," agreed Cherry, behind her. "He is not. Here— why don't you wear this one? I think it's charming."

Jacintha frowned. "It's very pretty, but— Isn't it rather dull?" she asked anxiously. It was the gown her husband had liked to see her wear when he entertained his most conservative friends.

"Oh, yes," agreed Cherry musingly. "It is a little—dull. Well then, wear this one. I'm sure you'll create a great sensation in it. And you may as well, after all."

The gown Cherry had chosen now was one she had bought the summer before when she and Martin were in Paris; it was made of velvet in the very fashionable solferino: a vivid purple-pink. Color could not be too rash or clamorous for high fashion. It was, in fact, the gown she had worn to the ball when she and Douglas had first met. But she felt shy about mentioning that now, for fear Cherry might think she was hoping to cast the same spell with it tonight. For, of course, she was.

It took an hour and a half for Jacintha to bathe, arrange her hair—with Cherry's help—and get dressed. All the while, they continued talking, but not about their host.

Jacintha had wanted to find out if Cherry knew him or

knew what kind of man he was, but, when she asked, Cherry only said:

"Yes, I know him. At least, I've spent quite a good deal of time in his company, which is all anyone can say about knowing him. People never agree about him—he seems one kind of man to one person, and quite different to another. So, you see, anything I might tell you would never match your own opinions. Wait—and decide for yourself. Now, let's not talk about him any more. He's a disturbing subject at best, which is what he loves to be, of course. Let me warn you of only one thing—don't be misled by his good looks or any charm he may choose to show you from time to time. He's not the Devil for nothing, you know."

Jacintha listened carefully and soberly, like a little girl receiving her first lesson in school, nodding her head from time to time. "I did think there was something—sinister, about him."

Cherry sighed heavily and gave a brush at the air with her spangled black chiffon fan. "He's all things to all men and women. Please—Jacintha, let's not discuss him any more."

"No. We won't. I'm sorry I ever brought him up. Tell me what they do here for amusement—"

"Well, let me see," began Cherry slowly. Now she was drawing on her long white kid gloves and buttoning them at the wrists. "There is a great deal of gambling, for instance."

"Gambling!" Jacintha stood before her dressing table, sorting among her jewels. "Is that the best way they can find to waste their time?"

Cherry shrugged delicately. "It's one of the best, at least. He invented it, you know. Then there is—"

"Cherry!" cried Jacintha and, holding something in her hands, turned and ran toward her. "Look! *Look* what I have here!" She was standing before Cherry and she held forth both hands to show her a wide lacy necklace and bracelet with heavy gold fastenings, made of Cherry's own red-brown hair. "Father wore a watch chain made of your hair for years—all my life, in fact."

Cherry looked at them with polite curiosity for a moment and then was forced to an involuntary shudder. One hand lifted to touch her hair. "How dismal. I had one, too—my mother's hair. We *were* morbid, weren't we?"

Jacintha looked at her treasures with disappointment. Cherry, it seemed, had lost many of her values, since coming to this place. She returned them to her jewel case and they talked, instead, about Jacintha's collection of blue china and how she had loved to draw and paint out of doors.

At last she was ready. Her hair was plaited and twisted and scrolled; she wore a cluster of three pale-blue ostrich tips at one side of her head. Her face was discreetly powdered and rouged, only as much and no more than was permissible for a lady of refinement. Her white kid gloves buttoned to her elbows and she carried a small fan of pale-blue ostrich feathers. She wore single diamonds in her ears, a pair of diamond-encrusted stars over her left breast, and a magnificent diamond necklace which had been Martin's last present to her.

Cherry and Jacintha complimented each other, with warm enthusiasm and sincerity, and they set out down the broad deserted gaslit hallway.

Cherry, in her black satin gown, small, soft, quick, vivacious. Jacintha in purple-pink velvet, somewhat taller, lustrous and tranquil. They strolled arm in arm, passing one closed doorway after another, their trains sweeping behind them, their murmuring voices fading in the vast dim silence. Out here, it was cold and empty and they appeared as diminutive figures moving down endless corridors. Occasionally, there was an outbreak of light shimmering laughter; it sounded as happy and carefree as if they were two young girls on their way to an eagerly anticipated ball.

They drifted along, traversing one passageway, turning the corner to confront another, moving down that one and, by degrees, progressing through the maze of galleries along which she had earlier followed the scuttling lackey. They did not pass another person and, when it seemed they had been walking more than half an hour, Jacintha turned to Cherry.

"Are we lost?"

"Oh, no. Don't be frightened. I know the way—we'll get there. This is a big place, you know. And he keeps adding to it all the time. He's constantly building. Nothing ever satisfies him. He builds more and more and more. Well—we don't care about that, do we?"

Both women laughed.

Now and then one of them gestured with a delicate round arm covered by a white kid glove, buttoned up tight to the elbow. Jacintha would flirt out her feathered fan, or Cherry make a sweep with her spangled black one. And as they moved, their pointed toes emerged from their skirts in easy continuous patterns, pink velvet toes and black satin toes, emerging and retreating.

Jacintha felt as if she were in a mild but delicious state of delirium, intoxicated, as it were, by some inner happiness, greater by far than any she had previously experienced. "I can't imagine what's happened to me," she confided. "I feel drunk."

She felt reckless, in fact, and that was not her nature. Though she had done reckless things, she was not of a reckless temperament. And the recklessness made her feel as if she were going somewhere in a great hurry, somewhere she had not chosen or planned to go, but to which she was nevertheless hastening with almost preternatural speed.

"One has to get acclimatized to any new place, you know," said Cherry, as if to minimize this frothy high-spirited excitement which had taken hold of Jacintha.

For the past several minutes there had been a murmuring sound, low and indefinite, floating all around them, so scarcely noticeable that neither had remarked upon it. Now, suddenly, a hideous shattering roar, like a blow of great physical force, came crashing at them. It lasted only a moment and then the murmuring was heard again, but very much louder now.

"Good heavens!" cried Jacintha. "What was that?"

"The lobby. It's around this corner. It's always frightfully crowded at this hour. Everyone comes before dinner to see and be seen, to gossip and flirt and find out what the others are doing."

They turned the corner and came to a set of double doors above which the motto WELCOME had been worked in pine branches garnished with clusters of pine cones. The doors were opened for them by two lackeys. Cherry and Jacintha swept majestically through, heads high, fans unfurled, arms held gracefully so as not to obscure the contours of their bodies, two women accustomed to commanding instant attention and breathless admiration.

The lobby was now packed full, from one end to the other—a mass of people, as far as could be seen in every direction. They stood elbow to elbow, toe to toe, face to face, back to back.

Now, they were all in evening clothes so that there was a dazzle of white shoulders and bosoms, diamonds glittering at ears and throats, aigrette and ostrich plumes waving, and elaborate fitted gowns which displayed little waists and swelling breasts and hips. The room burst with brilliant color, royal blue, garnet, purple, scarlet, emerald green. The fabrics were rich—satins, velvets, taffetas, laces, tulles, thick with bead and jet embroidery. They were ornamented, as well, by every conceivable arrangement of folds and frills, bows and tassels and ribbons and knotted fringe. Their elegance and splendor were almost stupefying. The men wore black and white dinner dress.

An incessant babble was carried on in high-pitched feminine tones and deep masculine voices, and the room split and crackled with laughter, as though lightning played through the atmosphere above their heads. Jacintha had never heard any group which seemed so excited, so amused by its own conversation, so entirely given to pleasure and hilarity.

"Oh," moaned Jacintha, and one hand went up involuntarily to touch her throat and rest on her bosom. "How dreadful that noise is!" She winced, for it seemed a physical assault, dangerous and wild. Their jabbering, in fact, was so piercing, it battered so hard at the walls and smashed so violently at the ceiling, that there seemed an almost literal danger it might blow the building apart.

"It's always like this in the evening. I hate it. But you'll get used to it in time. I think they make so much noise to keep themselves from thinking. They're all bored to death." Cherry shook her head. "I'm sorry. I don't mean to keep making those terrible puns. I just can't get over the habits of speaking that I used before."

"I don't mind it. What shall we do?"

"Let's stand here a moment. Look around you and

take stock of things, since this is where you'll be from now on."

"Oh, I'm not so sure," said Jacintha doubtfully. Her exhilaration was gone. "I may not care for it."

"You'll get used to it."

Jacintha turned, lifting her black shiny brows. "You mean—even if I don't, I can't leave here?"

Cherry slowly turned her head and they looked at each other for a moment. Cherry's eyes swept over her face a time or two, and then at last she smiled, a rather subtle smile of tolerant amusement. "Of course not," she said finally. "That's the—"

"That's the hell of it!"

And gleefully Jacintha threw back her head and burst into laughter. But then, just as suddenly, she sobered, clapped her white-gloved hand to her mouth and stared at Cherry, her eyes opened so wide now that they were round.

"You didn't really believe it, did you?" asked Cherry gently.

"No." Jacintha bowed her head, looking downward at the toe of her pink velvet shoe, peeping from the edge of her gown. "I believe I thought I was on a visit."

"Well! So here you both are!"

It was a man's voice, hearty and commanding, just behind them. The two women turned with a start, giving little involuntary shrieks of alarm and surprise. He stood grinning down at them, a slight sideways twist to his mouth.

He had on a double-breasted dinner coat with quilted black satin lapels, a soft tucked white shirt and black silk tie; there was black silk braid down the sides of his trousers, and he wore black patent leather shoes. He was even more awesome than he had been earlier in the day, for the contrast between this conventional formal style of dress, no different from that worn by every other man present, and his relentlessly virile good looks was so irresistible that Jacintha stood gaping, stunned. He seemed almost to blaze with savage glory.

"My, my," whispered Jacintha, transfixed.

How marvellous he is. How truly marvellous to see a man of such matchless and terrible beauty.

For the effect he produced was not merely the result

of his being incomparably handsome. It was, far more, the monumental energy he seemed to possess, volcanic and inexorable.

How wicked he is, she was thinking.

How evil— How cruel. How destroying.

She was so completely lost, so victimized and intoxicated, that several seconds had passed before she realized that, after the first quick glance at her, he had been looking only at Cherry.

His expression was appraising and proprietary, his eyes glancing up and down her body and across her face with a boldness which would have been shocking in any ordinary man, and which was shocking to Jacintha, even so. Cherry had, indeed, as she said, spent a good deal of time in his company. And the time had not been idle, either, occupied with polite talk or questions concerning her soul.

Now, all at once, Jacintha remembered a number of things she thought she had not noticed: Cherry's expression when she told her that she had met him on Roaring Mountain; Cherry's recommendation that she wear a simple and innocent kind of gown; Cherry's refusal to discuss him and the trace of alarm she had shown at Jacintha's frank statement that he was the only man here worth taking into consideration.

It was all quite simple now: Cherry had felt that wretched twist of jealousy, familiar to every woman upon the merest hint that the man she loves may pay flattering attention to someone else.

Her mother, then, was in love with the Devil.

How incredibly horrible!

She had, quite literally, been cast into a spell by him. Nothing could have been more obvious. The way she looked up at him, her beauty so intensified by eagerness and ardor that she had become almost iridescent. That much was bad enough—but it was not the worst. For Cherry's innocent proud little face now immodestly betrayed a sensual and wanton longing.

Seeing it, Jacintha felt a disgust and abhorrence which made her skin begin to crawl. It was almost unbelievable, and yet it was undeniable. They were smiling into each other's eyes with a monstrous intimacy, detestable beyond anything she had ever seen. Frantically, she longed to spring between them, give them each a violent slap, and break apart their private impure world. Never before had she felt such loathing and revolt.

She must do something!

At that instant her fan, which she had been furiously fluttering without being aware of it, fell out of her hand and dropped to the floor.

"Oh!" she cried and stepped back, looking down at it, helplessly.

It took a moment longer but finally he looked down, too. Then he looked up at Jacintha and slowly he smiled. She felt her face growing hotter and hotter. He made no move to retrieve it. What if he was going to force *her* to stoop and pick it up! Oh—how could she have been such a fool? She felt herself about to be overwhelmed by some tremendous unknown catastrophe.

And then, when her confusion and dismay had reached a pitch which seemed intolerable—just then he turned slightly, caught the eye of one of his hovering lackeys, and the fan was whisked off the floor and returned to her by a cringing fellow who bowed so low she could not even see his face.

Jacintha took it, her lashes lowered to conceal her eyes, still flushed over her face and neck and shoulders, and bowing her head she whispered. "Thank you. I'm sorry."

Then, to make her predicament even more unendurable, she heard Cherry's pattering laugh and felt her arm go about her waist.

"Poor child. You've upset her."

Oh! thought Jacintha, frantic. I can't stand this! I've never been so humiliated. What is she trying to do to me? She's making it worse—calling his attention to my state!

I wish I could die.

I wish I *could* die!

Jacintha's head was bowed so low that it seemed as if a strong hand pressed hard upon the back of her neck, making it impossible for her to lift it even if she tried. She wanted to pick up her skirts and run, out of the lobby and out of the building and away. But she did not know where to go. She would get lost. And she was afraid of being captured by Indians or attacked by wild animals or even of falling through the thin crust around the geysers and boiling alive.

Cherry's voice sounded lilting and gay and her arm tugged coaxingly at Jacintha's waist. "Don't be shy, darling. He *looks* much worse than he is." Jacintha heard both him and Cherry laughing at that, as if it were a very amusing joke. He must think he was extraordinarily handsome, to laugh so readily about it.

But the most mortifying thing of all was Cherry's buoyant and sprightly manner with him, the obvious result of deep intimacy and prolonged association. Jacintha felt that Cherry had been dishonest, had cheated her, in fact. For while she had earlier spoken of him with reservations amounting to actual resentment, now, in his presence, she was merry and frolicsome.

It must have been her relationship with him to which she had covertly referred when she said that this place had "other compensations." Jacintha now recalled her mysterious refusal to be more explicit.

And here I am—dressed like this, trying to compete with her! And she knows it.

All of a sudden she became embarrassed at her own embarrassment.

At the instant that happened she flung back her head, the red drained out of her face leaving her skin once more white and fragile and clear, and she stared at him directly, her large brown eyes full of sparkling hauteur and malice. She looked young and rather wild, like an animal challenged on its forest trail.

I'll never make that kind of fool of myself again, she promised.

She had the feeling that since he had spoken, saying: "So here you both are!" an age or more must have passed. It had been, of course, only a few seconds.

And yet, profound and permanent changes had occurred between her and Cherry. She felt a mournful nostalgia for that earlier and more innocent love which they had lost—as one is constantly losing things on earth, by the mere passage of time, altering continuously the balance within oneself and in relation to everyone one knows.

He was looking at Jacintha now and smiling. "Mother and daughter," he said softly, reflectively. "When one of you arrives—I always know the other will be along."

"Don't you think it's a little presumptuous," asked Jacintha tartly, "to 'always' know anything?"

Cherry gave her a look of surprise and then smiled proudly as if pleased by her quick reply. He threw back his head and laughed. Then, all at once, he left them. He touched Jacintha beneath the chin, grinned once more at Cherry, and was gone so swiftly that they saw him absorbed into the depths of the crowd with the same startled wonder they would have watched him swimming effortlessly downward to the ocean's depths. In a few moments, he had disappeared. They turned to each other, eyes wide, brows up, lips pursed.

"Well!" they said.

"He's an odd one, isn't he?" inquired Jacintha, thinking it a good idea to minimize his effectiveness with some such remark.

Cherry laughed, but the laughter was artificial, as Jacintha could not help noticing. And Jacintha heard her follow it with a tiny soft sigh, as of remorse or hopelessness. For a moment Cherry's lovely face seemed to droop and grow mournful. But then, almost before Jacintha could see it, she was smiling again and linking her arm through hers.

"Let's stroll around. I'll introduce you to a few people—if I see anyone I know."

"If you see anyone you know?" repeated Jacintha incredulously. "I should think you must know any number of people here by now."

"Fewer than you might think. Look at this crowd—could you easily pick out a face you'd seen once before? There is no rhyme nor reason to it, remember. This is the main lodge, but there are numbers of others and often, just when you begin to get acquainted with someone and to like them, he transfers them somewhere else. There's no accounting for anything he does."

"He's impossible," said Jacintha. She glanced at Cherry to see if that announcement would bring an expression of relief. It did not. Cherry only frowned a little, as if it troubled her.

"He is, I suppose," she said, softly and slowly. "I've grown rather used to his ways during the past twenty years. I don't expect anything of him any more—except what he gives."

"What he gives? What does he give? He looks to me as though he would never give anything."

"Let's not talk about it. I can't discuss him. He's not like anyone you've ever known." She stopped abruptly, turned and faced Jacintha. "You'll fall in love with him."

"*I'll* fall in love with him?" cried Jacintha.

"Perhaps you have already," said Cherry, and looked carefully into her daughter's face. "You won't be able to help yourself. Don't you see what mischief he is about now? We thought it was such a miracle, our finding each other as we did, the very day of your arrival. *He* did it. He put you in the room next to mine."

"But why? What does he hope for?"

Cherry drew a deep breath and stopped, closed her eyes briefly and then looked straight at Jacintha. "I love him, you see. No—you mustn't ask me why, or anything about it. When you love him, too, you will know. It will give him amusement to see what we do—what happens to us."

Slowly, as she listened, Jacintha's face had altered: shock, disbelief, repugnance showed in quick succession. Finally, there was defiance.

"That may be his plan—but he won't succeed."

"He never fails," said Cherry, with a sad and stricken little smile.

And seeing that look on her mother's face, Jacintha felt her heart break with tenderness and love. She swore that, since Cherry had lost the power to rescue herself from this ravenous and unruly passion, her own clear responsibility was to repudiate him entirely and at this moment. She clasped Cherry's hand in both her own.

"I promise you," said Jacintha, with intense fervor and devotion.

"Please," whispered Cherry. The noise was so great that Jacintha could only see her lips move. "Promise me nothing. We're in no place for promises—" She gestured. Then, with one of the swift magical changes of mood which so surprised and delighted Jacintha, her face flashed into brightness and animation. Her arm again went about Jacintha's waist.

"Not another word!" she cired.

"Not another word," Jacintha agreed.

They were in the midst of the crowd now. The handsome, fashionably dressed men and women were talking frantically into each other's faces, the women laughing and using their eyes and mouths as if determined to display their beauty to its utmost advantage, fluttering their fans, touching gloved hands to their hair, tapping a man's shoulder. They seemed, en masse, in a state of hysterical hilarity. The racket and din were clangorous, their voices raucous and shrill; their expressions were fantastically lively and their manner spirited to the point of desperation. The room had grown much hotter since Cherry and Jacintha had arrived. It felt as if the floor were sending up waves of stifling heat. The fans of the ladies beat faster and faster.

"They're all so eager!" cried Jacintha. "Each one seems to be telling a story that's the most important story in the whole world!"

"They're practically all of them talking to someone they've never seen before and will never see again. About the only time they ever do see each other is when they arrange an assignation."

Jacintha was aghast. "You mean, they talk a few minutes and then—*meet?*"

"Why not?" asked Cherry reasonably.

"But—doesn't it cause gossip?"

"They gossip, of course—but they don't censor."

"There's no need for secrecy or concealment?"

"Concealment from whom?"

"Why, from each other—from—"

Cherry smiled with affectionate reproval. "Come, Jacintha. Remember where you are."

"Yes," agreed Jacintha, feeling rather embarrassed and childish. "I know. I forget. And yet it's so much like real places where I *have* been." She was frowning, thinking over what Cherry had said as they made their way in the crowd, a few inches at a step, then a pause, then another slight forward movement. "But that must take away a great deal of the pleasure," she said, after a few moments.

"It does. It takes away most of it. At first, everyone is nonplussed to think of being able to indulge themselves limitlessly, with as many different lovers as they want and as often as they want and no one to so much as lift an eyebrow or care. But then, after a time, they find that it is completely meaningless. They no longer enjoy their romances and soon they cease to have them, except now and then, when a particularly attractive person turns up and they grow hopeful. But the end is always the same—there is no pleasure to speak of."

Jacintha had been listening with a growing horror and at the last, she gave an uncontrollable shudder. "How terrible! He's left everyone looking so beautiful, so tempting—and he's taken away the temptation and the delight of succumbing to it. And yet—he is the essence of temptation, himself."

"Exactly," agreed Cherry, and now her eyes took on a sly slant. She looked like a mischievous wily minx. "Don't you agree he's extraordinarily clever? There are people who believe that it is only physical love which makes being alive for fifty years or so endurable. How endurable do you suppose eternity will be—without it?"

"Oh! How detestable! It would be better if he tortured us!"

"Isn't that torture? No, of course you don't know yet —whether it is or not."

"I don't believe it!" Jacintha violently declared. "I won't believe it! There must be some way of finding pleasure here!"

"There is. And that is in his power, too."

"*What?*"

"Yes. You must have heard that. He can give a woman greater pleasure than she ever dreamed of. Now—I warn you—not another word about him. Here—I'm going to introduce you to two men over here. We've got to get our minds off him and onto something else. If you concentrate too long on any one thing it begins to make you a trifle daft, you know." She laughed, her same rippling merry lovely laugh, and Jacintha marvelled how she had contrived to keep up her spirits in this place which had begun to seem so vile and horrible to her.

It was true, however, as he had told her that morning on Roaring Mountain: She had forgotten her former life already—it seemed a dream she had had one night which had evaporated by morning, leaving her the most wispy and fragmentary recollections.

She and Cherry were inching, working, pushing, maneuvering their way through the throng. Now Cherry stopped with a sharp little cry of distraction and annoyance.

"Oh! Isn't that tiresome! They weren't the ones I thought they were!"

She stamped her foot and fluttered her fan. The noise seemed suddenly louder, as if a tidal wave of harsh clamorous sound had broken over them. So violent and crushing was its impact that they stood there, cringing inside, visibly wincing, both women feeling themselves bruised and wilted and dismayed by the tremendous booming roar. It rose around them, enveloped them, bore them down, pushed against them.

"Don't you see how aggravating it is to have everyone dressed in the latest styles?" asked Cherry crossly. "It makes it absolutely impossible to find anyone you know! He says we love fashion, so he provides us with it. But he doesn't do it to please us—he does it the way he puts those mottoes over the doors saying 'Welcome' and 'Thou, God, Seest Me.' He mimics our way of life—not from consideration for us, but contempt!"

She seemed almost ready to cry, tremulous and panic-stricken. On every side they were being jostled, jolted, bumped against, pushed and shoved.

"Shall we go back to our rooms?" asked Jacintha tenderly.

Cherry brightened instantly. "Yes! Let's! Do you mind very much?"

"I want to. I can't *wait* to get out of here!"

Holding each other by the hand, Cherry steering, for she knew in which direction an exit might be found, while Jacintha was hopelessly lost, they began the difficult and seemingly endless journey back. But Cherry's spirits had noticeably revived and she talked quite gayly as they went. Her eyes, Jacintha saw, glanced eagerly around, looking, searching, and of course the object of her search must be him.

But, though his height, being so much above that of most of the other men, would have made him discoverable, they caught no glimpse of him. Perhaps he had gone into the gambling rooms, which were off this main lobby and crowded at all hours, Cherry had said, with men and women so agitated and engrossed they were like creatures paralyzed or in a state of trance, aware of nothing but the turning cards and rolling dice. And, though they could neither lose nor win, they were helpless to rescue themselves from that trivial and sterile excitement.

Jacintha, seeing how covertly anxious was Cherry's search, watched her with wonder and pity. *She must love him desperately. She is so terribly afraid of having him see me again.* She felt profound sorrow and despair, and the shame she felt for Cherry's shame seemed her own dishonor as well.

"You'll find you have very little in common," Cherry was blithely saying, "with people born in another age. You strike up a conversation with someone who looks interesting and then find that he's a first-century martyr or a Renaissance priest or someone else you can't make head nor tail of. Pretty soon, you realize that it's almost impossible to find anyone of your own time and station and you stop trying. He's the only one who seems to find *some*thing amusing about everybody!"

Cherry kept saying that they must not talk about him any more, but she also kept referring to him—unflatteringly, it was true, but so frequently that it was obvious he was constantly on her mind.

Jacintha believed, from her own brief contact with him, that she could guess how he might stir an unappeasable appetite. But, once a woman had succumbed to the obviously mesmeric force of his personality, she would then be at the mercy of a restless vagrant nature, entirely given to its own caprice, pitiless, violent, arbitrary. She would have much to fear and almost nothing to hope for. And she would return, as if all the centuries of civilization had dissolved, to a defenceless servility, wholly in thrall to her own insatiable need. She would have lost the dignity and aloofness, the power to refuse, which a woman must have for her own protection, almost, it seemed, for her decent survival.

Thinking of these things, as they moved along, Jacintha found it more and more incredible that Cherry—dainty and sparkling, with her beloved winsomeness—should be in such servitude. The realization made her sick and a frantic powerless fury began beating inside her.

He's not the Devil for nothing, Cherry had said.

They arrived at the lobby doors without catching another glimpse of him; the lackeys flung them open and Cherry stepped aside, touching Jacintha's back ever so lightly to usher her through, glanced one last time over her shoulder, and the doors closed behind them.

Cherry was plainly relieved. She stood fanning herself, and Jacintha could see moisture on her forehead and little wisps of clinging hair. She sighed as if she had run a hard race, and then suddenly she laughed and lightly clapped her hands.

"We got out, didn't we? Every time I go in there I get terrified that I will never get out again!"

Jacintha felt a swelling burst of painful love, an almost overwhelming devotion and gratitude, and she kissed her, tenderly, on the cheek.

Cherry gave her a little glance of faint surprise, touched her finger to the spot, smiled softly, and her eyes filled with tears.

Then, without either of them saying anything more, they started back along the hallway.

When they finally reached Jacintha's room they decided that it would be much more comfortable to get out of their tight-fitting gowns and laced corsets and pointed shoes and into their graceful easy ruffled silk wrappers. Cherry dashed into her own room and was back in no time at all, it seemed.

"I hate to leave you," she happily confided.

"I hate to have you leave."

But she knew that the real reason for Cherry's haste was her fear that if she left her alone, he might appear. There was, to Jacintha, something infinitely pitiful and sad about Cherry's quivering dread, so ill-concealed beneath her carefree manner. It seemed to mock at everything which was most essentially her own spirit—all her delightful and impulsive little ways, precious to Jacintha with a value unlike any other. To see these beloved qualities betrayed was agony; she felt as if a lump of pain had frozen in her chest.

I must find a way to make her feel safe about me. I must convince her somehow that nothing he could do could tempt me. I must give her back her self-respect —at least as far as I am concerned.

With other women, she could bear it better anyway.

It is only with me that the jealousy would be intolerable.

Both women were now in their wrappers, loose and soft and flattering, billowed out by embroidered ribbon-decorated petticoats. They talked to each other in the mirror as they stood with arms lifted high, removing pins and combs and feathers from their hair, tossing them onto the dressing-table top which was massed with Jacintha's collection of cut-glass bottles and porcelain boxes, filled with oils and scents and lotions and pomades. Among these were her pincushions, shaped like hearts and swans and guitars, covered with crystal beadwork and bristling with jewelled pins. The lamps were burning, casting a soft and subtle light, the heavy crimson draperies had been pulled together, a brisk fire was going in the fireplace, and all the room seemed a warm and intimate and wonderful haven.

Surely, here they were safe from any intrusion upon their companionship and their happiness. Indeed, it began to seem the threat itself had been imaginary.

Had they ever been out in that wild treacherous place?

Had they actually encountered him and been forced violently, if momentarily, apart by his explosive and ominous energy?

Of course not.

This was where they had been all along, softly talking, moving their hands and arms as gracefully as if they were performing a ballet, smiling in the mirror and admiring, with equal pleasure, their own selves and each other.

Both of them had luxuriant hair, falling down their backs below the waist—Jacintha's shining black mass, waving and rippling and twisting into curls at the ends, Cherry's deep red-brown, almost the color of polished mahogany. They had the same eyes, big and dark and seeming to pour forth a splendid radiance. Their mouths were soft and pink and fresh. They looked very much alike and, at the same time, very different. For while Cherry was sprightly and spontaneous, both in looks and in manner, Jacintha, by contrast, had an unaffected pride and dignity which made her often seem unintentionally imposing.

"Come," said Cherry. "Sit down here and let me brush

your hair, as I used to do. Remember? Such a very long time ago—"

Jacintha sat on a small violet-wood settee formed of two gracefully curved attached chairs, carved around their scalloped frames with roses and grapes and upholstered with crimson silk plush. She tilted back her head and Cherry, with slow and rhythmical strokes, began drawing the brush down through her hair. For a few moments they were silent, Jacintha sitting with closed eyes, trying not to cry. Now that she and Cherry were together again, it seemed she felt more and more poignantly the significance of those years which had been empty of her mother's gaiety and tenderness.

Unexpectedly she shuddered, a sharp spasmodic shudder that began at her shoulders and travelled down her body. Then she laughed and gave Cherry a quick apologetic little glance.

"Something just reminded me of Father. I guess I'm still a little afraid of him. Do you know—he kept worrying that *I* would come down with consumption? He worried about it all my life and I saw one doctor after another every time I caught a chill or ran a fever or even sneezed. I believe he finally convinced himself that you actually *had* died of consumption."

"Hypocrite!" said Cherry with sharp scorn. "I hope he doesn't die until he's very old. Imagine how boring *that* would make things for him here!" They both laughed and then Cherry said: "Let's make plans. Let's talk about all the things we're going to do together."

"Yes!" Jacintha clasped her hands in her lap like an eager child, sitting with her back very straight, her feet close together. "Let's make plans."

"This is the most picturesque country imaginable, you know." For a countryside to be picturesque was its finest recommendation. "We can take a coach—a private one, or we can go in a public conveyance if we prefer—and travel about as much as we like. I haven't seen a great deal, for I simply never got around to it."

"Never got around to it! In twenty years?"

"The time went by so fast. It was gone before I knew it. I kept meaning to stir about—and then you arrived. We might even stay overnight and camp—don't you think that would be nice?"

ON ROARING MOUNTAIN BY LEMONADE LAKE 65

"But it must be dangerous—bears and panthers and wild Indians. Wouldn't you be afraid?"

"I suppose. Well, then—perhaps we can get together a party. Yes! That's what we'll do!"

They went on, talking and planning of how they would fill sketchbooks with every wonderful sight they saw (as each had done when touring Europe), of how they would collect flowers and press them—and all at once it seemed they had a dozen fascinating and vital projects.

"We'll be so happy!" declared Jacintha.

"The time will simply fly!"

"Now—" Jacintha got to her feet. "Thank you, and it's my turn to brush your hair."

"I'll run next door for my brush. I won't be a moment—"

She hurried with light quick little steps to the door, kissing the tips of her fingers to Jacintha as she went out. At the same instant Cherry disappeared, Jacintha heard an unexpected sound behind her and felt a rush of chill air. She whirled swiftly, her flesh cold and crawling with horror. Her stomach plunged as if a molten ball had dropped through it.

A door had opened in the floor at her feet and there was the obscene-looking coachman, Grant, grinning up at her.

She started as if she had come upon a snake. He grabbed her ankle.

"Quick! Before she comes!"

"Let go of me!" cried Jacintha. Frantically she began trying to break away, looking backward for Cherry, struggling furiously. "I'm going to scream!"

"I'll break your goddamned neck!"

He gave a jerk so violent and vicious that she was almost thrown to the floor. When he threatened to repeat it, she quickly started down the steep stairway, still looking backward, still expecting that Cherry would appear and save her and then—no more than five or six seconds after Cherry had left the room—he gave her a swift rude brutal shove that knocked her against the wall, reached up, and the door crashed down above their heads.

Jacintha cringed against the wall, watching him and shuddering. He had left a lantern at the bottom of the stairs and she saw a narrow wooden staircase not very different in appearance from that which had led into the cellar at home when she was a child.

Now she heard, from above, Cherry's voice, crying piteously. "Jacintha! Jacintha! Come back! *Jacintha!*" The voice rose on a mournful wail and then shattered into sobs.

Jacintha opened her mouth to reply. Grant clapped his hand across her face and held it there, fastening the fingers of the other hand into her shoulder and giving her a hard nudge in the small of her back with his knee. "Down the stairs!" She looked back and, at the sight of his anger-distorted face, picked up her skirts and went scurrying down as fast as she could. Even so, he gave her a shove that sent her sprawling the last half-dozen steps, spreading her arms and hands out wide to catch herself. She heard Cherry call to her once more, and then Grant had seized her wrist, picked up the lantern, and was rushing along a narrow winding passageway which seemed to have been carved out of stone far beneath the earth's surface. The air was cold and wet.

He went at such speed that she could only stumble frantically along behind him. Then, when she had begun to feel that her lungs were parched and shrivelled and that she could follow him no farther, he suddenly stopped, flung open a great arched door, and pushed her into a brilliantly lighted room.

She stood there dazedly, panting and blinking, massaging her aching arms. Her gown was dishevelled, her hair fallen about her face and over her breasts; she looked like a Victorian wood-sprite, chased here by a satyr.

Grant, meanwhile, was closing and locking the door and now he started to cross the room with his same furious stride.

"Oh, please!" cried Jacintha, picked up her skirt, and started after him. "Don't leave me alone!"

He stopped, turned slowly, and slowly stared her up and down. Under his look of contempt Jacintha stayed where she was, her eyes round and frightened, gazing back at him. Finally, he started on his way once more.

Thoroughly intimidated, she did not move, but watched

while he continued on his way and left the room by another door. She sighed.

Then, raising her head, she began looking curiously about.

Like everything else she had seen today, the square room was of enormous size. Otherwise, it bore no resemblance to any other part of the lodge.

The colors were brilliant—red, yellow, green, blue, orange—but they were not garish, for they were worked in tile set in complex geometric mosaics which covered floor and walls alike. There was a great central space opening overhead to a ceiling thirty or forty feet high, surrounded by a tiled walk from which opened out small recesses, each one lavishly furnished, and each entered through archways formed of carved and gilded pillars. Rich Oriental carpets were strewn about the floor. In the center of the room was a vast semicircular red velvet ottoman and above it, suspended by red silk cords, hung an enormous chandelier made of thousands of pieces of colored stones, twirling and spinning and altering design like a kaleidoscope. Fantastic weapons, carved and jewelled, hung upon the walls.

Jacintha stared and shook her head, turning a complete circle, looking up and down and all around, and finally she gave an unconscious cluck of her tongue: "Tsk, tsk."

She heard a burst of masculine laughter, jumped as if she had been hit with a rock, and, after turning excitedly this way and that, saw him standing twenty feet or so away. He had apparently just risen from a chair near the fireplace—which seemed itself the size of a small room.

"Oh!" she cried. "You scared me again! *Why* do you always do that?"

He bowed slightly. "I apologize. It sounded funny to me, and I laughed. You weren't expecting to find me here?" His voice grew mocking on that last sentence.

Disconcerted, Jacintha looked away, saw that her gown had fallen so that one shoulder was bare, and jerked it up again.

He had removed his dinner coat and tie and wore the black, satin-bound trousers and white shirt opened down the front. His hands were in his pockets, his head slightly lowered, and only the edge of his straight white teeth showed as he smiled at her.

"Why do you like to frighten people?" demanded Jacintha. "Why do you always appear by surprise?"

"Why do you regard surprises as necessarily unpleasant?"

"Why—I don't. I love surprises, nice ones." She gestured nervously and frowned. "What makes you ask such an absurd question?"

"If the question were absurd, you wouldn't be upset by it. You know what it is, Jacintha, as well as I. The human heart is always ready to fear misfortune—it is heavy with the weight of its own guilt."

"*If* we are guilty—it's you who makes us so!" She was surprised at the swiftness, and impertinence, of her answer.

But he only smiled, and then shrugged. She lowered her eyes and took up a blue satin ribbon which went around her waist, tied in a bow, and hung almost to the floor. She began rolling it into a ball, pretending to concentrate as she did so.

"You had no dinner?" he asked her after a few moments.

She slowly shook her head.

"Would you like something now?"

She shook her head more rapidly. But she could not look at him. She was thinking of the sound of Cherry's voice, and it seemed she could hear it as clearly as if she were crying to her this moment: "Jacintha! Jacintha! Come back! *Jacintha!*"

The memory of that pitiful pleading voice which had been like a piercing instrument down the flesh of her back, seemed to scrape along her bones—at the memory of it she turned cold inside and hugged herself to get warm again.

I must get away from here somehow—I must get away at once and go back and tell her that I am not her rival and never want to be—I must get back to her now, this moment, so that she will know there was not possibly time—

There she stopped, holding herself tighter, and closed her eyes hard:

I must get back before I look at him again.

It's part of his depravity to look like that—brilliant and compelling. Even if he weren't who he is, he is too fantastically beautiful to be trusted. Masculinity was never meant to be so seductive.

I won't be fooled by it. I won't be taken in. No matter what happens, I won't look at him.

But even then the desire to have one more glimpse was growing stronger. Only one quick glimpse—to convince herself that she had exaggerated his beauty and dangerousness.

He was a handsome man, it was true. But no man was irresistible unless you wanted him to be. Unless you gave him, for your pleasure and his, the gift of irresistibility. Douglas had possessed great power over her—and yet she had sensed then and knew clearly now that he had possessed it because her own need had endowed him with mystery and urgency.

If that was true—then this man could be no different.

I've let my imagination run away with me again.

While she stood, huddled into her own embrace, her eyes closed, frowning—he had watched her silently for a moment. Then he picked up a pipe, filled and lighted it, and drew a slow deep breath.

Jacintha opened her eyes and looked at him. At the moment she did so he exhaled a cloud of smoke, allowing it to curl slowly from his nostrils, and it seemed to her that he stood in a boiling mist. Despite the room's tremendous size, he somehow created the impression of being bigger than his surroundings, of seeming to extend the boundaries of his personality until the room contained him and nothing else. The illusion was shocking, eerie and supernatural.

She blinked her eyes a few times; when she opened them and gave him a long, intense stare she found, to her relief, that he was the same size he had always been —it was a clue to her state of mind and one more warning.

"That fellow Grant!" she cried. "I think you should get rid of him!" Her eyes looked big and bright and scared, but she faced him proudly and was determined to show him that he neither astounded nor dismayed her.

"He abused me coming here! He's cruel and loathsome and as ugly as a dead monkey!"

He laughed and his black eyes were glittering with malicious amusement. "His orders are to get you here without any noticeable damage to your beauty. If he gives you a few cuffs and kicks along the way—well, he serves me well and I have no wish to interfere with his little pleasures."

"You don't *care* if he hurts me?"

"Why should I?" he inquired in a reasonable tone. "So long as he doesn't leave you less beautiful to look at."

"Well!" That was the most outrageous thing she had ever heard. It was almost beyond belief. Certainly that, if nothing else, should make her despise him.

Slowly Jacintha drew herself to her full height, raising her breasts, lifting her head, and staring steadily at him with hauteur and disdain. "Do you know that every time I encounter you, you become more obnoxious to me?" It was her most awesome forbidding manner and yet somehow, even to her, she sounded like a little girl wearing her mother's shoes and talking to herself in the mirror.

His hearty burst of laughter did not surprise her very much, though it did embarrass her into dropping her arms once more and looking at him with all her assumed composure gone. He laid down the pipe and started slowly toward her.

She watched him. With each step he took, she found it more difficult to breathe. A terror began to run through her body, like wind chasing a prairie fire. Slowly, steadily, implacably, he was advancing toward her. The sound of his footsteps on the bare tile seemed to echo thunderously in the vast silent room. And now, once more, she saw him looming larger and larger, and was struck with a sudden terror that he would envelop and crush and annihilate her. She stood staring at him, shaking; her fear became a heedless stampede. She gasped and her hands reached out. She tried to cry aloud but only moaned, as in a nightmare.

His size and nearness faded abruptly; he blurred and vanished. At the same time, there began a distant ringing in her ears, and oddly it seemed to be occurring one sunny Sunday morning in a foreign city. Cold sweat broke on her forehead and over her face and neck. Her eyes closed and she swayed forward.

He took a few quick running steps and caught her in his arms, then tenderly held her against him, supporting her head with one hand. When, after a time, she raised her head, he instantly released her.

Oh, she thought unhappily, why does he make everything so difficult? Whatever is going to happen, should happen now. What is he waiting for?

She looked up at him once more.

He was shaking his head, slightly smiling, but the look of malice had gone. "You Victorians. Here— Sit down. Try to compose yourself."

Jacintha silently obeyed. She sat at the far end of the low, deep, red velvet couch he had indicated, backing up against the corner so as to feel its firmness. She sat very straight with her delicate hands resting relaxed and palms upward in her lap, her ankles lightly crossed. She looked as if she expected to be catechized. Still, she felt much easier. His gentleness had been reassuring.

And, even while she felt resentful that he had dragged her here in this unceremonious fashion, frankly admitting that he did not care if she was abused along the way, she found herself guiltily pleased to be with him, and full of eager anticipation for what each next moment would produce.

Warily, she cast him a sidelong glance. He gave her a quick flashing grin and, after a moment's surprise, she spontaneously responded with a childlike smile and a little laugh.

"Tell me," he said, after a moment. "Have you enjoyed your reunion with your mother?"

Jacintha's face grew suddenly red. She had been on the point of flirting with him. In fact, she had been flirting with him. That little laugh was one of her most valuable assets—she had never met a man yet who was not charmed by it. This was his sly way of reminding her.

Oh! He *was* horrible!

"Of course!" she tartly replied, arching her brows and looking at him disdainfully. "It's been a wonderful thing to find each other again. We thought at first that it was a happy coincidence, but then of course realized it was a trick of yours." Her eyes narrowed accusingly. "You know that she is madly in love with you—don't you?"

"I know that she says she loves me. I'm not sure what she means by it."

"I know what she means by it! If you don't know what love is, then I pity you! No wonder you're what you are—cynical and unhappy!"

"As it happens, I've never been altogether convinced that any of you know for sure what you mean by it, either. And remember—it's your opinion that I am cynical and unhappy."

"Of course you are! You're dissolute and immoral and I'm sure you're miserable!"

He laughed again. "I'm sure you hope I am."

He was watching her steadily and, as he continued to do so, the anxiety returned, mobilizing all her forces and then, it seemed, scattering them the next instant. This frantic activity, alternately drawing together her personal army and knocking it apart, left her in helpless consternation.

"You want to make me fall in love with you, too, don't you?" she demanded after a long pause. "Then you intend to amuse yourself by seeing how much trouble we will have about you! You know that's your intention—why don't you admit it?"

He raised his eyebrows in mocking admiration, but did not reply.

"We saw through your trick. Both of us did. I suppose that shocks you. You haven't anything to say, for a change. Most likely you think you're much too crafty for anyone else to understand."

That speech gave her a glow of pride and pleasure. She felt that her mind was brilliant, her emotions large and noble, her beauty sparkling and fresh—and that all in all, he must be more chagrined than he had ever been in his long and infamous career with women.

Still he had said nothing for a moment or so and then, slowly, he said, "After all, I have to occupy my time, too. I was, as it happens, curious to see what you and your mother would do if you both fell in love with me."

Jacintha, to her own surprise, gave a sudden gleeful little laugh and clapped her hands together. "You see!" she cried joyously. "I knew it! I saw through you!"

"So you did," he agreed.

But now she felt deprived of her triumph. It was as if she had been holding a red toy balloon in both hands and suddenly it was gone. How had he done that?

"Shall I go now?" she asked him, and stood up.

"Do you want to?"

"Of course I want to! You've just admitted—everything!"

"Go on, then."

"The door is locked. Grant locked it when we came in."

She had expected him to tell her to sit down and behave herself and felt as if she had been pulling on a rope with all her strength, only to have him suddenly let go and send her frantically staggering, trying to catch her balance.

"It's open. Run along."

He got to his feet and stood with his hands in his pockets again, watching her and waiting. The initiative was hers.

She must somehow manage to leave this room with dignity and pride and the firm conviction that, no matter what her present company and surroundings, she was nevertheless a Victorian lady, wellborn and well-bred. Accordingly, she drew herself to her most lofty stature and stood for a moment as if at a court function, regarding him with imperious disdain. But she could not rely upon this haughty attitude to last her long—it might dissolve in tears at almost any moment. She turned slowly, as on a dais, her gown swirling over the floor in a semicircle and, with her hair streaming, her ruffled skirt billowing, she started with stately steps to cross the room.

Her progress was an increasing humiliation.

She was agonizingly aware of him behind her, watching her with his black eyes which seemed, in her imagination, to blaze with mockery. Her steps echoed on the tile floor and sent forth, apparently, spreading circles of sound which filled the room and slowly rose toward the vast ceiling. Her flesh began to creep with a dreadful sensation of being followed by something stealthy and ugly and unknown. She felt as though the muscles along her backbone were spasmodically jumping, like keys on a player piano.

When she had gone about ten yards she stopped,

clasped her fingers hard together, drew in a deep breath—and turned to confront him. He was standing in exactly the same place, in exactly the same position, looking at her with exactly the same expression.

"Have you never had respect," she began, dismayed to hear the high quavering pitch of her voice, "for any woman?"

He smiled slightly, but, almost instantly, seeing how hurt she was, his face sobered and he shook his head.

"Respect," he said, in a pleasant friendly tone, "is a state of mind forced upon children by their parents. It becomes a habit and sticks. But what use would *I* have for it—having neither parents nor children of my own?"

"You have no children?"

That was the most immoral thing he had said yet and so shocked her that she had taken several involuntary steps toward him before she realized it and stopped herself.

"I have no children," he replied. "Surely you know my reputation—I never beget. That's another of my sins, perhaps the worst of them all in the world's eyes. Neither I nor my mistresses pay in any sense at all for our pleasure. When it ends, it is done. There is no aftermath of any kind—there is no new life to anticipate, or to dread, as the case may be."

While he talked to her Jacintha gazed at him with her dark eyes round and horrified, her lips apart, one hand to her throat. Her face had drained white and she was having difficulty breathing. There was something in the sound of his voice—something—something— What could it possibly be?

It was like a caress. The very tones seemed to stroke her arms and back and breasts, tenderly, steadily, voluptuously, making her grow warm and luxurious. She was scarcely aware of what he was saying and only yearned for him to continue speaking.

Then she remembered what he had said. By standing there, goggling at him like that, she had given her tacit approval to the wickedest speech she had ever heard: He was tempting her again—tempting her, this time, to relinquish everything which made her a member of civilized society. Everything, in fact, which gave dignity to her existence as a woman.

"You find that shocking," he said, still speaking in that easy friendly fashion. "But your head is an attic, remember, stuffed with worn-out furniture. You're in a new place, but you don't have a new self for it—and perhaps you never will. That takes quite an active imagination, and you Victorian ladies had yours smothered in infancy."

"If you regard it as showing a lively imagination to arrange things so that love and babies have nothing to do with each other— Well! It's a lucky thing you're where you are, then!"

"I am," he said quietly, "myself—and only myself. I do not break myself up into little pieces and distribute myself around in the form of miniatures. Nor have I any wish to do so."

"If other men felt as you do—if they had *your* vanity," she added contemptuously, "a woman would be worthless."

"Only if you believe that pleasure is worthless. Anyway, your men don't and they never will. They will continue to need you for the reasons they always have." His face broke into an unexpected dazzling grin. "It's they, if you ask me, who are the poor devils."

Jacintha shook her head. "You are—disgusting! That's what you are!"

He made a wry face. "Am I?" And he came toward her once more, covering the few remaining feet between them with a light quickness that was almost uncanny. He moves like an animal, she thought, as if that were one more thing to keep in mind against him. A gentleman should be graceful—but not as graceful, certainly, as a panther.

Jacintha whirled, turning her back on him, and covered her face with her hands. She was suddenly so frightened again that she began to tremble and the trembling steadily increased until it became uncontrollable and she stood there quaking and shivering helplessly, her hands over her face.

"Tell me," he said finally. "What are you afraid of?"

She felt his hand touch her left forearm, very gently, and the fingers closed with tenderness and care. Even if he did not object to Grant's abuse, he evidently had no wish or need to abuse her himself.

Gradually the trembling stopped and she raised her head and waited, alert as an animal in a field scenting imminent danger. Even the soles of her feet seemed to crawl with anxiety; she shifted from one foot to the other but then did not move again. Desire grabbed at her like a quick closing hand. She stood perfectly still now, waiting for what he would do. He seemed to loom behind her, boundless and unconquerable, as she shrank into nothing, becoming smaller and weaker and progressively more helpless.

Very slowly, still with that excessive weakening tenderness, he turned her to face him and now, at last, the mockery was gone. He was looking down at her from his great height and his expression was sober, though not unduly serious. He seemed to wish, to will, that she be afraid of him no longer. And there was nothing—now that she was so close to him, her head bent back on her white throat, gazing obediently upward—for her to fear. His resplendent male beauty seemed no longer a threat or a danger—but a generous benefaction, meant for her pleasure and enjoyment.

The edges of her mouth trembled upward in a tentative smile, and the smile was reflected in his face.

She continued looking at him, questioningly, afraid to trust him for fear the mockery would return, but, as it did not, her smile grew wider and wider until, at last, her lips parted over her white teeth, her eyes sparkled with merriment, and all at once she flung back her head and laughed. In another moment he was laughing with her and they were transported by mirth, rejoicing and exultant. There seemed some profoundly understood and shared secret between them.

But if their laughter had stopped suddenly and he, or anyone else, had asked Jacintha what had caused it, she would have had no answer.

Even as she laughed she was vaguely aware that this rapturous delight and exhilaration had resulted from nothing more remarkable than his taking her by the arm and turning her to face him. And yet that domination, accomplished, as it were, by tenderness rather than by force, was so complete that she had only one wish now: to please him in any way she could and so continue this marvellous sense of buoyant felicity which his smile, honest and devoid of mockery, had somehow produced.

She felt that finally he approved of her, that he found her most beautiful when she looked happy and content, without fear in her eyes or distrust in her expression. And his approval had mysteriously become the one thing which was important to her.

"There," he said at last. "How lovely you look now."

"I do?" she whispered. "Oh—thank you."

She knew that she had passed by imperceptible degrees into a state of devoted mesmerism. She had succumbed to him as completely as she had ever wished and believed she had succumbed to Douglas. He had cast some magical enchantment over her, though by no determinable means but the sound of his voice, his touch, his surpassingly handsome face and body, and the principle of heroic masculinity which he seemed to represent. But there *must* have been something—some necromancy. For surely those things alone were not sufficient to so magnetize a woman of her rather cool or, at least, composed temperament, who had found only one genuine passion during her life and that, but a few months before her death?

Well, then, she was a victim of sorcery. There was no use even to imagine or hope any longer that she could contest with him.

"Are you sure," he asked her, "that you have ever been in love before?"

"Before?" she repeated. "Before? Then you think that I am in love with you now?" She sounded bewildered.

"Aren't you?"

His hand left her shoulder and moved slowly around to her back, no longer gentle, but pressing hard against her flesh; his fingers fastened in her hair and drew her head backward, pulling with a steady strength. The pain became pleasurable so that she neither winched nor cried out, but only continued to stand with her head back, looking into his face with an expression of reverence and gratitude, humble almost to abjectness. She would have dropped to her knees at that moment and prayed to him, if he had not been holding her with too firm a grip, and was a little ashamed to realize that she actually wished to do so.

"I never felt before," she murmured, "as I do toward

you. It's—uncanny. I seem to have lost my pride; and I was always very proud. I was even proud of being proud."

"Then you were never in love. One thing a woman cannot keep if she loves a man, is her pride. Pride is a ridiculous encumbrance for a woman if she ever hopes to feel anything more than pleasant titillation. Pride is an emotion suitable to a man's sense of conquest—so what would a woman be doing with it?"

"I don't know," whispered Jacintha. "I can't imagine now. I think, though, that I was trying to get rid of it when I fell in love with Douglas. My husband was never able to take it from me."

He released her abruptly and she had been depending upon him so completely for support that she staggered slightly; he caught her by one arm to steady her for a moment, then let her go. He turned and walked several steps from her; then slowly he faced her again. She stood gazing wistfully after him, her brown eyes puzzled and hurt like those of a puppy whimsically deserted by its master. Her arms fell gracefully at her sides, the skirt of her ruffled gown swept across in front of her, like swirling water arrested and held static.

"I think," he said, and that slight mockery was back, "that you must have been quite eager to get here. What was it you heard about me that made you so anxious to meet me?"

She was astonished. A moment ago he had been making love to her. Now, suddenly he had abandoned her and gone back to casual conversation. Having conquered her so easily, perhaps he had lost interest and was not even going to pursue his conquest to its logical termination.

Jacintha longed to run to him, beg him to look at her as he had before, to touch her and kiss her. But she was afraid. As soon as he had moved away, something of her old pride seemed to return, warning her not to make a fool of herself, or he would lose any regard he might have for her.

Play his game, she warned herself. Smile and flirt and talk to him as he seems to want. Please him—and, if you please him enough—he will come back and give you what you want.

That's the terrible thing about being a woman. It's the

waiting. You can never take what you want—as a man can —but must wait for it to be given to you. All your life is spent in coaxing, wheedling, fawning, pandering, enticing, stimulating, flirting—all the petty roundabout ways a woman must travel to reach her goal.

And, even here, it is the same.

She smiled at him and made a pretty little gesture with one hand, tossing back the hair from her face, shaking her head so that its long springy masses swung and bobbed behind her. She answered his question in a soft low voice—the tone which Douglas had told her was as lulling and distracting as whatever song it may have been the sirens used to sing.

"I heard what everyone does about you, I suppose. What makes you think I was eager to meet you?" She spoke with pert provocativeness, offering herself by her manner, proclaiming her independence by her words.

"You've fallen in love with me so quickly. I have to conclude you were in love with me before we met." He shrugged, smiling as though in self-deprecation. "So there must have been something. You heard I was handsome?"

"I heard you were ugly."

He laughed. "You heard I was fascinating to women?"

"I heard you were the most repulsive evil-smelling creature there ever was."

"You heard I could give a woman greater pleasure than any other man?"

"I heard there was nothing more painful or horrible than to be—than to be—by you," she finished, blushing.

He was still laughing. "My God! These lying Puritans! So that's the way you were brought up! No wonder men were a disappointment to you. Well—I never have thought sex should be available to everyone."

"What?" she gasped.

"Of course not. I have a sense of the fitness of things, a sense of beauty, if you will, and it disgusts me to see the way things are managed on earth, where *every*one has both equipment and inclination. To picture the ordinary couple at their love-making is enough to gag you, isn't it?"

"Why, I don't know! I've never tried to picture anyone! I wouldn't even think of it!"

Now he was laughing as if the joke was one of the funniest he had heard, while Jacintha stood watching him, puzzled and unhappy, for she knew she was being made fun of, and was not sure what manner she should take about it.

"Well, I have. Frequently. And I don't like what I see. You wouldn't, either. I've arranged things differently here."

"You've arranged things differently? How, for heaven's sake?"

"In the only logical way," he said. "I don't let any unattractive women in, to begin with, because I can't stand the sight of them. And the unattractive men—I have them castrated. That way, I'm not offended by—"

At that instant, what he had just said sank into Jacintha's consciousness and she gave a scream of horror. "You have them *what?*"

"I have them cas—"

"No!" she cried, and was running toward him with her hands held out. "Don't say it again!" She had reached him now and stood looking up at him with her face completely outraged. "What a fiend you are!"

He laughed softly, while his eyes were searching about her face, in her eyes, over her lips, across her smooth skin. "You mean I should torture myself instead by letting them go on copulating for all eternity? What a silly little girl you are—scarcely grown up." He shook his head. "And to think you were sent here for your sins. I can assure you, you haven't begun to commit them yet."

Jacintha felt once more absolutely bewildered. He was so entirely unlike any man she had ever known. He had no standards, no values, no morality, not even ordinary consideration for woman as a handicapped creature. And that was the quality which puzzled her most of all. For the first thing you must count on in men is that they were carefully brought up to respect and cherish women, and even to be somewhat in awe of them.

Without that— Well, without that she would as soon have hidden herself in a convent.

"You seem to be shocked by me," he said now. "Are you sure that is altogether honest?"

She looked at him with bright suspicion. "I don't know what you mean."

"Are you sure that you are not gratified, instead, by what you call my immorality?"

"Gratified?" cried Jacintha. "How could I possibly be gratified?"

"Doesn't everyone want to be immoral?"

"Not I," retorted Jacintha. "Perhaps I was—but I never *wanted* to be."

He laughed, his hands in his trouser pockets again, looking at her with amusement and a kind of curious speculation. "I think maybe you wanted to be immoral—more than you wanted Douglas."

"Oh! what an awful idea! I loved Douglas!"

"Yes, I'm sure you did, so far as you knew. But you wanted to be superior to the time you lived in, too. It's the same with every one of you. You are all rebels, who come here. Petty ones, for the most part—when I consider my own rebellion." He shrugged. "Still, I suppose it's better than no rebellion at all." Now he was smiling at her with a look of brooding tenderness. "You know," he said reflectively, "you have a wonderful mouth. And that's very important to an earthy bastard like me."

Jacintha caught her breath and—though she stood perfectly still, gazing up at him with a rapt helpless childlike stare, her fingers laced together for support—seemed to feel herself go reeling about the room in swift spirals, pulled like a puppet on strings. Finally, when she stopped reeling, she gave a gentle sigh and lowered her lashes.

"Thank you," she murmured, then glanced quickly up to see his amused smile. He patted her arm.

"You are a little girl, aren't you? I marvel at how you Victorians bear babies while remaining virgins. Perhaps it's the result of regarding pleasure for its own sake as a sin."

"There is no such thing," said Jacintha stiffly, "as pleasure for its own sake." His smile and pat on the arm and that last remark had been a deep humiliation. "Except, perhaps, to you," she added scornfully.

"When you took a lover—weren't *you* looking for pleasure for its own sake?"

"But I had already had two children!"

"Oh, yes, I remember. Then that made it right for you?"

"Not right, no! That isn't what I mean. I mean—

After all, I had done my duty. I had been a good woman and— Oh! I don't know why, but there was no excitement with my husband, and there was, with Douglas!"

"Of course. Because you felt very guilty with Douglas."

Jacintha hung her head. "I did. I always did. I felt wicked and sinful and—" Swiftly she looked up and now her eyes had a brilliant mischievous sparkle. "And wonderful!"

Both of them laughed at her admission and, for the first time, she had a warm excited gratified sense of being on friendly terms with him. How comforting and how delicious it was.

"My husband thought that I had a cold nature," she added confidingly. "Of course, he thought I *should* have," she hastily amended, and that brought more laughter.

"You must have had a fine life with him. There's no such thing as a woman who is cold by nature. By accident, perhaps—but never by nature. That's a contradiction in terms."

"Oh, do you *think* so?" whispered Jacintha.

She was beginning to feel a reckless rushing excitement. Her breath was coming quicker; her lips were parted in eager anticipation; her hands were held before her breasts, palms together. Surely there was now something miraculous in the way he was standing and talking to her, with that easy friendly smile and manner, not mocking her, not speaking as if she were a pretty child: Telling her of all the lies which had ruled her life. It must be wrong to listen—and yet it was so entirely intoxicating. He might have been lying himself. It didn't matter. She would have believed anything he told her at that hypnotic moment.

"However," he continued, "you won't find any of your men admitting that, since it is the myth of female reticence and comparative coldness which bolsters their own crippled self-esteem. A man who is sure of himself—and there can't be many in your kind of world—knows that any woman can be brought to heel as eagerly as his hunting spaniel. To accomplish that is, naturally, the greatest pride of his masculinity. The others, who trust themselves less, must believe in a woman's inferior ardor."

She listened, absorbing the words, swept by a rapturous enthusiasm for this moment when they seemed so safely and honestly close together. It was as if she had been granted something for which she had longed her whole life, without knowing it: She had been welcomed into a man's friendly confidence and treated by him as if she merited individual respect. For the first time she realized that the men who loved her had always before kept the barrier of her femininity between them. He, on the other hand, had brought them closer together by some implied removal of that barrier—almost as if he had taken a delicate chiffon scarf and, while he was talking, carelessly tied it around both of them.

She had forgotten Cherry.

She no longer believed that he was evil or cruel.

She had become perfectly submissive, ruled by an unashamed and elemental adoration.

His beauty appeared to her more glorious than ever before, his power seemed prodigious: swift, vibrant, supreme. Her own face, entirely unselfconscious, since her attention was centered wholly upon him, now wore an exquisite look of aspiration and homage.

All at once his expression altered and for the first time she saw pure exultant lust in a man's eyes.

At the sudden appearance of this primal ruthlessness, she became aware that every man she had ever known, and the two who had loved her, had been liars. With one crash everything which had composed her pride, her feminine expectancy of respect and tenderness, collapsed into hopeless ruin. There was no more left of it, and no better hope of repair, than if a glass building had been rattled apart by an earthquake.

Several moments passed, very slowly, it seemed, as she stood waiting and transfixed, lost in surprised awareness of a new world, the existence of which she had never imagined. The quality of this man's desire was as little like anything she had encountered before as he, himself, was like either Martin or Douglas. She sensed in him a primordial ferocity, a thronging tyrannous lust which would surge over her like a herd of wild horses, maddened and shrieking, pound her into annihilation and sweep on their way, their universal fury still unabated.

At that same moment—seeming in uncanny fashion to be a part of her terrified image of galloping horses—she heard a distantly echoing roar, followed by sullen rumbling. Glancing toward a line of windows near the ceiling, she saw several spasmodic bursts of lightning. A storm was beginnning.

She reacted to this natural tumult with a further increase of excitement and painful anxiety, for it seemed to heighten her own faltering cowardice.

She wanted to turn and run away from him. She had a frantic vision of herself beginning to run, of him starting in pursuit, of herself dissolving through the wall as she reached it, leaving him baffled and helpless.

For she felt in his ravenous plundering desire the threat of her own final destruction. He would accomplish what her death had not and she found herself afraid of him with a mortal dread she had not felt when she knew that Martin was going to kill her. The difference might have been that her death had been sudden and final and she had somehow remained aloof from it. Whereas, if this man took her body, she would be forced to participate, to be continuously aware; she would have to experience whatever sensations he chose to inflict upon her. She would be his helpless and passive victim, with the great danger that he might arouse her so violently that she would, by some fatal accident, demolish herself through response to his enormous passion.

Her eyes, large and dark, full of anguish and pleading, gazed toward him and now, very slowly, her arms reached out, as if she were begging for charity. Her head was tilted slightly back so that the fine long line of her throat showed in clear relief, while the twirling chandelier cast changing multi-colored lights across her face and shoulders.

"Please—" she whispered. "Let me go— Let me—"

He took a quick step and was close beside her, looking down into her face, his own expression serious and brooding but mingled with a strange tenderness.

"Why are you afraid?" he asked her. "Why are you less courageous now—than when you were alive?" He smiled and was now so close that she felt herself almost engulfed: the clean and vigorous male smell of his body; the sheen across his white teeth; the texture of his skin which roused a sudden unbearable longing to touch it with her fingertips. She closed her eyes.

"Because—I'm in love with you." She was surprised to hear the words and wondered vaguely where they had come from and how it had happened they were spoken in her voice.

She waited and when, at last, she opened her eyes once more, she saw his face moving downward, still with that faint smile. His mouth touched hers, lightly and softly, but the next moment he had spread her lips apart and was threatening to devour her with convulsive greed. Suddenly terrified, feeling herself overwhelmed by a remorseless tidal energy, her hands reached up, fingers widespread, and one foot stepped swiftly beckward, to move away. But his arms were around her and she found herself locked against his body.

She experienced a moment of awful fear. She was caught and helpless. Her control over herself, her emotions, her sensations, had been snatched from her. She was weak and humiliated. She had a sense of profound and agonizing despair—then the plain premonition that in another moment she would disintegrate, sacrificed to his indomitable will.

Far above her, through the black windows, shone a blinding flash and there was presently a heavy sound of distant booming. The storm seemed to be steadily approaching, like a giant striding over the mountains.

Though one arm held her fast against him, immobilized, his free hand moved slowly across and down her back, leaving in its wake a spreading electricity that made her heart pound faster and faster, her body grow warm with an exquisite delight and, by imperceptible degrees, she passed from her earlier terror and suspense to a hunger as exuberant as his own. Her arms strained to hold him closer, her head turned restlessly from side to side as if, after coming near death from thirst, she had discovered the most delicious fountain. She made unconscious sounds of moaning and crooning and now seemed entirely lost in this warm rough wild embrace—as eager and ungovernable and nervously alert as a young mare. She was beginning, even now, to abandon her consciousness of self to an ancient and hitherto unknown craving for this mighty dominance.

By swift degrees the Victorian lady had vanished, been momentarily replaced by a tormented and eager woman, then even that much pretense had gone to leave her only a quickened and painfully avid female.

Lightly, easily, almost magically, she felt his hands unfasten her garments so that one by one they fell into a heap. He released her abruptly and, in a moment, had flung his shirt aside and then his trousers. Eagerly they faced each other. He now seemed to blaze with beauty and power, ravishing, victorious.

The storm grew suddenly louder and more violent. Streaks of glaring light illumined the windows and lashed through the room. Thunder raged and roared, blasting as if to blow the earth open, rattling the windows, increasing the fury until the explosions were deafening. The wind howled in piercing hideous tones; rain came beating and pelting against the windows, pouring and gushing down with terrifying violence.

His face wore a wild and brilliant smile which seemed part of the storm itself. He was the embodiment of everything primordial and unrestrained, fierce, overmastering, intemperate. Suddenly he laughed:

"Lust is a wonderful thing, isn't it?"

His arms reached out and drew her to him again. He swept the hair off her neck and put his mouth there. Jacintha moaned like an animal and her flesh crept in a swift-moving chill.

Yes, she whispered to herself. It is a wonderful thing. I never knew what it was before. I never dared to know —and I never met anyone who could show me.

Why do they tell such lies about it?

They stood together, his legs widespread. The passion mounted to a turmoil, raging and swelling like the storm; in moments it had grown unendurable. He seized her wrist in a light strong grip, twisted her about, and she was lying on the floor at his feet. For an instant she looked up and saw him as he seemed to loom gigantically above her—his face in darkness now, for she looked into the light—and felt an instantaneous paralyzing terror. He would destroy her absolutely, tear her body, burst her asunder. She covered her face with her hands and screamed.

But before she could move he had knelt across her. With one hand he took hold of her wrists, jerked her arms above her head and held them there. She screamed in frantic fear and despair, for he seemed to her now like a great eagle in flight, powerfully descending. Her scream, hysterical as the storm, stopped suddenly as her breath caught in a gasp, and then came sailing weirdly downward to a murmuring groan.

A sensation of incredible warmth and delight had flowed instantaneously outward to all the parts of her body, so that even her throat turned hot and her wrists seemed to burn. She experienced a sharp clear joy, a feeling of exultant well-being and utter aliveness and, with it, the sorrowful but unmourned recognition that she would never again be able to claim herself.

She had become his prisoner and must remain so until he chose to free her. There was a brief reluctance, a vague resentment, a passing desire to secure her freedom—then she yielded herself to him completely; for he had evoked, like some magician employing a magic wand, a carnality so intense and luxurious that, now fully responsive and ardent, she became ready to experience whatever was to happen.

Slowly he moved upon her, slowly, and, it almost seemed, thoughtfully. Her eyes were closed, though she could not have seen him for his face was hidden in her hair. Their breathing came and went simultaneously. Their bodies moved with the same rhythm. All sense of time, even of motion, disappeared, until there was only a welter of vivid fantastic sensation. She felt a seething and quenchless desire, a dim hopeless conviction that he had liberated a passion he could never satisfy and she envisioned herself desiring him forever with this same obsessive torment.

Her body seemed to swell and glow, to seethe with excitement. Gradually, almost imperceptibly, the sensations kindled, she experienced them with greater and greater sensitivity, there was a mounting tension, a heightening of emotion and sensuality. She began to feel that she had been mounted by a ruthless rider, despoiling and unmerciful, who drove her onward to unparalleled and possibly unendurable excitement.

She flailed and threshed, moaning, twisting her head from side to side, pleading, begging, gloating over this seemingly endless indulgence. She had lost entirely all sense of herself as Jacintha Frost—almost all awareness of herself as an individual. She was now only a creature experiencing feelings so violent, so ecstatic, so incredible that the end of them must be her own extinction.

She had some dim sense of the storm driving to greater and greater frenzy. Boisterous and tremendous, it battered the building, swept in violent gusts, rending, rioting, smashing. Nothing could survive its insane brutal rage. The building must crack apart, the land would be broken and devastated. The ceaseless crash and din and clamor would leave them deaf forever.

But as time went on she became increasingly unable to distinguish between the storm as it brawled around them and the storm which went surging, heedless and exhaustless, through her body. Even its source had become unknown, unseen, no longer caused by the invasion of one man but a seeming part of all vast and endless natural forces: she felt that the walls between their two bodies had been destroyed and that they wallowed, not in sweat, but in blood.

He was swift and brutal and as he rode on and on, like a man who will ride his mount to its death, she was seized once again by an overpowering terror that soon this would become unendurable and that, trying to escape, she would be shattered and whirled free into space, there to wander through eternity as one of the galaxies, her own identity as a woman lost forever and destroyed. Screaming, she began to struggle, trying to force him from her, clawing her nails down his arms and back, leaving rakelike welts; she tried to fasten her teeth into his shoulder but all at once he seized her arms again and she caught a glimpse of his face, dark and shining, with a strange triumphant smile.

There was a monstrous explosion of lighting and she seemed to feel that a tree was torn up by its roots, but could not tell whether it had happened within her own body or somewhere out in the storm. The pleasure was incalculably, demoralizingly, exquisite. She felt herself to have been struck by some shattering force, or devastated by the explosion. Her entire being, it seemed, trembled uncertainly between existence and annihilation and then swam surely into a welcoming oblivion. Her ears were ringing, her face and hands and lips grew cold. She lay perfectly still, her head fallen to one side, her eyes closed.

She lost the sense of time and did not know how much later it was that she returned, again swimming slowly back to the surface.

She lay a moment longer, quiet, surprised to find that she had survived and that, though she felt spent to exhaustion, there was throughout her belly a warm and wonderful sensation of spreading ease and fulfillment. She could feel the heavy pulsing blood in her legs and under her navel.

She opened her eyes, cautiously, and looked to find him. He was lying beside her, his arms crossed behind his head, looking sideways at her, smiling. His broad brown chest rose in a swelling arch, then sloped abruptly to his flat belly and hard-muscled tapering legs. Jacintha looked at him with wonder and awe.

Her fear was gone; there was only a deep and humble gratitude. The terror she had felt of being ravaged and extinguished, seemed now a foolish distant little girl's fear. They seemed to have gone on a long venturesome voyage together, to have shared its dangers and marvels, and to have returned with a common experience which would bind and hold them close forever.

Deeply and slowly and luxuriously she sighed. Her mouth formed a soft but peculiarly poignant smile. There was about her now a compliant and voluptuous languor which made her extraordinarily more alluring.

"I feel," she murmured wonderingly, "as if I had been dead and come to life again."

He rose to lean on one elbow, looking down at her, still smiling. "I don't think you'll have much trouble with your pride from now on."

She gave a delighted little laugh. "I'm sure I won't." Her head turned and her lips softly touched his hand which lay beside her head. "You know," she said, with a sudden air of longing to confide, and her dark eyes glanced up hesitantly, "I was terrified at first—I've never been so afraid of anything in my life—"

He bent and kissed her softly, and his mouth lingered just above hers as he answered. "If a woman doesn't feel some fear, she won't feel great pleasure, either."

She closed her eyes, feeling his warm breath upon her

lips, deeply inhaling its fragrance, and she had begun to grow irresistibly drowsy. "I'm only afraid," she whispered, and was but half aware of what she said, like someone sliding under anaesthesia, "that you will get tired of me."

He laughed softly, and the laugh sounded reassuring; then abruptly she had dropped off to sleep.

She had no idea how long she slept for when she woke, suddenly and rather startled, sitting up and looking swiftly about, everything in the room was exactly the same, even the slowly churning kaleidoscope of lights far overhead. But he was no longer at her side, his clothes were gone, and he was not in sight.

All at once she felt cold and frightened and there was a strong desolate sense that she had been abandoned in an alien place. To wake without him, expecting him to be there all the while she slept, then finding herself alone, was a profound and disturbing rebuff. For her entire being was filled with an awareness of him, so intense and strong and absolute that whatever it was she had once felt for Douglas seemed as trivial and superficial as an appetite she might have had for lollipops.

She got to her feet, moving lightly and with a fluent grace.

Now she found herself refreshed and volatile, brimming with miraculous optimism. She raised her arms above her head and stood on her toes and stretched, feeling that she could pull her body like taffy. She was completely relaxed and filled with a sparkling strength. The sensation was new and astonishing and, after a moment, she realized that it must be the gift he had left her, the residue of his imperial power which had, it seemed, entered into her blood and muscles. She laughed, amazed and delighted, as if she had discovered a treasure in a forbidden forest.

She looked down at her naked body. She had always admired her own beauty, but she now appeared to herself as incredibly lovely, soft and warm and desirable. He had transformed her, it seemed, and made her even more lovable to her own self. How fantastic that this man, and the powers he possessed, should be regarded as evil by the stupid and blind and insensitive world she had known.

It is they who are the dead, she thought. Not we.

She moved quickly about the room now, darting lightly, searching for him, looking into the various alcoves, behind pillars, between archways, hoping to find him asleep in one of the deep velvet divans. He was not. The room was empty and she had been left alone.

There was an unexpected sound. She turned sharply to see the door open and Grant come in. She shrieked and with a hasty feminine movement sought to cover her body with her two hands.

"Get out of here!" she cried. "Don't you dare stand there staring at me!"

He was staring at her, it was true, but with no more interest than he had shown when she was dressed. "Hurry up!" he commanded, and came strolling farther into the room. "Put your clothes on!"

"Get out of here!" she cried again. "I'll have you beaten! Things have changed since you saw me last!"

At that he gave a sharp mocking contemptuous laugh which startled her like a shot. There was some unpleasant premonition in it, she felt. At least, that was surely his intention. Now he was swaggering directly toward her and, seeing that she could not frighten him away, Jacintha ran to her clothes, snatched them off the floor and rushed behind a tall chair where she stood, putting them on and glaring at him over the top of it with her shining black eyes.

He rambled about the room while he waited for her, scuffling his feet, kicking at the carpets and furniture, a scowl on his face and his hands in his pockets like an ill-natured middle-aged brat, which was what he appeared to be.

"All right!" she snapped presently, reaching up her arms to draw her hair into some kind of order and shake it out so that it fell down her back. "I'm ready!"

He stopped his ramble, glanced at her as she stepped out from behind the chair, then shuffled toward the great door through which they had earlier entered this room, jerking his head to summon her.

She walked toward him, more sure of herself than she had ever been in her life. "I'll do as you say now," she informed him, speaking with the manner of a queen to her most despised subject, "but later—I shall tell him about you."

Grant listened indifferently, made a face and shrugged his shoulders. He opened the door and gave another jerk of his head to indicate that she should precede him. She swept disdainfully by and he picked up a lantern which threw ragged shadows about the black narrow passage. They came, very quickly, it seemed, to the foot of the stairs. There she stopped, suddenly white and cold, and feeling as if her heart was dead.

Cherry.

Cherry was at the top of those stairs. Waiting for her.

She had forgotten her so completely that it was now a greater shock to remember than it had been to meet her here after a separation of twenty years.

For now she recalled with agonizing vividness how eager Cherry had been to prevent what had happened. She could see Cherry's lucid little face, gazing up at him as they three stood together in the lobby. She could see the troubled look which had come into her eyes later, as she guided Jacintha away, back to their own rooms. She could hear her talking, merrily chattering, trying not to betray her desperate anxiety.

And then, Grant had summoned her and she had gone —against her will, firmly intending to remain faithful to the promise she had made Cherry and herself.

She had not only broken the promise; she had forgotten it.

She stood a moment, stunned and revolted to have found herself capable of such treachery. She would have been ashamed if the woman had been a friend— But Cherry!

She felt a rude hard shove at her back and stumbled forward, throwing out her hands against the steps above.

"Go on!" It was Grant!

She turned and there was his grotesque face, disfigured and discolored, just beneath her, waiting with his usual air of violent impatience.

"I *can't* go up there!" she told him tensely. "Don't make me go back up there, I beg of you! I'll give you all my jewellery—I'll—"

"Quick! I've wasted time enough on you! I've got other business."

She stood where she was, drawing herself now to her most commanding height, staring down at him with cold determination. But, after a moment, he gave a grunting laugh and, with a startlingly sudden motion, raised his arm and threatened to strike her across the face with his elbow. She gave an involuntary shriek and turned, started up, and the door was flung wide, as if blown open by a gale. She ran to the top as fast as she could and arrived breathless back in her own room. She had one last glimpse of Grant's face, grinning as he slammed the door down. She peered closely, but its outline had been lost in the riotous flower garden which decorated the carpet.

Then, swiftly, she turned:

The room was empty.

That was both such relief and shock that she began to tremble and sweat and, after a moment, had to sit down, weak and almost sick. She sat there and slowly shook her head, back and forth, back and forth. Tears dropped gently upon her hands as they lay folded in her lap.

In their excitement last night, they had forgotten to draw the draperies, and now the room was growing light. Slowly she rose and went to look out the eastern windows. There was a pink streak along the edges of the dark distant mountains, and in the vague milky light she could once more see steam rising—faintly blue and red and green. She leaned her forehead against the glass to feel its coolness, then pressed her cheek and finally her lips against it as she stood there, gazing wistfully out. She could hear the cawing of hoarse-throated birds, keeping up a steady complaint, and before her floated a magpie, his feathers so flippity that she had to smile at him with tender amusement.

She stood for several minutes gazing out, forlorn and perplexed. The time she and Cherry had spent together yesterday now seemed far longer than an afternoon and evening. Yet it had contained the real beginning, the culmination, and the end of their relationship as mother and daughter.

She had forfeited, through her selfishness and treachery, any claim she had ever had to Cherry's love. And now she must confront eternity alone—as she deserved—pitiable, comfortless, desolate.

Her feelings were muted—mournful disillusionment and regret, rather than any wild or passionate grief.

I'm too tired, she thought, to feel this as I should—and as I will.

When I've slept I will go to her and apologize, even though I know she won't accept it and shouldn't accept it. Still, it's my duty to humble myself. Or perhaps something else will happen which will make it unnecessary for me to do anything at all. While she was thinking about these things, she wandered from window to window, drawing the heavy crimson velvet draperies and when she had drawn the last the room was dark. She took off her clothing, got into bed naked and stretched out on her back, her hands flung above her head, palms open and fingers curled like a child's, eyes closed.

I'll think about him.

Now that it's been done, I can't undo it by refusing to think about him. I've done the worst thing I can already—and, in a way, that leaves me free—

These were strange thoughts to her, quite unlike any she had had while she was scheming to spend an hour or two or three with Douglas once every week or so. Then, she had brooded much over her sin, haunted by thoughts of how she had fallen from her strict upbringing, wondering where the evil streak in her nature had come from: Now— How great the difference was.

Even her remorse had in it some pride that he had summoned her the first night. She knew and admitted to herself that she would have been deeply humiliated if he had ignored her after their meeting on Roaring Mountain.

As she lay there, she found that she could recall him with startling clarity. There seemed not a detail of his looks, a tone of his voice, a word he had said, a gesture, any of the violent exuberant emotions he had made her feel, which she had forgotten. He was more vividly present, more an actual reality to her than the reality that she lay alone in bed.

She lay flat on her back and still, recalling with tenderness and gratitude everything which had happened between them from the moment she had turned and found him standing there smiling down at her, almost naked against the brilliant sun and white flashing earth of Roaring Mountain, to the last touch of his mouth as she was falling asleep the night before.

She remembered the crispness between her fingers of

the black curly hairs covering his chest. She smelled his breath and tasted his mouth. She felt the hard muscles of his back, spasmodically working as he pumped his vast energy and excitement into her. She recalled every sensation to which he had provoked her with such intensity that again and again she was swept by waves of feeling, rushing through her in wild joyousness. Her body became permeated once more with tumultuous erotic longings. Her desire for him had returned in full dynamic and demanding force, treacherously taken possession and now was threatening to drive her into frantic despair. At that moment she experienced a shocked and horrified revulsion and seemed to recoil from contact with her own self, as if she had discovered herself to be disgusting or ugly.

She felt sickened with love and yearning and dismay. I am bewitched or insane, she thought, and her eyes searched desperately through the dark room, seeking help. She was frightened and overcome with mortification.

Surely it is unhealthy for a woman to feel this kind of desire. It's immodest and—unladylike, and it takes everything of me away from myself.

It leaves me helpess and incomplete, a faceless unidentifiable female who must follow him wherever he goes, carrying a heavy burden. The burden is my own desire, which I cannot lay down or any way rid myself of, but only follow and hope he will turn and take it from me. When it pleases him.

Her face twisted. I must get over this ridiculous idolatry. Surely, the next time I see him he will repel me. No man can arouse such violent atavistic feelings without finally growing repulsive to you.

I think perhaps he is ugly, after all— Yes, I'm sure that he is—

The emotions he had evoked she now converted into disgusting and unnatural feelings. He had employed some trick to take away her femininity and pride and natural dignity and leave her infested with his own vile nastiness.

And he had succeeded. At least, he had succeeded until this moment when some lingering sense of decency had made her consider what had happened.

How stupid he must think I am!

How he must laugh at me and despise me!

I did everything he wanted—I had even begun to adore him, with absolute humility and devotion.

She brushed her hand through the darkness, as though to banish the malign and baleful influence of his image. He was not beautiful, irresistible, a creator of unparalleled excitement, supreme and commanding. He was hideous, repellent, possessing some uncanny but revolting power. He had enchanted her and she, alone and seemingly helpless, had nevertheless had both strength and courage to break the enchantment and set herself free.

Finally, she was enough at peace to fall asleep, and she slept without moving, until she opened her eyes and saw Cherry's face above her. She looked up, only mildly surprised, and then, slowly and softly, she smiled. For the moment she had forgotten everything but the fact that here was her mother.

Cherry was leaning across her, fully dressed, Jacintha noticed, as if for an outing of some kind. She even held a small closed parasol in one hand. Her gown, which fit her with fashionable tightness, was of bright green and red plaid wool, buttoned down the front, with a black velvet collar, and there was a little black velvet bonnet perched on top of her head. She smelled, as she always had those many years ago, of some fresh lilac fragrance, and Jacintha thought that she looked captivating.

"Aren't you ever going to get up?" asked Cherry in a tone of gentle humorous chiding.

Still smiling, Jacintha yawned and stretched and started to reply. Then she remembered. The smile disappeared, her dark eyes widened and, involuntarily, she stuck one forefinger into her mouth, like a little girl expected to be punished. Cherry continued to gaze down at her with that same smile, calm and compassionate, and Jacintha, unable to endure the absence of blame in her eyes, turned suddenly upon her stomach and hid her face in her arms, sobbing.

Almost instantly she felt the pressure of Cherry's bosom upon her back, and Cherry's arms went around her. Her hands began to stroke and smooth the tangle of her black hair, and her voice was light and comforting.

"No, no, no, no," she murmured. "Don't cry, my darling—please don't cry. You mustn't cry."

Jacintha, now sobbing frantically, turned swiftly and looked up at Cherry across her naked shoulder. Her face was wet with tears and her expression strangely mingled pleading and horror.

"You hate me now!" she sobbed, crying so hard that she could scarcely breathe. Cherry took a handkerchief from the little black velvet bag which hung at her wrist and began to blot Jacintha's face. "You do hate me! I *know* you hate me! And you should! You're right to! I deserve it! Oh!" she wailed in a sudden desperate frenzy. "I hate myself!"

Cherry, still blotting the tears which continued to pour down Jacintha's cheeks, answered gently. "No, Jacintha. I don't hate you. Of course I don't. To hate you—I would have to blame you. How can I blame you?"

"How can you *not* blame me?"

She had an almost furious need for Cherry's blame and hatred, for some swift shattering punishment. If only Cherry would recoil from her, speak to her with bitterness and contempt, abandon her to eternal loneliness and despair— But Cherry was warm and lovely and seemed no more disturbed than if Jacintha were still her five-year-old child, guilty of nothing worse than having broken by accident a favorite Sèvres vase.

Now Cherry gave her the handkerchief, sighed a little, and stood up. "It's a beautiful day. You must get dressed and we'll go for a stoll—or perhaps a picnic. They have delightful picnic places here." As she talked she was drawing the cords so that the draperies swung back and, as the brilliant light flooded into the room, Jacintha had to cover her eyes with her hands until she became accustomed to it. Cherry brought her wrapper to her. "Come now, darling—do get up. It's such a glorious day. It always is, here—when there's been a great storm the night before."

Jacintha, sitting on the edge of the bed, slipping into the sleeves of her wrapper, felt her face suddenly burn. Her face and neck turned red and there was a nervous prickling in her armpits; it seemed that her ears were literally erect and waiting for what she would say next. Though she did not know why, the storm seemed intimately connected with everything that had happened.

But Cherry said nothing more and went to sit in one of the great overstuffed crimson velvet chairs, looped with silken ropes and pouring forth cascades of silken fringe.

Jacintha stood up, drawing the wrapper about her, and, as she went into the bathroom, paused at the doorway, looking toward Cherry but not quite at her. "How long did the storm—" she began, and then stopped, afraid that Cherry would know why she asked. "How long did the storm last?" she finished recklessly, for she had an obsessive need to know the answer.

There was a moment's silence so that Jacintha, in alarm, glanced quickly at Cherry—and found her gazing directly toward her, smiling. But Cherry's smile now had nothing in common with any expression Jacintha had seen on her face before. This smile was subtle and mysterious, and tinged in some way with both cruelty and triumph. Jacintha's reaction to it was a quick flashing spasm of fear—and the sudden amazed recognition that this young and beautiful woman, Cherry Anson, who was her mother, was, furthermore, a complete human being, having areas to her personality altogether lacking in any reference to Jacintha. For this look which she now fastened upon Jacintha was oddly sinister, and caused her an involuntary shudder.

She tried to make a joke. "Someone must have walked over my grave." She laughed weakly and felt her cheek muscles begin to tremble with uncontrollable nervousness.

How strange it is—how strange and sad that Cherry should look at me like that. When only a moment ago she—

But a moment ago, of course, she must have been reminding herself that she is my mother.

Then this was what came of their meeting here—both the same age, and both at the height of their beauty. Mother and daughter, it was true, with the old profound and mystic devotion. But, because they were also young and beautiful and in full vitality and ardor, their personal private needs remained urgent and undeniable. Enthusiasm had not dwindled down, and neither had grown pessimistic concerning her own rights to vibrant experience.

"The storm," Cherry replied, "lasted for two hours and a half."

Jacintha's hand slapped to her cheek in horrified astonishment. Then she hung her head and started on through the doorway.

"I think you might be interested to know," continued Cherry's voice, still in that same soft but now, it seemed, peculiarly malevolent tone, "that it always storms when he is making love."

Jacintha gasped again and stepped backward in alarm. "It does!"

She turned swiftly, went into the bathroom, and closed the door. There she stood for several moments, leaning against it for support, her muscles quivering and aching, as if some poison had been poured into them.

Two hours and a half!

Two hours and a half.

My God!

How horrible! How unspeakably incredibly horrible. And to think that at the time— Oh, no, I won't think about it. I'll *never* think about it again.

Cherry knows what happened then.

She was struck with a new thought so humiliating that her legs collapsed and she began to sag toward the floor: Does anyone but Cherry know that I was with him last night?

Oh, this is dreadful. Worse than anything I imagined. It's a nightmare of everything I might ever have feared or despised.

But I must not stand here trying to solve things no one can solve.

I must take my bath.

Cherry is waiting for me.

We're going on a picnic.

She ran water into the tub and scrubbed herself, vigorously and angrily, as if she could scrub him off the surface of her body, at least. After that, she felt a little better, but still stunned that Cherry not only knew he had made love to her but knew for exactly how long.

She slipped back into her wrapper and returned to find Cherry sitting in the same chair, but now smiling affectionately at herself in the little fan-shaped mirror, preening, tilting her head first to one side and then to the other. Though it was her own beauty Cherry was admiring, she reminded Jacintha more than anything of a happy child with its favorite toy. The expression was familiar, the playful enjoyment and approval, for it was the look her own face assumed when she confronted herself in the mirror. The satisfactions of being a beautiful woman who knows she is beautiful, Jacintha had found to be considerable. It was almost enough, she believed, to have been granted in life.

"You do look lovely today," she said to Cherry, pausing a moment at the threshold, speaking shyly, like a little girl giving her elder sister a compliment.

How impossible it was—the way he had arranged things—for either of them to keep in mind that they were mother and daughter!

"Thank you, darling," said Cherry lightly, and smiled at Jacintha who saw, to her measureless relief, that there was nothing left of that subtle mysterious look she had shown her earlier. "I've ordered a lunch made up for us. My maid is getting it now. We'll find some pretty forest or meadow for our picnic—and we can do some botanizing, too. This is the most wonderful place for botanizing!"

Jacintha began to get dressed, as quickly as possible considering the layers of petticoats, the boned and laced corset, the dozens of hooks and pins.

And, as she did so, she marvelled once more at how Cherry—after twenty years in this place and with an eternity ahead to contemplate—could be so optimistic, so happy in her manner, so enthusiastic and gay. She felt an awesome admiration for Cherry, and a portent of self-disapproval.

She must try to match Cherry's light-hearted behavior, for fear of infecting them both with her own gloomy forebodings. She had been inclined—due, no doubt, to a vivid and active imagination—to spells of melancholy which drifted into her for no accountable reason, lingered awhile and drifted away once more, as softly as morning mist. They were considered by everyone she knew to become her and to add a mysterious fascination to her temperament. But here, where the cause of depression was so real and so terrible, she could not permit herself the luxury of such self-indulgence. She would harm Cherry, as well as herself, if she looked grave or seemed disconsolate.

And so, when Cherry spoke of botanizing, she took up the suggestion with a lively display of eagerness. "Oh, yes! I love botanizing! Father used to tell me how much you had enjoyed it and I loved it for your sake. Oh, I studied it very seriously, I assure you," she added, making a comical little face.

They both laughed, and Cherry came to lace her corset and then carefully arranged the curling tendrils along the nape of her neck. When she had finished, Jacintha turned with sudden impulsiveness—feeling the same overwhelming love she had the day before—and hugged Cherry close for a moment.

"Thank you! Thank you for not hating me!"

"Shh," whispered Cherry. "We won't speak of it any more. We *must* not speak of it any more," she added, with gentle emphasis.

Jacintha stood looking down, a wistful smile at the corners of her mouth. "How splendid you are! If only I could have had you during the years I was growing up—"

Cherry made a pretext of gay laughter. "But, if you had, we wouldn't be together here now, would we?"

Jacintha sighed. "No, we wouldn't."

"At least," added Cherry, "we would not be together —and both the same age."

Jacintha blushed at that delicate reminder of her betrayal. But, after a moment, she fought away her self-consciousness and looked directly at Cherry with the most intense and dedicated expression.

"I promise you, it will never happen again."

Cherry shook her head and turned away. "Don't make promises. Promises don't mean anything here. They never mean anything—when our strongest feelings threaten them. You don't know him yet."

"I don't know—" cried Jacintha, astounded that Cherry should say such a thing after what had happened. Then she stopped. "I know as much about him as I ever shall."

"Jacintha, please," said Cherry softly. "Let's talk about other things. There is only one subject dangerous to us. Why can't we avoid it?" She made a little gesture with her hands, palms up.

Jacintha nodded in silent obedience and finished her

dressing. Once more they began to talk lightly and frivolously and kept their conversation to harmless feminine interests.

"Thank heaven," said Jacintha, "whoever packed for this trip, put in my pincushions, even if they did leave out my photographs."

"What could you possibly want of photographs of people who are still alive? Oh, my dear—those earrings! May I see them?"

"Martin gave them to me for my last birthday. I loved violets, and I have a great deal of jewellery shaped like them. One of the worst things, Douglas always said, was that he could never give me anything."

Jacintha now wore a gown of finely woven surah with a pale-blue bodice, fitted tightly down over her hips. The purple skirt was swept to one side, caught and held with a knot of violets, and fell into rich sweeping folds. She set a bonnet covered with violets on top of her head and tied it with a pale-blue veil. She gathered her kid gloves, her beaded handbag, her parasol, and they were ready for the picnic.

The maid had brought in the lunch basket and, though it was light, they each took a handle and carried it between them.

"Do we lock the door?" inquired Jacintha.

"No one ever locks a door here. It wouldn't do any good if they did, I suppose. And anyway, it's so easy to replace something if it should be stolen. One can spend literally hours every day shopping for new things." Cherry gave a light little laugh. "Love-making grows tiresome here—but no one *ever* gives up shopping."

Jacintha laughed too and then suddenly sobered. "Is that true? How ghastly!"

Cherry glanced at her briefly as they walked along the hall, not dawdling as they had last evening, but moving almost briskly or, at least, as briskly as well brought up young ladies ever did move. "It's most fortunate, actually. There's so little else to do. Here—let's take this turn. There's a door just down the hall. We don't need to go all the way back to the lobby."

"But there must be *some*thing one can find to do!"

"You can do whatever you like, of course. There are no rules or regulations."

"That seems quite considerate."

"It may seem considerate—for a year or two. But, eventually, you'll find that since there is nothing you *must* do, there is nothing you will want to do." Cherry turned into another hallway and stopped before a heavy carved door. "We don't realize," she said, "how greatly we depend upon our duties."

It took both of them to get the door opened. And then they stepped out into a day so brilliantly clear and blue that they had to pause a moment and shade their eyes until they grew accustomed to it. They stood, squinting and smiling, thrusting open their parasols. They had come out on another side from the great entrance porch, and this gave them an entirely different view.

A thick natural untrimmed green lawn, filled with blue and yellow wildflowers, sloped away beneath them. They heard a swishing whispering rushing sound, as of a fast-running river, and a great cloud of steam blew suddenly across them, laden with sulphur fumes. They held their noses and made faces, laughing.

"This place smells to high heaven," said Jacintha.

"That's what he intended."

They both burst out laughing, as if at the greatest witticism. Jacintha had begun to realize already how much more precious laughter was than she had guessed during her lifetime, and knew they had now tacitly agreed to laugh at everything which could in any possible sense be made to seem funny.

The rushing swishing sound died away, the steam disappeared, and the air was fresh and clean and exhilarating. Whatever this place was, it had many charms and very great beauties. She and Cherry should be able to spend a long time exploring its possibilities—months, perhaps years—and then her imagination stopped, for she had been struck by a black horror. Even if they spent a hundred years, or two hundred, they would have done nothing at all to whittle away the eternity confronting them. No matter how long they spent at any project, they could do nothing to lessen the time. There was no goal, no limit—

But she must not think of it, for already she had begun to feel dizzy and swarming with anxiety.

"Isn't it incredible!" whispered Jacintha, eager to escape

her own thoughts. "The mountains in the distance—the boiling cauldrons—the sulphur and brimstone—everything as I expected it and yet so entirely different. And the air! It's more delicious than anything I've ever smelled or drunk!"

"Yes," agreed Cherry. "Living the way we did, like plants in a conservatory, all but immobilized, surrounded with two much warmth and humidity—" She gave a quick little shudder, as if the recollection disgusted her. "You get simply *wild* for something primitive."

They strolled down the sloping lawn, discussing whether they should walk to their picnic or take a coach. There was a line of coaches waiting, Cherry said, at all hours, and a driver who could drive you wherever you chose. They decided on that, since it would permit them to see more, and made their way across the high thick wet grass, dragging their long skirts, chatting idly and contentedly as they went and, from time to time, bursting into exclamations of delight or high trilling laughter.

The sun passed, it seemed, to and fro among the clouds, brilliant one moment and faded the next. In the distances they could see that other men and women were out today, too, though there were fewer than might have been expected from the size of the building and the fact that there were several other lodges in these mountains.

They circled a shallow steaming lake of brilliant smeared orange and rusty colors and Jacintha pointed with pleased wonder at the clumps of grass growing in the hot water. They walked by great craters filled with boiling water—one of them pouring forth a stream two hundred feet wide which meandered over white gravelled earth, trickling and bubbling and reeking of sulphur so that they daintily held their noses as they passed its rim.

They rounded a corner of the building and came upon the long line of waiting carriages, the drivers lounging or wandering about or gossiping. A gentleman very elegantly dressed in English tweeds was wrapping a beautiful young lady in a heavily embroidered carriage robe. Now he sprang into the open vehicle and they were off with a smart snapping of the whip and clattering of hooves.

Jacintha and Cherry watched them, standing quietly to one side, both their faces still and white and wistful, almost sad.

"Some women," said Jacintha finally, when the carriage was far down the road, "seem to make happy matches here."

Cherry shook her head. "It won't last. It looks very pretty today in the sunshine. But by tomorrow afternoon they may despise each other. Disappointments—especially sensual disappointments—are felt more keenly here, it seems."

The carriage was a fine one, opened on all sides, a small phaeton intended for two occupants. It was shiny black with red and yellow decorations, and four black horses, highly polished, stood ready to draw it. Jacintha looked at the coachman somewhat anxiously, afraid that it would be Grant, who she was beginning to fear might have been delegated her tormentor—but it was not. It was only some nondescript individual, though he wore a splendid livery. With great deference, he handed first Cherry and then Jacintha into the carriage and spread a handsome robe, embroidered with flowers and birds, across their laps.

The two women looked at each other with gleeful smiles, settling into their corners, making themselves feel cozy and pampered and prepared for a delightful excursion.

The coachman was waiting for their order. "Where shall we go?" asked Cherry.

"Heavens, I don't know. I haven't the slightest idea. You tell him."

"I've seen so little of this place, myself. Take the north road!" she instructed him. "We will guide you as we go along. Now—isn't this better than walking? You see how free we are?"

The coachman snapped his whip above the horses' backs, the carriage gave a quick lurch, and they were away at that same bewildering speed with which Grant had careened her through the forests and over the fields yesterday.

Yesterday?

Don't think about how long it has been or what has happened, she told herself. Think only of this very minute.

"How enchanting!" cried Jacintha. "I've never enjoyed anything so much! Do you remember how you used to take me driving on Sunday afternoons when we went to visit Grandfather Anson?"

"Of course I do. If you could have seen yourself, Jacintha! With your pretty ruffled dresses and long black curls and the sweet manners you had—even when you were two, you seemed a perfect little lady."

They burst into dainty laughter at that, for obviously she had been less a lady than she had seemed, and so had her mother. But it was even more humorous that Cherry should speak of how she had looked at the age of five, and here they were twenty years later and exactly the same age.

They went bouncing over the meadows, lurching in the deep ruts left by the other carriages, through brief forests, along the edges of low pine-covered hills, through steam which came rolling off a boiling pond, gray-blue and orange, so that they stared at it in wonder and craned their necks looking back. Everywhere the colors were intense but, also, soft and misted, giving an almost miraculous effect of purest reality combined with fantastic hallucination. At the foot of a rock-piled mountain they passed a little lake covered with water lilies floating bright yellow blooms among the pads. They saw deer and, always in the distance, a number of elk. There were also several iron deer and dogs, painted chocolate brown, exactly like those which stood on the lawns at home.

Over and over they exclaimed on the beauty of this place, its strange mystical unreality and the clear bright air which gave an illusion that it was possible to see infinity; even though, at the moment of conviction, a vast cloud of floating and whirling blue steam, outlined in brilliant yellow, would pass across their vision and they would find themselves staring only into its thick sulphurous vapors.

Occasionally they saw Indians.

Cherry said that they were merely passing through the place on one of their migrations—which was why papooses were the only infants to be seen. They did some hunting and fishing, in which they were frequently joined by him, for he seemed to like their company, their fine physical hardihood, and their freedom from the attitudes of his white guests. They never stayed long, though there were always some of them coming and going.

"I thought he was an Indian myself when I—" began

Jacintha and stopped abruptly, giving a little gasp and pressing her lips tight together. "Oh, I'm sorry!"

Cherry patted her knee reassuringly. "Never mind, darling. We can't avoid him entirely, of course. It's only that I think we should avoid him when we can."

"I intend to avoid him entirely!"

Cherry glanced at her and smiled. "You can avoid him only to the extent he is willing for you to. Do you honestly imagine that, if we were to round this corner and find him there, you would be able to ignore him? Remember —he offers the only hope there is in this crowded desolate place."

"He offers the wrong kind of hope for me!" cried Jacintha, hot all over with excitement and some strange eager anger.

"I wonder if you know," began Cherry slowly, watching her as she spoke, "that you are exactly the kind of woman he finds most appealing?"

"What?"

She was so stunned by what Cherry had said, particularly by the fact that it was Cherry who had said it, that she felt as if she were strangling. She stared back in pain and sickening confusion.

"I don't know what you mean," she replied in a voice scarcely audible.

"I mean what I said," replied Cherry and as Jacintha glanced stealthily toward her, she found Cherry's eyes fixed upon her with a look of bright watchful curiosity. There was no tenderness or softness—only the suspicion and malice of a distrustful animal. Jacintha wanted to leap from the coach and run, for she had a sudden conviction that she must escape before something terrible happened between them. Then the look changed, softened, and disappeared.

I must have been mistaken, thought Jacintha, still gazing toward her in helpless fixed fascination. It was not the look I thought it was. But, of course, she knew better.

"Certainly," continued Cherry. "You are proud and thoughtful and take things more seriously than they ever deserve. He has great sport amusing himself with women like you. You are always more ready to be his victim than any other kind."

Jacintha felt only a deep shocked horror. For, even though she had heard the words and Cherry's voice speaking them, she still could not believe that Cherry would be so willfully cruel. Then he was not attracted to her beauty or her gracious sweetness—but, rather, to her susceptibility to pain? He was interested not in the qualities she had which were tempting to other men, but only in those which made her most likely to suffer. She was not a woman to be cherished, but prey, to be molested at his whim and injured playfully.

That was what Cherry had been telling her. But, though for a moment she sat silent and sickened, Jacintha would not accept it.

Surely he was not like that. Or, even if he was, he would not be like that with her. The women he had amused himself by tormenting had not been her, had lacked qualities—certain undefinable qualities which Jacintha nevertheless felt to be strong and victorious within her, qualities which made it impossible for him or any other man to ill-use her: Shame, or some other mysterious inner force, would prevent him.

Last night, certainly, there had been no hint that he could ever do her harm. His tenderness had surpassed any she had ever known and had seemed, in fact, almost supernatural. While his passion, though coercive and unbridled, had given her voluptuous pleasure beyond imagining.

How could he intend her ill after that?

Cherry had been wrong but—Cherry had been wrong intentionally. She wanted to frighten her, since she must obviously fear that Jacintha had become as much his willing greedy victim as she was herself.

Then, to her surprise, there came a quick spasm of reminiscent pleasure which spread upward and out through all her body, seeming at last even to fill and expand her breasts, making them glow and tingle. And with sudden extraordinary clarity she recalled his commanding beauty, the power and sensuality he had which stunned the senses, immobilizing self-control and power of decision.

The sensation was so surprising, so unexpected, so pleasurable, that she paused, scarcely breathing, her eyes wide and sparkling. For, though it was the merest hint and mimicry of what he had made her feel the night before, still, it was not only memory but promise as well.

It was but a matter of seconds, vivid and intense though the experience was, before she caught herself with outraged astonishment.

How did *that* happen? How did he catch me off guard?

And, feeling her face and throat burn with guilty embarrassment, she cast Cherry a hasty glance, to see if she had been observed, convinced she must have given herself away. But Cherry, by the greatest good luck, was looking out the other side.

I'll never let that happen again, she promised, and gave a great sigh of relief.

For Cherry loved him and Cherry had loved him first. And, therefore, as between them, at least—he belonged to Cherry.

After all, she is my mother, the dearest person in all the world to me, now that I have lost Douglas. And she is, furthermore, all I will ever have to comfort me in this desperate place. For even if I could be so contemptible as to set myself up to be her rival—even if I had such a revolting capacity within me, I could not trust him. He may not be cruel, as she says, delighting most in women who are most vulnerable—but he has told me himself that he never loves, and I know it's true. So that even if he does not keep women about for the pleasure he takes in tormenting them, it comes to the same thing. A man you love who cannot love you—there could be no worse torture.

She wished she had not found so many reasons why it was to her profit to give him up—for the truth was, she would have given him up anyway. Her love for Cherry, surely, was greater than her love of herself.

Now, unexpectedly, Cherry's head turned and she smiled quickly and innocently at Jacintha.

"I only mention these things, darling, so that you may protect yourself."

Jacintha hung her head again and looked both shamed and grateful. "Thank you," she murmured.

They kept driving along at the same merry rapid rate, the coach jouncing and bouncing; from time to time Jacintha felt moist steam across her face and the smell of sulphur reached sharp raw tendrils into her nose.

Then all of a sudden Cherry cried: "Oh, look where we are! Have you ever seen anything so picturesque? Stop here, driver! We want to get out!"

The next moment she had flung aside the carriage robe and climbed down. Jacintha followed and they stood together beside the coach, staring ahead with awe and wonder and some discomposure at the scene before them.

They were on a high cliff, overlooking a vast spreading cascade of empty steaming while terraces, descending, one after the other, away into the far distance. A few dwarfed and warped pines were stuck about like artificial trees in a stage set, and there were some odd roots thrusting up from the chalky white earth. Other trees, stripped bare, were the color and texture of driftwood, and their branches twisted wildly about the trunks as if they had been caught and petrified while in a terrible writhing rate. The sun was so hot and so intensely brilliant as it came striking off the rocky white earth, that it brought tears to their eyes. The scene itself was both dismal and ominous. Though it may have been, as Cherry had said, "picturesque," it was also alien and ugly, and Jacintha could not look at it.

"It's hideous," she said, shaking her head. "There's something evil in it."

"Suppose there is?" asked Cherry lightly. "Evil is not without purpose."

Jacintha did not believe that such a remark was sincere, and therefore she must have said it for some other reason, which could only be a sinister one. Cherry had not forgiven her, that was plain enough. It would take a great deal of time and infinite patience, before Cherry would trust her again.

Jacintha turned and, slowly and thoughtfully, began to stroll toward the edge of a forest which lay on the far side of the blazing white plateau on which they stood. Dejected and unhappy, she did not notice if Cherry had stayed behind or was accompanying her. Until all at once she heard Cherry's voice speak in a clear light tone, just in back of her:

"Your first love is not always the one you thought it was, is it?"

Jacintha turned and looked around. Cherry, who had

been steadily approaching, now stood before her, face to face. "For instance," she continued, "you probably thought that Douglas was the first man you loved."

"Of course he was," replied Jacintha, trying to sound more confident than she felt. "I never loved Martin. I never even imagined that I did. I was a dutiful wife to him—until I met Douglas—but I never loved *any* man before Douglas."

"You never loved Douglas, either."

They stood where they were and confronted each other, two small figures against the harsh glittering white floor of the terrace, minimized even further by the distant mountains and high blue sky. Their silhouettes looked exaggeratedly female, breasts and hips accentuated by their corsets, and their skirts trailed behind them in the dry dust. They twirled their ruffled parasols, spinning them like pinwheels as they balanced them lightly upon their shoulders.

"Don't you see what's happened?" asked Cherry reasonably.

"Of course I don't see what's happened," retorted Jacintha.

Cherry laughed, half stifling it with her gloved palm, as if her amusement, at someone else's expense, were impolite. "But, my dear child—don't you see now that you were *never* in love before? That you fell in love for the first time when you looked around on Roaring Mountain and saw him standing there?"

Jacintha started to answer but could not speak. Her eyes were suddenly full of tears and her chin had begun to quiver. She turned and went on, convinced that something in this wicked landscape had infected Cherry, hoping that if she could lure her to the forest, its cool cleanness would restore her innocence and mercy.

Cherry, however, caught up with her, slipped one arm about her waist and spoke in a soft confiding tone: "Daring—don't be upset." She clucked softly. "How sensitive you are. My, my. If I hurt your feelings, I'm sorry, I apologize."

Jacintha brightened at this and turned to Cherry, her gloved hands clasped fast together. "I *don't* love him," she said with intense earnestness. "You must believe me. I *don't* love him."

Cherry gazed into her face a moment longer, searching carefully behind the desperate sincerity for whatever uncontrollable flickers might betray her. Then, as if she were in some way satisfied, she drew her onward toward the forest, still with one arm about her waist.

"I believe you, Jacintha. And for your sake, I hope you never will. He is, believe me, what I told you."

They had come now to the edge of the dark damp fragrant forest and, as they paused, gazing into its watery depths, they could hear, amid the silence, old trees creaking like rocking chairs. Clumps of bright blue flowers sprang energetically out of the thick moss. There was a little pool, so clear that the skeeters darting about its surface cast their dotted shadows on the sandy bottom.

Jacintha wanted to ask why, if that was what he was, he should be so important to *her*—but knew she must not. That was Cherry's secret and she must never try to discover it. Now, hearing a strange unexpected sound, she raised her head.

"What can that be?"

"I don't know," said Cherry. "Let's find out."

"Perhaps it's dangerous."

"It won't be. And, if it is, danger is one of the few antidotes to the interminable boredom of this place."

They followed the direction of the sound—a low rumbling—along the edge of the forest. The forest curved away abruptly, and they saw what had caused it: there was a crater the size of a small lake, filled with boiling ugly fighting gray mud. It was hideous, and they stared in fascinated awe and revulsion. Beyond, lay a meadow with sagebrush growing among the white and yellow and blue flowers.

"How horrible!" said Jacintha, strong disgust in her tone, as if the sight offended her.

"I wonder how deep it is?" mused Cherry.

Jacintha gave an involuntary backward start. "Don't even think of that! It must be bottomless!"

"Look! There's another!"

"I don't want to see any more."

Cherry turned and surveyed her with delicate surprised amusement. "Why, Jacintha—where's your curiosity? Come along. Seeing it can't hurt you."

The air was so thick with choking sulphurous fumes

that they had begun to cough and were making futile gestures of fighting them off. At Cherry's gentle insistence they passed the crater—half obscured by swirling mists—keeping a good distance away, and advanced with slow careful steps toward a low hillside from which had come even noisier and more mutinous sounds.

There, at its base, they saw a great cavern, like an open wound in the earth, and from it came furiously churning a headlong torrent of boiling gray mud. It rushed forth in angry and vicious turmoil, rumbling and hissing, sending up vast enveloping clouds of steam, brawling, raging, seeming almost to be alive and maddening. Rolling and heaving and splattering in all directions, it poured into a turbulent pool of hot gray mud, then plunged immediately back into a vent in the earth—penetrating it with frenzied destroying rage.

Here was a natural phenomenon which, to Jacintha, was sure indication of his existence in the vicinity. Tumultuous and devastating, it must be part of the general scheme for evil.

Jacintha stared at it in repelled horror, thinking that if anything should fall into this crater it would be swept down into the boiling mass which must be the earth's center. For this, she felt, was a part of its core, like oozing pus reaching the skin from an internal wound; this terror and rage and ugliness was what the earth's crust hid from view, and no wonder—shame, alone, would keep it hidden.

Involuntarily she was retreating from it, taking small uncertain backward steps, while Cherry made her way slowly forward.

It was a few moments before Jacintha realized that Cherry was steadily approaching that monstrous horror. The clouds of sulphur were now so thick they seemed almost literally to wrap and entrap them; it was like struggling in a gale with endless veils of chiffon. The fumes were harsh and clawed in their throats and lungs so that they coughed constantly and helplessly.

Suddenly, springing from her stunned silence, Jacintha screamed and rushed forward. She grabbed Cherry by one arm and began to drag her back. Cherry pulled against her and Jacintha pulled harder and harder, with all her strength. All at once Cherry stopped, and the change was so abrupt that it sent both of them staggering.

"What's the matter with you, Jacintha?"

They stood face to face again, coughing and rubbing their burning eyes.

"You'll be killed!"

"How could I *possibly* be killed?"

And Jacintha realized with unbelieving shock, that Cherry had spoken to her angrily. Now she shook off Jacintha's hand with such energy and disdain that Jacintha obediently let go.

"Don't do that again," she warned. *"I'm* going to explore. You can come along or not," she flung over her shoulder, as she started slowly forward again.

While Jacintha watched her, trembling, wringing her hands, Cherry moved nearer and nearer to the terrible boiling crater. "Oh, Cherry," she was murmuring. "Come back, please come back, please come back—"

But Cherry ignored her and, with sudden determination, she started forward herself, reached the place where Cherry was, and softly took her hand. Cherry turned her head and smiled and Jacintha felt she had been rewarded.

Now, together, carefully and experimentally, placing their feet with great caution, they moved nearer and nearer to the crater's edge. They grasped each other's hands so hard the nails cut and the knuckles turned white. Their faces were moist and shiny and their clothes stuck to them, wet underneath from their sweating bodies, dampened on the surface by the stinking steam. The ground could break through like a piecrust. Any step they took might be the wrong one. The nearer they approached, the greater their danger became.

And since they could not, as Cherry had just said, be killed by any such catastrophe—it must surely then be their fate to spend eternity bobbing about in that boiling hot mud, down inside the earth, without even air or sky to give them comfort. Cherry, it seemed, must have gone mad to insist on taking chances with such a possibility, on the theory that danger was her only antidote to boredom.

But Jacintha loyally took step for step with her.

She could not hang back—not only from the fear of showing her cowardice, but even more from the vivid sense of how intolerable it would be to survive if Cherry should be swept into the crater. If it was to happen to either, it must happen to both.

At last they came within five or six feet of the edge.

They stood and stared for several moments, speechless, until Jacintha grew aware of that sense of distance from herself which always came just before she fainted. She gave a timid little tug at Cherry's hand and stared at her in mute humble pleading. Cherry, in return, sent her the merest glance, apparently not even seeing her white sickened face.

"Isn't it exciting!" she demanded. "Look!" And she leaned forward, bending from the waist.

Jacintha felt her head whirl as if it had detached itself by a spring and took one swift turn in the air above her before settling onto her neck once more.

"I—" she whispered. "I—"

But she could not speak. Her ears were ringing and by now she seemed a vast helpless distance from herself. She tried again to tell her that she was fainting, but could say nothing. Time seemed to stretch and, for an endless period, she felt herself bending obediently forward.

Then Cherry let go of her hand.

Jacintha, shocked closer to consciousness, flailed out, searching desperately, and she felt the gentlest push at her back. Her arms flung wide, she gave a wailing lonely scream, and began to pitch forward—still strangely delayed in time, so that she seemed to sail endlessly toward the crater like a great bird in slow swooping flight over a canyon.

Then, as if she had been struck a violent blow, she felt herself seized and flung furiously backward. The next instant she and Cherry lay on the chalk-white earth, locked in each other's arms, wet, panting, and Cherry was sobbing in a strange dry hard tearless way that was almost indistinguishable from their coughing.

Jacintha lay on her back, her arms around Cherry, who lay beside her, turned onto one side. She was staring upward toward the sun which appeared through the steam as a flat orange circle. She seemed to be coming back from a distant journey, returning by a spiral along which she glided in smooth swift silence, sweeping nearer and nearer to the spiral's center and then, as she reached it, she emerged with surprising suddenness and was back in the present.

What was it that happened? she asked herself.

I must remember what it was—

But I *know*.

Cherry meant me to fall into the crater. She knew that I was fainting, she let go my hand and she—

No, she didn't. Of course she didn't. I imagined all that.

It was Cherry who saved me.

That is the truth.

If Cherry had not thrown her arms around me and flung us back, if she had not risked herself—I would have fallen into the boiling mud and been swept away.

That is what happened and that is what I must remember.

She felt Cherry stir beside her and then, moving very slowly, as if every muscle were stiff, Cherry sat up. Jacintha lay a moment, looking at her. Cherry was still coughing. Her hat had been knocked to one side and her hair was dusted with white powdery earth. Her face was wet and the white earth had made pasty smudges on it. Her gown was tangled and twisted and so laden with white dust that the bright plaid looked dim and dingy. Even her lashes had a sprinkling of white powder across their edges.

She was busy trying to put herself in order, patting and twitching, tugging and brushing, like a sparrow in his dust bath, so preoccupied that it was a few seconds before she looked directly at Jacintha. And even then her eyes went first to the lower part of Jacintha's face, experimentally, it seemed. Then quickly she raised them and they were looking straight at each other.

Now both seemed puzzled and the look that passed between them was one of questioning only. There was a feeling that someone was about to speak—when, with a tremendous rush of air and clattering of hooves, he arrived on his black horse and sat a moment, a cloud of white dust shifting around him, partially obscured by the restless hovering vapors.

Then he swung down abruptly and reached his hand toward Cherry, who extended her own and was whisked to her feet. Next he drew Jacintha up, lightly and swiftly, so that she seemed to rise by some marvellous feat of levitation—and all three stood looking at one another.

Today he wore the fringed and beaded leggings of the Blackfoot nation, a tribe believed to have got its name by roaming through regions destroyed by fire. His chest and shoulders were naked, brown and shining, and his black hair was ruffled by the wind. He wore beaded moccasins, but no headdress. His fists were on his hips and his white teeth shone in a strange half-grin which instantly made them wary. He was, quite clearly, in full possession of that alluring magnificence and unbridled power which had exerted such malefic influence upon them.

"What happened here?" he demanded. "An accident?"

Quickly, as if at a prearranged signal, both women opened their handbags and took out mirrors, peering into them, and began setting their bonnets straight, wiping their faces with embroidered white handkerchiefs, tucking wisps of hair back into place. They frowned and pursed their lips and appeared to be engrossed by this activity.

All at once he threw back his head and laughed, a hearty ribald laugh which was an insult to them both. They stopped, handbags still held open, arrested in gestures of rearranging themselves, and looked at him in openmouthed surprise and anger.

"Well!" he said at last. "Which of you is the guilty one? I can't tell by looking at you— Either of you could have done it."

Jacintha promptly turned her back and stood tapping her foot and staring toward the forest, where his horse had wandered for water and grass. Both their parasols had been flung away, and the sun beat upon her head and face with a steady insistence that made the blood throb and leap just under the surface of her skin.

The smashing and rumbling of the cauldron, only a few feet away, filled the air. Sulphur fumes streamed continuously about them. The heat was fierce and smothering.

Cherry burst into another coughing fit. "Guilty of what?" she demanded, coughing so hard she could scarcely speak, pressing the flat of one hand against her chest for relief.

"Don't play with me," he advised. "One of you tried to throw the other into that thing over there."

Jacintha shuddered to hear him call it "that thing," as if it were alive, for her own terror and imagination had made it a kind of subterranean monster, thrusting its head and mouth out of the earth in search of prey.

"Which one was it? Jacintha!"

And he gave her an impertinent whack on the buttocks, knocking a cloud of dust from her skirts. She jumped and reached back with both hands, but did not cry out.

"Come on," he said now, took hold of Jacintha's shoulder to turn her around, and slid one arm impersonally about each of their waists. "Let's get out of this infernal muck." The three of them started walking toward the forest.

Only a few steps brought them out of the oppressive fumes—through streamers of the smell wandered for some distance after them—and presently they had stopped coughing and rubbing their eyes and felt as suddenly freed as if they had been imprisoned back there against their will. It seemed now as if they had stayed an interminable time and been unable to escape until he came to rescue them.

"You always arrive," said Cherry, as they walked along, "at the most inconvenient times."

"Oh?" he asked, and his tone was full of mockery and amusement. "Then it *was* you."

Cherry stopped suddenly, whirled and faced him and, to Jacintha's astonishment, she stamped her foot and fiercely clenched her fists. "How dare you make such a filthy accusation!"

"You mean it was Jacintha, instead?" He had a lazy smile on his face and looked from one to the other as if this pleased him more than anything in a long time.

"No!" cried Cherry. Her face was red, her breathing hard, and she seemed so distraught she might be about to burst. "It was *not* Jacintha! It was not—"

Jacintha grabbed his arm. "What are you trying to do?" she demanded furiously. "Are you trying to make me believe that my mother meant to shove me into that crater? Are you trying to make us hate each other for your entertainment?"

He glanced at her briefly, started to return his attention to Cherry and then, as if caught by something in her expression, gave her a long steady stare, curious and amused. "Are you possibly naïve enough to believe that was not her intention?"

They stood there now, close to the forest. There were a few ravens in the sky; his great black stallion cropped at the grass; the air was full of a still and wonderful peace, though they could faintly hear the rumbling cauldron and, in the forest, small sounds of birds and crackling twigs.

Jacintha stared back at him for several moments, proud and defiant, but his expression did not alter. He continued to look at her as if this situation was comical in a way both she and Cherry should have been able to appreciate. There was even an indication that he pitied them for their lack of humor.

Then she turned quickly to Cherry. "Don't you see what he's trying to do? If he can find something to make him laugh—what happens to *us* doesn't concern him at all."

Cherry watched her as she talked, squinting her eyes a little because of the sun, but Jacintha could see the sorrow and pain in their dark depths. Slowly she nodded.

"I know," she murmured. "Of course."

Jacintha stepped before him and took hold of Cherry's hands, pressing them together, and spoke to her in a low intense voice: "I don't *want* to know if that was what you meant to happen to me. It doesn't matter—because you saved me at the last. Cherry— We must not let him trick us into abandoning each other!"

At the last, Cherry lowered her eyes.

They stood, Cherry looking down, Jacintha gazing eagerly into her face, holding each other's hands. He continued to watch them with mild interest—as if this were a performance staged for his benefit—standing with his heavily muscled arms crossed upon his naked chest. Finally, Cherry kissed Jacintha's cheek, very softly withdrew her hands, and they were walking again along the forest's edge, until—still silent—they reached that part from which expanded before them the blazing white floor of the upper terrace. Straight ahead in the distance, a small black silhouette, stood the phaeton with the driver in his place. The sight of it was a shock, like returning from a long hazardous journey and wild adventures, to find that during all the years of absence no single piece of furniture has been moved in one's living room.

Here, as if by mutual consent, they stopped again. Cherry, seeming unable to speak, put her arms about Jacintha and held her tenderly. Tears came into their eyes and, as they shut them, the tears spilled down their faces. After a moment he casually remarked:

"If you would forgive your enemy—first do him a wrong. That's a neat way of putting it, don't you think? It's an old saying—I forget whose."

Both women looked at him, still holding each other as if for mutual assurance and support. The sun threw sharp dark shadows over his face and his beauty seemed intolerable, a bitter mocking challenge; they held each other closer than ever. He had such hard assurance, such an excessive male vitality. Now, almost as if he had reached out and drawn them toward him, their bodies seemed to incline, helplessly; until suddenly they both became aware and stood erect, releasing each other. He smiled.

"Why do you want to hurt us?" asked Jacintha, her voice wistful and plaintive.

He grinned. It was unbelievable to them that he could take such cruel and callous pleasure in their unhappiness. "I don't want to hurt you," he said. "On the other hand, I don't honestly care if you happen to get hurt."

"That's the same thing!" snapped Jacintha.

He glanced at her briefly, and something of impatience and anger in his glance terrified her into instant silence. Her throat grew dry and her heart beat as fast as if she had suddenly confronted mortal danger. She hated herself for her fear, but could do nothing to banish it.

"You want, both of you, to have me be a part of your world, the kind of man you always knew—who pitied women, and feared them. I don't, and can't. Women are, along with hunting and fishing and gambling, my chief diversion—but I regard them neither with contempt nor with awe, and that's the mixture you're accustomed to. I have no hypocrisy in my feelings about you—and

I think it's that which you miss most and blame me for. You also want me to take your jealousy seriously and be considerate of you for allowing yourselves to be victimized by an artificial and irrational emotion. I am not even in sympathy with such nonsense. If you will be jealous—and it is not as inevitable as you both believe—then I decline any responsibility for your pangs." He smiled, first at Cherry, and then at Jacintha. "You are two extraordinarily beautiful and desirable women—it would not do me much credit if I avoided either one of you, would it?"

Jacintha saw that beguiling treacherous tenderness come into his eyes, an expression infinitely more dangerous, as she well remembered, then his anger.

She grasped Cherry's hand. "Quick! Let's get away from here!" She pulled at her.

Cherry jerked free and turned upon Jacintha with such a look of excited anger that Jacintha stared at her openmouthed and astounded.

"What's the matter with you, Jacintha? We can't run away from him! We're in his country—there's no place we can escape to! Running won't solve this—" She looked up at him once more. "You don't want to hurt us, but you don't care if we get hurt. Of course. I knew that. I've known you for some time now—haven't I?"

"Yes. You have." He smiled, and then chuckled softly, reminiscently. "We have," he amended.

He and Cherry were looking straight into each other's eyes, laughing—not loud boisterous laughter, which Jacintha could have scorned, but soft pleased conspiratorial laughter, which made her feel as lost and cold as if she had wakened alone in a dark strange room. She stared at them, growing more and more frantic, wondering what she could do or say to break this bond they had, to destroy whatever secret it was they shared, to attract his attention back to her.

"You're a liar!" cried Jacintha.

That stopped the laughter and turned them to her, so suddenly, and with such a complete erasure of humor from their faces, that she began a slow involuntary retreat, one gloved hand to her mouth, staring from him to Cherry and back to him again. And then, overcome with a strangling terror so great that she had to do something to release the tension, she picked up her skirts and began to run.

She ran blindly, stumbling along in her high heels, her purple silk legs flashing back and forth. Followed by a little cloud of white dust which seemed to scurry after her across the blistered plateau, she vanished from them swiftly, a pale blue and purple figure, growing smaller, disappearing toward the bright wide open sky.

She concentrated fiercely on only those things which came directly before her eyes: the dead white blazing earth, the boiling puddles of gray mud, the hovering vapors—on anything but the memory of their smiles, sharing something she did not know about which mocked her and made her ridiculous.

And then she heard them begin to laugh—his voice first, loud and hearty, that laugh which turned everything human into ridiculous sham and pretense, and, following along, weaving in upon it like a tenderer lighter melody, came Cherry's laugh. She stopped a moment and started to turn—but she could not face them. The laughter seemed to swell like an orchestra, filling the air with its sound, and she ran on, sobbing. She had run so far and so hard that she now began to gasp and her lungs felt raw and burning; there was a pain in her side like a thistle. The blood pounded in her throat and ears, roaring louder and louder, until it had finally drowned out the sound of their laughter.

At last, staggering, no longer able to run, she reached the coach and stood leaning against one of its yellow wheels, her chest heaving and swelling, one hand pressed to the stabbing pain in her side, the veins throbbing and jumping along her arms and legs. The pain and exhaustion had done what she wanted—she had forgotten them, for the moment, and she could not hear their laughter.

The coachman sat on his perch. He glanced at her once and then, with a grimace, turned back, to wait.

After some minutes Jacintha began, surreptitiously, to look for them. First she looked toward the forest. They no longer stood there and she looked toward the upward slope, beyond the edge of which the terraces descended. There was nothing in sight, in any direction, but the sick white earth, the blue sky, the black-green mountains out in endless space.

What a fool I was!

I turned, like a coward, and ran away.

How they must both despise me!

And now where are they? Together, somewhere. I accomplished the thing I most wanted to avoid.

Thereupon, she heard a piercing whistle that seemed to come from some distance and yet sounded so sharp and near that she covered her ears with her hands, wincing. The next moment there was a drumming of hoofbeats and his black stallion appeared, far ahead, galloping toward the horizon. They rose into view, walking up over the crest of the terrace, two figures looking very small from this distance, in black silhouette. She saw him lift Cherry swiftly onto the horse, swing himself up behind her, then the great animal wheeled and was off at a gallop, rounding the edge of the terraces, plunging downward, and disappearing, all in an instant.

So absorbed had she been in watching them that she was not aware she had begun to cry. She saw a tear splash into the white dust at her feet, dashed away the next with her gloved hand, and then realized they were her own. With a long melancholy shuddering sigh, she picked up her heavy dust-covered skirts and climbed into the carriage.

"Take me to the lodge," she called out, and immediately his whip lashed down, the horses leaped forward like jack rabbits, and the small coach went bouncing and joggling along.

To keep herself from thinking about what she had just seen or speculating on what it must precede, she opened her bag and looked at herself in the mirror, gravely shaking her head. Her hair blew in damp tendrils. Her face was reddened from the sun and smudged with white dust. Her body, inside the heavy cocoon of corset and petticoats and thick ruffled skirt, was wet and stuck fast to her clothing. She even smelled of sweat. She wanted to cry out of sheer chagrin and anger at being in such a state of unladylike disarray, which the wind, springing up all of a sudden, was making worse as quickly as she tried to put herself in order.

After several minutes she had made but little improvement. The coach bounced too much and the wind kept dragging loose wisps of hair every time she tucked them away until finally, disgusted, she dropped the mirror in her bag and sat holding onto the side of the coach.

She noticed that it had grown colder and drew the lap robe across her knees. Then, looking upward, she found that while she had been absorbed in repairing herself, the blue had faded from the sky and clouds had rolled across it, gray and stormy and shaggy underneath. The treees whipped smartly about, bending and twisting like dancers limbering up.

Jacintha shivered and put one hand to her throat to fasten her collar. There was a quick spasm of light. She glanced up, surprised, and heard a sharp rap, as of a giant's knuckles across the mountains. She drew the robe closer, snuggling into it, trying to snuggle deeper into herself as well. It's going to storm.

It's going to *storm!*

Her eyes opened wide, she sat up straight and began turning frantically in every direction, looking out both sides and then the back, with no idea of what she wanted to find. The coachman was lashing the horses, urging them faster and faster.

"Stop!" she yelled at him. He paid no attention. She yelled again, louder, and just as she opened her mouth, the thunder rattled. She shouted again and again, but he did not so much as turn his head. "It's going to rain!" she cried. "I'll be soaked!" On he drove, bounding across the meadows, through the ragged little forests, over the rutted dirt roads; he ploughed his way amid fields of flowers, went splashing through sulphur streams and tearing past vaporous boiling blue pools.

Finally, in furious frustration at her inability to make him obey, she gave up and sank back, waiting. The sky was flickering now, dark one instant and flaring brilliantly the next. The thunder rolled across the distance. Jacintha sat, her hands clenched tight together, and winced as if she had been struck at each flash of lightning and each thunderous report.

It will stop. It will stop, she kept repeating to herself. It won't storm. It's only threatening.

I can't stand it if it storms!

Oh, he's horrible—*horrible!*

Jacintha could see them together with hallucinatory vividness: Cherry's eager laughing merry face turned up to his, his big square-fingered hands pressing upon her belly and breasts, his mouth close to hers—she could feel within her own body their excitement, growing swifter and stronger and more demanding every instant, their reckless urgent need for each other— And now, as the thunder roared out suddenly, like a voice in universal rage, Jacintha wailed and closed her eyes, put her hands over her ears, and crouched in upon herself.

She felt something wet strike her cheek; then again, and the rain came splatting down.

"Oh, no!" she wailed in futile lonely protest.

Her little carriage rushed along, faster than ever, the driver beating the horses in a kind of insane frenzy. The rain increased so suddenly that it was as if she had stepped under a waterfall. The sky kept lighting up with such great white flashes that it seemed the world must be exploding, and each flash was accompanied by an instantaneous burst and roar of thunder.

Jacintha had begun to cry. Soon she was moaning and sobbing piteously. Like an animal seeking shelter, she crept down onto the floor of the carriage and crouched there, doubled up, knees and elbows together, beating her fists upon the floor in the total darkness, for she had pulled the blanket over her head and was completely covered by it.

It *could* not be true that her mother had deserted her, gone off with him—and was now advertising everywhere in the world their love-making.

It could not be true and it obviously was true.

She felt more scared and lost and filled with hatred than ever before. The tears teemed from her eyes like rain itself. Crouched down there in darkness with neither air nor light, jolted and tossed by the rocking coach, she sobbed herself into exhaustion.

And then, while the storm still snarled and clattered all around, wild and rude and dreadful, the carriage stopped short.

It took her a moment to realize that the rocking and pitching had ceased and then she looked up, puzzled, turned back an edge of the blanket, and found that they were in front of the lodge. With a gasp of horror she saw that people were standing there, dozens of them, hundreds, perhaps, talking and laughing together, sheltered from the storm under the vast porch roof, but watching it, pointing, jumping and bursting into excited laughter at each appalling crash of thunder.

Swiftly she flung off the blanket and sat in the seat once more, feeling the back of her skirt instantly soak through. Some of them had seen her. Two or three men were watching her with amusement; she lifted her chin high and stretched her neck long and stared at them haughtily. Then, after looking briefly for her hat, she decided it had been lost along the way, picked up her wet skirts, and started to climb down.

Two of the men, broadly smiling, sprang forward with offers of help. Jacintha refused to extend them her hand and got down unassisted, though with difficulty.

Her clothing was so wet that it dripped and stuck fast to her, the ruffles and layers of her petticoats clinging in soggy heavy masses to her legs as she moved. Her hair was smeared across her forehead and neck in an unsightly bunch. Feeling herself frightfully ugly, betrayed in every ugliness—imaginary or real—which she had ever tried to conceal to win the world's admiration and love, she ducked her head and shaded her eyes and made her way through the crowd as swiftly as she could.

In the lobby there was the usual acre or more of luggage waiting to be distributed, lackeys running frantically about, Indians wrapped in their blankets, some of them smoking pipes, others squatting on the floor playing dice, and numbers of well-dressed good-looking men and women.

Jacintha rushed through and among them, hoping desperately that if she did not look at them they would not notice her. But she could not help glancing from the corners of her eyes now and then and, whenever she did, she saw men and women observing her, glancing and then glancing away, with expressions of surprise, amusement, boredom, even faint outrage that such a bedraggled creature should be among them. She felt that it took her at least an hour to cross the lobby though, in reality, it was but a few minutes. And when at last she gained the hallway she started down it with a sense of tremendous relief, heading as fast as she could go for her own room, seclusion, obscurity, and, she hoped, some kind of forgetfulness.

But she could not escape the storm.

She could hear it still rolling and grumbling and banging up the world outside. As she passed windows she saw the lightning break again and again and the rain came down with shattering force. Shaking her head, whimpering, she ran on and on, down one corridor and then another, and at last reached her own room, flung open the door and rushed in, slammed it shut and leaned back against it, panting, still crying, still shaking her head from side to side.

The whole experience had been more torturesome than even those few minutes before Martin had levelled his gun at her. She had never been so frightened, so desolate, so thoroughly and unredeemingly humiliated.

Now, as she hung there against the door, she could see the lightning through the windows and she rushed to draw the heavy draperies. But she could not shut out the swelling drowning thunder, though she paced the room with her hands over her ears. Engrossed in her own violent participation in the storm, her hatred of Cherry, her wild fury against him—she started with a shriek when the door was thrown suddenly open. She had not lighted a lamp and the room was in darkness. A woman's figure stood silhouetted in the doorway.

"Who are you?" she cried.

There was a moment's silence while Jacintha stared at her, electric chills rushing along her arms and legs and over her body, so terrified that her breath had stopped.

"I am your maid, madame," came the timid quiet reply. "May I come in?"

"Oh!" Jacintha gave a sigh of relief so deep and intense that it seemed to wash through her as if a plug had been pulled in a basin.

She had thought, for the moment, that it was Cherry —and to confront Cherry now that she hated her, was the most terrifying experience she could contemplate. No matter how she prevented it or what she had to do—that must never happen.

"Shall I light the lamp, madame?"

Jacintha sighed. "Yes, you may as well."

There was a soft scratching sound and the next moment the big glass-shaded lamp on the center table flowered into a radiant glow. Then, seeing how the maid stood staring at her, Jacintha, after returning the stare with a moment's puzzlement, looked down at her soaked dress and glanced across at herself in the mirror. Her hair was strung out of the combs and hung wet and sodden upon her cheeks and neck, sticking fast to the bodice of her gown. Water dripped off the sleeves and skirt, and she could feel it running down her legs. She shuddered.

"Madame—you'll take a chill. Can't I build up a fire and help you to undress?"

"Yes," agreed Jacintha, grateful now for the companionship and for someone to help her with all the trivial things she had never done for herself. "Please do. What is your name?"

"Beth, madame."

Beth was busy setting the fire and, presently, it was going. "Come here now, madame, and let me undress you before this nice warm blaze."

Jacintha felt more tired than she ever had, it seemed, and she walked slowly to the fire and turned her back so that Beth could unhook her gown. The room was more cheerful now with the blithe leaping fire and, when she had removed Jacintha's clothing and rubbed her skin dry, Beth brought a dressing gown and held it for her to slip into. Jacintha sat in a chair, warming herself, and closed her eyes while Beth took the pins and combs from her hair, dried it as well as she could with a towel, and then began to brush it.

The stroking along her scalp was so soothing that presently, despite the incessant roar of the storm outside and the bursting thunder which was sometimes so violent that it seemed it must be the building itself cracking open, she began to have a luxurious sense of ease and pleasant drowsiness. She moved her head against the brush strokes, like a kitten being petted, and told herself that in this room it was so warm and softly lighted, so beautifully furnished, so complete a nest, as it were, that she did not care about him or about Cherry or about anything else but this exclusive delightful comfort.

"I love it here," she said finally.

She glanced up at Beth, who was bending over her slightly. Beth was a few years older than she and looked too common, thought Jacintha, to be pretty—though she was pleasant in appearance and her face seemed kind, if somewhat stupid.

Beth was shocked at this remark. "You *love* it here?"

"In this room, I mean."

"Oh, yes, the room," agreed Beth, as if relieved to have found that her mistress was not entirely mad. She was twining the ends of Jacintha's hair carefully about her fingers now and brushing them, while still slightly damp, into long loose full curls which hung almost to her waist. "The rooms *are* very handsome."

"So is the out-of-doors. For him—it is all perfect."

"For him, yes. But for no one else, madame. For no one else, believe me. I have been here a long while."

"You have?" Jacintha turned, gesturing that she could stop the brushing now. "How long have you been here?"

"Well—I don't recall how many years it's been. It's too many for me to add. But I remember when I died—it was March 12, 1643. I was burned for a witch, madame."

"Burned for a witch!" whispered Jacintha. Her brown eyes gazed wide and thoughtfully and somewhat awestruck at the maid. "*Were* you one?"

Beth gave a low chuckle. "No, madame. I was not one. They said I'd had intercourse with the Devil and they burnt me. And the humor of it all is, madame, that I had not then had intercourse with him, nor have I any time since I got here."

Jacintha blinked at that and then, suddenly, they both laughed. They laughed delightedly at the joke on Beth and, through the laughter, came to feel very friendly toward each other.

"Has he asked you?" inquired Jacintha.

"Never, madame. Not while I lived and not once I died, even though I died, as it were, for his sake."

"Tsk, tsk." Jacintha shook her head and got up. "It's like him. Do you think he ever will?"

"Never, madame. Or he would not have put me to this kind of work. Look at the difference between us. I'm not pretty enough for him. He likes a woman like you—or like Mrs. Anson, in the next room." Beth gave a nod of her head toward the wall and, at the mention of her mother, Jacintha felt her heart knot up, as if someone had squeezed it, and she walked to the window, drew back the drapery just enough to peek out—and saw that the storm was almost done. The light flashed across the sky far in the distance now, as if bidding them all farewell, fluttering a negligent sign as it disappeared across the mountains. The thunder gave a last surly mutter or so, and the rain was a mere spatter and trickle. Jacintha let the drapery fall to again and turned back.

"He likes Mrs. Anson, you say?" she asked, with elaborate idleness.

She walked to the dressing table, seated herself on the fringed and padded tabouret before it, and began to dust a light film of powder over her face, leaning forward to look at herself, smitten with her own beauty once more: He will not desert me, she thought, and was surprised at the thought's boldness and confidence.

Beth was moving about, lighting the lamps so that an intimate mellow glow now floated throughout the room. Then she began picking up Jacintha's clothing and taking it into the bathroom.

"*Like* her?" she asked, pausing beside Jacintha with a significant small leer as she was going by holding a wet petticoat in her hands. "He likes no woman, in the way you most likely mean. He likes a female body, that is all. And Mrs. Anson's seems to please him as well as any around here."

Jacintha felt a sharp little prickle of nervous shock and anxiety at that which almost seemed to lift the back of her scalp. "She does?" She did not look at Beth but continued watching herself in the mirror as she picked up a gold and crystal bottle of rose perfume and touched it to her ears and wrists and throat.

"He's been with her more than with anyone else, I think, since she came. Of course—that isn't to say he doesn't sometimes neglect her for weeks or months at a time. Perhaps even years." Beth shrugged. "But that's him. That's the way he is. It's not sour grapes, madame, but I'm glad I'm not the type for him."

Jacintha looked up at her. "You're glad? You mean

to say that you prefer to have neither joy nor pain? You'll do without the joy in order to avoid the pain?"

"That's what I mean, madame."

"You must have had more spirit when you were alive —or they'd never have burned you for a witch."

"It wasn't anything *I* did, madame. I had the ill luck to be born with one blue eye and one brown eye. And that was what brought about my burning."

"Only that?" demanded Jacintha, incredulous.

"Only that." Beth nodded vigorously, and bent down so that Jacintha could inspect her one brown eye and one blue eye.

"Thank heaven, I didn't live in such a barbarous age."

Beth went on into the bathroom. "Didn't you?" she asked as she went.

Jacintha watched her go, somewhat annoyed by the impertinent remark, then shrugged her shoulders and stood up, still studying herself.

She had never realized how alluring a dressing gown could be with nothing under it for, of course, even with Martin she had worn her petticoats and camisole. Now, its deeply opened neck showed her breasts, swelling out, tilted upward, the nipples soft and relaxed from the room's warmth. Jacintha took a pose, bending slightly and gracefully one way and then another, to see what the effect would be. Then, suddenly embarrassed, she straightened, drew the gown together, gave a toss of her head, and went to sit in one of the chairs, looking automatically about for some needlework to occupy her hands.

Of course, there was none.

Beth appeared once more. "What am I going to do?" asked Jacintha.

"About what, madame?"

"About my time. No one packed any books or any Berlin work or anything at all for me to *do*. Can I buy some materials somewhere?"

"Not that I know of, madame."

"You mean—the women don't do needlework or make things here?"

"Not that I know of, madame."

"Then what do they do?"

"Whatever they can think of."

"Well, I'm going to get some patterns and some yarn and begin to work something. I cannot be idle."

Beth was folding garments now, watching her with a look of curiosity and sadness. "You mean to do needlework all through eternity?"

"All through—" Jacintha stopped, overtaken once more by that sick plunging despair: *You mean to do neddlework all through eternity?*

"Well, why not?" she demanded. "What else is there to do? You mean, he's provided no diversions for us?"

"He's provided himself, madame—for some of you, anyway."

"I, as it happens," retorted Jacintha, "intend having nothing to do with him."

Beth gave her a sly smile. "You mean to say you prefer neither joy nor pain?"

"Don't talk to me like that!" cried Jacintha, and jumped up in a sudden flash of anger. "Use sarcasm on me and I'll slap your face!"

"Yes, madame."

"I mean it! Oh— No, I don't." She sighed. "I'm sorry, Beth. Of course I won't slap you. I'm sorry I was rude —but I'm out of my mind!" She was wringing her hands now. "To be here in this terrible place forever!" Her voice had risen to an hysterical wail. Beth came quickly and put her arms about her, holding her gently and patting her shoulders and back.

"I know, madame, I know. It's a hard thought to get used to. It's better not to think about it. Just go along from day to day—as you did before."

Gently, Jacintha disengaged herself and wandered slowly about the room, pausing now and again to touch a fringe on a chair, to examine a red velvet sofa covering, to tinkle the bead fringe hanging on a glass lamp shade. "If he doesn't provide for us, then I shall provide for myself. Tomorrow I'm going to go out and get some ferns and flowers and mosses and twigs, and set to work myself."

"What sort of work will you do with those implements, madame?" asked Beth, in honest puzzlement.

"Why, I'll make lamp shades and little boxes and things of that kind. And I'll start to collect curiosities— this is a fine place for curiosities. I shall begin a collection of pressed flowers, too. And I will set aside a certain time every day to go botanizing and educate myself on the plants of the vicinity. And I will—" She stopped, covered her face with her hands, and began to cry. "It was all right to do those things," she whimpered softly, "for the few years I was alive—I even enjoyed it. But who can do them forever—"

Then her sobs broke beyond restraint. Beth sorrowfully watched her, as if she knew that it would do no good to offer comfort. Jacintha stood with her face covered, her shoulders shaking, crying harder and harder. To have nothing to do—

We don't realize, Cherry had said, how greatly we depend upon our duties. She had also said: *He offers the only hope there is in this crowded desolate place.*

It had sounded fantastic at the time—now it seemed so clear and so obvious. That is why she was ready to destroy me when I threatened to take her place with him. And that is why *I* hate her now. We have come to be mortal enemies. It is unbelievable, and yet we have.

She heard a sound and looked up swiftly.

It was Beth, standing beside the doorway into the hall, holding it slightly ajar. She had given a soft hiss. Now she jerked her head. "She's coming!"

"Who?"

"Mrs. Anson! Quick! You can see her!"

Jacintha hesitated on the edge of a haughty refusal, but then she picked up her swinging ruffled skirts and rushed on tiptoe to the door. Of course she wanted to see her. She wanted to see how she looked. And, anyway—what else did she have to do? Idleness, interminable idleness, would produce considerable changes in her, she could see that now. For she had never before stooped to spying on anyone, no matter what the circumstances.

Jacintha stood beside Beth and peeked out. The hall, as usual, was rather dimly lit, but they could see Cherry hurrying toward them, moving with her familiar quick skimming graceful little steps. She was still only a dark figure but, after a few moments, she emerged more clearly and they could see that her gown was drenched, tangled and torn, her hair undone and hanging in wet coils across her breasts and over her shoulders. Her entire appearance was wild, dishevelled, at once rapturous and tormented. She had been, it seemed, entirely possessed and had not even now shaken free of the enchantment.

Jacintha was outraged.

She heard Beth give a little clucking sound and suddenly became aware of the girl's warm body and the faint unpleasant smell she had. She turned and gestured her away, ignoring the look of disappointment and pleading on her face. What right had that wretched creature to stand gaping at her mother's shameful appearance?

Cherry came along swiftly and, just as she drew opposite the door and passed beneath one of the gas jets, Jacintha saw that her face was white to the lips, as if she was chilled through, but that her dark eyes looked unbelievably large and glowing with a triumphant fire. She was wholly absorbed in her own thoughts and feelings.

Nevertheless, just as she passed, Jacintha stepped back and shut the door. After a moment she opened it again and this time took a step into the hallway. Cherry was opening her own door and now, as if at a signal, she stopped, turned slowly, and faced her daughter.

Jacintha gave a start as those dark eyes rested upon her and, feeling as if she had caught a culprit and, at the same time, been herself accused of a crime—she stepped hastily back and closed the door.

Breathing fast and hard, weak with some inexplicable terror, her heart pounding so that it seemed to shake her whole body, she leaned there helplessly. She felt convinced that something peculiarly horrible had been about to happen between them and that it would have happened, but for her own swift retreat. Cherry's face, so white that not even her lips showed, a white mask with those dark and glowing eyes, now persisted in Jacintha's vision as if she had gazed too long at the sun.

Beth crept nearer, like a frightened pup. "What did she do, madame? What did she do?"

Jacintha ignored her for a few moments, still fighting for her self-control. Then, suddenly enraged at Beth's whining insistence, she flared out: "Don't you know who she is?"

"Who she is, madame?" repeated Beth, trembling now,

as if Jacintha had threatened to beat her. "She's Mrs. Anson, madame—isn't she?"

"Oh, you're so stupid!" cried Jacintha, and passed her swiftly, disgusted to hear herself speak that way to a servant. She stood with her back to the fireplace and then addressed Beth very clearly, drawing herself as tall as possible. "Mrs. Anson is my mother."

Beth retreated from that as from a blow. "Oh," she whispered. "How cruel. How *cruel.*" She was shaking her head, and her distress was so genuine that Jacintha felt not only pity for her but honest affection as well, and she smiled, trying with gentleness to make up for the way she had spoken to her before.

"Yes, it is cruel, isn't it? I suppose it amuses him greatly."

Beth was silent a moment, thinking over this startling information. Then she lifted her head and looked at Jacintha once more. "Which of you will renounce him? Since even I can see that you love him too, madame."

"*I* will, of course!" retorted Jacintha, as if the mere doubt had been an insult to her integrity. "Who else? I have done it already!"

Beth shrugged and gestured, palms up. "God give you strength." And suddenly, realizing what she had said, she clapped both hands to her mouth, stared at Jacintha a moment with her eyes popped wide, and then they laughed together at the blunder.

"I think I'll go to bed now," said Jacintha finally. "I'm very tired and perhaps I can sleep."

Beth turned down the bed and went puttering about the room, straightening furniture and picking up odds and ends, a fan Jacintha had played with for a few moments, a hairpin she had dropped, and then she turned out the lamps. She left one burning, for Jacintha was still standing before the fire yawning and stretching, watching the flames, admiring their colors which kept blending and changing, like a fluid opal.

"Good night, now, madame."

Jacintha glanced across her shoulder. "Good night, Beth."

The door closed and the girl was gone. Jacintha sighed. She continued to stand, watching the fire, her left hand lightly poised on her hip, leaning with her right arm against the mantelpiece. Idly, her eyes travelled down to her toe and up her bare leg which emerged in a taut straight line from the gown's opened front, showing as far as her thigh. The light turned her flesh to a melting rosy tone which she could not help admiring, and then, impulsively, she slid free of the gown and flung it onto a chair, kicked off her slippers, and stood naked before the fire, luxuriously enjoying the heat on her skin.

How good it feels, she thought, smiling to herself. How wicked I am, too, she considered, to stand here like this, and was surprised to find herself indifferent to the discovery.

The fire seemed to eat into her skin, nibbling at the flesh, rousing urgent sensual and voluptuous longings. All this beauty, she reflected dreamily—and was filled with yearning to have herself desired, to watch a man's responses as he gloated over her, to see his mounting excitement and, finally to abandon herself to his mastery. It hasn't taken long, she thought, with an amused and rueful smile at herself, for me to grow accustomed to this place.

Slowly she turned, very slowly, for she wanted to surprise her own image in the mirror across the room, pretending—by casting her eyes this way and that way —that she did not quite know where she would encounter herself. And, with that same self-absorbed dreamy expression, her body languidly turning, she encountered him, instead.

He stood a few feet away—at the top of the stairs down which Grant had hustled her the night before.

He had one foot planted on the carpet, the other on the stairs, and he leaned forward so that one arm rested across his leg. He was fully clothed, wearing informal evening dress, as he had when they encountered him last night in the lobby. And he grinned broadly as she saw him—gave a shriek of alarm—and stumbled backward, almost falling.

Recovering herself, she rushed forward to get her dressing gown. But as she reached for it he moved swiftly, snatched it from the tips of her fingers and, now laughing, held it away from her. He kicked the trap door shut.

"What do you need it for?"

"What do I need it for? I'm—I'm naked! Oh—please give it to me! *Please!*"

She darted to one side and then the other, reaching, but he kept it teasingly out of her grasp. Suddenly he held it before him and, just as she had grabbed the edge, he ripped it apart, down the middle, and tossed the two rags at her, still laughing. He then began to wander about the room, his hands in his pockets, as if he had come on a tour of inspection. Jacintha stood there holding the pieces in her hands, shivering with helpless humiliation and biting her lips. Her embarrassment was all the worse, it seemed, because *he* was fully clothed.

He went prowling about, looking things over, his face amused but critical, as if anything found wrong or out of place might make him angry. He picked up one of her embroidered pincushions, examined it for a moment, and tossed it down. He looked at some of her bottles and boxes full of handkerchiefs and jewellery. He opened a drawer or two and closed them again with the toe of his shining black leather shoe. Finally he turned.

"Is everything to your satisfaction?"

"Oh, yes," said Jacintha, holding the torn wrapper before her and feeling like a fool. With all the beautiful clothes she had, all the things she would have liked him to see her in, and she must stand there holding up to herself two shredded muslin rags.

Apparently he found it as ridiculous as she, for now he crossed the room, snatched them away from her, tossed them into a heap and said: "Stop that nonsense. You've got a beautiful body and you know it. You're dying to have me look at you, so stop pretending. That's what I detest about you Victorians!"

He was right, of course. She did want him to look at her. And yet, she felt so helpless and absurd. "But I can't look dignified!" she protested, trying now to cover herself with her hands. "I—I feel awkward!"

His eyes swept over her swiftly, down, and back up. "You look," he said slowly, "as white and succulent as the flesh of an apple."

"Ohh—" breathed Jacintha, and turned suddenly weak. "I do?" Her hands dropped limply to hang at her sides.

Then she remembered what had happened this afternoon. It was incredible she could have forgotten for even a moment—except, of course, that he had appeared in his usual sudden startling fashion and caught her off guard. Now she had returned to her senses and would treat him as he deserved: with a full measure of hauteur, intimidating to any male upon whom she had ever turned its powerful beam. She would wilt his confidence, shrivel his despotic assurance, make him aware of himself as exactly what he was—a man beneath the contempt of any fastidious lady. Preparatory to impaling him upon her disdain, she lifted her brows delicately, faced him directly—and felt herself begin to melt inside like a wax doll.

For there he stood, perfectly calm and self-contained, not ashamed of himself and not preening, either—agonizing her with his hard virile powerful beauty. And all of a sudden she was swept with a memory so violent that its force seemed almost great enough to crush her.

"Thank you," she said humbly, "for the compliment."

"It's quite true," he replied, and it seemed as if everything she did amused him.

Still, he continued looking at her.

And the longer he looked, the less embarrassed she felt. Since he would not permit her to be shyly modest, there finally seemed no reason to pretend that she was. She began to enjoy standing there before him with nothing to conceal her from his eyes. Was it not, after all, exactly what she had been wishing for—only the moment before she discovered him?

She even had a sense that somehow, at this very instant, she was being permitted to gratify a wish she had cherished a long long while, though of course she would never have admitted it to herself. To be naked and stared at by a man—it was something she had not experienced before. Neither her husband nor Douglas had thought it proper to show undue interest in her naked body, though Douglas, being her lover, had had license to show greater and franker interest than her husband. With them both she had always assumed what even they knew to be an exaggerated shyness. Still, it was expected of her and they would have been puzzled and disappointed, if she had not.

Now—how delightful it was finally to have had her beauty discovered. It seemed to her that by his admiration and interest, he had made her truly beautiful for the first time. What meaning had her beauty had before—when it could only be covertly enjoyed, and must always be half ignored? And how great a pleasure it was to know that he would find no flaw, that she could only *please* his eyes.

Very slowly, in a movement as fluid as oil poured from a jar, she raised up on her toes, drew her ribs high so that her waist narrowed to its smallest circle, lifted her breasts and then raised her arms above her head, sweeping her long black hair upward. Quickly then, smiling at him with her head tipped slightly forward, she divided her hair into two sections and tied a knot. The gesture was simple, strangely innocent and childlike, but at the same time, entirely aware and provocative.

He did not move but only continued watching her and Jacintha felt a sharp painful twist inside. What was wrong? Why was she not exciting to him tonight? And then the humiliating reason struck her. Of course. He was satiated, replete from his afternoon with Cherry. Again, she had forgotten. Here she had been, confronting him, naked, wanting him to desire her—when the mere notion of a woman was probably tiresome to him.

And yet, they had said—had they not?—that he was insatiable.

Then what was he doing? Why was he here? Had he come to humiliate and torment her?

Something of her bewilderment and despair must have shown in her face, for, just as she was wondering how she could turn away from him and hide, just as she had begun to despise herself for standing there with that ridiculous smile, he seemed to come to her rescue.

"Yes," he said softly, nodding his head. "You are beautiful." He leaned back against a great marble-topped chest, slid his hands into his pockets, crossed one foot over the other, and smiled. "You're as beautiful as any woman I've ever seen."

"Oh!" cried Jacintha. "What a thing to say!" Her face now unconsciously had a look of pouting taunting petulance, like that of a very young girl first made aware of her effect upon men, frightened by the new knowledge and eager to try its power, all at the same time.

"You would have preferred that I said you were *more* beautiful?" he asked.

"I would have preferred," retorted Jacintha, "that you did not make any comparison at all. No woman wants to think a man is running his eye over his private collection while he is with her! She wants to pretend, at least, that there were no others!"

Then, like a child who has said its piece in school, she sat down abruptly upon a crimson velvet tabouret before the fire. She extended one leg straight before her, drew the other up to clasp her fingers about the knee, and leaned backward. She wished she could find a mirror to see if the position was a pretty one.

"You look fine," he said. "I wish you'd stop being so goddamned self-conscious. It's very strange," he added, and slowly shook his head.

"*What* is very strange?"

"You women are all alike—no matter what age you were born and bred in: All that any one of you really wants to hear are bons mots, bagatelles, and bullshit."

Jacintha gave a little scream of horror and clapped one hand to her mouth. *"What?"*

"That's right. You call it chivalry in one age. You call it gallantry in another. Sometimes you call it honor and sometimes you call it respect. It all comes to the same thing. Even passion is only a means to an end with you— the price you think you must pay in advance for the only thing you honestly value: bons mots, bagatelles, and bullshit."

"Well!" said Jacintha.

He had gone right ahead and said it again. And yet, now that she thought about it, it was funny and it was, furthermore, true. Jacintha put her fingers to her lips and giggled.

"You Victorians are the worst of all," he added.

His references to the Victorians had begun to nettle her. She raised her head and stared haughtily at him. "You seem to overlook the fact," she said, "that women are born under a handicap. There is something naturally rather ridiculous about us and our entire predicament. If we did not protect ourselves by disguising our own absurdity beneath many veils of romantic mist— men would treat us much worse than they do."

He laughed softly. "You're clever," he said. "Who taught you all this? Your mother died too young, though she would have been an excellent teacher—"

"Don't you dare mention my mother!" cried Jacintha, and seemed to hear the cry still in the air, shrill and rasping, like the sound of tearing silk, long after the words left her mouth.

The next instant she had leaped up and run to stand before him, her fists clenched, so furiously angry that she had lost all fear of him. He had not moved but continued to stand with his hands in his pockets, looking down at her, calm and indifferent but, at the same time, mildly amused. It was the look of amusement which blew her rage wide open.

"*You!*—" she began, in a frenzy of rage and hatred. She raised her fists and saw, as she did so, an image of how shocked his face would look when she struck him.

He seized her wrists with one hand, gave a quick twist which made her cry out in pain and sent her spinning half across the room. She regained her footing, staggering, but then whirled and rushed at him again. He was walking toward her, advancing slowly, and she stopped still, staring at him, then turned to run away, when she heard his voice, sharp and stern: "Come here!" She stopped, looked back at him across her shoulder, and stood where she was, trembling and waiting. When his hand took hold of her shoulder she began to quiver uncontrollably and, as he turned her around to face him, she raised her hands as if to ward off a blow.

A look of disgust crossed his face and he shook his head. "No," he said. "Don't do that. What have I ever done to make you think I'd hurt you?"

Her hands dropped and she was looking at him with wondering despair, unable to recall now exactly what it was that had happened so swiftly during the past minute or so.

"I don't know," she replied weakly. "I'm afraid of you. I think you're cruel—I think that you despise me. I think you came here to mock at me." She lifted her face higher and looked up at him now with perfect open honesty. "Why *did* you come—tonight?"

"I wanted to see you."

"No," she said sadly. "You came to remind me of what

happened last night between us and of what happened this afternoon between you and—my mother."

He stood looking at her, his eyes slightly narrowed as if he were concentrating closely—but not upon her face or body, rather, upon whatever she was as a woman. "You know," he said at last, "Your mother was no older than you when she died. But she has much more sense about men."

"Ohhh—" Jacintha gave a lonely sorrowful protesting little wail. She turned, covering her face with her hands, and dropped slowly to the floor at his feet where she sat on her heels, whimpering, like a frightened child.

I wish I could die, she thought dismally. I love him and he cares nothing about me. He prefers her—she knows how to please him better than I do. What does she do? What does she know? Everything I say and do is wrong. I defeat myself every moment, every time I speak or look at him. And yet, I do know better. I knew better with other men. It must be something in him that makes me do the wrong things.

She heard a soft sound and looked up. He had taken three or four steps away from her.

"Are you going?" she asked him, more in wonderment than desperation, as if she felt she deserved abandonment and was ready to accept it.

He turned when she spoke and paused, looking back at her. "I may as well." And now she felt as if her heart stopped its beating, swelled enormously, and burst within her.

There was nothing of that look of raw desire she had seen on his face last night. He was looking at her only as if she were a somewhat pitiful child. She had never felt such mournful hopeless anguish; she wanted to crawl away and hide, from him and from herself. How could she have imagined, last night, that only a few hours later he could look at her as if it had never happened or as if he, at least, had forgotten?

For that is the thing, she reflected, a woman can never believe—that once a man leaves her body he can be, again, entirely free of her. He can regain his self-possession as easily as he lost it. He can consider her or not, as he chooses, without reference to their intimacy. While she must remember always, and carry in her deepest self the awareness and the fact of having once been loved by him. There is no escape for her. There is no imprisonment—unless he seeks it—for him.

She raised her arms toward him. "I love you." She heard the words—spoken in a melodious throbbing tone she had never heard in her own voice before—with a sense of surprise and discovery, and relief, as well. For, by the tone even more than by the words, she entirely committed herself to him. The veils of romantic mist lifted and melted away and she was as devoid of coquetry and pretense as she was of clothing.

After a momentary shock, a surprised feeling that she had abandoned the battlefield to a rival general, almost, as it were, on a sudden impulse, unintentionally—after that, she was exquisitely glad that she need never deceive him again.

Still kneeling there in her arms extended, she looked up at him and now her face had the shine of a devout twelve-year-old at her prayers. "You see?" she murmured softly. "It's just as you said. I have no further use for my pride."

He did not move but continued to stand a few feet from her, his hands still in his pockets, his head slightly lowered, watching her carefully. There was a look on his face now that seemed close to compassion, certainly there was sympathy. But there was not, as she had hoped, either an answering love or a return of that sudden lust which had absolutely transformed him, and her, the night before.

"I should imagine," he said quietly, "you'll be much more comfortable without it. You will certainly be much closer to yourself as a woman."

"Yes," said Jacintha. "I am. I know that I am. Though I'm not sure it's going to make me happier."

"Happy is a concept I have never understood. Every creature should seek to experience most profoundly that which is its own essence. A woman, by nature, finds her greatest glory in defeat. Surely that must be worth something to you?"

"Yes," she whispered again. "It must be. Anyway—I can't feel otherwise now." She paused, "I don't even hold you responsible."

"Why should you?"

"I don't know." She slowly shook her head, gazing now not at him but at the carpet, tracing over a flower with one forefinger. "I don't know anything. It's strange though, isn't it? You are the cause—and yet you didn't do it."

"If I had—it would be a fraud. I would have bullied you, from my own insignificance, and you would find it out and despise me—and yourself, too. This way, it came about naturally, through your own desire, and so it will give you satisfaction. You will be regretful about some things, of course, but not about the way you most deeply feel."

She looked up at him again, her face touchingly innocent, shining with a winsome sweetness. She gave a faint long sigh. She kept waiting, expecting him to do something, but he did not. He only stood and continued looking at her and he seemed to her incomparably handsome, dark, brilliant, spectacular, and remote.

"What is it," she asked him finally, "that I am going to regret?"

"So many things, I suppose. You won't be able to help yourself and I can't help you, either."

"If you wanted to—" she began, in a light tentative voice.

He shook his head. "I don't want to."

"And you never will?"

"I never will."

Jacintha looked down again. Her eyes had begun to ache, as if the terrible intensity of her desire had concentrated there. She yearned for him with a tormenting ardor that she felt would be unendurable if it should not be appeased. But she was helpless, dependent upon him, while he was entirely detached from her. She would never be able to have the comfortable necessary feminine conviction of holding and possessing him. He would remain, as he was, inaccessible, appearing and disappearing at his own need, without reference to her. While she must somehow learn to endure the taunting loneliness of waiting, of patience, of brief joy and endless anxiety.

Could this possibly have happenened to her?

And had it, actually, happened only during these past few hours? Or had she been, as he had said, in love with him for a long long while and eager to reach her destination?

"No," she agreed. "I know you won't. And will you never love me, either—even if I do everything right?" Her voice was wistful, like a young girl's, rather than a woman's.

"You can't do everything right, since I have no definition for what is wrong. But you knew the answer—why did you ask?"

"I suppose I asked because I was hoping—"

"You were hoping that you would be the one exception since the beginning of time."

She lifted her head quickly, her face lively and alert, almost flirtatious, to conceal, if possible, her embarrassment and profound hopeless disappointment. "And I'm not."

"Of course not. I told you yesterday, when you asked me that—I don't fall in love. It's not one of the things that happens to me. You know—there is, naturally, always something which a given woman lacks. But I have never yet met one who had a deficiency of vanity." His expression had changed again, some slight hint of mockery had returned. He was amusing himself, she felt, at her expense.

"I know," agreed Jacintha apologetically. "It was foolish of me to ask. And yet, it was a natural thing to do, wasn't it?"

He nodded. "Perfectly natural for you to want me to love you. And perfectly natural for me not to do so. Good night."

"What?" she cried, in dismay. "Oh, you're not going!"

He crossed the room and gave a sharp stamp of one foot. Instantly, the trap door flew open and there was Grant, disgusting and offensive as always, with his uncanny grin. Jacintha shrieked and bent over, covering herself with her hands. "Get on down there!" he said sharply. Grant disappeared from view.

Jacintha leaped up and ran to him. Cool moisture came from the stair well and her flesh crept with the cold. "Take me with you!" she begged.

He descended two or three steps and regarded her as she stood there, clasping her hands together, looking desolate, and yet so beautiful in her eagerness and honest self-betrayal. "I don't think so," he murmured, still smiling.

Hopeful, because he had not absolutely refused, Jacintha reached out and touched his arms with her hands, her face almost on a level with his now; she was shivering in the wet cold. Grant had left a lantern on the top step and it threw upward strange sharp shadows which lit their faces and made them seem two dramatic conspirators meeting in desperation. "Please, please," she whispered. "Please."

His mouth was very near and her eyes closed, seeming to lower of themselves, unable to support their heavy burden of desire. Her lips parted and waited, waited endlessly it seemed until, at last, she felt the slow warm pressure of his mouth. She sighed and her arms passed swiftly and eagerly about his wide shoulders. Her breasts crushing out upon the stiff white front of his shirt. The memory of last night had tormented her throughout the day, in spite of everything she had done to banish it, and yet now that it was happening it seemed infinitely more exciting and rewarding, more completing to the intolerable emptiness she had begun to feel, than she had remembered.

Her passion sprang eagerly, like an animal rushing to greet its master, then crouching for a moment, obediently waiting for his sign. All at once he released her, moved apart, and, while she regarded him with startled eyes and increasing frantic despair, went down another step or two.

"No!" she cried. *"I'm coming!"*

She descended a few steps and stood above him, her face on a level with his. She stared into his eyes, pleading and scared, for she knew already that he did not intend to let her accompany him. He was smiling at her again, ignoring her desperation and smiling.

"Run along," he said, as if to a child. "Before you take a chill."

She continued to stare at him, determined to prevent his departure for as long as possible. Even if there was nothing more he would give her, she wanted his presence —only to look at him was a greater pleasure than any she had had with another man. But then his face changed once more, and she knew that he was through playing with her. She must obey. She turned and slowly, sorrowfully crept back up and stood at the top of the stairs, looking wistfully down, her hands folded. His face, turned up to her, with the lantern casting bold shadows upon it, was so spectacular that she could only gaze at him with longing admiration. She was not even angry. She gave another sigh, this one heavy and hopeless.

He had succeeded, again, in dominating her completely. But, whereas the night before, the domination had been accomplished through tenderness and, later, physical power—tonight there had been nothing more definable than his clear and absolute self-possession. He had no understanding of what it was to crave something inaccessible, to yearn, to lie in torment and anguish, waiting, lonely, frightened, angry, hating and loving all at once. These things belonged to another breed and in them he found nothing which was tragic or which obligated him—but only mild scornful amusement and some diversion.

"When will I see you again?" she asked him finally.

"I don't know."

Then—as she suddenly foresaw the night and the next day and perhaps a thousand more days or even years—she grew wildly frantic. "But what will I do while I wait for you?" she implored. "What *is* there for me to do?"

He shrugged.

"I asked my maid today and she says you don't even have embroidery needles here!"

He smiled. "She's right. I don't have embroidery needles."

"You don't have yarn or glue or paints or any of the things I must have to keep myself busy!"

"Is that how you kept yourself busy?" he inquired with polite sarcasm, as if vaguely wondering and admiring at this manner of occupation.

"Of course!" she cried, and the thought occurred that if she could engage him in a quarrel she could keep him with her a little longer and perhaps he would take her with him after all. "I was always busy! I was never idle! But no one packed my books or my paints or my Berlin work! I have nothing to do! You have provided nothing for our diversion!"

He listened, and his eyebrows flickered slightly; his mouth turned down in a momentary grimace. "On the other hand," he said, in an eminently reasonable tone, "how could I provide for your diversion? Each generation of rich women has a different way of wasting time —and the poor spend theirs with babies and drudgery, neither of which is available to them here. In fact, the poor women who are pretty enough to get in here have an opportunity to dress and live like the rich. They think it's heaven, for a century or two. No, Jacintha. I have not provided for your diversion. The problem here is one of too much leisure, and each of us must solve it in his own way. You will have to find what means you can of passing eternity. You can regard it, if you like—and I think it will be helpful if you do—as a challenge, a problem in imagination and resourcefulness. I don't mean to sound pessimistic, but I've been here a long while and from my own experiences and what I've heard of others', I don't think it is possible to succeed in that task. Things are quite pleasant here, as I'm sure you will agree—" He gestured to indicate the handsome luxuriously furnished room. "And yet, everyone is dissatisfied—myself included. I'm afraid the truth is that any heaven would become hell if it lasted too long. Good night."

He descended rapidly several more steps, reached up with one swift movement of his arm and brought the trap door crashing down. Just at the last instant, as she moved forward, crying out, he gave her a flashing half-smile which appeared upon his somber dark face so unexpectedly, shone brilliantly for such a brief space, that now, with the door fast shut and its outline lost once more in the carpet's intricate pattern—she continued to see the gleaming black eyes, the trace of white teeth beneath his scarcely parted lips, the look of tantalizing challenge.

Then, as the image slowly faded, she thought perhaps he had not been there at all.

And yet he had. For his kiss had brought to intense urgent focus all her desire for him, and now he was gone, leaving her turgid and full of uneasy discontent.

The fire was burned down. The room had grown chill and she realized that she was cold, even shivering. She turned out the lamp and crept into bed where she lay with her teeth chattering, stretched out straight and flat, staring into the black room, eager and intent and alert, still convinced that he had been teasing and that he would return to her. She waited, so intent on listening that she scarcely gave any thought to what he had told her at the last, or to what kind of predicament she was in—only listening, her neck taut and strained, for she scarcely dared lay her head upon the pillow, her muscles tight and ready to leap. The time passed slowly and she continued waiting, refusing to believe that he would not return. Suddenly there was a sharp crack and she gave a violent shuddering start.

"Yes!" she cried, and sat up straight. "Who is it? Who's there?"

She waited, her heart pounding, not knowing whether to be scared or happy—whether he was returning, as she had known he certainly would, or whether someone had entered the room to harm her. At last, unable to bear the suspense any longer, she got out of bed and lit one of the lamps. The room was empty.

I was falling asleep, she decided, and it was the fireplace, cooling off, that made that sound. She turned out the light and went back to bed and continued to listen until, slowly, against her will and almost without her knowledge, her muscles unknotted, slipped into relaxation, and she fell asleep.

When she woke, Beth was bustling about the room, the fire was going, the draperies were drawn back part way to let in some of the dashing brilliant sunshine, and, as she opened her eyes, Beth cried cheerfully: "Good morning, madame!"

Jacintha sighed. She glanced at the clock and it was only nine. She had not slept very long and she was tired. But worse than that, she felt overwhelmed by a morbid hopeless gloom, as heavy and inescapable as if she had been crushed flat beneath a giant hand.

"Good morning, Beth. Have you been here long?"

"An hour or so, madame. I should say. I've sent for your breakfast. It will give you something to do, so I thought you might like to have it. You can sit by this window and look out—it's *such* a fine day!"

Jacintha gave a low moan. "It seems always to be *such*

a fine day in this place! Isn't it ever dreary? Where's my wrapper? Oh—" she said, as she remembered.

Beth apparently had seen it already, for a roguish mischievous grin spread over her face and she picked up the two shredded rags and held them before Jacintha: "You had a visitor, I see."

"Stop that!" cried Jacintha, and clapped her hands together. "You're the most impertinent creature I've ever had for a servant! Get my wrapper!"

"Yes, madame. I'm sorry, madame. I thought we'd have a laugh together."

"I can't imagine, what there is to laugh at," muttered Jacintha, as Beth brought her another dressing gown and held it. Her slippers were there, just beneath her toes, and she stood up, tying the sash, throwing back her head and shaking out her long black hair, running her fingers through it.

"Only that it's exactly like him, madame, to do a thing of that kind. And though I'm sure you were warned against him many times, as we all were, you let him dupe you all the same. But I'm sorry if the mention of it offends you, madame." She hurried across the room and began to clear the little tulipwood desk which stood between the two big windows.

Jacintha watched her moodily, sorry for her, angry that she should dare be on such familiar terms with her, a thing she had never before permitted in a servant, and glad, too, for the mere fact of her presence. Now there was a rap at the door and Beth went to get the tray which one of the lackeys delivered. On it was Jacintha's breakfast and, as Beth bore it swiftly by her and set it on the desk, she could smell the buckwheat cakes and sausages and coffee. Beth arranged the pretty hand-painted dishes, placing each one as if it gave her pleasure, then stepped back with a little gesture for Jacintha to take her place.

Jancitha sat down humbly. "Thank you. I won't—I won't—be rude any more, Beth."

"Oh, I don't mind, madame. I know your nerves must be strung like a harp. He *is* a hard one, isn't he?"

Jacintha, spreading the napkin in her lap, lifting up the silver covers on the dishes, nodded her head. "He is," she agreed with a sigh. "He is. The only thing—they never mentioned the way he looks. In fact, they pretended he was ugly."

"Of course! If women knew what charms he has— what use would they have for other men? He makes all other men look ugly and seem like dullards, doesn't he?"

Jacintha nodded, picking indifferently at her plate. "He does, that's true. But he's capricious and he's cruel. He taunts and mocks and ridicules, and I can't and won't endure that kind of treatment." The words sounded to her like the delayed echo of something spoken long ago in a hollow room.

"Still, madame," said Beth, as she turned to pull the blankets and sheets off the bed and make it up fresh, "what else is there for you to do?"

At that, Jacintha put down her fork and sat with her cheek on her fist, staring out the window, across the meadows with their whirling steam and rushing torrents of hot water, across the low pine-covered hills to the dim bordering mountains. A kind of languid stupor seemed to invade her; finally she sighed.

Then, resolutely, she got up. "I'll find something to do!" she announced. "I'll begin by taking a bath!"

She made as much of the bath as she could, lingering in it until she was all but immobilized by the heat. Then she dawdled over getting dressed, searching up and down her closet, discussing this gown and that one with Beth. Finally they selected one made of bright-green wool with black stripes running up and down the bodice and crosswise over the folded and gathered skirt. Beth took some time to put up her hair. Then there was the business of selecting gloves and a hat and jewellery and a parasol.

But, the closer she came to being dressed, the slower her movements got and the more her hands and, it seemed, her whole insides, began to tremble with apprehension. She grew heavy in every muscle, as if her arms and legs dragged great weights: *Why* should she go out? What was there to do?

She stood now and faced herself in the mirror, staring with hostile indifference as though at an unwelcomed stranger. She looked enchantingly beautiful, and she despised the sight of herself. She wore her hat, her black kid gloves, carried her parasol and handbag in her right hand, and a fan in her left. Her face, white and oddly tragic, gazed back at her. She stood in this way for several moments while Beth hovered about, looking vaguely frightened and full of concern.

"Madame—" she whispered at last, and reached forth one hand tentatively. "Are you ready?"

Jacintha sighed and nodded. "Yes. Shall we go now?"

Slowly she walked to the door and Beth opened it. She went through the doorway, took two steps, and then turned and looked toward Cherry's door.

She had been trying all night and since waking this morning to keep Cherry out of her thoughts. They loved the same man and hated each other. There was no place in their lives for companionship or even tolerance. They would never meet again, never speak to each other—everything was as it had been, when Cherry had died.

She felt a recurrence of that old desolation, the emptiness, the hopeless longing for her mother's voice and smile and comforting arms, the warmth of her love and devotion, and the terrible knowledge that although she could not at that moment understand or believe it, those things were henceforth denied to her—a loss she would only learn fully to understand and to make a part of herself, as the years went by. Later on, it was as if she had taken her memories of her mother into her own body, carefully wrapped and shrouded, and concealed them, held them there as part of herself, cherished and tenderly cared for. But, always, they had been a part of herself subject to the most terrible and intense pain, which must not be touched, which must be left a kind of hollow to float in so that nothing could break open its cocoon and set free a swarming anguish she would never have been able to bear.

Must I do all that again?

I can't.

Jacintha turned, shaking her head, went past Beth, who turned slowly to watch her, walked back into the room and sat down beside the window once more, her black-gloved hands shielding her face as she rested her elbows on the desk top.

"I'm not going out," she said to Beth. "I can't."

She felt so peculiarly foreign to herself, as always when pain became intolerable. It was as if she retired into a dazed seclusion and waited until she could admit the pain, little by little, permit it to enter her and establish itself. She could not allow it to rush in all at once, like a trampling giant, and demolish her. The pain was a horrible spectre, an ugly tremendous goblin, which must move into her house little by little, slowly making room for himself, nudging and edging with his feet and shoulders, pushing other feelings out of the way until he had the space he needed. At that moment, of course, he might grow obstreperous and rise up, fling his arms wide and spread his feet—and destroy the entire fabric of her being. That had almost happened on the occasion of her mother's death. And yet, just at the moment when he threatened to break down the boundaries of her being entirely, she had tamed him, forced him to squat obediently and let her grow a bit larger in order to contain him. And he had lived with her ever since.

Until the moment she and Cherry had met here—when he had departed.

But now he was back again, bigger and more terrifying than ever, threatening, pounding to get in, demanding his admission. She sat there, pretending indifference, pretending not to hear or be aware that he was battering away at her private personal domicile once more.

We were so entirely happy, she thought. For a day and a half. It almost seemed we made up for all the years after she died. The instant we found each other here I suddenly experienced, for the first time, that kind of mystical happiness which is contentment and conviction, blended together of tenderness and mercy and compassion, arising from something deeper in us than love for a man.

As she sat there, her head in her hands, Jacintha sank into a kind of stupor in which she left almost entirely the awareness of her present physical self and seemed to drift backward through the centuries, the thousands of years, following the long subtle intricate tracery which had produced first Cherry and then herself. It was that blood continuity which seemed to her the only true eternal value, and which she now perceived with unbelievable clarity was significant only as it had passed from Cherry to her, then to her own daughter whom she had so recently left—it seemed without genuine relevance to her father or to any of the men down through the centuries. They had been, as it were, accidental factors in the long line of mothers, giving life to one generation after another.

I must go and talk to her.

Jacintha was caught up in a sudden excitement and conviction, and awareness of her relationship to Cherry and to all the women whose bodies had given *them* life —she felt a tie stronger than any she had realized before, a relationship existing on levels which no relationship with a man ever touched. There was her loyalty —there was her link with all humanity. The accidental passion was of no comparable significance and no longer could it be permitted to interfere in the deep oceanic love between Cherry and herself.

If only she were not a beautiful woman my own age—

But, almost as the thought entered her mind, Jacintha shook her head. No. I still want the advantages for myself. I wish she were older than I, beyond her youth and loveliness. Of course that would make it simple. She would be resigned, in the practical sense at least, and I would be gentle with her and perfectly in command because of my own youth and beauty. I am selfish. I deserve to be unhappy!

We have met each other honestly here—each of us at the height of our beauty and energy and desirability. He wants to destroy our love—not for any purpose, only to entertain himself with his brief mischief, but we must be cleverer than he. We must not permit him to do it.

I'm going this moment!

Jacintha leaped to her feet and whirled about, to face Cherry coming through the doorway as Beth backed out, bowing her head and closing the door behind her.

The two women stood confronting each other.

Cherry looked calm, almost serene, and there was a slight smile on her lips, a smile which had no mockery or cruelty in it, but only tenderness and love. Jacintha stood with her body tense, arrested in the act of whirling about, her arms held stiff and far back at her sides, her eyes big and staring. And then, after a moment, with a little moan, she ran forward and Cherry came to meet her. They flung their arms about each other and held each other close. Jacintha was crying and Cherry stroked her back and petted her and clucked and murmured soft cherishing reassuring words.

After two or three minutes Jacintha stopped crying and turned to take a handkerchief out of a drawer and blow her nose.

"We won't let him do it, will we?" asked Cherry softly, standing still and watching her. Jacintha dabbed at her cheeks and blotted the tears from her thick black lashes, sniffling a time or two, like a little girl. She shook her head vigorously.

"No, we won't! I'm sure he thinks he's succeeded already. Why didn't they ever tell us that this was one of his vilest tricks—to separate a mother and daughter?"

"They are so much more concerned with sex back there."

"And even about that, they tell you lies. They say how he hurts you and how repulsive he is and—" Jacintha stopped, blushing.

"Yes, I know. They say everything that is the exact opposite of the truth, don't they? I would have preferred, actually, that they had been right."

"How dreadful that would have been! To spend eternity with a monster!"

"Perhaps he is more a monster this way. I've known him much longer than you, Jacintha, and I think I can say with reasonable authority, that he is actually worse than he was painted. Oh, not in any obvious way, for he is, after all, so tremendously attractive and desirable and exciting. But we are accustomed to one way of life —and he to another. Don't you see?"

"I'm—not sure," admitted Jacintha.

Cherry sat down in one of the crimson velvet chairs, crossing her delicate ankles, holding the handle of her parasol in her gloved right hand which was stretched outward from her body in graceful negligence, while her left hand rested lightly with palm upward in her lap. Her small bonnet had a veil which tied across her face and cast tiny dots of shadow upon her nose and cheeks. She looked delightfully young and fresh and winsome as she talked to Jacintha. Once more, now that they were together, Jacintha found it impossible to keep in mind that this vivacious merry girl was her mother.

"While it is happening," said Cherry, speaking in her

soft gentle tone, "it is impossible to do more than react to him with enormous gratitude. After all, he makes one feel things never even imagined before. But later—doubt and dissatisfaction begin. It is over. There is nothing left but anticipation of the next time—and that, because of his capricious nature, turns to anxiety. In that way, he robs us of the future. He has also robbed us of the past, for what is left of it but a tenuous memory, only enough to taunt, but not enough to satisfy? Don't you see what is wrong with this kind of love?" She tilted her head to one side as she regarded her daughter who stood before her, twisting the lace handkerchief about her gloved fingers, looking perplexed and unhappy. "It is too strange to our ways for us to accept: There is neither punishment, nor reward. And so it is useless and worse than useless. It depresses and frightens and disgusts us in the end. And yet—" She opened her free hand and gave a slow-moving outward gesture. "We have nothing else, here, where he is absolute master."

Jacintha was silent for a moment, listening, thinking intently about what Cherry had said. "We have each other!" she burst forth at last.

Cherry smiled. "We have." She nodded slightly. "We have each other, of course. You know that I love you, Jacintha. I know that you love me. We would not, either of us, willingly hurt the other. But we have hated each other already. And I'm afraid we shall again."

"No!" cried Jacintha. "We won't! If you want him—have him! I don't—" She began to gesture excitedly, almost as if his image had appeared before her eyes and she was trying to brush it away. "I don't want anything more to do with him! I've seen him clearly—I know what he is now! I—give him to you!" Unaware of what she was doing, Jacintha, at the moment of speaking the last sentence, seemed to gather a gift into her two hands and then leaned forward with a sweeping bow, as though presenting it to Cherry.

Cherry threw back her head and laughed joyously. "Oh, Jacintha! Jacintha, *darling!*"

Jacintha, shocked and offended, not certain what had caused this immoderate glee on Cherry's part, straightened swiftly, dropped her hands limp to her sides, and stared down at her. "I beg your pardon?" she coldly inquired.

"You're so sweet, darling. And so innocent."

Jacintha did not like to be treated in this fashion, as if she were a naïve and possibly rather dull-witted child. What right had Cherry to laugh at her intensest desire to please, at her absolute renunciation of future pleasure with him? Why should she not be humbly grateful that her daughter was willing to give up so much for her? How dare she laugh, in fact?

"Don't sweetheart," said Cherry teasingly, and pursed her full pink lips. "Don't look so cross with me. I think you're charming and touching and adorable. But *how* can you give him up? Tell me: While we are alive, what is it which is the source of most of our joy and much of our hope?"

"Why—I suppose—"

"That's not a difficult riddle," said Cherry briskly. "You know what it is as well as I. It is physical love. Nothing else. Oh, we pretend that it's a great many other things and if I had lived until you began to grow up I suppose I would have been hypocritical enough to tell you that it was many other things. Neither of us would have been fooled, of course. Well—that is still true here, at least where he is concerned. Now what have you to say?"

Jacintha stood for several moments, staring at her in turbulent confusion, shocked, at first, by what she had said, and then angry, hurt, dismayed. She took it, finally, as a challenge.

"I don't believe you!" she cried.

Politely and coolly, Cherry lifted her brows. "You don't? Why not? What is it, then, we value more?"

Jacintha felt that in some profound and disturbing way, she had been first tricked and then cheated. All her life she had believed in her mother as a virtuous and noble woman, a paragon of ladyhood. And this was what she was? These were the things she believed?

Well, then—it was her duty to break up that false image and set herself in its place. She had not sought the opportunity. It had come to her unbidden and most certainly against her will. Cherry had given it to her, was insisting, almost, by her smile and her cool detached challenging manner, that she accept it. Very well. It may be my strength, after all, that will save us.

The thought that she would not merely reveal Cherry as a woman of selfish and sensual inclinations, but that she would actually rescue them both, gave her a conviction of strength and a capacity for self-abnegation she had never known herself to possess.

"There is very much more," she said, speaking soberly, solemnly, intensely. But she felt such tremendous excitement that she was quivering and her big dark eyes, directing their gaze into Cherry's, seemed to light and flame with violent conviction. "What you have mentioned," she said slowly, speaking with careful disdain, like a lady lifting her skirts as she passes a dirty and stinking puddle, "Is not the greatest, but the *least* of the glories of humanity!"

She spoke so fervently that she had convinced herself and thus had forgotten not only the time she had spent with him but his virile and challanging and monumental beauty, as well. Everything which had to do with him she thought of as both ugly and evil, and terrifyingly cruel.

Cherry lifted one eyebrow, slowly twirling her ruffled parasol as she balanced its tip against the floor. "Indeed?" she asked softly. She looked amused, but tolerant, too. There was also something of pity in her expression, and that made Jacintha even more frantic and determined.

"You look at me as if you think I am a silly child! You have no right to do that! There are so *many* noble things in life—" She flung out both arms in a furious gesture and turned and walked to the window, nervously beating her gloved hands together. The blood seemed to be rushing through her body in a torrent and she could feel herself begin to sweat with anxiety and fear. She whirled and turned back. "There are so many things!" she cried again. "To begin with—there is a mother's love for her children!"

"Yes," agreed Cherry, still sitting as she had, straight on the crimson velvet chair, her head high and alert, proud and yet gently humorous. "But your children are not here."

"But yours is!" cried Jacintha and then stopped, horrified, feeling that in some way she had betrayed herself.

Something terrible had happened.

She had said the wrong thing.

What was it?

She had meant so well, had felt herself to be exalted and ennobled—and yet suddenly, without warning, there had been some hideous self-betrayal. Sick and weak, she waited for what Cherry would say now, expecting that she would take this opportunity to destroy her, since she had somehow witlessly subjected herself to such an attack. If only she could know what she had said wrong!

But Cherry did nothing of the kind. She lifted her brows and briefly glanced away. When she looked back at Jacintha she was smiling. "Ah?" she asked lightly. "So you are. And, since you are, I suppose I should be the one to—"

"You should not!" broke in Jacintha, for she felt she must not hear her implication put into words. "There are many other things, as well! There is honor and justice and loyalty and consideration and generosity and self-respect and—"

She would have rushed on, enumerating them one after the other, striking them off on her fingers as she went, but Cherry interrupted gently, still with that urbane little smile: "And all the virtues in the world cannot make you forget the passage of time—as we both know he can do."

Jacintha stopped, hung her head, and turned away. She had been so filled with conviction, she had had an almost religious sense of virtue and pride, a great determination and violent wish to martyr herself in this cause between them and come out once and for all as the nobler of the two.

How could she ever have guessed that she harbored any such ambitions against her mother? She was ashamed of herself, as intensely as, only a few moments earlier, she had been determined to shame Cherry.

Now Cherry spoke again. She still sounded entirely in command of herself, calm and light and sweet. Apparently this scene was not of the cataclysmic nature to her that it was to Jacintha. "There is no value here in being good, don't you see? No one respects it, no one pretends to practice it. We are all of us in the same desperate situation and must fight our battle with time any way we can. And sensual love is the only thing which can eternally give us pleasure—for it is new each time it happens. We forget, and so it always comes as a marvellous surprise. For a while, at least, we do not count minutes."

Jacintha listened meekly, knowing that everything she said was true, and was only amazed that she should have rebelled against him. She would be, as he had told her, dissatisfied by many things, but her feeling for him, involving her being to its last cell and vessel, was of such a nature that she believed it would last forever, even if it happened that she should never see him again.

She still, however, had made no reply, and so Cherry continued: "Come, now," she said. "Let's not be dishonest with each other. You would not be here, if you had not been a courageous woman."

Jacintha shook her head, still staring down at her tense moving fingers.

"Of course," said Cherry briskly. "You had courage enough to love a man and act on your love. It takes less courage to remain faithful, after all. I don't expect you to give him up for my sake. If you try—you won't succeed in anything but learning to hate me. Perhaps, together, we can outwit him."

Jacintha looked up with sudden alertness. *"How?"* she asked in an eager whisper. She crossed the few feet between them and now Cherry stood and they faced each other, Cherry's hand seeking her daughter's and holding it.

"He thinks, no doubt, that he has separated us already. He probably laughs to himself every time he thinks of us (if he ever does) hating each other—meeting after so many years apart, and hating each other because of him." Cherry was talking in a quick crisp manner now, something like a general ordering his troops about the field, confident and self-assured. "He has been outwitted before, you know—but only by guile, never by force. We must be cleverer than he."

"But how? *How* can we be more clever?"

Cherry released her hand and turned away and began to pace around the room. "I'm not sure. The best we can hope for, probably, is to remain together when he expects us to hate the sight of each other. There's no way of ever predicting him. He appears when and where you least expect him—and disappoints you if you're waiting for him. We shall not wait, or mope, or quarrel with each other, but keep very busy with a great number of things. We shall botanize and shop and get some paints from the Indians. We will get a harp, too—there are all kinds of musical instruments around here, since they are among the things *he* likes—and we will play and sing duets. We will be very busy, at all times—"

"Yes, we will!" cried Jacintha eagerly. "We will keep ourselves so occupied that he will be amazed! Let's go out this very minute! Let's begin to do other things and find new interests! Let's not lose a moment! Are you ready?"

They rushed to the mirror and peered into it, lifting their arms in unison to adjust their hats, pulling down their tight bodices so that they fitted without a crease, turning to observe themselves this way and that and then, taking each other by the hand, they skipped from the room in a flurry of laughter and rustling petticoats, naïvely excited as two children off on a picnic.

They sped down the corridor and out the side door by which they had left yesterday afternoon, picked up their skirts and went rushing across the meadow, their gowns bright and colorful against the grass—Jacintha's green with black stripes, Cherry's black and red checkered wool with scrolls of black braid and terraces of black fringe. They ran on and on, glancing at each other now and again and bursting into fresh laughter, and they continued running until they rounded the corner of the building and found the line of coaches and horses. They climbed up immediately.

"Go anywhere!" cried Cherry. "Hurry!"

She and Jacintha looked at each other and giggled delightedly as the driver snapped his whip and the horses leaped forward. They sped along, past the steaming open vents in the earth, across the flower-laden meadows, down the narrow forest lanes. They saw motionless buffalo in the distance. They passed startled deer which gazed at them for one instant and then disappeared with miraculous speed. Half-naked Indians went galloping by on their ponies. Cherry and Jacintha bounced up and down in the coach, laughing gleefully, pointing to the marvels of the place as if they were seeing them for the first time.

But a practical thought had occurred to Jacintha and, the answer. She put off asking time and again, but at last she could delay no longer. She turned to Cherry, whose face looked radiant and fresh, her skin pure and smooth and without a flaw in the sunlight, everything about her so felicitous. She was almost heartbreakingly lovely and vital.

"What if he tries to make love to one of us again?" called Jacintha, for they were going so fast, the horses' hoofs clattering so loud, the crack of the whip sounding again and again, the wheels banging over the rocky path, that she had to raise her voice.

"Why think about that now?" countered Cherry, as if the question had genuinely surprised her. Then her eyes travelled once very swiftly across Jacintha's face and she smiled, but turned her head away and looked at something out the other side of the carriage.

"We must decide!" Jacintha insisted. "If we don't decide what we're going to do—then we're no better off than we were before!"

"We're no better off anyway," replied Cherry, "if you must know the truth."

"Well!" Jacintha felt as if she had been pushed in the stomach. "Then what were all our plans for?"

"Darling, please," crooned Cherry, and clasped her daughter's hand for a moment. "No one expects to actually carry out every plan he makes, don't you know that? We made them as much for the sake of making them, as for any other reason. They brought us together when we were on the edge of something disastrous. That, in itself, justifies them, doesn't it? We will carry them out as well as possible, of course. But things are no more certain here than anywhere else."

"You mean—you'll change your course, depending on what happens?"

"Why, *certainly*, darling."

"Well," said Jacintha again, and sank back deep in the seat. At last she leaned forward once more. 'Then if he tries to make love to you—you intend to let him!"

"I intend— Oh, Jacintha. Please. Let's both intend nothing more than good will toward each other. With that as a beginning, we must improvise as we go along."

"Oh, Cherry." Jacintha solemnly shook her head. "Cherry—you're not like my mother, at all. If you want to know the truth I'll tell you: I think you're very immoral."

"You think I'm—" burst out Cherry and then, unable to contain herself, threw back her head and gave a laugh of such surprised delight and exuberance that Jacintha stared at her dumbfounded. "Oh, Jacintha!" she cried, when she could get her breath. "You think I'm immoral! You honestly do, darling, don't you?" She seemed not only amused but pleased, as if Jacintha had said something clever.

But to Jacintha it was beginning to seem that almost every moment she grew older and Cherry younger. She seemed to feel herself growing more prudish, more prim and narrowly critical, more tightened within herself, restricted from the allurements of femininity. What was happening to her? Was she giving up? Was she prepared to relinquish him altogether and let Cherry have him, after all?

Her earlier determination to martyr herself for the sake of their mother-daughter relationship seemed considerably less grand in design to her now than it had half an hour or so ago. It seemed, in fact, to have been more cowardice than generosity.

I wonder if I'm beginning to look any different?

While Cherry was still laughing, Jacintha quickly opened her black velvet drawstring bag and took out her mirror. As she lifted it toward her face she had a dreadful premonition that she would find herself grotesquely altered. She expected now to confront a thin-lipped woman with her mouth drawn into a straight puritanical line. She expected to find all the astonishing luminosity of her brown eyes—her greatest beauty, beyond a doubt —dim and dull. Her skin would no longer be white and clear with a sheen of fresh youthfulness, but most likely had turned some ugly grayish hue. Her thoughts must have shrivelled her.

Preparing herself for a shock, she closed her eyes briefly, then looked.

She looked exactly as before. Still somewhat dubious, she turned her head this way and that, narrowing her eyes a little, as if she believed they were deceiving her. No. She was the same. She felt she had miraculously escaped some terrible threatening danger.

With a guilty little start, she glanced sideways at Cherry who was still looking gay and pleased, her head now tipped to one side as she regarded Jacintha with faint amused curiosity.

"You're looking lovely," she said. "Were you doubtful?"

Jacintha nodded, embarrassed. "A little."

"I know. So was I, for a time. He loves to do that—tear a woman's vanity to shreds."

And that, of course, she realized the instant Cherry said it, was exactly what he had done. He had sent for her the very night of her arrival, had behaved toward her with that marvellous tenderness and passion—then, he had promptly abandoned her to go off with Cherry and had appeared next only to stand around tormenting her with his beauty and presence, but giving her no satisfaction from it. Of course she had begun to feel ugly.

Jacintha sighed. "If only he were different. Why is he like he is?"

"He probably wonders why we are like we are. Except that he doesn't, of course. He doesn't care." Then, at the same instant, they turned to face each other with a look of profound surprise and alarm, twisted about in their seats, and saw a swarm of mounted Indians round a corner and come galloping straight at them.

"Faster!" screamed Cherry. "Faster! We're being overtaken!"

They did not for a moment doubt that these Indians, unlike the others who had passed today, were pursuing them. For they rode at such a frenzied speed, feathers flying everywhere, covered with bright paint, sending forth a continuous quavering howl which rose and fell, swooping eerily up and down the scale, and their horses came on faster and faster so that it seemed certain in another moment they would go sweeping over them, trample them into the mud, and swarm on their way, still mournfully howling.

The two women, now kneeling on the seat and facing backward, clung together and stared in fascinated horror at their steadily approaching pursuers. Their teeth were chattering, they shook from head to foot, and their throats were dry and tight.

"We'll be scalped!" yelled Jacintha, grabbing her hat.

"They have the most horrible tortures!"

"Will they rape us?"

"That's the *best* we can hope for!"

Cherry turned her head. "Faster, you idiot! Drive faster!"

The horsemen were not more than fifty yards behind them now and still gaining. Their hoofbeats sounded like continuous thunder. They were all of them grinning, a sight unbelievably horrifying for the grins appeared to have been pasted across skulls painted black and white and green and red and yellow. They held their bows ready to shoot and swung tomahawks around their heads. The howling soared and wavered, rising and falling, shrill, uncanny, wilder and more savage than any sound they had ever heard.

Cherry and Jacintha were now too scared to move or speak.

Suddenly one Indian broke free of the group with such a tremendous burst of speed that he seemed literally to fly toward them.

Without an instant's hesitation they both turned and crouched down low in the seats, doubled over, and hid their faces in their laps, throwing their skirts up over their heads. There was a shout and their coach came to a jolting stop which threw them forward off the seat. They clutched at each other to avoid pitching onto the floor and then, as the carriage stopped still, did not glance up, but immediately covered their heads again.

He began to laugh.

They looked up at the same moment to see him there astride his black stallion which moved restlessly about, pawing the earth and lifting his forefeet as though eager to be on his way. Once again he wore a loincloth, beaded moccasins, and a vast feathered headdress. He lacked only the paint to be in Indian war regalia. And as their expressions quickly shifted from astonishment and fear to relief and then furious indignation, he threw back his head and laughed more than ever.

"What a pair you are! Frightened of gnats. What *else* can happen to you?"

They glared at him while still holding each other firmly by the hand. Once they glanced at each other briefly, as it for reassurance and a bolstering of their anger, and then stared again at him, straightening their backs, raising their chins and eyebrows—though their faces were still white and they could not stop shaking.

The Blackfeet had arrived and, while they waited, began immediately to pass the time by running races across the meadow, staging mock fights on horseback, leaping off and on their horses with astonishing ease and swiftness, playing practical jokes on each other, watering their horses in a meandering little stream. They chattered incessantly, gestured and laughed and seemed in jubilant high spirits. They must have enjoyed terrorizing the two white ladies for now they kept glancing at them and chuckling.

He sat facing them, his hands on the pommel of his handsome carved leather saddle, heavily decorated with silver like those the Spanish rode in California. His chest was heaving from the strenuous exertion, his brown skin glistened with moisture—he looked a symbol of unbridled temptation, indomitable, boundlessly sensual. His eyes, as he watched them, were hard and glittering and his smile had turned into scornful amusement.

"You're stubborn, too, I see."

Cherry let go Jacintha's hand and leaped to her feet. Now, as she stood in the carriage, she was at a greater height than he on horseback. Imperiously she gazed down at him.

"We are stubborn," she said, or proclaimed, and Jacintha watched her with chills of admiration twitching her flesh. "We are stubborn and we are loyal. You will not find *us* like the others. We know that we must trust each other—since there is no one else to be trusted here. And there is nothing you can do to change that!" She spoke in a tone of dedicated conviction, with such a thrilling ring to her voice that Jacintha wanted to applaud, as for a great performance.

He, however, only continued watching her and smiling and whether he listened or not it was difficult to say. His eyes were travelling slowly about her body with the insolence and assurance of a conqueror considering whether and when he shall plunder his captive. When she concluded her speech he gave his mouth a slight twist. His face looked somber and moody, as if there were plots in his head, cruel and sinister and designed for their affliction.

Now Jacintha, too, sprang to her feet. "Why don't you let us alone?" she cried, and heard herself first with surprise, an instant's fear and hesitancy—and then pride that she had not left it to Cherry to face him alone. "We can be happy if you'll let us alone!"

At that he gave a short and unpleasantly contemptuous laugh, wheeled his horse so that momentarily it stood almost erect, and raising one arm in a sweeping gesture he shouted a command in their tongue and he and the Blackfeet were off at their earlier terrible speed.

His departure had been so sudden that Cherry and Jacintha stood for a moment and stared after them. Then they turned and looked at each other, puzzled, not altogether sure of what it was that had happened, until all at once they smiled, threw their arms about each other and stood embracing and laughing.

"We won!" cried Cherry, like a gleeful little girl.

"We won! We won!" they shouted.

They sat down again.

"You see how easy it was?" asked Cherry. "We have nothing to fear from *him*—only from ourselves. He won't do anything to us we don't invite or permit. It's strange—" she added reflectively. "That's something I've always known and yet I only realized at this moment."

"How good it makes you feel!" declared Jacintha—and both their faces had become almost iridescent.

Cherry leaned forward and spoke to the driver who had all this while continued sitting with his slumped back toward them, completely indifferent to everything: his physical surroundings, the arrival of his master with a band of Indians, the two women talking. He seemed absorbed within his own wordless world, stupid, or, at least, stupefied.

"Where were they going?" she asked him.

"To the rendezvous."

"What's that?" inquired Jacintha.

"They were held years ago," explained the driver. "Before either of you were dead. He lets them gather now and then for old times' sake. The Indians, of course, not being dead yet but only passing through here, just go for the hell of it." He smirked over his shoulder to call attention to his clever remark.

Cherry and Jacintha made a face at each other, and Cherry delicately pinched her nose.

"Are we invited?" she asked.

"No one is invited. Anyone in the area may go."

"Then let's go!"

Once more the lash curled back and swept hissing down, the coach bounded forward, and they were away in the dusty eddying trail which still moved and whirled about the path like aimless ghosts to mark where their horses' hoofs had passed. Here and there, in the shade, were left deep puddles of mud from the recent storms.

"I've heard about the rendezvous," said Cherry. "There hasn't been one since I arrived, but all the old-timers are still talking about the last one." She flared out her fan and inclined her head to whisper behind it. "They say it's incredibly wicked!" She pursed her lips and nodded once, an impish little smile on her face, her dark eyes glittering with eager naughtiness.

"*Is* it?" breathed Jacintha. "What do they do?"

Cherry flicked her wrist once to snap her fan together. "Everything," she stated succinctly.

"Every—" began Jacintha and paused, considering. Then, after a long minute's silence, she clasped Cherry's hand and looked her straight in the eyes, their faces close together and bouncing up and down, up and down, with the motion of the carriage. "We mustn't go!" she cried, with an urgent intensity which took Cherry quite by surprise.

"Whatever are you talking about, Jacintha?"

"We mustn't go!" she repeated, and her voice and body seemed literally to vibrate with conviction. "I know it, I feel it!" She put one hand against her breast. "I feel it, Cherry, and I know I'm right! If we go, we may destroy everything. Don't you remember that look on his face? This is a trick—a trap he's leading us into! He wants to test us in some way! He is angry with us for having defeated him—and he means to destroy our devotion, once and for all!"

"I thought we just agreed," replied Cherry with an air

of cool annoyance, "that we had only ourselves to fear, not him."

"We aren't the strongest women in the world," Jacintha reminded her.

Cherry laughed with delight. "No, we're not—thank God. Jacintha, for heaven's sake, he can't hurt us if we keep our wits about us. I actually don't believe he wants to hurt us, anyway. It's the difference in our standards that makes us feel pain at what he does."

"I'm afraid," insisted Jacintha gloomily. "I'm afraid that he will separate us forever. And I could never bear the loneliness of this place, if that happened. Don't forget—it may be a long time before this is over."

Cherry laughed softly and affectionately. "It may be," she agreed, with a humorous little look. "But it will seem even longer, if we begin to refuse opportunities for diversion because they may contain some possible danger for us."

Jacintha was gazing into Cherry's face, her own still sorrowful and full of unhappy foreboding. Nothing but trouble could come of their following him to a place of license and wickedness, where everything must be in conspiracy against their vows.

How could *they* be good where everyone was being bad?

And yet Cherry seemed so entirely unconcerned. She seemed, in fact, to be almost unaware of these dangers, and Jacintha began to feel uncomfortably that she must be evil herself to worry so much about the possible influence of evil. If Cherry could face this rendezvous with optimism and tranquillity, so could she or so, at least, should she.

"Very well," said Jacintha. "We'll go and we *won't* let it destroy us."

"That's a good girl," said Cherry, as if Jacintha were, indeed, a child who vows she will go to the dentist without further protest.

And so they continued through the small forests and across the meadows, past the steaming spurting geysers, through the spreading rushing warm streams that piddled here and there, alternately sniffing of the fresh fragrant pine and wildflowers and the thick stinking sulphurous vapors. Some of the geysers spurted three hundred feet into the air. Others poked up tentatively like drinking fountains, muddled up and down for a few moments, and sank quiescent once more. They passed warm shallow pools, colored rust and buff and yellow or the purest blue, and skirted along spreading opalescent terraces, half liquid, half glistening white mineral.

There were grazing buffalo and, in the distance, they saw the antlers of elk and moose standing chest-deep, feeding among the luxuriant meadow grasses. Both women shrieked with laughter and delight to see two black bear cubs—one leaning drunkenly against a low bank with his paws full of white and yellow daisies, as though he had sat down to rest on his way to pay his sweetheart a call. The other waddled a few steps after their flying carriage, hoping no doubt to be thrown some nuts, and then, disappointed, he collapsed suddenly in the middle of the path and gazed forlornly after them.

Whereupon they rounded a corner and arrived with unexpected abruptness in sight of the rendezvous which, they saw, was being held in the meadows spreading before and about Roaring Mountain.

The carriage was still perhaps a quarter of a mile away, but Cherry called to the driver to stop and let them look for a moment: they were on a slight rise and could see it as though it were an enormous painting of camped armies. To the right, as it were, of their canvas, rose Roaring Mountain, a vigorous aggressive thrusting mountaintop, its sides furrowed and whitened, steaming from thousands of vents; from this distance it appeared to have burnt down, turned to ash, and to be still smoking hot. Here and there, vast clouds of vaporous steam broke loose and rolled with the wind; one could imagine a population of ghosts. There was something about the mountain which seemed extraordinarily ferocious and temperamental; it has a look of wickedness and of being the cruelest most malevolent trick nature had ever played.

Lemonade Lake lay before it, a pallid shallow yellow-green pool into which had fallen bare broken trees, to rot in the poisonous water. It seemed possible Lemonade Lake had somehow contested with Roaring Mountain, struggling for supremacy or, perhaps, equality, and now lay supine and helpless, absolutely defeated, a small delicate unhealthy body of water. Nevertheless, the glaring spewing glittering white mountain and the sickly little yellow-green lake combined into a gorgeous sight.

Toward the center of the canvas, stretching all the way left and out of the painting, spread wet green meadows full of purple, white, blue, yellow and pink wildflowers. There were small groves of dainty aspen, their leaves trembling in the sun as though someone had cast a shower of sequins upon them, tall handsome straight dark pine, and many blue and silver spruce. Still farther in the distance was a mountain spotted black by its cover of pine, looking as if it crawled with ants.

This was all as it had been when Jacintha had first seen it, a moment before she had ascended the mountain and confronted him—standing there naked with feathers wheeling in a great white and scarlet circle about his head.

Everything else, however, had changed.

From the edge of Lemonade Lake, all across the vast meadow and to the foot of the pine-covered mountain, were gathered at least two thousand people, Indians and whites, braves, squaws, children, mountain men and traders. There were, furthermore, hundreds of horses and dozens of dogs. Everything was in motion, running, walking, leaping, crawling, riding, hurrying, lolling, swaggering, prancing; everything busy, occupied, energetically engaged.

The tents and tepees of the Indians stood in an irregular circle which straggled around the entire plain, and to each pole a flag was fixed. Horses and mules were gathered, for the most part, at the outskirts, but many were wandering inside, some roaming riderless, others mounted by braves showing off their skill.

Many squaws wore red calico dresses and white stockings. The Indian men were almost naked or, like the trappers, wore fringed black buckskin. Colored feathers blew and floated everywhere. The sun struck bright blinding spots off silver bracelets and strings of mirrors hung around the squaws' necks. Even the clouds seemed to go hurrying along. Innumerable campfires burned, the smoke rising in thin straight lines.

Cherry and Jacintha sat staring like children at a circus, their lips parted with breathless wonder and surprise. At last, their heads turned slowly and simultaneously, and they gazed at each other.

"My!" said Jacintha. "It's beautiful!"

"Isn't it! Driver—go ahead—but slowly!"

As they got closer, they heard the noise. Wild war whoops were let out by exuberant Indians. Horses neighed and gave forth piercing shrill nervous whinnies. Excited dogs yelped and barked incessantly, prancing about the horses, rolling and tumbling together. Some of the trappers were singing the songs they had brought with them long ago into this new wild country. Babies cried. Children ran and yelled and shouted deliriously to one another. Drums were being beaten and the sound seemed to move over the vast camp, steadily murmuring, pulsing like blood through the body of a giant. There was laughter and shrieking, coarse-voiced male bellowing and high-pitched women's chatter.

Slowly, their carriage approached.

The Indian's horses were decorated with many-colored beads and glittering metals. Squaws, some of them alarmingly pretty, apparently no more than fifteen or sixteen, rode astride, laughing and shouting in loud voices which seemed very vulgar to Cherry and Jacintha. It was getting more crowded every moment. Lines of mules passed them, bearing tin kegs, and Cherry said that was the way they transported alcohol in the mountains. From the numbers of mules and kegs, this promised to be a monumental debauch. Indians were still arriving, afoot or on horseback. Their dogs dragged travois, loaded with their belongings, and similar contrivances were pulled by horses. Trappers rode along, slowly jogging, rough full-bearded men in greasy buckskin, their eyes showing the peculiar light of men who have escaped civilization and laid hold of their own kind of freedom. Fashionably dressed men and women from the hotel were appearing in phaetons and Concord coaches, gay and laughing, waving everywhere and pointing and calling around, as if they had come on the jolliest outing. The crowd was now so thick on all sides, their carriage had come to a standstill.

"Let's get out and walk!" said Cherry, shot her parasol open and climbed down. Jacintha hesitated a moment and then followed.

"Will you wait for us?" asked Jacintha uncertainly, turning and looking up at the driver where he now lounged picking his teeth.

"I'll be here," he muttered, in a tone which implied they would be lucky to find him.

"He doesn't dare go away," said Cherry. "He has his orders. Now—let's not lose each other."

"Heavens *no!*"

Holding their parasols, they took each other's hands and set timidly forth, into the outer eddies of what appeared to be a most enormous and ferocious maelstrom.

"I'm still afraid," said Jacintha, looking warily about, "that he means this for us."

"Nonsense. I assure you, neither of us has entered his head, except for that one moment back there."

"I'm not so sure," replied Jacintha dubiously. It seemed to her that this great and wicked festivity was a plot designed explicitly to test their loyalty to each other and to demolish, once and for all, whatever was left of it.

She refused to believe the driver's story that these gatherings were held now and then, "for old times' sake." The explanation was nothing so simple as that. This was too grand and terrifying a spectacle, not to serve some sinister end.

"Remember what you said," she vaguely reminded Cherry.

"I remember, I remember," agreed Cherry, slightly impatient.

They were aware of being stared at: Heads turned, male and female, Indian and white, as they walked along, making their way gingerly among dogs and children, swaggering braves and flirtatious active young squaws, wrinkled old men sitting beside their tepees gossiping idly together and smoking. Trappers ambled about, thumbs hooked arrogantly in their belts, throwing out their feet as they went like men accustomed to considerable room in which to move. Sometimes their passage left a quiet little wake, a toning down of the babble and racket for a moment or two. But then, immediately after, they would pass some rude gigantic mountaineer who gawked them up and down, spit a brown squirt of tobacco—once so close that Jacintha had to hop aside—and threw back his shaggy head with a burst of ribald laughter.

Gradually, they began to walk a little faster, holding tighter to each other's hands. Jacintha was thinking: Even if it isn't *meant* to test us, it will—so it all comes to the same thing.

Every man they passed was armed as if for war. The trappers carried rifles or had knives and pistols stuck in their belts; the braves had bows and arrows and tomahawks slung at their hips.

"Oh, look!" shrieked Jacintha, clutching hold of Cherry's arm and pointing.

"What?" Cherry was glancing about eagerly and nervously.

"That— That thing! It must be a—"

"Scalp!" yelped both women at once, picked up their skirts and started off at a run, away from the tent beside which had hung a fresh bloody scalp with clotted hair hanging from it in a tangled mass. Laughter followed them and that scared them more than ever so that they kept going, not daring to pause or look back.

And as they ran, all the latent fear increased suddenly to monstrous proportions, becoming hysterical as they dashed along, holding their skirts up, racing against some unknown terror, in flight from something unbelievably horrible and strange. They had to dodge this way and that, around the tepees, shying from the horses which went prancing by—jingling with bells, waving with feathers, wheeled and maneuvered by some proud naked brave. They sprinted past rudely constructed booths surrounded by trappers getting drunk on the poisonous brews for sale—honey and alcohol, water and alcohol—big dirty men who poured the liquor down their throats as if they had been thirsty a year, spilling it on their beards, laughing and cracking each other across the shoulders. They darted this way and that to avoid stepping on the Indian babies and children which swarmed everywhere. Dogs barked and came bounding gleefully along beside them, yapping and taking playful snaps at their flying ruffles.

They ran faster and faster, rushing with frantic haste, skimming and flitting, feeling themselves pursued, followed, hovered over, breathed upon. And then they heard a shout: "Hey!" and a form stepped swiftly before them, holding his arms spread wide to stop their flight; they ran smack into him and almost literally bounced back.

"Grant!"

They stood staring at him, panting, their chests heaving, shaking, frightened, and saw his rude grin. Slowly, both of them turned and looked around, back to whatever it was they had been fleeing from. They saw nothing to fear. Everything was as it had been. Nearby, a group of trappers and Indians squatted on the ground, gambling. Three or four squaws joined them, sitting cross-legged and careless, chattering, bold and vivid and provocative.

Jacintha and Cherry looked at each other and began to laugh. "Aren't we the ninnies!" cried Cherry.

"Afraid of our shadows!"

Grant had stood, during the past few seconds while they discovered they were in no immediate danger, regarding them sourly. Now he gave one of his harsh jerking gestures.

"Stop gaping! Come along!" He started off but they hesitated a moment, still holding each other's hands, turning their heads to consult each other's eyes. He glanced back, saw them still hesitating, and his face squeezed itself into an expression of outraged fury. *"Come along!"* he bellowed.

"We'd better!" whispered Cherry and, holding up their skirts once more, they started after him.

He moved nimbly among the tepees and campfires, among the trading booths surrounded by yelling trappers and Indians, bargaining for moccasins and buckskins, coffee and liquor and tobacco. Stinking bloody beaver pelts, smelling as if they were still raw, stood piled in enormous bundles, and whenever they passed them both women held their noses and turned a little green. There were hundreds of bolts of brightly colored calico and the squaws were rummaging over it in frenzied excitement, unwinding it and wrapping themselves like mummies, pushing and shoving, tearing and hauling, loud and violent, until it seemed none of them could emerge with a length fit for future use.

More and more ladies and gentlemen were arriving from the hotel. The gentlemen looked suave and elegant in their Norfolk jackets and knickerbockers of brown plaid, their yellow and brown knitted socks and white linen spats. Others wore lounge suits made of blue serge with wing collars and polka-dot bow ties. The ladies were in gay, garish colors—green, royal blue, purple, garnet, plum, electric blue, scarlet. Their gowns seemed pasted to swelling breasts and hips, while the skirts burst forth into cascades of ribbons, tassels, knotted fringe, pleated flounces, bows and frills. They minced through the meadow on their high-heeled pointed kid slippers, their lifted skirts showing bright-colored stockings. They carried their opened parasols in daintily gloved fingers, for the sun was hot and damaging to a fine-textured skin. They wore bonnets perched on the curls that massed over their foreheads and they peeped about with curiosity and coquettish smiles, squeaking with alarm, giggling with shocked delight, clinging to their gentlemen, gawking eagerly about for all the wickedness they had been told to expect. The encampment grew more populous every moment, until now it had begun to resemble the most crowded thoroughfare of a great city.

Big clumsy black ravens floated about, lighted teetering so that they seemed to be drunk already, then took off again with much flapping and ado and circled overhead as if to get a better view of these strange goings-on.

There was a grizzly chained to a stake, restlessly prowling his half-circle, besieged by a pack of snarling wolflike dogs which had succeeded in tearing open his nose and drawing blood from his paws. One of them flew suddenly at him, confident, as if he expected to kill him instantly. The grizzly reared and gave him a swiping blow that sent him hurtling through the air, howling as he went, but dead when he landed. The grizzly turned and reared, roaring in a voice that seemed almost a physical explosion, challenging his tormentors. Mountain men, rambling by in their black buckskins fringed along arms and legs, stopped to watch and place bets.

Not far away, squaws knelt about campfires, cooking up noisome messes from which Cherry and Jacintha fastidiously averted their eyes and turned away their noses.

Even this early, the camp was acquiring its peculiar characteristic smell: meadow grass, torn and trampled; the ironlike smell of new mud; crushed fragrant flowers; the decaying flesh on the beaver pelts; manure fallen in fresh yellow piles; unwashed bodies of trappers and Indians, greasy, sweating; whiskey and wood smoke and burning buffalo chips; the delicate straying scent of pine and fir; boiling coffee. All the swiftly accumulating slop and filth of two thousand humans and half as many animals.

The sun had moved higher and shone down with unusual brilliance. The sky was purest blue, scattered with the whitest clouds. The movement and color was everywhere so bright, so sharply detailed and vivid, that it seemed unreal. The mountain air was giving both women a curious lightness and lethargy combined with that dizzy exhilaration Jacintha had experienced the first night.

As they followed Grant they were looking around more and more boldly, more and more eagerly—no longer sharing each sight and sound and feeling, but taking them in separately, each responding in her own individual way.

Jacintha was still apprehensive. Some of the trappers, all of whom looked like reckless ungovernable giants to her, were reeling and singing in loud unmusical voices, knocking into each other, grabbing hold of the Indian women who giggled and struggled, while they looked around to see if some stern male relative was nearby to object or demand adequate payment.

There'll be trouble before we get out of this, she warned herself.

All at once Grant stopped and pointed. "There he is!" They followed his finger and saw that he had led them to the base of Roaring Mountain, though now the crowds and tepees were so dense they had not realized it until this moment. "Go on!"

Looking up the smoking white rocky mountain, they saw him standing on a great jutting ledge, a strange rocky lichen-covered formation, somewhat like a speaker's platform. Though they could not see his face clearly in the distance he was easy to recognize because of his size, the magnificent proportions of his naked body, the way he stood, with his legs spread and fists on his hips, the circle of braves—many of them chiefs, judging by their war bonnets—standing around him.

Now, once more, they must confront him together.

How much simpler it would be, if they could see him separately. Or would it?

If she went alone, I would be in agony, thought Jacintha—wondering what was happening, what they were doing and saying. No, this is better. I think I would lose my mind entirely if I had to go through what I did yesterday, when they rode away together.

She glanced quickly and covertly from the corners of her eyes and encountered Cherry's own swift glance. For an instant their eyes met, questioningly; and then they started up the mountainside, picking their way among the rocks and between steaming vents, dragging their trains in the white dust. The mountain seemed so full of activity, hissing and murmuring, sending out boiling clouds of steam and vast whirling vapors, that it must be about to blow itself wide open. Spindly, straggling little pines were stuck around, forlorn objects in the desolate whitened earth which gave them no nourishment and no hospitality.

Slowly they ascended, watching their footing but, also, keeping a wary eye on him. He appeared engrossed in his conversation with the gesticulating chiefs, some of whom wore scarlet military coats of European make, with epaulettes and gold lace, trousers and towering shakos. Everyone was in high spirits and there was much laughter and excited babbling. Apparently they did not consider it necessary to assume for him the rigid bearing and stern decorum they often used to impress white men.

Finally, when they were ten or fifteen yards away, Jacintha stopped. They were breathing hard with the effort and their heavy gowns had made them sweat so that they took out handkerchiefs to dab their moist foreheads and cheeks.

"I think we should wait here, don't you?"

"I suppose. He must have seen us, even though he pretends he hasn't."

They looked into their mirrors, tilted their heads, touched their curls, straightened their hats, glancing toward him every few seconds. The laughter and talk went on. Cherry and Jacintha could understand nothing since they all talked in some barbaric Indian tongue. Close by was a noisily boiling cauldron which now and then sighed heavily, making them glance at it in swift alarm, for it seemed to be warning them that its patience was near an end and it might spew forth a torrent of horrid little creatures at any moment.

And presently, since he continued to ignore them, they began to take less interest in their faces and how they looked, how hot they were and how breathless, and to watch the scene below, touching each other on the arm to point out new marvels, laughing at something comical, gasping when they were surprised or shocked, pleased and amazed by the whole sprawling panorama. It was much more enjoyable now that they were safely out of it.

Even from here the camp was mercilessly noisy with barking dogs, whinnying horses, the shouts and cries of children, roars and laughter of the trappers, beating drums, wailing Indian songs and incantations, the shrill yammering of the squaws, the howl of prairie wolves loitering enviously about the edges of the camp, the sharp report of a rifle going off now and then, shot into the air, shot at a dog, or perhaps shot at a friend in a quarrel.

"Oh, look!" cried Jacintha. "Look at that magnificent horse!" She pointed to where a naked brave went prancing proudly by Lemonade Lake on a white horse decked out in feathers and bells and ribbons, turning and wheeling in magical obedience to the touch of his rider's knees.

"Look! There's a fight beginning! Over there! Oh, somebody's going to get killed, I know it!"

"Look how everyone's running to see it! *Aren't* people bloodthirsty and dreadful!"

They were leaning forward, hands on their knees, peering toward the fight which, from here, was a twirling kaleidoscope, colors and humans blending and rushing together, when suddenly Jacintha felt a hearty whack on her buttocks and gave a cry of surprise at the same instant Cherry was saluted in like manner and both girls straightened abruptly, their hands going backward as they turned, looking up indignantly— There he was, grinning down at them.

"How do you like it?" He nodded toward the camp.

"Well!" said Jacintha, staring him severely up and down, by way of reprimand.

But he was smiling at Cherry; and Cherry was returning his smile.

And now she must watch it again: He was looking at Cherry with that speculative intensity, amused and gloating at the same time. While Cherry returned his gaze, her chin tilted provocatively, her eyes liquid with yearning and adoration, her entire face flowering into radiance through some enchantment worked upon her by his mere presence.

To see them like this, not touching, not moving toward each other, and yet so intimate, so unashamedly sensual and luxurious, was an almost unbearable torment to Jacintha. She stood there twisting her handkerchief into hard knots, and longed to flash out at them both, striking each one so hard they would never again dare to look at each other with that rapt, tenacious ardor.

He does it to hurt me! she thought.

No, she corrected. He doesn't. He does it because he is attracted to her. And why not? She is using every charm and wile she knows to make herself alluring—while *I* stand here like a disapproving maiden aunt!

What's the matter with me?

What makes me act like this when I see them together? What happens to change me?

It's her fault! She has somehow made me think—or feel, at least—that he is hers by right of first claim. Because she got here first. But that was only an accident. I might have been *her* mother—and then I would have been here first and seen him first and have the right to him.

But she told me, didn't she, that she didn't expect me to give him up, and knew that I couldn't.

Well, then—

I won't.

And, upon this resolution, Jacintha's expression and manner slowly changed: Her mouth relaxed and parted just enough to show the edges of her teeth. Her eyes seemed to darken and melt until there appeared a danger they might literally overflow and pour down her cheeks. Her head tipped back so that her throat looked fragile, almost breakable, and strangely tempting, with the pulse beating at its base, the impression given of life being concentrated and vulnerable within that slender pillar. She did not speak but only looked at him, thinking now, not of how Cherry was sparkling and subtly challenging him, but only of how intensely and recklessly she loved him herself.

He turned, after a moment, and glanced down at her.

A quick look of surprise crossed his face, and then there crackled like a flare of summer lightning, the momentary glitter of that earlier lust. Jacintha saw it with exultant joyous pleasure. Slowly and delicately, her tongue moistened her lips. Her head tilted still farther, and her face broke free into a wide vivid smile, wanton and inviting.

She did not look at Cherry, now that she had this triumphant instant of her own, but knew that Cherry must be as hurt, as puzzled, as helpless and infuriated, as she had earlier been.

He smiled and shook his head. "I would pity the man who had to choose between you."

Then, he slipped one arm about Cherry's waist, the other about Jacintha's, and the three of them started down the hill. "Let's take a look around," he said. "You've never seen anything like this before, I can assure you."

Jacintha laughed. "Oh, we know *that!*" she cried, as if she were being very witty. "Don't we, Cherry?" Smiling, she leaned forward to catch Cherry's eye.

Cherry smiled back, also leaning momentarily forward. "We do, indeed!"

And Jacintha had found out what she wanted to know. Cherry was angry—and Cherry was scared. That meant that she was successful in Cherry's opinion, as in her own. I've won, she told herself. I knew I would, and I have.

And yet—the triumph sagged abruptly and, like a deflated toy animal, crumpled into nothing. She felt ashamed of herself. She had, somehow, committed a wrong, done something for which she must pay later.

I had no right. I love Cherry—I want her to be happy. I cannot be happy myself at her expense. She felt puzzled and dazed and wished she could have a moment to be alone and think about this and somehow conclude what was right and what was wrong.

But there was no time, of course.

They were descending the mountain now, slowly and carefully. He attended them like the most courteous gallant, taking first one and then the other by the hand to help them over difficult places, warning them of holes and dangerous spots, smiling and chatting, looking magnificently at ease within the great fortress of his male arrogance and confidence. He talked to them, as they went, about the rendezvous, why it had originally been held, and how he had decided, after listening to the nostalgic tales of the old trappers who had been sent here for their sins, to give them an occasional brief whirl at it—for his own amusement, of course, no one else's.

"Everyone has the time of his life," he concluded, chuckling.

But Jacintha could not get free of that look she had seen in Cherry's eyes. I'll never forget it, she thought dismally. Never at all.

It seemed to Jacintha that the sun was moving across the sky more swiftly than usual. Perhaps, because everything was new and exciting and dangerous, her sense of time had been lost. She had an extraordinary sense of being hurried forward, rushed along, toward some destination already determined and beyond her control. There was a steady stealthy force which seemed to be tracking her down, overtaking her, and which was, perhaps, about to break up and destroy the entire organization of her beliefs and trusts and expectations.

But there was no time for considering that, either. The force itself thrust her forward, rushed her like an impetuous hand at her elbow guiding her. Something, in fact, like his hand at her elbow, guiding her, and Cherry, through this riotous circus.

For it was, beyond doubt, noisier and more unruly than when they had passed through on their way to climb the mountain.

Not only was the time hastening forward, but every movement seemed to have speeded up, as well. The horses pranced by at a livelier clip. The young braves running races were dashing along as if they had wheels tied to their feet. The three of them stopped to watch a circle of dancing Indians, their naked bodies painted vermilion and blue and white, and animal masks over their heads with horns and feathers and streaming animal tails. They were shuffling and stamping, giving forth sudden terrifying whoops, then raising a sad ululation which went quavering outward, to be eagerly seized and imitated by the coyotes.

He led them to a liquor booth about which men stood seven or eight deep, shouting and quarrelling, laughing and shoving to get at the counter, big, dirty, bearded, ferocious mountain men. Cherry and Jacintha hung back, fearful of the men, for they were drunk now and roused in them an intense female fear of the inhuman savage which lies beneath civilized man, a murderous rapist without morality or respect or self-control. They hung back but, at the same time, tagged timidly along, for it was he who now seemed their only protection in this violent boisterous place. And he had begun to shoulder his way among them.

The men turned at the pressure of his body and, seeing who it was, parted instantly to give him room. Both they and the Indians behaved as though he was a highly respected member of their own group—respected for the same reasons any other would have been: for his size, powerful strength, skill with weapons, horsemanship. Nothing in their manner suggested that they set him apart as an object of awe or reverential fear. There was comradeship and admiration, but in his presence they shouted and sang as loud as ever, swore as fiercely, and in no way mitigated their rioting recklessness. They must have good reason to believe he approved of them.

Cherry and Jacintha followed him down the opened path to the counter, the men shuffled and moved and the pathway closed. They stood stiff and unmoving behind him, clenching each other's hands, darting their eyes from side to side like two young fillies in nervous terror.

The men were close, so close they could not move an inch without touching them, and, cringe and twist about as they would, they could not avoid being rudely jostled. It seemed they were surrounded by all the men in the world, and would never get free again. There was no cool quiet feminine retreat for them here, even in imagination; no place they could avoid the painful jarring roughness of masculinity. They became breathless, and their terror grew greater and greater; in a matter of seconds, it had become almost unendurable.

They felt oppressed by a massive remorseless weight which seemed to lean in upon them, slowly, steadily, mercilessly, and would soon crush them to pulp. Their ears roared with noise, exploding and bursting like shells —deafening, hideous, stupefying, so that they shrank from it, covered their ears and closed their eyes, but still felt as if they were being pounded and beaten. Worst of all was the pervasive stench, a rank and musty smell of sweating bodies and polluted breath, a smell so thick it seemed to fall upon their skins and clothing in droplets, clinging and contaminating.

"Have a drink!" they heard him say and both women glanced up at once, hands over their ears, their large frightened brown eyes staring at him. He was still grinning broadly so that it was obvious he was not only enjoying this delirious bedlam but was hopeful it would get even worse.

How wickedly pleased he looked. How he seemed, all at the same time, to participate and to remain aloof. How superbly powerful he was!

They stared at him in helpless enthralled wonder.

"Come on," he insisted, and thrust a half-filled tin cup at each of them. "Drink it! You both look scared to death—and there isn't a damn thing here to be afraid of. Quick! Everything will look different to you once you've swallowed that."

Doubtfully—like two little girls not at all convinced the medicine they are advised to take will do them the good claimed for it—they continued looking up at him a moment or two. Then, all at once, as if they had held a private consultation, they lifted the cups, each holding hers in both hands, and drank the contents in three or four convulsive gulps. The next instant they burst into a fit of coughing and choking and sputtering, gasping as if their throats had been seared by acid, weeping, shuddering, while on every side the men—he, too—rocked on their heels and roared with laughter. Finally, when they had more or less recovered, they stared at him reproachfully.

"What is it!"

"I know it was poison!"

"I'm going to be sick."

"No, you aren't. You'll feel much better. Come on—let's take a stroll and see what they're up to. Some of these fellows are rather ingenious."

"I can imagine!" said Jacintha.

The whiskey still burned her throat and had heated her stomach. For a few moments it filled her with such nausea she was afraid she would not be able to keep it down, but then the sickness ebbed away and she could feel the heat in her stomach begin to spread and work outward, through all her body, until presently she was so warm the ends of her fingers were tingling.

I like it, she decided then. He was right. I'm not afraid any more. I'm not afraid at all.

He and Jacintha and Cherry had emerged from the mass of men which, only a minute or two before, had seemed to hold them captive, so easily that they did not even notice how it happened. And now the three of them sauntered along, one woman on either side, each with her arm linked in his.

A circle of Indians and trappers sat on the ground, playing a game. They stopped to watch.

The players squatted or sat cross-legged around a heap of objects: strings of beads, buckskin shirts and leggings, fringed doeskin skirts and blouses, mirrors, bells, feathered war bonnets, scalping knives, medicine pipes flaunting feathers and braided ribbons, tomahawks, ruffled silk garters. All attention was focused upon one trapper. He held his closed fists before him, chanting. Now he raised them above his head, swept them around behind him, shot them out at either side, never once pausing in his monotonous weaving chant, while the others stared avidly, following each gesture, swaying from side to side, chanting along with him and keeping up a steady low hypnotic moan. They looked like drunken participants in some weird religious ritual.

The spell was broken by a sudden furious howl as one of the trappers seized his squaw by the wrist and shoved her onto the pile of gewgaws, as his forfeit. She stumbled and fell and knelt there, waiting passively, watching the man who had resumed his gestures and chanting.

"Oh!" cried Jacintha. *"Don't* let him do that!" She grabbed hold of his arm. "Stop him!"

He ignored her for a moment and then looked down, his face serious and contemplative. He grinned so swiftly and with such contempt for her squeamish morality, that she blushed and hung her head and the squaw went to sit beside the man who had won her. They strolled on.

"Look around you," he said. "Things are just warming up. In another hour, maybe less, there'll be no way of telling which are savages and which are civilized men."

"How disgusting," remarked Jacintha, more from a

sense of duty than present conviction. He seemed to realize that and glanced down at her with an amused and tender smile. Jacintha, for once, was not looking at him but off in another direction. I'm drunk, she thought. I'm actually drunk. Next thing you know I'll be reeling.

Wherever she looked, things were blurred. She might have been under water, so wavy were the outlines of people and tents and trees. Everyone else looked drunk now, too. Their eyes appeared to be out of focus and their faces were lopsided. Her ears rang steadily, so that she could not hear outside noises as plainly as before. That was a relief. There seemed to be a steady hum or buzz moving along her veins, vibrating throughout her body. And she walked without reference to her feet or the ground, paying no attention to either, pleasantly surprised to find it was not necessary. She sailed along quite nicely, independent of her bones and muscles.

It was hot.

Her dress was buttoned to her throat and she wore many layers of clothing. Impulsively she reached up, took the pins out of her hat, untied the veil and handed it to a passing Indian woman who received it eagerly and, babbling her thanks, promptly set it upon her greasy black hair. Jacintha tossed back her head and gave it a shake of freedom. It felt suspiciously as though it might come off.

She was beginning to feel as if parts of herself might loosen, jar free, and fall along the wayside. If that happened, she would certainly never find them again. An Indian would put on whatever it was, as part of his costume.

She leaned against his arm and closed her eyes, feeling the beating hot sun upon her head and face, so hot that her lips began to throb. *Ohh*—and she sighed heavily—what do I care?

She hard Cherry's laugh, and that made her eyes snap open. Across his handsome naked chest she saw that Cherry had not only thrown her hat away, but taken the pins from her hair as well and allowed it to fall in a waving mass over her shoulders and back. Jacintha lifted her arms, removed the pins, and let her own hair fall.

"I'm so glad we came!" cried Cherry.

"So am I!" sang Jacintha.

They were walking by five or six trappers who stood in a knot or squatted on their haunches, holding great dripping lumps of meat in their hands, sawing and hacking with knives, greedily sucking the cracked marrow bones, smearing their beards and shirts and hands with blood and juice. Jacintha glanced in their direction, saw with horror this filthy repast and, instantly sickened, looked away. At that moment one of the men, who had been gnawing a quivering hunk of raw liver, had it snatched out of his grasp and, with a howl of rage, leaped and sprang upon the other, knocking him to the ground, and they were rolling over and over, locked together. A crowd began to gather, appearing around the clawing, grunting, kicking, biting, snarling men, so swiftly that when Jacintha turned to escape, she had already been surrounded.

They rolled over and over, one on top and then the other. Men were yelling and howling like fiends. Jacintha and Cherry suddenly and unexpectedly found themselves clinging together, clutching each other as they would clutch a log in a stormy ocean. They stared at each other.

"Where is he?"

At that moment, a howl of agony rose from one of the men and they looked back to see the one astride thrust his thumbs into the corners of the other's eyes, give a quick hard gouge, and the man's eyeballs popped from their sockets. A dog had sneaked through and now stole swiftly forward, was caught by a man's boot and went sailing through the air, piteously howling.

Jacintha, who stood nearby, turned, and, before she could stop herself, swung her handbag at the man's head. Her teeth were bared, her eyes blazing; she meant to kill him.

Something seemed to warn him and, the instant before it would have struck his head—a light little bag, not nearly substantial enough to effect her murderous intentions—he whirled and grasped her wrist and she found herself captured by a huge bearded sweating man who pulled her against his greasy chest and stuck his wet mouth fast upon hers. Feeling as if she had been caught by a grizzly, she began to fight hysterically, her arms flailing out, her head twisting and turning. She planted the heel of her hand against his chin, trying to force his head back, then raked her nails down his cheek. He seized her arm, twisted it behind her, and she heard him laugh.

His fetid breath was reeking of decayed food and alcohol. He smelt like weeds rotted in water. His mouth was avid, gnawing and licking at her face and lips, as if he would devour her. She opened her teeth and his tongue plunged into her mouth; she bit down until she tasted blood. He roared and let go of her as she brought her knee jabbing upward into his groin. He howled in rage and pain and gave her a shove so violent that she went sprawling several feet away and landed on her stomach, knocked breathless.

She lay there, feeling the waves approach and recede, fading out, slowly returning. She rolled with them, helpless, hoping to be rescued, then finally gave up and let herself sink to the dark depths.

It seemed that hours went by—though in reality it was no more than thirty or forty seconds. Then she rose again to the surface and, still with her eyes shut, felt the wet grass beneath her palms and began to explore and stroke it, kneading it with her fingers, as a sleepy kitten does. She was relaxed and contented, as if she had awakened early and looked happily forward to another few hours of sleep. She decided that it must not be grass, after all, but the cool sheets of her own bed, and this a dream materialized—for there was Cherry, bending above her. Jacintha began to smile, slowly and peacefully, as she lay with her face sideways against the grass, looking up at Cherry with one half-opened eye.

But Cherry's face, she now saw, was white and tense with anxiety and, the next thing Jacintha knew, Cherry was roughly shaking her shoulder and crying over and over again: "Get up! You *must* get up! Get up, Jacintha! He'll kill you! *Get up!*" There were tears in her eyes and she began pulling at Jacintha, trying to haul her up off the ground.

Responding to Cherry's frantic desperation, she got to her feet, though Cherry had to help her, tugging and pulling, struggling with Jacintha's inert weight.

"For a minute it seemed as if everything had been a dream," Jacintha was murmuring. "As if Martin had never shot me and I had never come here—"

"Jacintha! Stop daydreaming! We'll both be torn to pieces!"

Now that Jacintha was on her feet, though unsteadily, Cherry seized her hand and began to pull her. "Come! Before he see us!"

"Where is he?" Jacintha was turning, looking in every direction.

"He's over there! Don't look—he may see you!" Cherry was almost hysterical now, running a few little steps away, returning, trying to drag Jacintha.

But Jacintha had to look. She must see him. She must see what he looked like and what she had done to him. After a few seconds, she found him. He was ten or fifteen yards away and other people were continuously passing between them—but she caught one quick sufficient glimpse: He was huge and ugly and his beard was smeared with dark blood. He was doubled over with his fists jammed into his belly, pumping his legs steadily up and down, his face hideously contorted. He grunted and groaned so loudly they could hear him above the noise.

Jacintha stared at him for an instant, fascinated, feeling some strange and savage satisfaction. It even seemed she had somewhere before witnessed exactly that same sight but, before she had time to think about it, Cherry succeeded in almost pulling her off balance—and the two women started running together.

They ran as fast and as hard as they could in their dragging clinging skirts. Their petticoats were wet and stuck to their legs; they kept twisting and turning their ankles in the pointed-toed high-heeled shoes. The handbags slung over their wrists swirled wildly about, until a quick-moving Indian severed the cords to Cherry's as they went by and held up his treasure behind their backs, grinning. Their hair blew streaming around them and tendrils clung to their wet red faces. They felt as if steel claws raked through their chests. But they kept on and on, taking one turn and then another, following a devious route, heading toward the outskirts.

The sun had passed overhead and it was the hottest time of early afternoon.

A few trappers and Indians and squaws and babies slept in the shade of tepees or cottonwoods. Everyone else was noisier and drunker than ever. As they ran, white-faced and wild-eyed, trappers reached out, laughing, to grab hold of their skirts and hair. They twisted away and slapped at them, as if at enormous insects, and their dresses got torn. Complimentary obscenities were shouted. Three reeling mountain men linked hands and, staggering, dodged back and forth, trying to capture them, but Cherry and Jacintha ducked under their outspread arms and escaped. Agile and fleet, they ran until forced to slow down and finally stop from exhaustion and then stood slumped over, their chests heaving and aching, gasping for breath, their hearts pounding frantically. They had come at last to the camp's edge.

Cherry sat, then lay on her stomach and Jacintha stretched out beside her, on her back, with her arm flung across her eyes. They lay speechless and panting for several minutes.

Finally they recovered enough to sit up, shaking out their hair, and look about. They were beside a tepee and being watched with interest by an old Indian woman smoking a pipe and a naked baby which had crawled up close and gazed at them in wide-smiling wonder. Tentatively, they smiled back, first at the old woman, then at the baby, and Jacintha reached out to pat the baby's head. Cherry looked for her bag and found only the two tied strings. They combed each other's hair and wiped their wet dirty faces.

"Well!" said Jacintha finally. "There can't be any doubt about where we are after today!" She got to her feet and tried to smooth her skirts. "I've had enough of this! Let's find the carriage and go home."

She reached down to help Cherry. The breech between them had been completely closed, it seemed, by Cherry's action in rescuing her. She had thereby undone whatever it was she might have done yesterday, at the boiling gray crater. But there was nothing for either of them to say about it.

They were in a safe retreat, here with the baby and the old woman, while all around the uproar continued. It was as if they had found a quiet spot in a battleground, and might be overswept at any moment. Pandemonium was everywhere about them.

Jacintha lifted her arms and held her hair up high to let the breeze cool her neck. Cherry blew childishly down the front of her dress. Suddenly she seized Jacintha's arm and pointed in the direction of the boiling churning hysterical mob.

"Look at that!"

A few feet away, a trapper had grabbed a squaw around the waist, reached one hand beneath her skirts, and swiftly ran it up between her legs. The next instant he gave a yell of rage and let her go. He picked her up in both hands, raised her, kicking and protesting, above his head, and, with a mighty heave, sent her hurtling through the air. She landed, flat on her back, with a crash that seemed sure to break every bone in her body. Even as she struck the ground, Cherry and Jacintha were running forward to help her. And then, since her skirts had been flung up high, they stopped with a simultaneous shriek.

"It's a man!"

"Dressed like a squaw!"

"How horrible!"

He lay unconscious. A passing trapper gave him a kick. There was noisy laughter on every side and Cherry and Jacintha turned hastily away and started off.

"We won't even *think* of helping anyone again," vowed Jacintha. "No one in this place wants help anyway."

"We'll only help ourselves," agreed Cherry. "But where is the carriage?"

"Good heavens! Don't you know?"

They stood in the midst of the agitated crowd and confronted each other, looked first one way and then another, turned about, were buffeted and jostled, flung together and apart, and finally looked back at each other, hopelessly.

"I have no idea. I was so sure I could find it— But everything's changed since we got here. So many more people have come— Oh! What will we do?" She put both hands to her head and pressed hard and then began to wring them together.

"We'll find someone from the hotel and ask him—"

They started walking. Now, of course, there seemed to be fewer hotel guests than before and, whenever they would catch sight of one and start after him, the crowd would roll and revolve, others would get in the way, and he would disappear. But, finally, they came upon two well-dressed gentlemen, though drunk. Eagerly and seriously gazing up into their faces as if it were a matter of life and death, Cherry asked them where the coaches were waiting.

The two men looked them up and down, teetered backward and forward, looked at each other and then suggested that they all have a drink together.

"Don't be impertinent!" cried Jacintha, sure of herself with men like these, even if they were drunk. "Answer our question!"

The men looked at each other once more, simultaneously lifted their eyebrows, simultaneously smirked, and then, with elegant though unsteady bows, pointed in what they said was the direction of the carriages. It led back through the encampment.

It was not as hot as it had been. Already, the sun was halfway down the sky, still moving at the preternatural speed Jacintha had noticed early in the day. And, as the sun sped, every Indian and trapper, horse and dog in the camp, seemed to move faster and faster, growing more and more frantic, galloping, scampering, sprinting, scurrying. All seemed to be in crazy gyration. The noise had become a continuous deafening uproar, blustering and raging everywhere.

The drums beat louder. The dogs bayed. Coyotes raised their mournful tremulous howl. Here and there Indians and white men were dancing, shuffling and trampling about the fires, their eyes glassy and stupefied with ecstatic madness. There was vomiting and brawling, swearing and yelling, fighting and maudlin reconciliation. The young squaws sauntered and paraded, bargaining for bells and vermilion and calico. Above everything bobbed and swayed the feathered bonnets of the chiefs. Guns went off every few minutes.

All the while they were looking for him.

They had not mentioned him since his disappearance, but both had been aware of him, and wondering.

Now, though they looked for the carriages as they had agreed, neither intended to go without seeing him. Or, perhaps, to search for the carriages gave them something to talk about while they searched for him.

They both suspected, without mentioning this, either, that he was teasing them, that he knew where they were and what they were doing and knew, furthermore, that they were seeking him. For they could feel him, the compulsion of his power, very strongly. There was an incessant nagging awareness of his presence, sensual and hungering, exciting and tantalizing them. He was a continuous tormenting allurement, dragging them about this maddened meadow, compelling them to wander helplessly to and fro, searching, will-less, as if he maneuvered them by means of a rope tied around their waists.

Every tall chief seemed to be him, from a distance. Every crowd must have him at its center.

He may be here—he may be over there.

We may have just missed him.

Perhaps he passed there, while we were looking over here.

"You look that way," said Jacintha. "And I'll look this way. We may miss them if we both look the same way."

There was a sudden piercing scream of warning, quick screams from several others, a rush of thudding hooves, and he came galloping toward them. A way was opened for him with seemingly miraculous swiftness, the people parting so swiftly, leaping backward with such magical skill, that there was an illusion of parting waves, between which he came riding. Clamped fiercely between his knees, the stallion halted beside Cherry and Jacintha and reared back, pawing the air, while the two women clung to each other and ducked. He slipped down and stood before them laughing.

"Well! Have you found amusement?"

"Oh!" murmured Cherry. "You shouldn't have left us!" She stepped softly away from Jacintha's clasp and nearer to him, looking up into his face. "We were in terrible danger. Where did you go?"

He turned, raised one arm and pointed off in the distance—toward the pine-covered mountain—where Indians and trappers were running races on foot and horseback, wrestling and jumping, shooting arrows and rifles. "I went for a breath of fresh air." He glanced back, still grinning. He was breathing hard and his body looked wet and shining.

They gazed up at him, subdued, admiring, their faces wistful and waiting. Each was thinking: If only he would choose me. If only he would take the initiative, so that I could not be guilty because I hurt her.

The squaws looked at him and at them, their faces openly envious, their smiles sly and malicious. The women from the hotel looked at him, too, their eyes sweeping greedily up and down. A young squaw going by reached out boldly and stroked one hand across his chest. She had three fingers missing, and the mutilated hand caused both women to shudder as it lay for a moment against his broad black-haired chest.

"What mischief have you been into?" he asked them. His manner was hearty and somewhat violent, full of the exuberance of strenuous outdoor exertion.

It seemed quite plain to them both as they looked at him, strong, proud, magnificently independent, master of himself and them, that he would make no decision for either one, but entertain himself by waiting to see what each was able to contrive.

"We haven't been in any mischief!" said Jacintha. "But we *were* in danger—"

"A horrible beast of a man attacked her and kissed her and—"

"Kissed her?"

"I bit him! I bit him and kicked him and—"

"Sounds like you've been pretty well entertained."

"Oh, really!" pouted Cherry, looking at him with playful crossness. "This whole thing is disgusting. It's—it's bestial!"

"It's obscene!" cried Jacintha. Both women had been talking so quickly they were now almost breathless. "The most vicious things are going on everywhere!"

He turned down his mouth in a comical grimace of mock surprise. "They are?" Then he shook his head. "There is no such thing as being civilized until you can thoroughly enjoy, now and then, the return to savagery."

They looked at him soberly and solemnly, and then together slowly shook their heads.

"Oh, no," said Jacintha softly.

"You're quite wrong," said Cherry.

"You, of course," Jacintha informed him, "would like to destroy civilization. You—being who and what you are despise everything we have achieved, since it threatens your supremacy."

He threw back his head with a sudden burst of laughter. "I would hate to see your civilization destroyed. I find it a very good show—and that's more than either of you can say for it."

"Tsk, tsk," agreed Cherry and Jacintha.

He smiled. "You didn't enjoy it as much as you're trying to pretend—or what are you doing here?"

They gave a surprised gasp and turned to look at each other, as if for consultation.

"What's this?" they heard him exclaim and, the next moment, he had left them and was running with his lithe easy gait, which seemed to merely skim the earth, toward where a crowd was gathering with phenomenal rapidity. They were converging from all directions, streaking toward a common center, like bits of metal shot together by a strong magnet.

Cherry and Jacintha hesitated only a moment, and then followed him. Picking up their skirts, they went paddling through the mud as fast as they could go and caught up with him just as he reached the crowd. They got behind him and stayed close and once again, at the pressure of his body and shoulders, the others drew apart and the three of them arrived easily at the circle's inner edge.

There was a man and a woman on the ground, the woman beneath with her legs spraddled, the man on top, sawing vigorously back and forth. They looked like one huge agitated beetle.

At the sight, Jacintha's mouth fell open and her eyes popped. She felt stunned, as if she had been struck with violent force, knocking her momentarily insensible, and had then instantly come to in a blackened room where a sudden glaring light revealed this scene. But she was not conscious, after the first astonished moment, of other people about her. The voices, noisy and profane, shouting words and expressions she had never heard before, faded to a distant thunderous roar. She was being constantly jostled but, though she accommodated herself to it, moving, regaining her footing when she was given a hard shove, she felt nothing. She stood and stared, growing hot across her face and throat, and her heart was pounding like the hoofbeats of a galloping horse. She began to breathe in quick shallow panting gasps. Suddenly, unexpectedly, she moaned and covered her face with her hands and when she looked again the man had gotten up, was grinning sheepishly at the crowd and cinching his belt while the woman sat, hanging her head, looking as if she expected to be beaten.

Jacintha shook herself and looked around for them. They were not in sight.

"Cherry!" she cried.

She began twisting and turning, lifting on her toes, craning her neck, calling out again and again, her voice becoming more lonely and piteous with each repetition.

"Cherry! Cherry!"

The crowd was breaking up and she found herself painfully aware of everything around her: the moldy smell of the men's greasy shirts; the sour alcoholic taint of their breath; a man's eyes peering at her—she escaped by ducking down and skittering away; the embarrassed laughter of the well-dressed women; the fading sun, now only a faint red disk sunk into a bank of clouds along the horizon. The air was chilly and she buttoned her dress to her throat. Soon it would be dark.

The crowd had broken apart, into separate invididual units, moving about as aimlessly as before. Men and women passed her on all sides. She was half running now, peering and searching frantically. They were nowhere in sight. They had disappeared, departed from her side as if they had been insubstantial ghosts and faded into the air itself.

"Cherry!" Suddenly she stopped still, cupped her hands to her mouth and screamed as loud as she could: *"Cherry!"*

While she had been gawking, blinded, helpless, stupid, they had run away and left her, laughing at her, no doubt, making fun of her, holding each other by the hand and running to some private place where they could enjoy each other, as that sight had most certainly suggested to them they should do.

"It's my punishment. It's what I deserve. I never should have looked. How *could* I have looked?

A flare of lightning crossed the sky and there was a sharp report of thunder.

"No!" wailed Jacintha, lifted her widespread arms, and felt a drop of rain pelt her cheek. "No! *Don't!*"

The sky darkened in an instant. It thundered again,

a deep and direful sound. Immediately the camp was drenched with a massive drumming downpour.

The drunken Indians and trappers, laughing and shouting, turned up their faces and opened their mouths, and, as they got wet, began to scrub at their snarled beards and hair, rubbing their arms and chests, standing ankle-deep in quickly formed puddles. Jacintha ran into a tepee, following three or four men and women from the hotel. Several Indians were in there, farther back, and the ladies and gentlemen gathered nervously together at the opening of the damp, dark, nasty-smelling tent.

Around her, Jacintha heard them gossiping: "Who do you suppose he's with?" "I saw him only a minute ago, watching that couple." "Where can he have gone?" "He has his hiding places, you know." "He's got more pride than a dog—he doesn't take a woman where he'll be watched." "Ugh! What a stink this place has! I'd rather get wet!"

"What's the matter with *you* standing there looking so gloomy?"

This last was addressed to Jacintha. She gave a quick hostile glance out of the corner of her eyes at the man who had spoken. Her face and hair and clothes were wet; her gown was torn in many places. She looked, indeed, no longer a Victorian lady of proper upbringing, but a wild wood spirit dressed for a comic masquerade who had fallen into a pool on the way, or, perhaps, merely decided to swim to the party and only now come up for air.

She stared at him a moment with a hard direct gaze, contemptuously flicked one shoulder, and returned to staring out-of-doors.

She peered moodily out at the storm and the antics of the Indians and trappers, though many by now had retired into the tepees and the noise that came from them seemed even louder and more alarming than before. The storm had produced a new and additional frenzy, it seemed, had made them all restless and impatiently lustful at once.

The man at her side moved nearer, pressed his body suggestively against hers. Jacintha stiffened with loathing and rage and closed her fingers around the hilt of a knife which had been sticking in the lopped-off tree just inside the tepee. She did not turn or glance at him again but he had seen her take hold of it, and promptly left her.

The storm continued. The rain swirled by, accompanied by a moaning sound of wind; the thunder crackled and then roared. But, though it was loud and violent, there seemed almost a merry playful quality about it today.

Behind her, it grew quieter and Jacintha began to have a horrid feeling that if she looked around she might find them all turned into beetles. Softly, she stole out of the tent. She slogged alone through the mud, letting her skirts get filthy, letting the rain soak her hair. She felt ugly and felt, furthermore, an almost lecherous need to feel uglier still, to look ugly to everyone who saw her—ugly enough to horrify and frighten them. Dogs ran by at a frenzied rate, splattering her with mud from their scampering feet, barking and chasing one another. All around, the tepees seemed literally rocking with activity.

"I'm alone, she dismally reflected. I'm alone now and for the rest of eternity. I shall be completely miserable —I shall take care never to be anything but miserable. I shall gather up misery and hold it close like a lover and slobber over it like that man slobbers over his joint of meat. The sights around her were no longer horrifying or disgusting, but seemed only an external manifestation of her feelings. Now that she saw them, outwardly expressed, and permitted herself to recognize and admit ownership of them, she moved among them almost unconcernedly, taking them for granted, it seemed.

The storm was waning. The crowds were reappearing, creeping out of their tepees, gathering once more about the liquor booths. She passed men gnawing on maggot-infested meat, drinking melted lard and vomiting it up again, smearing themselves, wallowing in the guts of a great buffalo they were carving. A crowd had set two dogs to fighting and were yelling and betting on the outcome while the animals tore each other to bloody carcasses. Squaws were getting the fires going again, waving blankets over them, and heavy sodden smoke drifted through the camp, making everyone's eyes burn and smart. In the distance, trees looked like bouquets held in the fist of a hidden giant. The sun came out quickly and very hot, for the last few minutes before it sank behind the mountains.

Jacintha had reached the edge of Lemonade Lake and stood gazing into it pensively, one forefinger in her mouth, listening to the ferocious sounds from the encampment and the strange wistful contrast of a bird on a branch above her head, singing as if to burst his throat. She watched him, tenderly. And then she heard a woman's laughter.

She glanced up, looking around in every direction, then stepped back instinctively to hide herself behind a fallen trunk and knelt down, waiting. It had been Cherry's voice. She heard it again, that same merry, spattering little laugh, which she had loved so well.

This was where they had been—together in some secret cave in Roaring Mountain, hidden from her and from everyone. While she had wandered alone. She is not my mother any more. From this moment I reject her. Perhaps she never was my mother, anyway. How do I know that she is? I have only her word, and his—and I think it is a trick he has played, to torture me. She is an imposter, I *know* she is! And I hate her.

She continued to search for them, feeling that she moved her eyes with an actual physical force, turning them slowly along the edge of Lemonade Lake, then lifting them up the slopes of the gasping white mountain. She knelt with her tense stretched fingers balanced in the trampled grass, scarcely breathing, all her body still and stiff.

They might still be in the cave.

And yet, the laugh had sounded quite near.

She heard the laugh once more and then Cherry's voice, gay and playful, cried: "I never said that in my life!" And, a short distance up the mountainside, Cherry appeared. She rose into view, as if stepping upward from an underground hiding place and stood there alone for a moment, luxuriously raising and stretching her arms, then folding them behind her head and smiling toward the sky. Suddenly, with a wild and exultant, but still feminine gesture, she flung her arms wide, as if to embrace infinity in her happiness. The white mists moved and shifted about her, making her almost invisible for the next few moments.

Jacintha continued to crouch, watching.

Your mother was no older than you when she died. But she knows a great deal more about men.

The vapor circled upward and, as it lifted, she saw that now he was standing just behind Cherry, one arm about her waist, his hand spread across her belly. He bent his head and kissed her on the mouth. They stood a moment, looking at each other and smiling.

Jacintha sprang to her feet, even before she realized that that was what she meant to do. She stood, staring at them accusingly, waiting for them to see her. She stared straight at them, her eyes glowing with fury, and seemed to feel herself literally swell and grow bigger with hatred.

They came slowly down the mountain, his arm still about her waist, talking softly, laughing continuously, and Jacintha knew, of course, that they were laughing at her. They might have passed her, it seemed, without even noticing, so absorbed were they in each other. But when they drew nearer she took a few steps and stood straight in their path, gazing at them with alert shining hostility, like a forest creature challenging unwelcome intruders.

Cherry gave a start of surprise and the smile quickly faded away. He glanced up, his face rather grave for a moment, and then he smiled.

"Why, Jacintha," he observed drolly. "Aren't you drenched?" He peered narrowly at her, mocking.

Cherry had regained her composure and now she was smiling, too, standing beside him as if perfectly confident of possessing him, vibrantly aglow with the extraordinary effect produced by his love-making, which seemingly had the power to increase and emphasize a woman's beauty to incredible degrees. The look of her face, soft and shining, relaxed and vivacious at once, struck Jacintha like the most insulting unbearable blow. Her body, easy, composed, graceful, full and voluptuous, secretly enfolding the spreading pulsing warmth he had left her—her body, with these attributes, roused the most violent intense hatred.

At that moment Jacintha discovered the knife she held in her right hand.

She had taken it, of course, from the tepee but had been unaware all along that she had it. The three stood staring at one another, motionless and silent for several moments. A conviction of fierce boundless power seemed rushing in her veins. She grew increasingly nervous and eager and could feel her heart beating throughout her body. She trembled and shook and suddenly the need for action became uncontrollable. She started toward them, filled with a lust of hatred and violence, hoping and expecting to destroy them both. She believed at that moment she had strength and rage great enough for any act.

As she started to move, he came slowly toward her, Cherry walking at his side.

Slowly, one step and then another, they shortened the distance between them. Cherry's expression was changing. The radiant confidence and languishing contentment had passed into curiosity and was now becoming a sad poignant pity. As they drew nearer, Cherry impulsively held forth her hands and opened her mouth to speak.

It was the look of pity on Cherry's face which made Jacintha, uttering a strange deep moan, start to run, moving lightly and swiftly, slightly stooped, her eyes gleaming. As she reached them she swept back her arm, held the knife poised for only an instant, then brought it sweeping downward. Cherry screamed and, inadvertently, Jacintha changed the direction of the blow, flashed it sideways—visioning how it would tear open his face and throat.

For the fraction of a second she was fixed greedily upon that vision. She shut her eyes, felt a shattering blow across the side of her face, and fell at his feet, the knife flying out of her hand like a hummingbird.

Cherry turned to him, her fists clenched and her eyes filled with fury. "Oh, I despise you! You knew she was hysterical! You've hurt her!" He gave her a look of disgust and shook his head.

Cherry knelt, tenderly raised Jacintha's head and held it cradled against her breasts, rocking gently backward and forward, crooning: "Darling— My darling— Jacintha, speak to me— He didn't hurt you, did he— It was my fault, my fault, forgive me— Jacintha, please forgive me—"

Jacintha lay with her eyes closed. The hatred was gone, as though he had knocked it out of her. Her jaw was aching as if it had been broken and the bones in her neck and shoulders ached. A tear splashed onto her face, causing her vaguely to wonder why Cherry should be crying.

It was dark now and as he stood looking downward at them, his fists planted on his hips, his legs outspread, he seemed to rise gigantically, filling the night itself with prodigious power and ruthlessness. They appeared small and helpless at his feet, subdued to his will, ineffectual delicate creatures who could no more challenge him than could Lemonade Lake challenge Roaring Mountain. Across the encampment, dozens of fires smoked and sparks shot toward the sky, appearing to mingle with the stars which were emerging in miraculously quantity.

Jacintha lay without moving, strangely comfortable in Cherry's arms despite the conviction that her face had been crushed; she lay perfectly still and reflected with some surprise and some pleasure, despite her grief, that he had degraded her to a condition where she had lost not merely her pride—which seemed inconsequential now —but whatever dignity her status as a human being might once have implied. He had defeated her absolutely by revealing to her, through the medium of his cruelty and trickery, that her self-respect had been a myth.

How I hate myself. How despicable I am. I'm glad he struck me. I wish it had been possible for him to kill me. I would kill myself, if I could. I am nothing of what I pretended to myself to be. I have seen myself now and I am beneath even *his* contempt.

She considered these things in a detached and philosophical way, with only mild concern. She felt that she had had an important revelation, one which would change all the future for her.

At last, slowly, she opened her eyes and looked up at Cherry, who had continued crooning and rocking as Jacintha lay considering her reasons for self-hatred. The instant she did so Cherry burst into tears and began frantically kissing her face.

"Oh, my darling darling darling little Jacintha. *Forgive me*— Forgive me—"

Jacintha looked at her, marvelling that it was Cherry asking her forgiveness, and was about to ask her why, when his voice spoke sharply, rapping out:

"Stop that! Let her go—and get up!"

Cherry looked swiftly about, raising her head. He stood motionless, an awesome black shadow against the smoking white mountain which murmured and hissed behind him and shone in the dark like silver. She stared at him defiantly.

"Get up!" He gave a swift hard jerk of his head.

"But you've hurt her!" cried Cherry. "She hasn't been able to speak! Have you gone—"

He leaned down, seized her by the shoulders and snatched her to her feet. With a cry of anger she tried to pull away from him and return to Jacintha who was now sitting upright, her palm against her face, touching it experimentally: strangely, it was only numb now and did not actually hurt at all. But, as Cherry struggled to rejoin her, he held her and, the next instant, a shrill painful whistle sounded above the camp's riotous noise.

In what seemed only a few seconds, they heard a clattering of hoofs and racketing of wheels and their carriage drove swiftly toward them, stopped, and he almost literally pitched Cherry into it, still violently protesting:

"I won't leave her! I won't leave her alone with you! I won't—"

"Shut up!" He spoke sharply, but without real anger, like a stern parent to a troublesome child. "Drive her a hundred yards or so along the path and wait!" The driver snapped his whip and, while Cherry was still trying to get out, still insisting that she would not leave Jacintha, the little carriage quickly disappeared into the dark.

"Don't you dare hurt her!" Cherry cried once more, leaning over the back of the seat and holding forth her hands. Then she could be seen no longer and the noise of the carriage was drowned in the din from the camp.

Jacintha sat still, staring toward the ground. She had not even glanced up as Cherry was put into the carriage and sent away. Now she waited and felt herself willing to accept whatever he would do to her. Both were silent for several moments.

All at once Jacintha, with an uncontrollable shudder, covered her face with both hands. "I don't care," she whispered. "I don't care what you do—I couldn't help myself—"

His hand touched her shoulder and she glanced up in a

sudden terror which belied the listless words. She gave a violent start. "I won't hurt you," he said softly. "I'm sorry that I hurt you before—but there wasn't much time." His voice sounded faintly amused, though it was too dark to see his face. Now he bent, slipped his hands into her armpits, and drew her slowly and gently to her feet, then held her against him. Helpless and stunned, her heart beating fast with fear, she stood stiffly, waiting. She did not doubt that he would do something terrible to her, and that he was enjoying her agony of suspense.

I don't care, she reassured herself. Whatever it is, I don't care.

He continued to hold her against him and, very carefully, slowly, tenderly, his hands stroked her hair, her back, her arms, her face. The stroking was infinitely soothing, almost healing, she felt, and was without sensuality. Trustingly, she relaxed, closed her eyes, rested against him and found herself being slowly restored to her normal strength, serenity, self-confidence. The pleasure was great, though not voluptuous, and she wanted to linger there forever, shut into her dark private world, aware of nothing but the continuous slow caress of his hands. She sighed.

Then, still with great care, he released her and, to her surprise, she found herself standing alone, only a few inches from him, though it seemed a great cold distance was between them. Alarmed, she moved toward him.

"Go back with her," he said.

"Go back?" she repeated in wistful bewilderment. "Back where?"

"Go back to your rooms."

"I want to stay with you."

She looked toward him, trying to see him, but it was too dark. He was only a dim massive figure before her, and a powerfully felt presence. Even more, she wished that he could see her. For she felt that her beauty might persuade him where her words could not—though, of course, it had not been persuasive last night.

"Please—let me stay with you. I won't ask for anything or even expect anything—"

Having defeated her, she believed that now he was obliged to be responsible for her.

They heard a restless heavy trampling nearby and Jacintha started nervously. "What was that?"

"Only my horse. Go on—go back." He sounded impatient.

"But I must—"

"Good-by."

He turned swiftly, moved away and, almost before she knew what was happening, she saw his vague shadow mount the black stallion. He raised one arm to her in a salute, and was off at a furious gallop, down the forest pathway, away from the rendezvous, in the opposite direction from where Cherry was waiting. Jacintha stood and stared. Now there was nothing, not even the sound of hoofbeats.

He's gone. He was here—she held out her hands—and he is gone.

The noise from the camp blasted in her ears and she covered them, cowering. Then she picked up her skirts and began to run as fast as she could go, toward the carriage. The dark was suddenly populated by a hundred hostilities—Indians creeping toward her, prowling wolves, trappers insanely drunk, tremendous bears, silent swift mountain lions. She ran as fast as she could go and she began to call Cherry's name, calling louder and more wildly when there was no answer.

Then Cherry must have heard her through the noise. "Jacintha! Here I am, Jacintha! Here I—"

Finally she got to the carriage and stood beside it, panting, trying to get her breath again. Cherry reached down.

"Where is he?"

"Gone. He rode away."

"What did he do to you?"

"Nothing," Jacintha said, her voice soft and light and bewildered. "He was kind to me—I think he pitied me." She felt lost, powerless, deprived of everything but the need to be with him.

She was shivering and realized that it had grown very cold.

"Get in," said Cherry. "It's freezing here at this time of year. The nights are always cold. Let me bundle you up." She was wrapping Jacintha in a buffalo robe, lined with scarlet wool. She told the driver to take them back.

The two women sat side by side, close together, with their arms linked and their hands clasped. They were silent for what seemed a long while, rushing through the darkness. It would be useless to ask the driver to slow down and they were more afraid of whatever might be lurking for them than of his heedless haste.

Cherry was the first to speak. "Will you be able to forgive me, Jacintha?"

Jacintha gazed steadily ahead. "I would have done what you did."

Cherry gave her hand a warm grateful pressure. "How honest you are! I'm proud of you. But I am ashamed of myself. I should have been able to be less selfish."

"I don't think so. Considering what he is—how could you be?"

"Look! What's that?"

They looked up as Cherry's hand darted forth and seized a snowflake; it melted as she touched it. And then they saw that the snow was sifting down, great soft floating flakes, circling overhead, aimlessly drifting, and settling, even now, upon the trees and earth.

"Does that mean—" asked Jacintha hesitantly, "the same thing a rainstorm does?"

They turned toward each other and suddenly Cherry laughed. "No. It means something quite different. It means that he has gone away."

Jacintha sat up straight, a quick hot flash striking the back of her neck and then the pit of her stomach. "Gone away!"

"Not forever," said Cherry soothingly. "He always leaves here at this time of the year. We'll be snowed in, you know—for months."

"He'll be gone for months! Oh, no! He can't be!"

"He'll return in the spring. Or, if not this next spring, then probably the following. Someday, at least, he will come back." Cherry's voice was very warm and delicate as she spoke, saying the words slowly, as if to accustom Jacintha gradually to the shock. "Until he does," she added, "we shall comfort each other."

But Jacintha sat heavy and stupefied. It was the one thing she had not expected. Almost nothing else could have surprised her now—but she had never anticipated his prolonged absence. After all, this was his domain, was it not?

"Why does he go?" she asked finally.

"No one knows *why* he does anything." There was a brief pause and she added: "You will be surprised at how lasting those memories are."

Jacintha felt her face grow red. "Will I?"

"It's very wise of him to leave, actually."

"Wise?"

"Of course. Think how *glad* we will be to see him!"

Cherry's voice was again gay and cheerful, and it seemed she had quite recovered from the confusion and exhausting excitement of the day, as if she had even recovered from and already forgotten the terrible scene which had occurred so recently, and had recovered from the announcement of his departure, as well.

No matter what happened, it seemed that Cherry's natural gaiety and resilience would reassert itself almost immediately.

But not Jacintha's, and she knew it.

She had a picture of them together during the months ahead: Cherry busy and lighthearted, chattering and merry—while she sat forlornly brooding, staring into herself at the memories of which Cherry had spoken. She would only wait—while Cherry passed the time to her own satisfaction.

"Jacintha, darling," continued Cherry. "Don't be sad. We'll have so many things to do. Why—we'll make spatterwork lamp shades and pretty little boxes out of bark and leaves. We'll be together. We'll entertain each other, won't we?"

The snow was settling, steadily, falling thicker and thicker. The trees were fringed with white and the earth was white. The air was both cool and warm. Like death, thought Jacintha. As I remember it.

"Yes," she agreed, but without enthusiasm. "I suppose we will." She turned to Cherry again. "Where does he go?"

"Heavens, darling. I don't know where he goes. No one does. Don't keep thinking about him now. What good can it do you?"

"I'm not doing it for the good it does me. I love him."

Cherry became instantly sober, slipped her arm about

Jacintha's waist, and hugged her close. "I know you do. And he loves you, too."

Jacintha turned her head and looked at Cherry. Their faces were close together, almost as white as snowflakes, and their dark hair rose about their heads, flying in the wind. Their dark eyes gazed together with steady intensity.

Finally, Jacintha shook her head. "But he chose you—not me."

"I think he did it to torment you. He's cruel, you know. It's part of his great fascination."

"Cruelty—fascinating?" Jacintha frowned a little.

"Of course. Always. Particularly to women. Come, darling—" She hugged her again. "We must do what we can to comfort each other. I waited for him alone before—you wait *much* longer, that way."

Jacintha glanced away, ashamed of her self-absorption. Then, quickly and impulsively, she smiled and kissed Cherry's cheek: "We'll be so happy together," she declared, "that we won't care if he comes back or not!"

"Of course we won't!" They held each other's hands tighter than ever.

Cherry reached up playfully and swiped with one cupped hand at the snowflakes. "Look!" she cried with delight. "I've caught a dozen of them! Here—" And, very carefully, concentrating seriously, she tried to pass them to Jacintha who gave the effort her entire rapt attention and—when the snowflakes escaped them—they began eagerly grabbing for others, half standing in the carriage, bouncing up and down, their laughter ringing out in the dark cold night.

TWO

The Silent Land

THE WHITE plaster frame, with a white plaster dove perched on top, was the exact size and shape of a girl's face. Within it, Amoret's features were exquisitvely lovely, even though it was early morning and she had not yet defined them with cosmetics. Her eyes, large and clear blue, with thick lashes, gazed solemnly and intently. Her round soft pink mouth was parted, as if she breathed rather quickly, which she did, in wonder at her own image. The small mirror did not have space to reflect a rich fall of golden-red hair, parted in the center and reaching below her shoulders.

"The most beautiful child, Mrs. Ames!" "What a beautiful girl!" "The loveliest woman." Amoret Ames. She drew a quiet little breath and smiled. How nice, how pleasant, to be so beautiful. No one had ever minded her beauty, either. It was so great, that apparently the world regarded it as a contribution.

She wore a black chiffon gown and, over it, a floating black lace robe. Now, sitting at her dressing table, she began to brush her hair, slowly and luxuriantly, enjoying the crisp strokes of the brush against her scalp.

Behind her, the bedroom, with its big double bed still unmade, was fresh and sparkling and sunny. That effect was partly the careful decoration, and partly Amoret's influence over her environment. Though she was seldom in any environment which might be unbecoming to her and, when by chance she was, she left it as soon as possible for something more in harmony with her nature and appearance. Other people, too, had cheerfully conspired throughout her life to see that her surroundings were suitable to her. This room, for instance, which her mother had so lovingly and painstakingly designed for her, with the aid of the best possible interior decorator.

The wallpaper had a black ground, flowered and latticed with pink and cream. White curtains, polka-dotted pink, blew softly back from the windows. Some of the chairs were bright pink quilted chintz and there was a gleaming black satin chaise longue. The room glinted with silver and crystal, and there were several vases of pink roses and white bouvardia. Amoret thought it the prettiest bedroom she had ever had.

Now she put down the brush and with soft graceful fluid steps, crossed the room to look out the windows. The apartment was located so high that New York was misty and enchanted in the distance. Her parents had suggested giving her a house, but Amoret had not wanted to be that close to the street.

At a sound behind her she turned and, with a faint sense of surprise, saw her husband come out of the dressing room, shaved and wearing a dark-blue suit. Of course. It seemed a little strange she had forgotten that he was still at home, but she did not stop to wonder about it and ran gaily toward him. He wrapped her into his arms and stroked her hair and put his mouth against her cheek. Finally she stood back and looked at him, her face radiantly smiling.

"I hate to leave you," he said. "I'll call you as soon as I get to the office."

"Don't forget," she begged him. "Call me *right* away. I'll just stay here and think about you. Oh, Donald—why do honeymoons have to end? We were having so much fun."

Amoret and Donald Paige Jennings had been married five months ago, in what everyone agreed was the prettiest wedding they had ever seen, and then they had gone to Europe for their honeymoon. They had arrived home last night, and now it was time for real life to begin.

Donald was much taller than Amoret, dark-haired and

very handsome. His family was as rich as hers. He was twenty-six, six years older than she, and he had a brilliant future in his father's law firm and would surely someday be a senator, a judge, or perhaps a great statesman. They stood at the edge of a glorious life, two of the luckiest people on earth. Their friends and acquaintances and many other who did not even know them but who had merely seen their pictures or read about them, wished them the realization of all dreams common to mankind. People were not jealous of Amoret. For one thing, she had always had every good fortune the world could give and she took them so much for granted, that others were forced to do the same. She did not, by any subtle hint of doubting her own claim to these things, permit anyone else to doubt, either. It was as if she had it all by divine right.

And, also, there was her charm. The expressions of her mobile face, the sounds of her voice, the movements she made, the aura she cast of little-girl delight with everything about her, insured that her beauty and privileges would be welcomed, not begrudged, by others.

Donald was kissing her, holding her close and kissing her fervently, but not with violent passion, for he had the premonition that passion might be a strong wind which could sweep her away. She was somewhat too fragile for it, at least now. And anyway, what she aroused in him was love and protection, much more than lust. Lust would not be any more suitable to Amoret than cheap clothes or housework or dingy furniture.

"I've got to go," he said finally, with intense reluctance. "Oh, Amoret, I hate to think of being away from you even an hour."

"Take me with you," she offered.

"I can't do that— Oh," and he laughed. "I see. Can I take just part of you?"

Smiling up at him, she made a little gesture of closing her hand over her left breast, and then presenting him with her heart. He took it, wrapped it carefully in his white handkerchief, put it into his pocket, and left without another word. She followed him to the door, blew a kiss down the hall, then shut the door and locked it.

She wandered back to the low crystal table where the maid had earlier set their breakfast, poured coffee into one of the thin china cups, and began to sip it slowly. She looked around the room, moving her eyes beneath the lashes, covertly.

I should call Mother, she thought. I should call her this very moment. She'll be waiting to hear from me. But if I do, she'll come right over. (Mr. and Mrs. Ames lived only five or six blocks away.) And I want to see *him* first.

She finished the coffee and went to look in the closet, down the long line of dresses and skirts and suits and coats, hanging neatly in their cellophane containers. She had dozens of dresses, dozens of gloves and hats and suits, drawers full of lace and silk, racks lined with shoes. Sometimes she thought she must have more clothes than anyone in the world. Whenever she saw something she knew—and her instinct was infallible—would illuminate some slightly different facet of her personality or beauty, she bought it. She gave things away all the time, but she seemed to get more than she gave and closet space was a constant problem no matter where Amoret lived. Her mother had imagined she might have solved the problem in this apartment, but there were still to be unpacked all the things she had brought from Europe.

She stood for several minutes, contemplating what it was she wanted him to see her in first—after so many months.

That would, of course, partly depend on where they met. Maybe the Park would be best. It pleased her to think of him coming to meet her there, seeing her approach from a distance— Or maybe she would get there first and as he walked up she would be standing watching the seals, with a bag of popcorn in her hand, holding onto Mio's leash. The more she thought of that, the more she liked it better than for them to meet in private. That was too obvious, too much as other people would do it, not enough like them—who had never done anything conventionally in all the time they had known each other.

And that had been a long long time.

She had fallen in love with him three or four years ago, though she could not remember exactly. It had been violent love-at-first-sight for them both, whenever it was, a thing wonderful enough in itself, but the best of all was that it would never change. They would love each other forever, as much as they had in the beginning. That was like having a secret little flame to light up your world when it grew dark, or some magical unknown flower with a perfume never fading or cloying, which you could hold and sniff when you felt lonely or sad and bring peace into your life again. No one would ever have guessed that Amoret might have need of such comforts, but she did.

Surely, she could not give up anything so precious, just because she was married?

They met as she had decided: Amoret, wearing a dark green tweed suit with a yellow sweater, her head bare, stood in Central Park watching the seals, holding her little gray clipped poodle by his green leash, nibbling from a bagful of popcorn. The sky was blue with many clouds and it was a cold early November day. The leaves had fallen during her absence, something she discovered to her dismay, for she had anticipated watching them change color, grow crisp, and fly from the trees. A few children, with their nurses, played nearby and she talked to them. Amoret had always marvelled how much easier it was to carry on a conversation with a five-year-old than with a grownup. They seemed infinitely more understanding. Whatever happened to them later?

That was the picture she presented when he appeared, softly spoke her name, and she turned delightedly, looking up to see if he had changed and if he loved her as much as ever.

"Miles—" she whispered. Miles Morgan, it was.

He looked exactly the same. There was no one else in the world like him. He was not, perhaps, any handsomer than Donald—probably no man could be handsomer—but he had other qualities Donald did not have. He had fieriness and gaiety and a sense of poetry in everything he did. He was her perfect lover, untarnished by familiarity, new and fresh to her each time they met. She looked into his eyes now, to see what color they would be this time. She never knew in advance for they kept changing, chameleonlike, as did his personality. Today they were green, speckled with bronze; she thought she liked that combination best of all.

They stood a long while, smiling at each other, remembering so many other meetings; both of them content, as they could only be together.

"Did you miss me?" she asked him softly.

"Of course I did. You're more beautiful each time I see you."

"Even now that I'm married?"

"What difference could that make?"

"It seems to make a difference with other women. They're never as pretty, once they get married."

"Maybe. I hadn't noticed. But nothing that applies to other women, could apply to you. You know that."

She laughed delightedly and took his arm. They began to stroll along, past the old people sitting on benches to soak up the last of the year's sun, past the playing children, the busy squirrels, the leafless trees which Amoret felt sorry for. She felt a perfect happiness. They had never once quarrelled, never questioned each other's moods or behavior, never exposed each other to anything of cruelty or ugliness. When they were together, they lived in a world totally unrelated to anything but each other.

"How do you like your husband?" he asked.

Amoret gave her brows a little lift and glanced up at him mischievously. "He's very nice— He's altogether different from you, of course. Down-to-earth, you know, and practical—like lawyers always are. But still—for a husband, he's fine."

Miles laughed. "But are you good to him? Do you love him?"

"I'm good to everyone, Miles, you know that. And I love him as much as I could ever love anyone but you."

They selected a bench along a rather deserted path and sat down side by side. Amoret flung out bits of popcorn to the squirrels and they laughed to watch them romping after it.

"Miles—where have you been?"

"To Africa," he said. "On safari."

"On safari!" She clapped her hands with delight. "Oh Miles! Isn't that wonderful! Tell me about it!"

Miles had been all over the world, but he kept going back to places where he had already been, or discovering new ones. And he did many different things. Like the color of his eyes, his activities kept changing, too, and she never knew when she saw him, what marvellous new adventure he would have to tell her about. They were much better than the stories her father had told when she was little.

Miles Morgan was rich—she could not imagine anyone interesting being poor—and he did whatever he wanted. He worked, too, when he found something that suited him or was sufficiently challenging. He was certainly not lazy, for he had an intense, though quiet, energy.

Now he told her about his safari and all the things that had happened to him—how he had photographed tribes which had never been seen before by a white man, and had recorded their music and songs. "You must hear it, Amoret," he said. "You'll understand it, I know—I'm not sure about anyone else."

"Oh, I want to, Miles. I can't *wait* to hear it. But the fever—" She turned to him anxiously, pressing his hand. "Were you very sick? Oh, if only I could have been with you to take care of you! I'm such a good nurse. When did you get back?"

"Yesterday."

They looked at each other, smiling and shaking their heads. "Isn't it amazing?" murmured Amoret.

"No more amazing than everything else. Everything between us has happened by the wildest coincidence. Even our meeting—remember?"

"Our meeting. How *did* we meet? Oh, yes! Of course!"

She had been travelling with her mother and father in Italy, and their first night in Venice had sneaked out of the hotel alone and set off in a gondola. She went drifting through the lagoon, happy to be out of her parents' sight for a few minutes, lying back and gazing up at the houses which were closed on the lagoon side, with soft light spreading through the shutters; caressive sounds of music and voices floated above the water. At each corner, her gondolier sang out a warning.

All of a sudden another gondola had appeared and— before she knew what was happening or could scramble out of the way—its sharp prow began to climb swiftly upon her. While the two gondoliers fenced madly with their poles, shouting and swearing, the occupant of the other leaped into hers and shoved back the prow, saving her from being seriously mauled and perhaps injured rather badly. Amoret lay breathless and trembling and weak with shock. Shuttered windows began opening and other Italians participated energetically in the discussion.

As a window above them burst open, Amoret got a look at her savior—the strongest handsomest man she had ever seen. She gave a little gasp of shock and delight.

He handed money to his own gondolier, gave directions to hers, and sat down beside her, back in the shadows.

"Are you all right? You weren't hurt?"

"No," whispered Amoret.

He had strong regular features, masculine and commanding. His skin was tanned deep brown, his teeth were white and straight. His black crisp hair had one faint wave, and his eyes were the purest blue of any she had seen but her own. The night was hot and he wore only slacks and a white shirt, opened, so that she could see how magnificently muscled were his shoulders and chest and arms. She simply stared at him with her lips apart, helpless. She felt as though a god had come to visit her.

"You shouldn't be out alone at this hour. Tell me where you live. I'll take you home—" And now he was gazing at her with that same helpless fascination.

That had been the beginning. Neither her mother nor her father nor anyone she knew ever met Miles Morgan, or even heard his name. He was her secret, kept safe from everyone else in her life; she did not intend to let any question or criticism touch him. But they had met, from time to time, ever since, and both knew they would continue to meet until the end of their lives.

Miles belonged to her, and she to him, in a sense too profound and meaningful to make necessary any of the usual devices for securing another person to you. They belonged to each other because they believed in each other and, in a sense, were each other. Nothing more was needed. And, perhaps, anything more would have been fatal. Fortunately, they both knew this. They had the understanding that a perfect thing must not be handled carelessly or roughly. Their love was delicate, fragile, ethereal, even when it was most exuberantly physical.

Now, when they had finished talking of his safari, they did not discuss her honeymoon.

"Maybe *I'll* get married," said Miles.

Amoret looked at him thoughtfully. "You know," she

said after a moment, "it might make you even more attractive."

He laughed. "Who should I marry?"

"Someone exotic." She wiggled a little on the bench, like an excited child who watches its father unwrap a gift. "Now, let's think it over very carefully—"

They began to discuss possibilities: The black-haired Russian countess who had been in love with him so many years? The famous movie star whose pictures appeared everywhere? The English ballet dancer? The Eurasian daughter of the great Chinese merchant? The East Indian maharanee who wore a diamond in her nose? The cruel gorgeous Spanish gypsy who electrified sophisticated audiences with her dancing? All these were women he had mentioned, and each of them she was able to imagine the possibility of having been, herself, in some previous or some future incarnation.

They talked them over but could not decide. "I know," said Miles triumphantly. "I'll surprise you!"

"Yes!" she agreed, with ready eagerness. "That's what you must do. Surprise me. I love surprises more than anything." She glanced around wistfully. "I must go, Miles. I haven't seen Mother yet. She'll be hurt."

"Run along, then."

They got up and stood looking at each other, holding hands.

"Amoret—little love—"

"No good-bys," she whispered.

"We've never said good-by. We never will."

"Never," she murmured fervently. And she was gone. They never turned, either, or watched each other leave. They met and parted as easily as dissolving mist, without the tears or poignancy of other, more ordinary, meetings and partings. Their love, being anchored securely in the deepest core of their being, was free from such usual accompaniments of emotion between men and women, or parents and children. Amoret could never cease being grateful for this one relationship which let her be herself, and left her to herself, without demands for special behavior, or punishment for failure to meet expectations.

She went directly to her mother's house, running in as when she was a little girl coming home from school, giving a joyous cry of welcome to whoever might be near, letting go the dog's leash and laughing delightedly as he dashed ahead. She ran up the stairs, pausing halfway to lean across the banister and wave to two of the maids who had appeared, calling merrily: "I'm back, Margaret! I'm back, Mary!" They smiled and waved and greeted her with affectionate enthusiasm. She rushed on, up the stairs, down the hall, knocked at her mother's door and went in almost before she heard the answer.

"Amoret!"

"Mother, darling!"

They flew to embrace each other and then her mother stood back to look at Amoret. Mrs. Ames was about forty-three, and still a considerable beauty herself, though everyone agreed the daughter had surpassed the mother by infinite degrees.

"Oh, my darling, I'm so glad to have you home! Tell me—are you happy? Are you really and truly happy?"

Amoret flung aside her sealskin coat, tossed away her gloves and handbag, kicked her shoes off, and curled up in a chair to talk to her mother. They had always been, people said, more like sisters than like mother and daughter, and strangers sometimes so mistook them. Amoret had confided everything that had ever happened—with the one exception of Miles Morgan—to her mother.

"I am happy, Mother," she said serenely. "Donald is so good to me, you can't imagine how good he is to me."

"Why shouldn't he be, darling?" asked her mother gently.

"He's so sweet. He simply adores me. I adore him, too, of course. And Mother—we had the most wonderful trip! When we were in Paris—" And for the next three hours they discussed the trip, the things she had bought, the places they had been, the people who had entertained them. "It was heavenly!" concluded Amoret.

Her mother sighed. "I'm so glad. I knew from your letters that you were happy, but to hear you tell me and see how you glow—you know, Armoret, you're everything in the world to me. You, and your father. And sometimes I think that my child is even more important to my happiness and peace than my husband."

Amoret went to stand behind her mother's chair. Her mother looked up and Amoret, leaning down, gently kissed her cheek.

"How lucky we are," whispered Amoret. "How nice to have everything." She wandered away and stood looking out the windows. After several minutes she turned back. "There's only one flaw," she said.

"What's that?"

"I don't like Donald's mother."

Mrs. Ames laughed. "I suppose that's natural, darling. What difference does it make?"

"It does make a difference," insisted Amoret, her face serious for the first time. "I not only don't like her. I hate her."

"Hate her?" Now her mother sounded shocked. She got up and went to face Amoret, whose lower lip was thrust out in a stubborn childish pout. "You don't hate her, Amoret. Why—you've never hated anyone in your life."

"I do."

The two women stood watching each other, and something new and puzzling confronted them. Amoret's life had been so smooth, so happy, with everyone laboring for her contentment—this disturbing element seemed almost tragic.

"Perhaps I can talk to her," said Mrs. Ames.

"What good could that do? She doesn't know it. She likes me as well as she can—but she's furiously jealous because Donald belongs to me now."

"Amoret—" said her mother, tenderly chiding. "Darling—" She reached and took her daughter's hand. "Something like this always happens in a new marriage. But it will solve itself, in a little while. It's not serious."

"It will solve itself," agreed Amoret. "I'll see to that."

Her mother peered at her closely. There had been an ominous tone to Amoret's voice, hadn't there? No, not possibly. This innocent child of hers was incapable of even understanding such a concept as hate. She simply did not realize what she was saying.

"I must go for a fitting," said her mother, having decided the best way to deal with this was to ignore it and trust that it would heal of itself, as it surely would. "Shall we have lunch together at the Plaza and then you come with me?"

"Yes!" agreed Amoret happily. "Let's do that!"

Mrs. Ames dressed and they went out and spent the afternoon together and no further mention was made of Mrs. Jennings. By evening, when they parted, her mother was convinced that Amoret had spoken carelessly, out of momentary pique, and had already forgotten what she had said. Amoret had been that way all her life, and there was no reason to suppose she had changed now. Mrs. Ames had long since ceased to remind her daughter of remarks which had disturbed her for, when she did, Amoret invariably looked at her with such perfect incomprehension that no one could doubt she did not remember; and, as often as not, Mrs. Ames would decide she must have imagined hearing Amoret say it in the first place. Sometimes the effect was a little eerie, and Mrs. Ames did not care to question her own memory or rationality oftener than necessary.

Amoret, however, had no intention of having her life spoiled by one woman—or, in fact, by anything at all.

"Mrs. Jennings," said Amoret, leaning with her hands on her dressing table and staring at herself in the dove-topped mirror. "Deborah Jennings—you are not going to interfere with my life." She spoke clearly and decisively, in a tone which doubtless would have surprised her mother or Donald or anyone else who knew her, except Miles who understood everything and condemned nothing.

These things were not as difficult as people thought. For the world was not exactly what it seemed. It was, for instance, far less solid than it gave the appearance of being. And the people in it were far less inevitable or permanent than they appeared to be. If you knew how to go about it, knew exactly what you meant to do, then there was no problem about doing it. Other people put up barriers between themselves and the accomplishments of their ends —Amoret had never admitted the possibility of any barrier between her and what she desired.

She could lean close to the mirror, stare deep into her eyes, and see so clearly the capacities she had to effect her wishes. Only Miles, of course, understood that such things were in no way weird, supernatural, uncanny, or even immoral, but only the most perfectly logical and also the simplest way of dealing with your environment.

Perhaps that was why she and Miles, of all people she knew or had ever known, were the only ones who did not compromise, who demanded and got, who molded life and were not molded by it. They two, alone, were superior to the usual laws and regulations of the universe. How fine and wonderful it was to know this power within you!

For when she had told Miles she did not like her mother-in-law, he had not been surprised, and he had not said that the situation would straighten itself out, either. He had nodded and smiled and said: "What are you going to do about it?"

"I'm not sure yet," Amoret replied. "Have you any suggestions?"

"Get rid of her."

"Oh yes—of course. But how?"

"Take away her ability to recognize you, or remember you," he suggested, matter-of-factly. "Will her not to see you when you are present, not to hear you when you speak, not even to remember your existence. Establish a no man's land between you, and patrol it yourself. Then she can be around—since she will, anyway—without being any bother to you."

"Miles! You're wonderful! I knew I could count on you. But—" She put one finger to her cheek, thoughtfully. "Suppose it doesn't work? Suppose I—leak through to her—someway or other?"

"Now, Amoret—" He smiled, the same confident challenging-the-world smile she gave herself in the mirror. "If you let yourself have doubts— It takes some effort of will to create your own world."

"Of course! What's the matter with me? I've been away from *you* too long!"

She left him then, and only remembered later that in her eagerness for his advice, she had forgotten to ask if he was married yet and which one he had chosen.

Now that everything was settled, Amoret began looking forward eagerly to the first night since their return that she would see Donald's mother—the last night, of course, that Donald's mother would see her. There was to be a dinner party, given by Amoret and Donald in their new apartment, for members of both families and some of their oldest mutual friends. Amoret and Donald had grown up in the same general group which was, nevertheless, large enough so that they did not meet until a year and a half before they were married.

They were playful and gay together, as they dressed for

the party. While he stood shaving, she lay in the tub snipping at the bubbles which foamed to the tub's top, each with a miniature rainbow in it. She told him what she had done during the day: she had gone shopping with her mother, had lunch with her dearest friend, Sharon, who was coming tonight, then she had had her fingernails and toenails lacquered and her hair dressed and her body massaged and her face treated. Donald, meanwhile, had been busy with some law cases.

Amoret had, like a good little girl, begun early in their engagement to ask Donald about his business. Her mother had impressed her with the importance of a wife's concern in her husband's professional life. She had, herself, been the very greatest help to Mr. Ames in everything he had done, and considered it one of a wife's most important functions to be the gentle guiding spirit of a successful man.

But perhaps it was the way Amoret asked—much like a child asking her father—or perhaps Donald genuinely believed that women should not fill their heads with such things; whatever it was, they seldom said anything about it; except to make jokes. Amoret deeply respected Donald's ability to memorize those long words and complicated phrases and put them together into something which made sense to him, at least, but she also had an underlying conviction that law was the most comical thing in the world. She could not get over the feeling that lawyers and their clients were playing a fantastic game. All business, in fact, seemed like a game to her. How did people ever manage to take it seriously? Sometimes, when she thought about it, she felt sorry for men that they had to be interested in things so far removed from the significant part of life.

And so they were never serious. At least, Amoret was never serious. Donald, sometimes, tended to be a little solemn and thoughtful about things like world affairs or national politics, but she could always coax him out of it and into a cheerier frame of mind.

"There's enough trouble in the world, darling," she would say, sitting on his lap and kissing him, "without *us* worrying about it, too. Let's have fun!" Life must be fun, if it was going to be anything at all. Amoret never had been able to stand the sight of a sober face or the sound of a complaining voice. She detested unhappy people, and would not allow them near her.

Nothing had ever happened yet that she could not, somehow or other, turn into a joke. And she was sure that if everyone else would do the same, the whole world would be much better off than it was.

It must be a relief to Donald, she was sure, after a day of listening to people whine and fret about their taxes or their marriages, to come home to her and know that she would greet him gaily and happily. He said it was, too.

She got out of the tub, slipped into a great terry-cloth robe which dried her instantly, kissed Donald good-by and went into the bedroom, wondering: How shall I look tonight? She rummaged around far back in the closet a few minutes, and came out carrying across her arms a short-skirted evening gown, floating dozens of yards of black lace.

Donald was dressed, handsomer than ever in his dinner jacket, standing in the middle of the room with his hand in his pants' pocket, smoking a cigarette and looking at her with one eye squinted to keep the smoke out.

"Oh!" she cried. "Aren't you gorgeous!" She ran to him, tossing the gown over a chair, and flung herself against his chest. She had forgotten him again, while she was back there in the closet: but, in a way, it was nice that she did, because the surprise was so pleasant each time when she saw him again. "I can't get used to you!" she declared, throwing back her head and smiling up at him, standing on one bare foot and holding the other ankle, swaying back and forth, pretending she was about to fall and giving a little squeal as he caught her.

They played together a few moments, running and leaping around the room, laughing, chasing each other—then suddenly Donald stopped still.

"We're late!"

"Late? But we're here already!" She burst into a peal of laughter.

"I know. And so is everyone else. Now, I'll go out and see about drinks, and you hurry like a good little girl, will you?"

She fluttered her fingers at him. "Go along," she said. "I'll hurry."

A few minutes later she entered the living room, threw

her arms about each guest in turn and kissed them, told them all how marvellous it was to see them, asked if they had everything they wanted, and stood with her arm linked through Donald's, thoroughly happy and delighted.

The room was beautiful: pale shell-pink walls and a mauve-beige carpet. There was one enormous sofa upholstered in mauve silk, chairs covered with dotted damask or beige-and-mauve striped silk, two smaller sofas with pale pink leather. There were dozens of pink roses and many sparkling crystal lamps, several mirrors and much polished silver. Amoret loved all shining shimmering dancing things, everything which gleamed, cast prisms of light, or made a tinkling sound.

They were drinking pink champagne, and now a toast was proposed to Donald and Amoret. His arm circled her waist and they gazed at each other during the toast. Then she went about the room, talking to her guests, and her father persuaded her to have a sip of the champagne. Amoret had never formed the habits of drinking or smoking, for she did not think they would become her, and whatever she wore or said or did must make some positive definite contribution to her attractiveness.

It pleased her to see how well her guests were looking, how handsome most of them were and how well-dressed. The instant they entered her house they belonged to her, and she took pride in them if they were a credit, and was annoyed with them if they were not. Tonight, they were a credit. They should be, of course—they had been carefully hand-picked. It was important to her to be able to feel pride in her guests, more so than ever now that she was married and in her own home, for she could no longer brush whatever she did not like of the guests off onto her mother. Now, if they were unsatisfactory, it was Amoret who would be tarnished by them. She must be exceedingly careful.

That was why Donald's mother presented a difficulty.

Mrs. Jennings was a good-looking woman, several years older than Amoret's mother, but stately and dignified, soft-spoken and well-bred. All that was fine. She even gave every indication of being pleased with Amoret, proud of her, and glad to see her son so happy.

If that had been all there was to it, of course there

would not have been a problem. But Amoret knew there was a great deal more.

For Amoret had an ability which no one knew about, and which they might have refused to acknowledge, if they had. She could, whenever she liked, communicate with other people's secret hearts. And she had been in communication with Mrs. Jennings' heart.

Mrs. Jennings did not know this, and undoubtedly would have done everything in her power to put a stop to such traffic if she had. But it went on, at Amoret's discretion, in Mrs. Jennings' presence and most assuredly against her will. This capacity of Amoret's was the source of a great deal of surprising information, sometimes very unsatisfactory information—as in the case of Mrs. Jennings—but nevertheless it kept Amoret supplied with knowledge no one would willingly have imparted to her in any other way.

When Amoret and Donald had announced their engagement, for example, Mrs. Jennings had kissed Amoret and said that she could not have hoped for such good fortune, either for her son or for herself. Amoret, suspecting this display of good will might not be entirely genuine, used her own method of communication.

"You talk a lot of pretty words," she said. "But you don't mean them. You never wanted Donald to marry anyone—certainly not me."

"Of course I didn't want him to marry anyone. He belongs to me. But you'll have less of him than you think. You'll only be his wife—someone he met after he'd lived more than a quarter of his life. You'll never mean to him what I do." And she had laughed, mockingly.

Even now, when they had been married several months, and anyone could see that Donald was so madly in love with her he didn't care about another thing on earth, she kept it up: "It's only an infatuation he has for you. It's not the same as what he feels for me. I'm not even jealous of you, you poor silly little creature." All this while she had one arm about Amoret, and was beaming upon her.

They went into the dining room, laughing and good-natured, the way people always were in Amoret's presence. She expected the best of them, and they gave it. Now, she sat and looked over the long table and was exceedingly pleased—except, of course, with Donald's mother. But she would not continue to disturb her for long.

The dining room was deep mauve and white, softly lighted, enormously flattering to everyone, but particularly to Amoret. The tablecloth was silver lamé, with two gilt swans in the center and gold service plates. On console tables at either end of the room stood pyramid-shaped camellia trees, laden with pink blossoms, each tree more than three feet high. All during dinner the servants continued to pour pink champagne.

Amoret was gay and gracious, talking to her father on one side and Donald's father on the other. She never talked too much, especially with men, but encouraged them to talk instead and seemed so interested and so impressed that they outdid themselves.

"Just to think," said Mr. Jennings, "that now you are my daughter, too." He took her hand and pressed it warmly. "I feel as if I'd included a fairy princess in my family."

Amoret smiled at him tenderly, for she knew that he meant exactly what he said. She also knew that occasionally he would look at her and wish that he had met her somewhere else and that she had not been Amoret Ames but a poor little girl who would have loved him, instead of Donald, in return for a beautiful mink coat. But she did not mind that, he was such a nice and good man.

You never learned anything significant by conversation, Amoret knew, since it was in talk that people concealed themselves. Only by establishing direct contact with their secret being, could you learn what they honestly felt. There were no lies told then. And they could not be on guard against her discoveries, either, for they did not know she had this power and—amusingly enough—would probably have refused to believe her if she had told them. Others might wonder about the secret of Amoret's perfect success in life—this capacity was her secret.

Even her mother did not know. Only Miles Morgan. And he had the same supersensitivity, himself. Which was one reason why they never tried to fool each other—it would have been useless.

At this very moment Mrs. Jennings was talking to Donald and once, during the conversation, Donald looked down the table to his wife and smiled as their eyes met.

Mrs. Jennings turned her head and glanced briefly. She smiled, too:

"If I could change places with you. If I could have your beauty and your red hair and your youth again and have this man who is my son but who should have been my lover—"

That's what she wants, thought Amoret. I knew it. And now she's admitted it. How ugly! She'd kill me if she could.

But she won't get a chance. If she tries, she won't even be able to find me.

It turned out, of course, that Miles had been right. Everything was so perfectly easy. Amoret did not bring it about suddenly, for then others might have noticed and wanted to know what was going on. She was subtle. Little by little, she withdrew herself from Mrs. Jennings. She took away the sound of her voice; then she removed her image, as easily as stepping away from a mirror. Finally, at the end of the evening, she took away Mrs. Jennings' memory of her. When it was concluded, Amoret breathed a deep satisfying sigh.

How much nicer. How much clearer and cleaner. Mrs. Jennings could no longer tarnish or smear her with her tawdry jealousy and envy.

When Mr. and Mrs. Jnnings were leaving, Donald kissed his mother good-by and Mr. Jennings kissed Amoret. They went out. Amoret noticed how Donald glanced at her, curiously, a little warily, probably wondering if she had noticed that his mother had neglected to tell her good night or to thank her for the party. Perhaps he expected that Amoret would be concerned, or might even pout and find fault and blame him. Nothing of the kind happened. She smiled and took his hand and they went back to join their other guests.

Early the next morning Amoret went to Miles' apartment. They had met there a time or two since her return from Europe and he opened the door himself to let her in. She had on a flame-red tweed skirt, almost the color of her hair, and a turquoise-colored sweater under her sealskin coat. She had rushed out in such a hurry that she had not even remembered to bring Mio.

They stood inside the closed door, and when they kissed it was all the kisses Amoret had ever wanted since she had been a little girl. There was a flavor and fragrance almost intoxicating; a warmth which promised to stay with her forever, even when she was no longer warm herself; there was tenderness and fervor. Miles was not so careful with her as Donald. Now, he reached under her sweater and pinched the nipple of her right breast. She winced and gave a little cry and they both laughed.

"Your husband's probably too much in awe of you for that."

"He is. He thinks I'm delicate. Poor darling. He doesn't know much about women." She glanced around the living room. Miles, naturally, lived in a beautiful apartment, filled with things collected from all over the world. "What were you doing?"

"Getting ready to leave. Remember, I told you the government might want me to do a job?"

"Oh, yes! Can you tell me about it?"

He smiled and shook his head. "Not yet. I shouldn't even have told you that I'm going."

"Is it dangerous, Miles?" she asked him eagerly, feeling cold little chills run over her skin as she thought of it.

Miles shrugged. "I suppose."

"Are you afraid?"

"No. When you get afraid, you get careless—and that's when it happens. Sit down over here."

Miles sat on the sofa and Amoret spread herself at the other end, arms behind her head, legs crossed at the knees, aware of exactly which lines her body showed him in this position, and watching the changing expressions in his eyes. Today, they were blue, like the first time they met.

"How did it go?" he asked her.

"Miles—you wouldn't believe it! I just disappeared from her, that's all. I didn't even have to try very hard. Why, it was wonderful." She opened her hands. "I'm so free!"

"You won't get the habit, will you?"

"No." She shrugged. "I can't think of anyone else I don't like—or who doesn't like me."

"But now that the air's cleared of her, you may find some others, you know. Be a little careful, Amoret. Sometimes it can happen almost against your will. Suppose you did it by mistake sometime, and found you'd lost someone you wanted back again? A power like that has dangers in it for you, as well as others."

Amoret shook her head. "Don't worry, Miles. I'm not

careless. Nothing happens against my will. Miles—Miles, what do you suppose it is that makes you and me different from anyone else in the world?"

"Mostly, I suppose, it's the fact that we think we are."

Amoret jumped off the sofa and came to stand over him. "No, Miles. Because we *know* we are!"

His arms reached up and went around her waist and she slid down upon him, then slowly turned until his body covered hers and they lay together on the couch. "Oh, Miles," she murmured softly. "I love you, I love you." Her hands stroked his hair and face and the slow demanding warmth began to crawl in her body. "Why can't Donald make me feel like this? Why doesn't it seem real when Donald loves me?"

"Maybe you're a little afraid of Donald—" His mouth moved over her face and neck, his hands started chills wherever he touched.

"I'm not afraid of you, though. Am I?" And then, after a moment, she sighed deeply. "Oh, Miles, I wish— I wish I knew someone like you—"

There was no doubt it might be a good thing Miles had to go away for a while.

She was coming to depend upon him more and more —she slipped away to him almost every day now, much oftener than before she was married. She seemed to need increasingly the companionship they had, the perfect understanding, the gaiety and poetic quality of his spirit, tuned to hers in a way Donald's could never be, the peculiar dangerous security he gave.

For she had begun to realize that there was something—still vague—which disturbed her real life with Donald. It was not only Donald's mother. There was something else, which she had not yet discovered, but which she knew made Miles Morgan more and more necessary to her.

She sat naked on her bed, legs crossed, one elbow on one knee, forefinger between her teeth, trying to think what it might be. She had come out of the bath and was about to get dressed to meet Sharon, when she began to think about it. And there she sat, and did not know how long she had been sitting.

Donald is expecting something of me, she decided. There is something he wants, which he hasn't told me about. Yes—that was what it was that had disturbed her. Well, then, if that's it, I can find out easily enough. I'll ask him. Not in words, of course. But suppose I find out and I don't like it? Suppose it's something I can't give him?

Suppose he wants the kind of love I give Miles? Suppose—why, it could be anything!

She jumped off the bed and went to look at herself in a full-length mirror. How beautiful I am, she thought, and gazed at herself with objective pleasure. Her breasts were firm and pointed and pink-nippled, her waist remarkably small, her hips and buttocks round. Her skin was white, with nothing to break its pure expanse but a small soft dark triangle.

What *more* can he possibly want?

Looking at herself made her angry with Donald. What was the matter with him? Didn't he realize how lucky he was? Didn't he know how many men would give anything to have the privileges he had with her? He must be crazy. If he wasn't careful, if he didn't appreciate his good luck, it might not last.

There was a knock at the door and she started.

She slipped into a negligée and went to open it. There stood Sharon, blonde and stunning, smoking a cigarette, wearing a mink coat. "For God's sake!" she said.

Amoret stepped back. "Come on in. What's the matter?"

"I waited half an hour!" Sharon flung off her coat. "I called and the maid said she knocked and your door was locked and you must be in the tub. Are you all right? I was afraid you were sick!"

Amoret listened in amazement. She looked at the clock. She *was* late. But she had not heard any knock. She began to laugh. "Sharon, I'm sorry. The water was running and I didn't hear a thing. Don't be mad at me. Sit down. I'll be ready in a minute."

Sharon shrugged. "I'm used to you being late. But you're later than ever these days. Amoret, talk to me seriously."

Amoret was sitting at the dressing table, making up her face. "About what?"

"About you. Are you—happy?"

"Happy, Sharon? Of course I'm happy! How can you ask such a thing? Isn't it obvious?"

"I suppose it is. I'm sorry. Forget I said it. But you—"

Amoret turned. "I what?"

Sharon sighed. "I shouldn't have brought it up. I wish I hadn't. But since I have— Well, sometimes, Amoret, I feel as though I'm losing you. Oh, I don't mean that the way it sounds. I know I'm not losing your friendship. I mean that sometimes you seem to disappear—you'll be right there and then you're not. I must sound crazy."

"Oh, no, Sharon. I do disappear. But I'm surprised you noticed it, because I don't disappear from everyone—certainly not from you. Just from people who bother me. And then they can't even remember me any more."

Sharon's eyes opened wide and she was staring at as if Amoret had said something fantastic. *"What?"*

Amoret turned back and began to brush on her lipstick. She should have known better than to tell Sharon. What if they had been friends all their lives? That didn't mean that Sharon had the capacity to understand anything as subtle as that. No one in the world could understand it but Miles Morgan.

"Let's not talk about it. And please don't tell anyone I mentioned it to you. But sometime, if you like, I'll show you how it works. On someone unimportant, of course—because once it's been done, it can't be undone. Now let's not be serious any more, Sharon. Let's have lunch and go to the galleries and have fun."

Sharon, however, still looked perplexed and, in fact, very much troubled. "All right," she said softly. "We will."

One thing, Amoret found, led to another.

That very afternoon, as she and Sharon were strolling along Fifth Avenue, they happened to meet an old beau of Amoret's. They stopped and talked and he kept looking at Amoret as if he had not given her up yet. Amoret became annoyed and decided that the best way to handle him was to disappear from him and she did.

In the middle of some story he was telling, she was gone. She was still with Sharon, but not with him.

"What in the hell happened to Amoret?" he demanded of Sharon. "Did I say something to make her mad?"

"Mad?" Sharon glanced at her friend. "She doesn't look mad to me. What gives you such an idea?"

Amoret withdrew herself even further and the next thing he said was: "Now, who were we talking about?"

"Amoret," said Sharon severely.

He screwed up his face. *"Who?"*

"Robert Maitland! Are you out of your mind?"

"Look," he said, and gently patted Sharon's arm. "I've got to meet someone. I'm late right now. I'll give you a ring one of these days. Nice to have seen you—" and he hurried away.

Amoret gave a peal of high happy laughter, slipped her arm through Sharon's and they strolled along among all the other mink-coated aimlessly wandering women.

"You see?" said Amoret. "Isn't it fun?" As Miles had said, it could easily become a habit.

When you got right down to it, there were so many people who could be disposed of. It didn't hurt them, after all, so there was nothing to feel guilty about. And it relieved you of a great deal of unnecessary annoyance in life. It made your surroundings that much pleasanter.

By the time Miles came back, after Christmas, Amoret had quite a story to tell him.

"It works on all kinds of people!" she said happily.

Miles smiled tolerantly and stroked her cheek. "Who, for instance?"

"Well—after Donald's mother, there was Bob Maitland. You remember—he was an old beau of mine. I met him on the street one day and he was standing there thinking that he'd always wanted to sleep with me and never had and now someone else did and he was wondering about it and imagining himself in Donald's place and it made me so mad that I disappeared from him. He'll never think about *that* any more!"

"Who else?"

"A policeman. I drove through a red light and he came to arrest me and I knew Donald would be furious and I just disappeared right under his nose and he had to tear up his silly ticket and throw it away and then I drove off."

Amoret and Miles laughed hilariously.

"To think," she said, "of all the years I've let people

see me and hear me and know me and pester me—when I could have disappeared from them!"

"But anyone might bother you in some way or other, sometime or other, darling. I've told you—you must be a little careful. This is strange medicine—the more you use it, the stronger it gets. You may disappear someday from someone you'd later regret."

Amoret was perfectly confident, intoxicated with her new power. "That won't happen. And, if it does, I'll always have you. Did you get married, by the way?"

Miles snapped his fingers. "By God, I did."

"Which one?"

"A surprise, like we decided. I married an international spy I met on this trip."

"Where is she?" Amoret looked around the room.

"Working, I suppose. Why? You don't want to meet her, do you?"

"I should say not! But I guess it eases my conscience a little—knowing that you're married, too."

He gave her a wry smile. "That's probably a kind of reasoning that no one but you and me could follow."

"Well—" said Amoret, "I hope you'll like being married better than I do." She drew on her gloves. "I must go, Miles. You know, I think that perhaps Donald is beginning to guess something about you and me."

"What gives you that idea?"

Amoret sighed, drew her mink collar up close, and gazed pensively down at the small bunch of violets she held in her black-gloved hands. "He asked me if I had ever loved anyone but him. I told him no, of course. But I suppose that he can tell by now that I don't love him with all my heart and soul, as the saying goes. Why is it men are never satisfied with whatever amount of love you can give them?"

"Because there's no such thing as enough love, I guess. What else did he say?"

"He said that it was bad enough what I had done to his mother, but now he's afraid I'll do it to him, too. I guess he thinks it only works on his family!" At that, she threw back her head and laughed joyously; so did Miles.

"You're a natural-born sorceress, aren't you? You really enjoy it."

"Of course! It's what everyone wants to be, isn't it?"

"But there's a catch nowadays. Among the primitives —and I've spent a lot of time with them, as an anthropologist—they are held in awe and fear and given places of great honor. But we're more civilized, and among us they wind up in the booby hatch."

Amoret laughed harder at that than almost anything she had ever heard. He said it so offhandedly, with such blithe detachment, that it struck her as one of the funniest notions she had encountered.

"Not unless they catch you. I'm sure no *clever* witch was ever burned at the stake."

Miles bent and kissed her gently. "Be careful, darling. You're so impetuous—sometimes I worry about you."

"Don't worry, Miles. Just go somewhere and keep busy." She kissed her fingertips to him and left.

Amoret had always been the neatest cleanest little girl. She could never stand to have things out of order. And this new accomplishment of hers made it possible to keep things in better order than ever.

And so she proceeded with the gradual perfection of her world. She did not propose to perfect the world for anyone but herself since, after all, each individual has his own private and wholly personal image of what he wants the world to be. She could not have perfected it to the satisfaction of any other person if she tried and, knowing that, she knew a great deal more than anyone but Miles Morgan.

One day she heard a knock at her bedroom door and absently went to answer it, forgetting that she was naked. There stood the butler. Of course, after that there was nothing to do but remove herself from his knowledge and memory, and presently he had to be fired because it made giving orders too difficult. But things of that sort were a minor inconvenience, trivial compared with the great gains she made.

She got rid of a couple of women friends, who had annoyed her for years by coveting her looks and personality and clothes. She disappeared from the sight of an impertinent elevator boy and thenceforth he was forced to take up and down in the elevator someone he could not see. When the dentist hurt her with a novocain injection, she vanished from the chair. And occasionally, out of sheer mischief, she removed herself from someone who had not even bothered her, just to see the surprised look on their faces.

Miles Morgan warned her several times that it was beginning to get out of hand, but she would not pay attention. "Don't tell me you're a moralist!" she chided him. "I'm having fun!"

A few weeks later, she met Miles' wife.

Amoret and Donald went to a big cocktail party at the home of friends they had known for several years. The husband was a publisher and the wife a painter, and both had inherited considerable money. All kinds of people were there. Amoret and Donald got separated and Amoret strolled around, talking to friends and acquaintances, and finally she was introduced to Miles' wife. The woman was not using Miles' name—in fact, she was introduced as Miss Marianna Knight, which was not even the maiden name of Miles' wife. Amoret had never seen either his wife or a picture of her, but nevertheless she recognized her instantly.

Miss Knight, on the other hand, pretended not to have the slightest idea who Amoret was. Her dissimulation, of course, was expert, as a result of her training as an international spy.

"Why isn't your husband here?" inquired Amoret.

Amoret was looking unusually beautiful. Everyone said that she was more exquisite than ever these days and that marriage apparently agreed with her. She wore a short silvery gown which lay upon her body like metallic wax. Her red hair, parted in the center, was drawn sleekly across her ears and fastened at one side with two white water lilies.

Miss Knight was a rather beautiful woman herself— the most beautiful in the room, next to Amoret. That could have been why she looked at Amoret with polite hostility, except, of course, that it was actually because of Miles.

"We don't go around together much," said Miss Knight coldly, "now that we're divorced."

Amoret smiled.

"Why do you ask?" continued Miss Knight, evidently not liking Amoret's smile, which was designed to indicate she saw through her and would not be fooled. "Do you know him?"

"I know him very well—naturally," said Amoret. "There's no point pretending you're divorced. After all, Miles and I discussed getting married, but decided we'd be happier together this way."

"Miles?" demanded Miss Knight sharply. "Miles Who? My husband's name was Bill. Bill Randall."

Amoret shook her head gently. "No. His name is Miles. He may have told you it was something else—but that was only a joke. Miles love to play jokes on people."

Miss Knight's eyes were beginning to shine brightly and she breathed a little faster. "Look, here, Mrs. Whoever-youare—"

"Mrs. Donald Jennings. I was Amoret Ames. That's my husband over there."

Miss Knight glanced around. "He keeps a watch on you—I think I can understand why."

"Because he's madly in love with me, that's why. He loves me more than anyone in the world and I love him more than anyone but Miles. And my mother."

Miss Knight gave a slight gasp. "Would you excuse me, please? I—I have to make a telephone call."

Amoret gave a gracious little wave of her hand and turned away. Then, abruptly, she turned back. "Just a moment, Miss Knight. I hope you won't spy on *me!*"

"Spy on you? Why in the hell should I spy on you?"

"Just as a matter of habit, for one thing. And because of your jealousy, for another. I wanted to let you know that it wouldn't be any use. If you try, you won't be able to find me."

"I assure you, Mrs. Jennings, I shall try *not* to find you!" She walked swiftly away.

Amoret smiled to a man who had just come up. "Eccentric sort of woman," she said, indicating Miss Knight. "Who is she, anyway?"

"I think she reads television commercials. Amoret, do you know that you're more beautiful every time I—"

Amoret smiled up at him, listening happily to his compliments. But then, out of the corner of her eye, she saw Miss Knight talking to Donald and excused herself to go break up the conversation. Miss Knight saw her coming and was gone when she got there.

Amoret slipped her arm through Donald's and gave him her most brilliant smile. Donald smiled back but he was looking vaguely worried again. He looked worried rather often recently. Amoret hoped that he was not working too hard and making himself sick.

"What was that woman talking about?" she asked.

Donald shrugged. "Nothing in particular. Why?"

"Was she talking about me?"

"What makes you think she was? She said you were extraordinarily beautiful."

"She said more than that, Donald," teased Amoret. "Tell me what it was."

"She's jealous of you. Let's go have dinner, darling. I've got kind of a headache."

"You had a headache last week," said Amoret, and pouted. She did not like to have people be sick any better than she liked to have them be gloomy. "Have you a fever? All right—let's go home. I'll make you well," she assured him.

They had dinner served before the fireplace in the living room. But, even though Amoret put on her new sapphire-blue negligee which he had never seen before, and twirled her hair on top of her head with diamond clasps to hold it, and told him funny little stories and talked with their own special language to him—in spite of all that, Donald continued to seem worried and abstracted. Finally, when they were alone, she curled up on his lap and kissed him.

"What is it, darling? You have a secret from me. Has something gone wrong at the office?"

"No. Everything's fine." His head was against her cheek and his arms held her close. He sighed.

"Donald! What is it? Tell me!" She tugged at his lapels. "You must tell me!"

"It's nothing, Amoret. Just that damned fool woman."

"What did she say? Tell me, tell me!" She was beginning to sound frantic.

"Well— She said— Okay. She said that she had the most interesting conversation with you about her ex-husband. She said you used to know him very well. I didn't like the way she said very well. That's all. Forgive me, Amoret. I know I'm jealous of you and I'm sorry."

Amoret looked at him seriously a moment, her eyes

big and thoughtful, and then suddenly she laughed and hugged him. "Oh, Donald! How nice of you to be jealous! But you know you have no reason—don't you?"

Donald regarded her soberly, carefully, but as she continued to gaze back at him with her wide blue eyes, his face changed and he caught her against him once more and began kissing her as if he wanted to eat her up. "I know it," he muttered. "Of course I know it. But if you ever loved anyone else—if you ever left me—God, I think I'd die."

His kisses became more violent, more demanding, and in a sudden panic-stricken moment, fearing that some terrible disaster was about to overtake her, Amoret started struggling. He freed her instantly and she got to her feet, reaching up to put her hair in place, straightening her low-cut gown. She felt somewhat as if she had crawled out of a train wreck, stunned, and gradually discovered with intense, pouring relief, that she had not been injured after all.

"I'm sorry," he said apologetically. "Did I hurt you?" He looked drunk, though she knew he had not had a drink all evening.

Donald continued to stare at her for several moments and she stared back at him. Her face had the look of a wild animal, fascinated by a briliant light turned suddenly upon it. She was beginning to realize what it was which had been disturbing their relationship, which she had tried to avoid discovering. Donald wanted her completely for himself. He wanted to possess and envelop her, take away her freedom of choice and action, absorb her personality into his and reduce her to a condition where she would be helpless without him.

He would even take Miles Morgan from her if she let him—move, himself, into the space which Miles occupied, and gradually crowd him out. Donald would do those things without even knowing of Miles' existence, but merely by his own persistent demands and his love which was like a great mantle flung over her, growing heavier and heavier, blotting out everything else in her life, leaving her nothing but a dark breathless space to be shared with him.

He wanted to kill her!

He called it love, but it was her death he sought.

As she stared at him, finally realizing these things, she had begun to hate and fear him as if he were a ravening monster. Donald was still watching her, his face heavy and yearning, as she had never seen it before.

"Oh, I love you so goddamned much," he said now, as if he suffered some kind of pain. "Amoret—Amoret, when can we have a baby?"

There.

That was proof.

"What would we do with a baby?" she asked innocently, trying to conceal her panic.

Donald laughed. "Take care of it, of course. Love it and bring it up. What else do you do with a baby?"

She could scarcely breathe now. She had a terrified sense of having been rushed backward in time to become the baby herself, floating in liquid warmth, struggling with frantic rage and energy to escape into the open. She would not go back there! He could kill her, but he could never force her to go back!

But she must be very canny. She must not say or do the wrong thing, give him any clues. She felt convinced that he would suddenly take her into his hands, crush her down to the size of a baby, and force her back to that dark airless terrifying death from which she had once emerged. If she let him know what she was thinking, he would be so furious that he might do it.

Walk very lightly, she told herself.

Softly and lightly.

It's the only way out.

Make him think it's a game and we're both having fun. Then—he'll look the other way.

"But Donald—" she protested, laughing now, "I'm not old enough!"

"Not old enough?" he repeated incredulously.

"I mean, our marriage isn't. Let's wait a little longer. I know!" Suddenly she clapped her hands and leaned over him as if the most delightful notion had just occurred. "*I'll* be your baby!"

Donald shook his head, not in denial of her suggestion but to ward off some private thought; then he smiled. "All right, honey. We won't talk about it any more. You are my baby, aren't you?" He stood up and took her into his arms again. "I guess I'm still afraid of losing you."

"Oh, no, Donald!"

As Donald held and stroked her, gently now, he knew that what she had said was true: she was his baby. She was still a child. And a child could not give birth to a child. There was something indecent in the very thought of Amoret pregnant, as he considered it. But he would be patient, and in time she would grow up. Just now, however, she did not know anything of serious adult emotions and did not want to. He hoped that he had not made a mistake, trying to treat her like a woman too soon.

Miles was away on another trip. This time, he was in Mexico, doing some archaeological work among the Aztec ruins for the Museum of Natural History. Amoret sent him a wire and begged him to return immediately.

Miles looked grim when she told him what Donald had said.

He had flown back, piloting his own plane, and he arrived with a deep tan and a week's growth of beard, black and bristly, like that her father used to have sometimes at their summer camp when he decided not to shave. Amoret thought that Miles looked handsomer than ever, standing with his hands in his pockets, his dark broad hairy chest and shoulders bare, for she had come early and he was only half-dressed.

"That's the way you should look all the time! I've never seen you so handsome. You look like a pirate!"

Miles was scowling. "Now, what's this business about babies?"

Amoret sighed. "Donald mentioned it the other night." Her panic was gone. She felt so safe, here with Miles, that she was actually sorry for Donald. What a blunder he had made. But, after all, there was no way he could have known about Miles. It had been a natural enough kind of blunder for someone who lived in the workaday world which Donald inhabited, completely blind to all the other more mysterious, fascinating worlds about him.

"I don't like that," said Miles. "He's got a hell of a nerve."

Amoret laughed. "That's what I thought."

"After all, he only has you—or as much of you as he does have—on *my* sufferance. Maybe it's time for him to find out about me."

"Oh, no, Miles," said Amoret gravely. "You don't know how much he loves me."

"He loves you less than I do—and you love him less than you do me."

"Yes," agreed Amoret. "Very much less." She glanced sideways. "Half of our trouble is that he loves me too much. When you love me, Miles, it doesn't make me unhappy the way it does when Donald loves me. Being loved by you is nice—it's like being loved by myself."

"Well, after all," said Miles. "When you get right down to it—" His eyes, she noticed, were black today.

Miles sat down, spread his legs wide and leaned forward, elbows on his knees. He stared at the floor, thinking, and Amoret watched him, breathing a little faster. He looked strong and vital and taut with magnificent recklessness. Miles would do whatever came into his head. He was not like Donald, slow and thoughtful, taking care not to act too swiftly. No, Miles was just the opposite of that.

"Maybe I'll take you away from him," said Miles, still staring at the floor, not glancing up at her.

"But we decided long ago that we wanted to keep what we have and not wear it out by using it every day."

Miles gave an impatient smack of one fist into the palm of the other hand, and stood up again. "What's the matter with him, anyway? Wouldn't you think a man would have some realization of how much his wife belongs to him, and not try to force her to give more than she can?"

"Perhaps he does, Miles. Perhaps that's why he wants—"

"I think I'll take you back to Mexico with me. He's beginning to abuse his privileges, and once he starts that, there'll be no stopping him."

"Would I like Mexico?" she asked dubiously. "I've heard it's dirty."

"Not where I'll take you. You'll have everything just as you like it there. When you get tired, or I do, we'll leave."

Amoret's eyes sparkled with happy excitement. "Oh, Miles, we'd have a glorious time, wouldn't we? But what about Donald? He's going to miss me."

"He won't miss you," said Miles slowly, "if he's already forgotten that you exist."

"You mean—I should—" Amoret's voice was a whisper, tentative, frightened. She had never taken herself from anyone who loved her. "Oh, Miles—" she breathed. "I'm scared. It's what you warned me about. He could never have me back again." She shook her head. "Poor Donald."

Miles walked over, hands still in his pockets, and stood staring out the great ceiling-high windows at the blocks and spires of the city, misted with fog and smoke. Amoret followed him. The muscles of his jaws were working, flickering impatiently. She had never seen him more angry or determined. There was a ruthless quality to him now. The lightness and poetry had gone. It was only the other side she could see—the side composed of darkness, savage egotism; there was an almost sinister mystery about him. And yet, she would rather abandon herself to that, than submit to the greater tyranny of Donald's loving devotion.

"I'm going with you! Donald will forget he ever knew me!"

There.

It was done.

She stopped, her hand to her heart, almost as if she had felt it pause in its beating. The next instant Miles caught her up and swung her off the ground and held her high in the air, and she was laughing down at him, her hands reaching out to touch his rough bearded face. In their eyes was the perfect triumph they had accomplished over anyone—not only Donald—who would ever try to part them or to put something new between them.

"I love you, Amoret!" Miles' voice rang with authority and passion.

"I love you, Miles! He's lost me!"

It was true, as Miles had said. The Mexico he took her to was not dirty or tawdry. They lived in a camp his men had set up under his instructions, quiet swarthy obedient men, who accomplished almost instantly every command he gave them. They were silent and soft-moving as cats, or as figures in a dream, except when they sang their strange uncanny music, and then their voices were melodious and clear and strong. Amoret would lie in the silken tent, which was her home now, listening to them for hours, without any realization of the passage of time.

The countryside about them was fantastic. It looked like nothing she had ever seen or heard of before.

On one side of their camp—a vast city of tents striped every imaginable color, some of the colors gleaming and irridescent—was a desert, reaching away into what must have been eternity. No mountains were to be seen in the distance, only the broad flat monotonous expanse of pale yellow and orange sand. About the desert cropped great cactus bushes, sallow green in color, taller than Miles, thick and juicy-looking, with malignant spikes which were believed to contain fatal poison. No one ever dared touch them, for the tales of those who had were terrifying enough to preclude curiosity. Strange bones, phosphorescent white, littered the desert, but no one knew to whom or what they had belonged or how they came to be there, or even how many ages had gone by since their original owners had died.

The other side was very different. There, it was green and fertile, the meadows spangled with flowers, yellow, brilliant orange, deep blue. Streams went rushing through the fields, lively, capricious, tumbling and dancing. The silence of the other side was broken here by numberless bright little birds which darted and sang the sweetest imaginable music. There were groves of glimmering trees, waterfalls which seemed to come from nowhere, but fell splashing down great heights.

Between these two very different worlds, Amoret and Miles made their home.

Miles went away early in the morning, on his archaeological expeditions, and came home with the sunset or sometimes not until the moon was out. Occasionally, he was away for two or three days at a time, but Amoret never worried about his absences or grew fretful. She had enough to keep her amused and entertained, and she had every comfort and luxury which could be provided.

Often, he brought her presents, found in the ruins—grotesque little statues which made her laugh, strings of turquoise and silver to hang about her neck, rings to decorate her toes and fingers, broken vases for the flowers she gathered. He almost always returned with something to surprise her.

And Donald seemed so far away, she scarcely thought of him.

"I had no idea," she told Miles, "how bored I was with

my former life. Now it seems so silly and pointless. Oh, Miles, thank you for bringing me here!"

They were in their tremendous tent, made of heavy silk, striped yellow, red, green, orange, purple, blue. There was no furniture in the tent, only enormous mattresses, deep and soft, covered with velvet in all the brilliant shades of the silk. Crystal lamps burned on pedestals, when it grew dark. There were several chests, filled with silks, spilling forth plumes and jewels. A single low broad ebony table carried their dinner, bowls full of succulent fruits and dishes seasoned with unknown spices, served to them on ancient silver plates. Amoret never wondered how Miles accomplished these miracles; she took it for granted they were no problem to him, but came about as a result of his will that they should exist for her pleasure.

There were no other women in the camp—only Amoret. Perhaps that was what made it seem so restful, without sharp sounds or quick jagged movement.

Miles lay stretched on one of the scarlet velvet mattresses, watching her and smiling. They did not need to talk very much, only to be together, each feeling the other's contentment and happiness. And, though Miles worked hard all day at the ruins, he was never tired at night. His energy seemed inexhaustible, his strength even greater than she had realized, or perhaps it had increased since their arrival here.

"No wonder you never stayed long in New York," she told him, plucking great full black grapes from the cluster she held, putting first one into her mouth and then one into his. She knelt beside him on the cushion. Amoret was wearing emerald-green pants, purposely ragged below her knees, and a gold cloth top which did not quite cover her breasts. Little gold bells tinkled about her ankles, her eyelids were painted gold, and the ends of her hair were caught with dozens of small gold rings. Every day she created a new costume, to wear for Miles and surprise him. It was one of their favorite games, seeing what Amoret would have on when he came home at night.

"I can't stay long in any one place," said Miles. "We seem to have been here for some time now."

If Miles was getting restless, then they must move. "Perhaps I'll go back and visit my mother," she said.

THE SILENT LAND 245

"She'll probably want to know what you did to Donald and why you did it."

"I'll just tell her that I had to. She'll understand."

"I'm not so sure. Haven't you noticed how seldom it is that people will leave each other alone to live as suits them best?"

"Of course I have, Miles! That's why I love you!"

And she flung herself upon him, kissing him, stroking his naked chest and back, smelling the strong male odor of his skin. He caught her roughly and as he kissed her the sharp edges of his teeth cut into her lips, not enough to raise a welt or draw spots of blood, only enough so the kiss was partly a struggle, token of his physical dominance. When Miles made love to her it was with violence and exuberant passion; there was an undercurrent of fury in it, and the constant reminder that he was her master. He was even a little cruel, bruising her arms and thighs, ploughing into her, spending his full strength and violence until she sobbed and beat his shoulders with her fists, begging him to kill her.

"Sometime," he once said, "we'll die together."

"Yes, Miles—we will!" cried Amoret, grateful and humble.

And then, deep in the night, they would get up and wander about the desert, bemused by the moonlight which shone so strangely there, or walk in their bare feet across the meadows and bathe in cool streams.

"This is what I've wanted all my life," she said. "Now I know that I was never happy before. I adore you."

When she talked that way, he would smile, and all his tenderness would return. That, perhaps, was why she loved him so much: this shifting of his personality between violence and tenderness. For between these two extremes, and all the subtleties of which they were composed, he gave her the conviction of being fixed, by his will, in time and space.

"You," she told him, "are the only god I have or need. Religion was never meant for women, was it?"

"It may have been meant for women who can't love a man." He was smiling down at her as he spoke.

Amoret burst out laughing. "Aren't we bad? Aren't we naughty, though? We say and do and think everything that's wrong, don't we? How delightful it is! How I wish I'd begun to be bad much sooner!"

"I'll fly you back," said Miles. "You can see your mother, and I'll see my wife."

"Your wife! I'd forgotten all about her! Oh, Miles, isn't that the funniest thing?" And they laughed together, until their stomach muscles ached, about Miles' wife.

When Amoret walked about her own apartment again, she found that several changes had occurred during her absence. The living room, for instance, had a great many huge trembling crystal lamps, which she certainly had not ordered. She looked at them carefully, admiring how beautifully they were made, wondering whom they were supposed to replace.

The same thing had happened in the bedroom, too, and, to a lesser extent, in the dining room. The apartment was peculiarly silent, except now and then when a breeze touched the crystal drops and made them tinkle.

"Mother," said Amoret, and frowned slightly, "why have all those lamps been put around?"

Her mother looked puzzled. "What lamps, darling? There aren't any new lamps."

"Of course there are," said Amoret. "But if you don't want to discuss them—" She shrugged. "I don't care. Though I do think it would be nice if I were consulted about changes in my own house."

"It's been a little difficult to consult you about anything at all recently, Amoret."

Amoret noticed now that her mother looked tired and she felt a quick anguished pity. She kissed her gently. "What's the trouble, Mother? Is something wrong?"

Her mother sighed. "I don't know what to say, Amoret. I'm afraid that anything I might say would upset you."

"Why should it?" asked Amoret. "Surely you're not angry because I was away for a little while?"

Her mother closed her eyes. She looked so sad, so sad. I must think of a joke, thought Amoret. And yet, she felt a little sad now, too. She wondered why.

"Is it Donald?" she asked softly, and knelt beside her mother's chair, looking up at her. "Is it Donald that you're worried about?"

"Why did you do it, Amoret? *Why* did you do it?"

"I had to," said Amoret. "It didn't hurt him—"

"Darling, you hurt him a great deal. He loves you so very very much. And he thought that you were perfectly happy together. *Why* did you do it?"

Amoret had begun to suspect that other people were not only incapable of contacting one another's secret thoughts and feelings, but that they also lacked ability to perceive what happened when she withdrew from one of them. They had not her instinctive knowledge of the world's arrangement. Their vision was warped, their hearing faulty, and their recollections out of proper focus. They knew, therefore, only as much of reality as they could permit themselves to know, and that was very little. She pitied them for having been condemned to so small an area of space and time and experience.

But she would not mention it. No. She would be kind and considerate about that.

"Donald was not satisfied with what I could give him. He wanted much love—I've forgotten by now what it was. But it was something I couldn't give him. And I knew that he would keep wanting it and from time to time would try to make me give it. That's why I went away from him. I had to, because of—" Suddenly she stopped, horrified to realize that she had been about to mention Miles Morgan. It was as if she had run to the edge of a terrible abyss and halted there, teetering, sick with fear and the yearning for her own destruction, which now she clearly recognized for the first time. Panic-stricken, she backed away, feeling as though her body had been wrung out like a rag, and she sank down onto her heels, letting her head fall forward. No. She would not make that leap this time.

Her mother touched her. "Because of whom, Amoret?"

Amoret twisted away. "Because of no one. Because of myself. That's all."

"Amoret—if you would tell me—"

Suddenly Amoret looked up, her eyes bright and hard and full of fear. "I've never lied to you!" she cried. "What are all of you trying to do to me? You've got to stop it! I can't stand to be badgered and pulled at! You must leave me alone or I'll—die!"

She flung herself onto the floor, covered her face with her arms and began sobbing. I'll cry until there's nothing left of me, she vowed. I'll cry until none of them can find me. Then they'll let me be, they'll let me have a little peace. But it was not only her mother she feared, or Donald, or her father, or her friends. She did not really fear them at all. It was those others. The ones who were searching for her, who would find her and capture her and take her with them to some wild remote place and there torture her until she died.

Her mother knelt on the floor beside her, her arms about her, stroking and petting her as when she was a little girl. Amoret's sobs grew quieter, her terror melted, and at last she lay exhausted in her mother's arms.

"There, there, darling," her mother crooned. "I'm sorry. I'm sorry I upset my little girl. Don't be angry with me, Amoret. We have all been—worried."

Amoret lifted her wet face, which was now earnest and pleading and intense. "But you mustn't worry about me. I was very happy. Don't any of you worry, please. I can't stand to be worried about."

When she told Miles, he was not at all surprised. "I expected that, Amoret. People can not let each other alone. They clutch and paw and try to suck each other dry. They're all so frightened. They're not as lucky as we are."

"No," said Amoret thoughtfully. "They aren't. We have the very thing they want." She gazed at him seriously, and then she whispered: "They'd take it away from us if they could, wouldn't they?"

"I suppose they would. They would think they were doing it for our own good, you know." He smiled, looking rather sardonic, and Amoret admired the expression which struck her with awe.

"It's becoming very quiet," she said, after a few moments. "Wherever I go, it's quieter now. It frightens me a little, Miles. What do you think causes it? Why should the world grow still? It's unnatural. Noise is part of life, isn't it? If it grows completely still—will I be dead?" She asked the questions wonderingly, softly, but she was, as she had said, beginning to be frightened.

"I don't know," said Miles seriously.

Amoret sighed. "I was always so happy. I was such a happy child, my mother said. Now, I'm only happy when I'm with you." She glanced up at him. "Perhaps I should stay with you all the time, and never go back to them at all."

"You can't, Amoret. You must go back sometimes."

"Yes," she agreed, and turned to leave. "I know I must." She paused at the doorway and looked up at him again. "I wonder why?"

"You know why. That's your real life—you can't leave it altogether."

"Can't, can't," murmured Amoret. "Even you say 'can't' to me."

But then they smiled again and he kissed her and presently she was gone. That was the day Sharon lost her. It was Sharon's own fault, of course.

By now it was early spring and they had lunch together and then went shopping. Amoret's passage through a store was like that of a butterfly through a garden. She lit briefly and delicately at one counter after another, directing which things were to be sent home. She made jokes with the salesgirls and they with her; a carnival might have arrived. People watched her, wistful and admiringly at such beauty and the reckless abandon with which she spent money. She never had to give her name, for they all knew her. But today she bought some shoes from a new salesman and, when he asked for her charge, she said: "Amoret Ames."

Sharon nudged her, and Amoret looked at her in surprise. "You gave him your maiden name," whispered Sharon.

"Well?" said Amoret. The man was waiting, holding his pencil, and Amoret told him her address. As they walked away Amoret asked Sharon what the trouble was.

"You gave him your maiden name," repeated Sharon.

"Why not?"

"Haven't you been using Donald's money? You always did before."

"That was before Donald lost me," said Amoret.

They had come out of Bergdorf Goodman and walked to the edge of the plaza. Now they stopped and looked at each other.

"Amoret—please tell me what's going on. Everything's so damned mysterious. Donald acts as if it's the end of the world and your family is upset and Donald's mother told me she didn't want to go to Europe but Donald insisted. What's it all about?"

Amoret started to walk on. Flocks of pigeons waddled aside for them or flew off, to settle again a few feet away, nibbling and pecking, bobbing their heads forward and back. Amoret smiled tenderly as she watched them.

"Sharon, you're like everyone else who takes the world for what it seems to be."

"For what it seems to be? I wish I could. I'd be glad to. I feel as if the world's breaking up—the world we've known, with our friendship and our families and the things we've always counted on. It *is* breaking up, Amoret. And you're the one who's doing it!"

They stopped again, in front of the Plaza Hotel now, and while people came and went up and down the steps, talking loudly, saying hello and good-by, getting in and out of taxicabs, Amoret and Sharon faced each other with hostility, for the first time in their lives.

"You won't leave me alone, either, will you?" asked Amoret.

Sharon's eyes filled with tears. "Amoret—please. It's getting harder and harder to talk to you. I feel as though you're disappearing right before my eyes."

"I will, unless you stop bothering me. I've never hurt anyone, Sharon. And I'm not hurting you, unless you think so. You want too much from me."

"I only want your confidence and trust." Sharon was begging. "I've always had it before. Why take it away from me now—when perhaps I could help you?"

"What makes you think I need help?"

"Of course you do! Oh, Amoret—if you knew what your mother's been through! And your father! And you know what you've done to Donald!"

Amoret glanced sideways, thinking over what Sharon was saying, idly watching three young girls who talked and laughed nearby, wondering how they came to have so few problems in life, when hers seemed to be multiplying almost by the moment. She felt a great pressure begin to weigh upon her, as if God had leaned down from heaven and were using her as an arm rest. Her chest felt the pressure from inside, too, and she was afraid that if she tried to draw a deep breath she would not be able to do so. She was too afraid even to try, for fear of finding that she had begun to smother.

"I haven't done anything to Donald," said Amoret with quiet firmness. "I haven't done anything to any of you. It is you who are *trying* to do something to me. But I won't let you. I refuse to have you do it. There." She gazed levelly at Sharon. "I warn you—stop trying. Anyway," she added, "I had a right to be in Mexico for a little while."

Sharon's eyes snapped wide open, and so did her mouth. "Mexico? You haven't been in Mexico since your parents took you there when you were eight years old!"

I never should have mentioned it, thought Amoret. I can't imagine why I did. What am I apologizing for? She's got me on the defensive. The first thing you know I'll be explaining to her that I had to make Donald give me up because of Miles. And if I once do that—I'll have to leave them all.

She continued to gaze calmly and serenely at her friend: Sharon is saying only part of what she really means. I wonder if I should find out what the rest of it is.

No, she decided. She had become increasingly reluctant, these days, to communicate with the secret hearts of her family and friends. I'd rather not know. I'm sure not to like it. It's something ugly—I can tell that, even from here.

"All right," said Amoret. "Suppose I haven't been to Mexico?" It was only a test, of course.

Suddenly Sharon grabbed her friend's arms and gave her a quick light shake. "Amoret!" she cried.

Amoret stared at her steadily. You won't leave me alone, will you? This is only the beginning, I can see that. You'll bother me more and more. Our friendship is gone. You don't want to be my friend any more. You want to pull at me and torture me and make me answer your questions. Well, I can't do it. I can't, and I won't. Good-by, Sharon. Good-by.

"Amoret!" cried Sharon again, and now her voice had a terrified piercing sound. People turned, to look at the two beautiful young women standing confronting each other. After several moments the girl with the red hair, wearing a sleek fitted black suit and carrying a pale mink stole over her arm, turned and walked away.

"Amoret!" cried the other girl, then put her gloved hands to her mouth, suddenly began to cry, and ran up the stairs and into the hotel.

When Amoret got home that night she found that there were more tinkling crystal lamps in the apartment. The place was beginning to look like a crystal forest, and the faint music which the drops made as they lightly touched, was the only sound she could hear. The silence was very soothing, and yet she grew steadily more afraid. She wanted to find Miles and talk to him and have him comfort her, but he had gone to Europe to write some articles on the war situation for a great national syndicate.

"It's too quiet," she said to her mother, when she and her mother and father and Donald sat down to dinner that night.

It seemed a little strange to her that Donald remained even though he could no longer see her or hear her voice or even remember her. She, of course, continued to see and hear everything he did. Perhaps he was staying until he could find a new apartment.

Her mother, nowadays, hastened to agree with her most trifling comment. "Yes," she said eagerly, and smiled. "It is quiet, isn't it? Shall we turn on the phonograph?"

Donald promptly got up and went to turn on the music. He came back and asked Mrs. Ames if she liked it, and Mrs. Ames asked her daughter.

"It's very pretty," said Amoret, and sat back to wait for the maid to serve the next course. "I liked it better the way they eat in Mexico," remarked Amoret, thinking of how she and Miles used to lie on velvet cushions, romping and making love with their meals.

"You didn't like it at the time," said her father jovially. "Don't you remember how you thought the tortillas were made of cardboard?" He laughed, and Amoret looked at him directly, wondering why he should bring that up. Mrs. Ames glanced at him and frowned. Amoret noticed it.

"I don't mean to be rude," said Amoret, "but I think that all of you are behaving very strangely these days. Even Sharon. Has something happened that you won't tell me about? Has anyone been hurt or killed?"

Amoret's mother gave an involuntary little gasp, and

Donald suddenly seemed to choke on his food and got up and excused himself from the room.

"Amoret—" said her father. She looked at him. His face and tone were grave. "If you've been playing a game—don't you think you've carried it far enough?"

Now *he* was going to begin.

"You've always loved to play pranks on people, I know, darling. But they're beginning to hurt. Donald is desperate, as you must know."

"And, sweetheart," added Mrs. Ames, "Sharon came to see me this afternoon almost in hysterics. You know how much she loves you."

"Why use love as a weapon?" asked Amoret.

Both her parents sighed.

"Perhaps we indulged her too much," said Mr. Ames in a low voice to his wife.

"Hush. Don't say such things."

"I don't mind," said Amoret.

"Now, Amoret," said her father, his voice stern again, "listen to me. We must all learn to do certain things which may not please us. That is one of the laws of life. Your mother and I protected you from unpleasantness as much as possible. Even as a child you had very little tolerance for anything but beauty and gaiety and we, naturally, found that charming and tried to avoid the entrance of anything unpleasant into your life. But now you're a grown woman and married, with your own home and responsibilities. And part of the responsibility of a grown-up is to accept some measure of concern for others. Can you tell me why you should find that such a difficult thing to do?"

"Why, Dad. You're talking to me as if I were five."

"Darling," said Mrs. Ames to her husband. "Why don't you leave Amoret alone for now? Can't you see she's disturbed?"

"No, Mother, I'm not disturbed. It's you and Dad and the others who are. I'm sorry for all of you, but I don't consider myself to blame. My own life is perfectly happy."

Her father got up and excused himself from the table. Amoret watched him leave the room: He won't be satisfied until he's badgered me into a corner, either.

"Do you realize," she asked her mother, "that it's come to the point where I have only one person who does not try to tear me apart to find something in me they hope to find?"

"Who is that person?" asked her mother gently.

"I'll never tell you. It's my secret—it's wrong to try to discover other people's secrets. You have no right to my secrets, just because I'm your daughter."

Mrs. Ames sighed heavily, and closed her eyes. Amoret watched her and felt sorry. But it was so perfectly obvious that all these people were bent on making themselves unhappy, and wished to drag her into it with them. Her father had gone too far already. She would have to leave him. Certainly she would not face the prospect of being lectured and put on a stand to defend herself every time he saw her. The simplest neatest way around that was for him not to see her. Then he would not trouble himself about it and he would not trouble her, either.

Her mother did not give up. She wanted Amoret's secret and she continued to try to discover it. Amoret suspected that she watched when she left the house, where she went, and when she returned. She asked her many subtle questions, and sometimes even pleaded for her secret.

"*Why* do you want to know?" demanded Amoret finally, in exasperation.

"I want to help you, darling."

"I don't need help. And, when I do, you can't give it."

"Oh, Amoret—what are you saying? Whatever has happened?"

"Life is getting too serious. People don't have enough fun. I don't like it this way. When Miles comes back—"

"Miles," repeated her mother cautiously, and even her voice seemed to go into slow motion, as if she had tracked her prey to its hiding place and now would coax it far enough out so she could pounce upon and seize it. But Amoret knew what she intended. "Who is Miles, dear?"

She got up and walked away. "I didn't mention anyone named Miles. You imagined that I did." She turned and looked directly at her mother, with her blue eyes wide open and guileless.

Miles, fortunately, returned soon after that. He had had a tremendously exciting trip, even got behind the Iron Curtain for a few days and, after many dangerous escapades, had got out again and written his articles, which were considered to be the most important contributions to international understanding so far attempted. He told her about his trip; and Amoret told him about the forest of crystal growing in her apartment, the deepening silence, and the people she had had to dispose of during his absence.

"There is only Mother left now," she said. "And the other day, I almost went away from her, too. If she doesn't leave me alone soon, I will. It's becoming intolerable, Miles. There is that terrible constant tension—I can't stand it."

Miles was tender and concerned. "My little darling," he murmured, and held her close and stroked her. "If only I could protect you from them."

She looked up. "Can't you, Miles? Can't you?"

"You know I can't. I wish I could, but I can't."

"Everything's so strange these days. Everything seems unreal, and everyone seems unreal—only you are real to me now. We thought before that they were my real life, remember? But we must have been wrong. Because now it's you who are."

"I'm real to you, Amoret—but I never would be to them."

"Even if I told them about you? Perhaps I should tell Mother. She wants to know so badly."

Miles shook his head. "You mustn't tell her, Amoret. What if she wanted to see me, then? And I'm sure she would."

"I'd say you were away somewhere."

"But sooner or later, I'd be expected to come back, wouldn't I? She would keep insisting on seeing me. No, that isn't the solution. We'll have to find another. Or perhaps," he added thoughtfully, "there isn't any."

"But then what will happen to me?"

"I don't know."

"You used to know everything, Miles. Or did I just think you did?"

"You thought I did. When you knew more, it seemed that I did, too."

"Oh, Miles—I'm scared!"

She began to cry. While Miles held and petted her she cried as she had not cried since she had been a very little girl, in the days when any small thing seemed large and terrifying, when pain was out of all proportion to its cause, when the world was full of terror and mystery. How did it happen that now, when she was grown-up and married, she should seem to be returning to those old lost days she had never wanted back again?

"I meant always to be happy," she said. "My mother and father and my friends and everyone meant me to be happy. But one of them must have changed his mind. Who do you think it was, Miles?"

"I don't know," said Miles again. "I don't know."

"But if you don't, Miles—then *no* one does!"

She was still crying, when her mother came to visit her late in the afternoon. She tapped lightly at Amoret's bedroom door and, when Amoret answered it, her face wet, her eyes red and swollen, she gave a horrified gasp and took Amoret into her arms.

"Darling! What is it? What's happened? What are you crying about?"

"I don't know," said Amoret. "I wish I knew, but I don't."

Finally they sat down, and Amoret stopped crying. But she still drooped mournfully, her hands open in her lap, her head to one side, gazing toward the floor. She seemed to be thinking of something very distant from them both. Her mother watched her with pity and anguish, helplessly.

"How strange," said Mrs. Ames. "How strange. Everything is the exact opposite of what it has always been."

Amoret lifted her head and looked at her listlessly, almost as if she did not see her. "The opposite?" she repeated. But she did not seem interested in inquiring further into her mother's meaning.

Then, after a few moments, Mrs. Ames got up and began to move briskly about, spraying perfume on herself, closing a window where the curtains blew, opening her compact to powder her face. "Darling—" she said, her back to Amoret, "what did you do today?"

"I was out," said Amoret.

"Shopping?"

"No."

"Did you lunch with someone?"

"No."

"You don't care to tell me where you were, or whom you were with?"

"No."

Her mother came and stood before her, her face gentle and soft, though still troubled. "Darling—you never used to make up stories. You didn't even leave your room today, did you?"

Amoret looked up swiftly, her eyes suddenly bright and gleaming. She leaped to her feet and took a few running steps, turning once more, half across the room, to face her mother, as if she had been cornered by a dangerous beast. Her mother had been following her and now had discovered her hiding place. Her secret would be torn from her.

"I was out!" she cried. "I didn't lie!"

Her mother moved toward her but Amoret, in terrible panic, moved backward a step with each forward step her mother took.

"Darling—I didn't say you lied. I'm not accusing you of anything. I want to help you. Oh, my baby—please—let me help you!" Her mother held forth her arms, pleadingly.

"You've been spying on me! I knew you were! How did you know—" Amoret felt as if, at any moment, her body might fly into pieces and she would disintegrate, never to be found or put together again. She would have been glad to have it happen. She must find some escape—some place she could go where no one would follow her. Perhaps the only true escape was to die.

"I asked Edna, as I came in. She said you'd spent the day in your room. That's all."

"That's not all! You told her to spy on me! I knew she was! I knew someone was! I'm going to tell her—" But, as she rushed across the room, her mother stepped in her way and Amoret stopped still again.

"Amoret— Let me talk to you. I asked her to tell me. But I wasn't spying, darling. Believe me, I wasn't spying. I had to know. I *had* to know."

"You didn't have to know! You have no right to know! You can't know!"

"Oh, Amoret— It can't be anything so terrible. Whatever it is, I'll understand. I trust you, darling. I love you. Can't you trust me any more?"

"No! You want to take him away from me!" Amoret's hands went to her head; she twisted her neck as if someone else were holding her fast, trying to imprison her. "Miles!" she cried, and her voice rose to a mournful screaming wail. "Miles! Help me!"

"Miles," repeated her mother, very gently. "You've mentioned him before. Tell me who he is. Shall I call him and ask him to come?"

"No! You mustn't call! He'll come when I call him! He won't come for anyone else! And I go to him—he doesn't come to me!"

"He's— He's someone you love?"

Amoret and her mother stood staring at each other, and Amoret knew that it had finally happened. Her mother had discovered her secret. The one person she had loved best in all the world, except Miles, must lose her now. She'll never see me again, thought Amoret, and felt a terrible pain, as though a hand reached into her body and tore out her heart.

"Good-by, Mother," she whispered. "I'm sorry. I'm sorry. Good-by—"

"Amoret!"

Her mother rushed toward her, but it was too late. Amoret was gone. She saw her mother sobbing and crying, reaching to try to catch her and hold her, but the thing was irrevocable. It had happened, and it could never be undone.

"Now," she told Miles, "there *is* no one but you."

Miles sighed heavily, as if the responsibility was a greater one than he had expected.

"We never thought this would happen, did we?" Amoret asked him.

"No. We never did."

She stood on tiptoes and raised her face to his. "Do you blame me? Are you sorry?"

"No, of course I don't blame me. But I'm afraid it's going to be very lonely for you. I'm afraid *you* may be sorry."

"I won't be lonely, Miles. I'll wait for you when you're away and I'll always know that you'll come back. And sometimes—can I go with you sometimes?"

"Whenever you like."

"Oh, Miles!" Suddenly she laughed and clapped her

hands. "It's not going to be lonely! I won't be sorry. We'll have fun! We'll play and make jokes and love each other and we'll have a wonderful time! You know, Miles—I didn't realize it, but I think this must be what I wanted all along."

Miles smiled at her, tenderly, like a father smiling at his capricious little daughter. "I think perhaps it was, Amoret."

"But what about your wife?" she asked him suddenly.

"I'm not married any more," he said.

"You're not? How wonderful! What happened?"

"She caught a fever," he said, "in Sicily, and died."

"Oh, too bad. But I suppose it's for the best."

"It seems so now, doesn't it?"

Now that Amoret and Miles, were finally, and perfectly, alone, they enjoyed life more than ever before. Amoret found that she did not miss anyone at all, not even her mother. Miles Morgan filled her wants and suplied all her needs completely. The world turned out to be a vastly more exciting place than she had ever imagined.

When they wanted to go somewhere, Miles flew them in his own plane. There was no tedious waiting around airports, and Miles could even get through customs without delay or opening their baggage, which was a good thing, because they collected all manner of souvenirs on their travels: bells from India that pierced the soul with the sweetness of their sound; silks and gorgeous gold and silver cloth for Amoret; statues from ruins in Pompeii and Siam and the jungles of Yucatan; brilliant plumaged birds, some of them able to carry on quite an amusing conversation; earrings from Persia that reached below her shoulders, a golden snake that wound from her wrist to her armpit, crystal necklaces that fell almost to the ground. They brought strange flowers and planted them on Miles' terrace, masks that would have struck terror into anyone else but which made them laugh delightedly, amulets and charms and bottles of love potion they stored in a cabinet and were sure they would never need.

Sometimes, when they sat at breakfast—Miles in slacks with his brown upper body naked, Amoret wearing, for example, a skirt of silver fringe with her breasts bare and the nipples speckled with silver flakes—Miles would ask where she wanted to go next. One of the things Amoret liked best about her new life was that she did not have to wear the monotonous unimaginative clothes which people living ordinary lives must wear. She put on whatever her mood or whim suggested might be both becoming to her and entertaining to Miles. And she never wore the same costume twice.

"Where *shall* we go?" she would repeat, sitting with her legs crossed beside the black enamelled tray on which their breakfast had been set, leaning slightly forward and sipping her chocolate.

All at once she laughed. "You know," she said, "we live the life the gods must have lived, before people made the world so dreary and proper that they got bored and had to move to heaven."

Miles laughed, too. They looked at each other admiringly. There was never a moment that Amoret did not watch him with wonder and awe. He was so magnificently handsome, strong-bodied, vital and spirited, taking violent joy in everything he did. Miles had no patience, he would never permit either of them to be bored or only half-aware, but he had endless resourcefulness to see that they were not. Amoret followed him gladly and gratefully, and longed for nothing else.

"Let's go to Haiti," she said. "It's just a short trip. We can learn about voodoo."

Miles was on his feet instantly. "Let's go!" Off they went, after first putting on the kind of clothes they needed in society.

Amoret had no idea how much time went by with those pleasures and amusements. Once in a great while she would wonder how the others had arranged their lives without her, but she was not curious enough to find out. Since they could not remember her, her absence could not hurt them. She had no responsibility, therefore, no reason to concern herself with them. They had all got along before she entered their lives, and they could get along now that she had departed.

One day, however, Miles asked a disturbing question.

"Suppose," he said, "that one of them got sick. What would you do then?"

"Why, Miles! What makes you ask me such a thing? No one's sick!" She looked at him closely. "Or *are* they?"

"Not that I know of. But I don't want you to completely

forget what they have meant to you. You could regret it, later."

"But I've given them up, Miles. I don't exist for them any longer, and they don't exist for me." She frowned, and put her closed fist thoughtfully against her mouth. "I wish you hadn't brought that up. Now, someday, I'll probably think I have to find out."

"You don't have to find out unless you want to. Are you coming with me to Tibet?"

The Dalai Lama was lost, and Miles Morgan was the man best qualified to find him. It was important that he be located as soon as possible, since vast political schemes hung on his whereabouts, and Miles could not delay.

"Of course I'm going!" she said joyously. "I wouldn't miss it for anything!"

But even so, on the plane she was sometimes abstracted, and would sit quietly, looking out the window, wondering about what he had said. I wouldn't mind so much, she thought, unless it were my mother.

Presently, she ceased to wonder about it.

They were very busy on that trip, which was one of the most exciting they had yet taken. They flew over dark wet jungles and great mountains covered with jagged peaks of ice that glittered blue-white in the sun. They came down, occasionally, at secret hidden airports where uniformed men, in the service of one of the numerous countries involved in this project, greeted them obsequiously and set to work to prepare the plane for further flight. At each of these landings Amoret would sit at a dinner table lined with men, listening to them discuss desperate plans, filled with admiration for the way Miles conducted himself, modestly, always, and yet with absolute control over the entire situation. Then they would be bowed on their way again and the men would cheer and wave their hats as the plane skimmed off the runway.

"How glorious you are!" Amoret said, standing beside him as he piloted the plane. He smiled at her lazily, twisting mysterious dials. "To risk your life for other people—and not even ask them a favor!"

"What favors do I need?" he inquired softly.

"None. None at all. You have every one. Oh, Miles—" She reached over and delicately touched his wrist, circled with a heavy silver chain. "Miles— If I were not me, I'd want to be you." And again they burst out laughing. It was one of the happiest things between them that each always knew exactly what the other would consider funny. No jokes ever went wandering. Whereas Donald, to his own eventual misfortune, had more often than not to pretend he thought she was funny.

When they reached Tibet Miles flew directly to a place which no other white man knew about. He had discovered it on an earlier trip, three or four years ago, and been sworn to secrecy in order to escape with his life. It was then he had met the Dalai Lama and come to be on friendly terms with him.

Miles had attended the Dalai Lama's coronation, disguised, necessarily, as a monk with a long black beard in which he concealed a camera, and thus he obtained the only photographs ever to appear in *Life Magazine* of this sacred ceremony. He smuggled the negatives out of the country and abandoned his disguise, pretending now to be a lost aviator; he was promptly taken to the Dalai Lama. Language was no barrier to Miles, who overcame it instantly with his smile and simple, though commanding, charm. His quickly established friendship with the new religious leader made it possible for Miles to buy up all the coronation postage stamps and sell them at home for a great deal of money which, of course, he did not need, being so very rich already.

With this background, Miles returned confidently to Tibet.

The altitude was at least twenty thousand feet and very cold and he and Amoret wore great hooded fur jackets and fur mittens tied at the wrists. Miles opened the plane door and jumped down.

A swarm of Tibetans, with bronze faces and thick-lidded eyes, stood about in their padded brilliant-colored costumes, silently watching to see who had come. Many of them carried guns.

"Which of you can I talk to?" demanded Miles.

They glanced at one another and some of them shrugged. No one understood him. Reaching into his pocket, he brought forth some small object which he exhibited to them. Amoret could not see what it was, but its effect was magical. Immediately they bowed low, and then knelt. Miles left them there, while he returned to the plane and held out his arms for Amoret.

"What did you show them?"

"A charm the Dalai Lama gave me. They'll take us to him now."

They started walking, Miles and Amoret surrounded on all sides.

They were on a high vast icy plain; far in the distance stood even greater peaks. There was not a sign of any human habitation, and it was impossible to imagine how all these people had appeared the instant their plane landed. The smell they had was a vile one, as Amoret could not help noticing every time she took a deep breath, but she enjoyed the brilliant colors of their costumes and thought it was fun walking among them here on top of the world, farther than she had ever been from home.

Night began to fall swiftly, making everything about them purple for a time, and then it was dark. The sky filled with stars.

One of the men approached, holding rags in either hand, which he proposed to use as blindfolds.

"Not me!" protested Amoret. "It's bad enough this way!"

"You'll have to, darling. I think we must be almost there."

And so she submitted to having her head bound with the rag. Miles had always told her that adventure was not a comfortable way of life, which was why more people did not go in for it.

Then, when she had decided they were fated to walk forever blindfolded across this remote icy plain, another hand touched her elbow, making her pause briefly, and they began to ascend steps. Up and up and up they went, almost as far up, it seemed, as they had come on the flat surface. There was a wet mouldy smell in the air now, fetid and rank, as if bodies were decomposing, and the steps felt slippery with slime.

I'll be asked so many questions, she thought dismally.

At last they stopped. Suddenly the man beside her shouted something in a quick fierce terrifying tongue, and there was a sound of great hinges moving. The bandages were whisked off, and they stood in a vast brilliantly lighted hall.

"I've been here before," said Miles, and she gave a little sigh of relief.

The hall seemed so enormous that it could not possibly be enclosed by a building; it must be part of the landscape itself. But there were walls, hung with gorgeously colored draperies, vermilion, vivid green, painfully bright blue, and a ceiling painted gold from which depended more tinkling crystal lamps than Amoret had imagined there were in the world.

He's got rid of an awful lot of people, she thought. I wonder if we'll be up there next.

Great as it was, the hall was crowded.

There were no women present, except Amoret, but hundreds, or possibly thousands, of men stood against the walls. Most of them wore long straight padded gowns, heavy with embroidery and jewels. A few had sweeping black robes, startling in contrast with the vivid hues. At regular positions stood men in full armor holding enormous axes sharpened to a hairline. They were all talking among themselves and the sound they made was like the murmur of a distant ocean on a windy night.

The clear center space, an acre or more, was scattered with glittering gems.

Far ahead was a throne of gold, broad enough for ten men, high enough for a giant. In the midst sat a figure no bigger than an elf.

As they began to walk forward, slowly, they stepped on the gems and occasionally Amoret kicked at one, sending it skimming.

The Dalai Lama sat cross-legged, wearing a robe of gold with strings of diamonds and rubies and a crown three feet high. He was a boy, no more than fifteen, at the most. In one hand, lying across his arm, he held a very long scepter and this, too, was crusted thick with jewels. These Tibetans must be both the richest and the most evil-smelling people in all the world.

"Hello," said Miles. "I guess you know why I'm here."

The boy nodded gravely, barely inclining his head, for if his crown should topple off, all the cities of the Orient would collapse into ruin.

"Will you come back with us?" asked Miles.

The Dalai Lama looked sorrowful. "I cannot."

"You know what the sitation is," said Miles, speaking in a significant tone.

"Of course. But what can I do? I am not my own master—only the master of all these others and several millions more."

"I promised to bring you back, and that's what I'm going to do." Miles glanced around. "Do any of these others understand what we're saying?"

"Only one. This fellow here." He indicated an enormous man who stood beside his throne, arms crossed, glowering.

With one quick motion, Miles drew a revolver from his pocket and shot the man dead. Amoret screamed and the hall burst into frenzy. The men, yowling and shrieking, rushed forward. The Dalai Lama cowered in the far corner of his throne, clutching his crown. Miles fired half a dozen random shots, hitting a man each time. The hideous greedy faces loomed closer and one of the men seized hold of Amoret's jacket and began dragging her toward him. "They'll find out!" she screamed. "Miles! Miles! Oh— *Don't* let them torture me, Miles!" Miles grabbed Amoret about the waist, kicked off the man who had seized her, and leaped onto the throne. There was sudden complete silence.

"Will they touch us while we're on this throne?" asked Miles.

"No. But the moment we get off they'll rip you to shreds and trample you into the stones."

"Tell the strongest ones to pick up the throne and carry us back to the plane."

Once back, Miles directed them to place it beside the plane door. Amoret crawled in first and Miles kept the Dalai Lama standing there while he warmed the engine and prepared for flight. At the last moment, they dragged the Dalai Lama into the plane and slammed the door. Before it could be wrenched open by his snarling subjects, Miles rushed up front and they took off, knocking a few of them helter-skelter as they went.

Amoret, looking out the window, laughed aloud. *"That was the grand-slam rescue of all time!"*

He only smiled. Miles never bragged about his accomplishments, because he took it for granted they would be successful.

They delivered the Dalai Lama into proper hands and went on home.

But, like some bad dreams, the memory was not easy to get rid of. It clung like a strong persistent odor, and now and then she caught a whiff of it, usually at the moment when it was least expected.

Whenever she saw the swarming ugly faces approaching her, the long-nailed fingers reaching out, abysmal terror would sink through her like a tremendous weight, seeming to push her almost literally into the earth.

Then she would go, wistfully, to Miles.

"They meant to kill me. They would have tortured me first until I told them—and then they would have killed me. Oh, Miles, they'll try to find me. Every time you go out and leave me alone I'm terrified!"

"They can't find you here, darling. They're in Tibet."

She shook her head. "Don't pretend with me, Miles. They're not *only* in Tibet. They're here, too. They're everywhere. Sometime they will find me and take me, won't they?"

"Not while I'm here."

"Can you *always* save me, Miles?"

"I don't know. I'll always try."

Neither of them was blithely happy, as they had been. Miles would not admit it, of course, but something in his quieter, soberer manner told her that he was afraid for her, too. The shadow was lengthening and had begun to fall over even her life with Miles. Sometimes, it seemed almost to be an actual, not an imaginary, shadow—but she could not tell whose. Occasionally she had a kind of wispy tenuous premonition that someday that shadow would stand in the full light and she would recognize it. That terrified her more than all the swarming evil faces which could, at least, be seen for what they were.

Miles said that he was going to stay in New York for a while and do some work.

She decided to see how things were at home—not her own home, but her mother's, for she no longer thought of the apartment as being her home in any way at all. She had turned that over to the crystal lamps, since they had invaded it and obviously did not intend to leave. They must have filled it completely by now and, in fact, she found a certain pleasure at the thought of their monopoly over the place where she and Donald had lived. They were certainly the cleanest least troublesome tenants she could have, and now and then when she pictured them standing there, sparkling and dancing, tinkling and chiming, she found the effect both soothing and restful.

Though it was midafternoon of a beautiful early summer's day, her mother was home, in bed, lying flat on her back and very still, her eyes closed. Amoret stood and looked at her, filled with horror and pity and sudden remorse.

I've done it! she thought. *I* made her sick!

She turned and ran out and found one of the maids. "What's the matter with my mother, Margaret? Is she sick?"

Margaret looked gravely at Amoret. "She hasn't been very well recently, Miss Amoret. You know that."

"I didn't know it! How could I know it? I haven't been here—"

"No, Miss Amoret. Not since last evening—"

"Margaret—whatever has happened? I feel as though none of you understand the simplest things any more. Are *you* well, Margaret?"

"Well enough, Miss Amoret."

"But you look sad. You used to look so happy to see me. Mother has another of those migraines, doesn't she? She didn't have them for years—not since I was a little girl. And now she has one again."

Margaret reached out impulsively and took gentle hold of Amoret's hand. "Miss Amoret, listen to me. You say that you haven't been here in a long while, that you weren't here last night—and yet you know why your mother's sick without anyone telling you."

Amoret gazed back at her thoughtfully. "Yes," she admitted after a few moments. "I did know, didn't I? That's odd. Is she sleeping?"

They went back to the bedroom and stood beside Mrs. Ames' bed, looking down. Amoret's throat began to ache as she watched her mother lying there. Miles told me, she thought. He told me I should find out and I didn't and she's been sick and she needs me. I could always play and make jokes and get her into good spirits when no one else could at all.

"Mrs. Ames—" said Margaret softly. "Mrs. Ames—"

Mrs. Ames opened her eyes slowly and looked up. There were fine lines in her smooth forehead. "Mrs. Ames—your little girl's here—"

"Margaret!" cried Amoret.

She stared at the maid aghast, wondering how she could possibly have been either so stupid or so callously cruel. To tell Mrs. Ames that her daughter was there, to have her look and try to find her and not be able to— The woman must be insane to do a thing like that. For surely she knew that Mrs. Ames no longer even remembered that she had a daughter. Or did Margaret know that? She could not be sure about these people. Sometimes they seemed to know almost nothing of what was going on.

Amoret turned from Margaret and back to her mother once more. Her mother was looking directly into her face, tenderly, wistfully, with what seemed to Amoret the saddest expression she had ever seen. Even though, after a moment, she smiled, Amoret knew that something terrible had happened during her absence, and she was stricken with guilty anguish for having gone away on her own adventures and left her mother alone, without even the comfort of her daughter's memory.

Now, quite obviously, the system had begun to break down.

Amoret could feel it happening: Her mother was looking at her. She saw someone standing there, perhaps she saw Amoret, there was no way of being sure. And then slowly, as if she swam under water, Amoret emerged and broke the surface, appearing once more to her mother's consciousness. She had willed it to happen, for firm as her intention had been never to allow any of them to see or remember her again, she could not bear her mother's suffering. She must try to help, if she could.

"Amoret—darling," said her mother softly. "You recognize me?"

Amoret's throat swelled with pain until it seemed to split. She took her mother's hand and knelt beside her, weeping. "Oh, Mother—you've been sick and I wasn't here!"

She touched Amoret's head. "You're here now, darling. Thank you for coming."

"No! Don't thank me! I should have been here long ago! If I'd known you were sick I'd have come right away —no matter how much fun I was having! You know that, Mother! You do know it, don't you?"

"Yes, of course I do." Mrs. Ames glanced at Margaret, who left the room; she was crying, too.

Amoret then began to talk gaily and cheerfully, and presently her mother's headache had disappeared and she put on a hostess gown and made up her face and they were as companionable as ever. Amoret was grateful that her mother did not scold or ask where she had been, or mention anything at all about Miles.

But, as it grew later, Amoret began to wonder if her father and Donald and Sharon and all the others would be able to see and her and remember her, too. Her heart started beating fast, her stomach writhed, and she found it difficult to breathe. The worse she felt, the gayer she pretended to be; she was afraid that if her mother knew how scared she was, her headache would return. It was she who had the responsibility of preventing her mother from getting sick again and, great as had always been her hatred of responsibility, she had now responsibility for her mother's well-being, and thus was imprisoned by this room into which all the others might presently walk and discover her among them once more.

Her father was sure to be home between six and six-thirty; she anxiously watched the clock.

What will I do? What will I do if he sees me? I won't be frightened. Even if he does, even if they all do—they can't make me stay. I can go back to Miles whenever I want to.

The door opened and her father came in. He went directly to kiss her mother and to ask how she was feeling, and as he passed Amoret he gave her an affectionate pat on the head. Amoret, sitting on the floor with her legs crossed like the Dalai Lama, looked up in astonishment.

He's not even surprised to see me again! Maybe he didn't notice that I was away! I tell you the truth, sometimes I wonder about these people.

Or—maybe—when I disappear I disappear so completely that they even lose track of the time and when I return, they take up again at the same moment of my disappearance. It was very puzzling. She must ask Miles to explain it better.

"I'll wash up," said her father. He turned at the doorway and grinned at Amoret. "Any shopping today?"

Amoret hung her head. "Not today, Daddy."

"Oh, well! Don't be discouraged. There's tomorrow!" And he went out, laughing.

Amoret glanced at her mother. "What does he think is the joke?"

"He likes to tease you, Amoret. You know—he always has."

"Oh," said Amoret, as if she had learned something new. "I suppose Donald will be here?"

"Of course, darling. Why?"

Well, then, the system had fallen apart. The flaw in it, unforeseen by either her or Miles, had been her mother's illness.

"I know!" cried Amoret gaily. "Let's have a party. Not a big one—just all of us and Sharon. Shall we?"

Her mother looked so pleased, and relieved, and surprised, Amoret felt exhilarated by her own kindness and generosity.

When Donald came he kissed her and, though she noticed that from time to time he gave her an odd little anxious look, he did not say anything. Neither did Sharon, when she arrived. The party was a great success and they were all as happy together as they had ever been. The only thing which made Amoret uneasy was that now and then she would catch one of them looking strangely at another, and she sensed that it had something to do with her. She did not like to see these looks being passed about, like secret coin, but was afraid to mention it for fear of bringing up the entire subject of her recent absence. People are so tactless, she thought, and it made her rather unhappy. If any one of them had half the sense that Miles has—

Amoret and Donald and Sharon left together and walked along the street toward Sharon's house, Donald on one side and Sharon on the other. They think they're escorting a prisoner, thought Amoret.

"Can we have lunch tomorrow?" asked Sharon. She sounded more anxious than the simple question warranted.

"I think so," said Amoret kindly. "Let me call you in the morning."

As Donald was fitting his key into the door of their apartment, Amoret asked: "Are there many more crystal lamps?"

"What?"

"Never mind. I'll see for myself."

There were. The living room, as she had anticipated, was filled with them, softly chiming and tinkling in the faint summer breeze. Amoret sighed and turned away and walked down the hall to their bedroom. Donald followed and, as soon as the door was closed, took her into his arms.

"Amoret—darling. Have you forgiven me?"

"Forgiven you, Donald? What did you do?"

"I don't know. I never did know."

He was kissing her face and she allowed him to do so, but made no returning caress. She stood with her fingertips lightly touching his shoulders and seemed to be waiting for him to stop.

"Will you make me a promise?" he asked.

There. He couldn't wait two minutes before he must begin to extract "promises." Donald had always wanted more promises from her than anyone she had ever known: promises that she would marry him, that she would love him, that she would never love anyone else, that she would love him forever. It would be impossible to remember all the things she had promised Donald merely to keep him quiet.

"What promise?"

"Will you promise not to put me out of your life again?"

He looked worried and anxious, the one expression she could not tolerate. She touched his lips with her fingers. "Shh, Donald. Let's not have so many promises. Come, now—can't we play and have fun?" And she took his hand, as if they would set off on a picnic, or a walk through the woods catching butterflies. Donald had never been the easiest man to have fun with. He always seemed to be thinking about something which might trouble him in the future.

Now, however, he laughed, and she knew it was as good an imitation of light-heartedness as he could give at that moment. She felt a tender appreciation of the effort, and a sense of pathos at what it cost him. The laugh reminded her unpleasantly of the great difference between him and Miles, between all this life and the life she shared with Miles.

She crossed the room, unbuttoning her dress as she went. Then she turned and looked directly at him and, for the second time that day, something disastrous occurred. The first had been her mother's illness, which had brought her back into all their lives. Now, without intending or even wanting to, she suddenly found herself in direct communication with Donald's secret heart.

She had taken care all evening, seeing the strange looks that went about, to avoid letting that happen with any one of them. But now it happened so suddenly, almost as if she were walking on a flat and safe meadow, stumbled, lost her balance, and fell into a deep pit.

He was watching her intently, and he was thinking:

She seems all right, again. Maybe they're wrong. But the lamps—what can she mean by that? She could talk to the doctor, at least. It couldn't do any harm. But which one of us has courage enough to ask her to do it? It should be me—I'm her husband—

Amoret felt her chest suddenly narrow and grow so tight she could scarcely breathe.

How terrible!

Her family! Her husband— All of them plotting to send her to a 'doctor.' She knew, without asking Donald, exactly the kind of doctor he was. She had a swift vision of all the faces, evil, greedy, demanding her torture and death.

She was too ashamed, when she saw Miles, to tell him what she had learned. She pretended, instead, to be merry and frolicsome.

She tossed her wide black straw hat onto a chair and stood smiling up at him, smelling of the long-stemmed red rose she had brought. "What have you been doing?"

"Helping the museum people put together some of those Mexican shards," he said, smiling back at her. "They had them hopelessly mixed up."

"Was it fun?"

"For a while. It's niggling work, though. I finished last night." His hands were in his pockets, his head a little to one side; he drew a deep breath. "I was afraid they might capture you."

Amoret sat down, stretching out her legs and crossing them delicately at the ankles, regarding the toes of her shiny black pumps. "You know, they almost did. I think they believe they have." She laughed mischievously. "They want me to face up to my responsibilities." She shrugged. "Can you imagine anything more tiresome?" She looked around. "How I love it here! Oh! What's this?" She got up and ran over to an easel which stood near one of the great windows. "It's bare!" she announced, as if he might not have noticed.

Miles strolled after, smiling. "I know. I thought I'd paint your portrait."

"My portrait!" She clapped her hands together. "What a wonderful idea! I didn't know you were a painter, Miles."

"I studied in Paris for a while."

They scrambled about the apartment for an hour or more, dressing Amoret, assembling the props, Miles preparing his paints and brushes, laughing and gay and busy as two children in a sand pile.

Against a deep blue curtain he placed a bench that was long and low with the front legs and head of some weird imaginary beast carved in gold. There was also the animal's hind legs and circling tail, while between front and back, where the body would have been, was a thick dark blue cushion with gold tassels at each corner.

Amoret reclined upon it lightly, seeming scarcely to touch its surface. She wore a transparent gold tissue gown which draped across one shoulder and under the opposite breast and clung as if wet down to her ankles. Upon her forehead he set a vast green enamel headdress, sprouting up and out like a tree, tipped with colored blossoms, drooping with quivering chains and beaded pendants. One bare foot touched the edge of an ancient Etruscan basin which had long ago been used for catching sacrificial blood.

There was a misshapen dwarfed tree growing from the basin and pomegranates scattered about the floor, some of them cut open. Nearby squatted a blind and deaf musician playing upon some peculiar flutelike instrument, setting off in careful tentative fashion notes and sounds which she had never heard before and which lingered in the air so long after he had produced them that they seemed almost to become solid matter.

Miles stood looking at her thoughtfully. "I'm going to call it: Portrait of the Sense of One's Own Uniqueness."

Amoret threw back her head and laughed joyously. "Miles, you can't imagine how different it is, here with you. I'm *never* going back!"

Miles raised one eyebrow, still studying her. "There!" he said. "That's the look I want—" He went swiftly to work, painting with confidence and energy, knowing precisely what he wanted and how to achieve it. Appearing in this way, he told her, she was the elusive eternal mystery of femininity, and he would capture whichever of its elements were sufficiently determinable to be captured.

She held a mirror at arm's length in her right hand. It had roses twined about its frame and gnarled enamel stems for a handle. But when she looked into it she saw Miles' face, rather than her own—the frame was empty.

"Miles!" she cried, twisting it this way and that, trying to make it reflect, as a mirror should. "The mirror's broken! There's no glass. I see *you*—not me!"

Miles was mixing paints on his palette. He made no move to take it from her and did not even glance up; he merely smiled.

"Well?" he said. "What difference does that make?"

Amoret frowned and for just an instant something inside her was afraid. But it did, surely, make a difference? It made a great difference.

"I'll paint your face looking through the frame," he said.

Amoret sighed with relief. "Oh. You meant it that way, then?"

"Of course. I don't have accidents, you know that."

But still, he *was* the only thing she had left in life. By that very fact, she must have become his prisoner.

Was it possible that Miles, whom she had met whenever she pleased and parted from whenever she liked, had actually become her jailer? But he had not wished it or asked for it. She had come to him, escaping from the others. She could not go back, though; she could no longer leave him when she took the notion. And instantly she realized that she was even more helpless, more trapped, than she had ever been before.

Now—whose was the responsibility?

She had entered a spiral, which had no beginning and no end.

She continued gazing through the mirror, seeing nothing but his face; until suddenly she could stand it no longer and she hurled the mirror across the room. To her horrified amazement it broke and shattered. There had been a mirror in it, after all—some trick mirror which had deceived her.

She jumped to her feet. "Miles! What have you done to me!"

The deaf and blind musician continued playing and, for a long moment, Miles even continued to paint. Amoret, feeling herself abandoned and betrayed, pressed both hands to her head and moaned. Miles, with a look of alarm, dropped his paints and rushed to her. Carefully, he removed the headdress, setting it aside, and took her into his arms. She held onto him desperately.

"Why did you do it, Miles? *Why* did you do it?"

"Why did I do what?"

"The mirror. You told me I saw you because it was empty. But it wasn't empty. And then you left me all alone. You knew I was scared and you kept on painting. Oh, Miles—*You* don't love me, either!"

"Of course I love you, Amoret. There's something you're afraid of. What is it? It can't be me."

Amoret gently disengaged herself and turned away from him, slowly and sadly. "Maybe it is, Miles. Maybe it's you I've been afraid of all along. Neither of us ever thought of that, did we?" She glanced back at him briefly, raising her brows, her old expression of flirtatious archness returning for just a moment. Then she sighed again and shook her head. "Every day it's more bewildering." In sudden anger she kicked at the squatting musician. "Can't you make him stop that noise?"

Miles tapped the musician on the shoulder. He got up, obediently, and crept from the room.

Amoret continued looking out the windows for a few minutes and then she swung about and addressed Miles in an accusatory tone. "Why did you decide to paint my portrait?"

He was cleaning his brushes and he glanced across at her with a look of mild surprise. "Why—I don't know. You're very beautiful. I thought it would be a nice thing to have."

"A nice thing to have when I'm gone?"

"Gone where?" asked Miles calmly, still cleaning his brushes but no longer looking at her. "Are you going somewhere?"

She ran toward him and stopped, breathing fast. "When I'm dead!"

He shook his head a little. "Amoret. Don't talk that way."

"You expect me to die, don't you? Miles—don't lie to me! That's why you're painting my picture!"

Miles shook his head again, regarding her solemnly, but he made no answer. Amoret left the room and went to wander about the great apartment, which had several rooms she had never been in. *He does expect me to die. He has a premonition. So do I.*

It had all been decided, somewhere else, by someone else. There was nothing she could do, or Miles. At least they *can never ask me any more questions or ever discover my secret. And wherever I'm going next, I'll be a long time getting there. I won't hurry. I'll take my time. And I'll make up a story on the way. I'll be ready when they start to ask me.*

She strolled along a hallway, moving with soundless fluidity, and as she went she began to feel a sense of soothing peace. The hall was broad and tall columns stood at intervals, each surmounted by an armor breastplate, enamelled white; they stood there like a series of truncated men. Each wore a garland of pink roses hung about its shoulders and, from the neck opening, brilliant butterflies, fixed to quivering wires, spurted forth. The walls were black. Between these figures, on other tall columns, stood innumerable great crystal lamps.

So that's where they came from, thought Amoret, but was not very much surprised. *Miles took them from here and set them in my apartment. I think, in a way, I knew all along that he was the one doing it.*

She opened a door and looked in. The room was vast

and empty, painted gold, floors and walls and ceiling. She closed it again. The next she opened was painted silver, and it was also empty. She shrugged.

At last she opened one and stopped on the threshold, feeling some strange sense of dread beginning to steal upon her, but could not tell why.

This room was, to all appearances, endless. There were no walls, or, at least, none that she could see, though it was somewhat misty in the distance. Overhead was a vague blue, like an early evening sky, which might have been only a skillful representation. The floor was checkerboarded with great black and white squares. She stood staring, first with apprehension, then with abrupt plunging despair. Three distant unrecognizable figures drifted from the mist and moved, very slowly, toward the horizon. She wanted to call out, ask them to wait for her to catch up, not to leave her alone—but something prevented her.

Then she heard a sound and turned.

There was no longer any door by which to enter or leave.

A great white stallion, heavy-bodied and of extraordinary size, went slowly by her and started across the checkerboard floor. His ponderous hoofbeats set up an echoing vibration which seemed to spread through space like circles of limitless sound.

Amoret stood watching with anxious fascination as he advanced toward the three misty vanishing figures. He might have been following them, though at a great distance, or it might only have been that they all had the same destination.

"How *terrible!*" breathed Amoret, and gave a violent convulsion shudder.

She did not know why it was she felt such morbid ominous dread. Yet, as she watched him, her horror and loathing increased. Her heart beat faster and faster until its pounding shook her body. She quivered and trembled uncontrollably. Her hands tore at her throat, and she gasped for breath.

The great stallion continued moving away from her; his hoofbeats resounding, slow—heavy—inexorable.

"*No!*"

She heard herself scream.

I *can't* listen! The sound of his hoofs! Oh, the terrible terrible sound of his hoofs!

She was running toward him, naked.

She reached him swiftly, grasped his white mane in her two hands and, enormous as he was, leapt upon him.

"Now!" she yelled triumphantly. "Ride!"

Instantly he reared and whirled, tossing his head to break her grip, his nostrils flaring and blowing spume, his eyes rolling wildly. The three figures turned—then fled into the distance and disappeared. Amoret clung desperately, shrieking with terror, yet overwhelmed by a boisterous convulsive excitement infinitely beyond anything she had ever experienced! She knew he would kill her.

He set out at a sudden gallop and, swift though he started the gallop got faster and faster and faster, while she clutched his body between her thighs and howled exultant defiance.

On they rode, his hoofs crashing the floor like thunder. She was utterly helpless, without control over her actions, her emotions, or her eventual fate. He would determine everything. She sensed all this but vaguely—for much stronger was a shocking detestation and rage against the stallion, which filled her with savage glory. She longed to kill him, to suddenly discover a knife in her hand and plunge it into his great quivering body, wash in his blood. She could hear herself wailing, but felt no responsibility for anything she did.

Abruptly he stopped, skidding and sliding with frightful awkwardness upon the polished floor. Amoret was flung off sideways.

He reared and his hoofs plunged downward. She saw his flaming nostrils, his maddened frantic eyes and then, as his hoofs struck her, they burst into flame and consumed him in an instant.

Miles appeared from nowhere and swooped to pick her up. It *was* Miles? And he had appeared at the instant the stallion vanished. Could it be—

But then she grew sick and could not remember . . .

Amoret lay upon the black satin chaise in her own bedroom. Her eyes were closed, her face touched delicately with cosmetics, her red hair brushed and spread over the cushions. She wore a white silk gown, and an opened negligee of pleated white chiffon, fastened at the throat and wrists with black velvet ribbon. Her ankles were crossed, one satin mule had dropped off. Her right arm lay against her side, while the left had fallen from the chase and hung straight and limp, its curled fingers touching the floor.

Her mother knelt on one side and Donald on the other. Her father stood with the doctor. Sharon had been led out by Edna when her crying became hysterical.

Mrs. Ames was sobbing, her head rolling from side to side, as if denying over and over again what had happened. Mr. Ames stared but did not see. Donald had bowed his head without a word when the doctor pronounced Amoret dead. No one spoke for several minutes.

Then suddenly, as if she had realized anew that Amoret would never again open her eyes or speak, play any of her little jokes and games, confide her secrets, smile or sigh or laugh aloud, her sobs grew uncontrollable. Mr. Ames started toward her but the doctor touched his arm, restraining him.

She looked across Amoret's body to her husband, piteously imploring. Her face was smeared and wet and haggard. "Why did she do it? *Why* did she do it? We were good to her, weren't we? We were! And she was always such a happy little girl, running and playing and laughing!" She held out her hands. "She *was* happy—wasn't she?"

Mr. Ames stared implacably. "I will never believe that she killed herself. It was an accident. It must have been an accident."

The doctor spoke softly. "Perhaps," he said.

"Of course it was!" His voice rose angrily. Then he appealed to Donald and, as he turned to him, his tone softened again. "Don't you remember how we all were last night? Amoret was gayer than she had been in months."

Donald glanced up at him for a moment, tried to answer, but bowed his head once more. "It's my fault," he muttered. *"I* should have known—"

"Donald!" cried Mrs. Ames. "Don't talk like that! *Don't*—I can't let you talk as if you murdered her! You loved her as much as we did! It was something else—something else—" Her voice grew faster and more frantic, and rose almost to a scream. "I called today but she had told the maid to let her sleep! I should have come— I should have known— We all knew it!" She stared from one to the other. "We *did* know! It's our fault—every one of us! We were cowards! We knew she was sick and we were afraid to tell her! Not one of us had courage enough to save her—"

Though Miles had walked into the room and now stood directly before Mr. Ames, only Amoret saw him, and spoke to him.

"Yes," she said, while he stood with great solemnity, silent, looking down at her. "I am dead, Miles. I was dying all day and now I am dead. But I have a moment or two, before I must leave you."

"I'll go with you—"

"I knew you were going to say that, Miles. I knew *you* wouldn't desert me." She spoke softly, tenderly, kindly. "Even though I think now that it was you who killed me. Never mind. I believe I knew all along that you would—that you must, I mean."

Miles continued watching her, but made no answer.

"Miles—it *was* you I was afraid of."

Her mother picked up a hand mirror which lay nearby, shattered, as if it had been flung angrily against the wall. The frame was a wreath of roses and the handle its twisted stems.

"Remember—" said Mrs. Ames, and touched it caressingly, wonderingly. "We gave it to her long ago and she always loved it and kept it with her. *Why* did she break it—"

"Miles—do you know that at the instant when you burst free of life there is a single gladsome, expansive moment? I *hoped* there would be." Now there was a touch of sorrow about her lips and in her voice. "That's the last discovery I can ever tell you, isn't it? We learned so many many things together—and that is the last." She sighed. "I have no more time, Miles. No—" she said, as he made a move. "Don't come with me. It makes me glad to know that even though *I* must leave you forever—you will be alive to give someone else the happiness you have given me. I bequeath you to the world."

She smiled a little, to reassure him, and then closed her eyes, so that he could no longer see her:

"Let me be generous. Good-by—"

"Good-by, Amoret," he answered softly, and only her mother, her father, Donald, and the doctor remained in the room with her.

THREE

In Another Country

ERIC STOOD leaning against the bar, his back to the room. He finished the shot of bourbon and gestured to the bartender, who promptly poured some more. As Eric picked it up the man swiped a filthy rag across the counter; Eric looked at him and smiled faintly and the man smiled in return, as if they both thought there was something funny about the rag. He took another swallow and leaned his elbows on the damp bar again.

The room behind him appeared only half-finished. There was a small yellow plaster fireplace in one corner and, in another, an old-fashioned upright piano, out of tune. The floor was cement, partly concealed by an Indian rug; the furniture, two ugly chairs and a couch, was covered with cracked brown leather. An icebox stood against one wall with a small artificial Christmas tree on top of it, still decorated, though it was now mid-February. In the doorway sat a mongrel dog, licking at a great open sore on one leg and, occasionally, scratching his head.

"This place has charm," Eric had told himself ironically, the first day he saw it. Perhaps that was why he had stayed as long as he had. It was such a mess, he felt it suited his present state of mind.

A man and woman sat on the couch, sipping drinks and

talking. The woman was tall and fat with popping eyes and wore a stiff white cotton suit with a bandana tied round her head and a sombrero perched on top. The man was much smaller and had a perpetual look of weary discouragement; for the most part he listened while she talked. Eric knew they were brother and sister.

There was one other person in the room, a man who invariably dressed in a dirty white sailor suit and blue beret. Eric had nicknamed him Mephistopheles, because of his dark color and the neatly clipped black beard which hid the lower part of his face and gave him a look of sinister secrecy.

All three of them had been at the hotel when Eric arrived, almost a month ago, but he had refused to let himself be drawn into conversation and had no idea who they were or what they were doing there. A few other guests had come and gone, North Americans, busy with their cameras and Indian baskets. No one seemed to mind his aloof indifference or tried to separate him from it and the days flowed along, one washing over the other in slow-motion dreariness. He felt as if a kind of spell had been cast upon him, and began to hope it might be of a healing nature. At any event, he held himself in suspension.

The place was quiet and cheap, which it should have been since it was like a fifth-rate hotel in the States, but the countryside was beautiful. For these reasons, it suited him very well.

A thin white cat now came into the room, sidled along the wall, and leaped suddenly onto the bar beside him. He glared at it and turned away, facing out into the room but leaning his back against the bar. When it came closer, however, and nudged his arm, loudly purring and holding its tail straight in the air, he gave it an impatient shove with one hand and the bartender, smiling again, picked it up by the scruff and set it on the floor.

A girl and a middle-aged woman walked up the steps, through the bright doorway, and into the room. The girl was laughing, but as she paused a moment, looking in at that silent solemn group, her laughter ceased abruptly.

Eric had not seen either of them before and now, unaware of himself or his expression, he stood and stared at her in outright unashamed amazement. The others stared, too. She was, without any doubt, the prettiest thing he had seen in his life and her beauty was all the more astonishing, having appeared so unexpectedly in these surroundings.

Her light blond hair reached her shoulders. Her skin was unbelievably fine and clear, gilt softly by the sun so that it seemed almost to glimmer. Her figure, in a yellow linen dress, was small and delicate and supple; her legs were bare and she wore flat black sandals. But the special enchantment which she had beyond her beauty and which, perhaps, made it so extraordinarily appealing, was some magic blend of youth, a kind of gentle vivacity, and her expression of perfect natural sweetness and simplicity. This last quality, occurring in combination with such loveliness, impressed Eric most of all.

"Well!" she said, as if somehow she had been taken by surprise. "Hello." She was talking to no one in particular, or to all of them. The others nodded. "Can we get a drink here?" She looked at the older woman, waiting now for her to do something about it.

"What would you like, señorita?" asked the bartender, and he leaned forward, smiling. The man in the dirty white sailor suit got up and left, as if the atmosphere had become unsuitable to him; but he stood outside near the door, like some rascal lurking in a dark corner at midnight.

"Two Coca-Colas," said the older woman briskly. "Have you ice?"

"No, señora. No ice. I'm sorry."

"All right. No ice, then. Where are we? What's the name of this place?"

She looked as though she disapproved thoroughly of the place, for herself and the girl as well. The girl, still watched by Eric, bent down to stroke the cat. She was about to touch it when the woman turned sharply.

"Dulcie! What are you doing? The animal looks sick."

"I'm sorry, Mother. I was just going to pet it." She glanced at Eric and smiled, very freely and sweetly, without coquetry. She did not seem at all aware of his looks, which surprised him and, in some obscure way, pleased him, too. It was one of the few times he had met a woman who did not instantly flare her nostrils, sniff, and come bounding at him.

"This is the Hotel Tzanjuyu," said Eric, addressing the mother rather than the girl.

The cokes were set on the bar and the mother picked them up, handing one to her daughter. The girl took a sip, made a little face, murmured, "It's lukewarm," set it back on the bar and walked outside again. Eric wanted to follow her but decided it was best to stay with the dragon who must, of course, be a very careful guardian for such a rare treasure.

"Are you stopping here?" he asked her politely, after a moment or two.

She was a woman of perhaps forty-five, carefully dressed in pale-blue sport clothes, with a soft sweater carried over one arm, like an accessory or afterthought. She was small and not so very pretty, but had her daughter's look of fastidiousness and gentle breeding.

She did not reply at once for she had been examining the room, casually, but carefully. Now she looked at him. "No. We were out walking and it's hot, so we thought we'd get something cool." She glanced at the warm drink, of which she had taken two or three sips, and set it down. She opened her bag, paid the bartender and left, nodding good-by to Eric.

He hesitated a moment and then followed her.

Dulcie was standing down in front, talking to Señorita Montero who, with her brother, owned the Tzanjuyu— an energetic young woman with pocked brown skin and long straight oily black hair, she spent the days riding, swimming in the lake, and telling the Indians to feed the birds.

Far in the distance, surrounding the lake, were great blue mountains. There was no grass near the hotel and two Indian boys sprinkled the bare earth several times a day, as they were doing now, to keep the dust down, then swept it with tree branches. Somewhere indoors a radio was playing American jazz. Everything was blowing: the women's dresses, the pepper trees and poinsettias, the plants potted in ceramic bowls and tin cans, the hollyhocks and palms and hibiscus. A turkey stalked back and forth, doing his best to ignore a black and white puppy that wanted to play with him. The lake drifted serenely.

"It's getting late," said Eric, addressing himself to the

mother again. "If you have far to go, I'll be glad to walk back with you."

Then he realized that the girl was watching him and that she had, probably, actually seen him for the first time. He glanced at her and saw that she was staring at him, her blue-green eyes opened wide and full of honest innocent admiration, as if she were looking at a painting which moved her, or some fine building.

He was darkly tanned and the sun had made his blond hair even lighter than usual. He was one of those men so extraordinarily handsome that women thought of him more as an object to possess than a person. But his good looks were in no way soft or pretty. He was over six feet tall, with a broad muscular chest and shoulders and back, lean hips and strong legs. He seemed to take his looks for granted and to regard them as something he wore, accepting them without vanity.

During the moment they stood looking at each other, the pock-marked Spanish girl looked first at Eric, then at Dulcie. "How beautiful you both are," she said wistfully. "Are you related?"

Dulcie laughed delightedly. "We've never even met."

"I am Mrs. Parkman," her mother said. "This is my daughter, Duclie."

"My name is Thorsten. Eric Thorsten."

For a moment each of them seemed to consider shaking hands and then to decide against it.

"Thank you, Mr. Thorsten, but we'll be home before dark," Mrs. Parkman said. "We don't have far to go."

She started off and Dulcie lingered a moment, still smiling at Eric. Then, as if her mother had summoned her, she turned quickly and took two or three little running steps to catch up with her. They walked along together and Eric and Señorita Montero watched them. She turned once, and waved. Eric looked at the woman and found her smiling at him.

"Can I borrow one of your Indians?" he asked. "I want to find out where she lives."

Señorita Montero laughed. "I know where she lives. She told me. She and her mother are staying about a mile from here—I can show you where it is myself."

He was surprised and wondered for a moment if she had given the information intending it to be conveyed to him—but promptly decided that that was an absurd notion, suitable for other women he had known, but quite unlikely for her. She was unaffected and friendly, and had mentioned it naturally in the conversation.

"She's so beautiful," repeated Señorita Montero. "The most beautiful girl I have ever seen."

"What do you suppose they can be doing here?"

"Travelling. The father died six months ago. They are on a trip together to forget him." She excused herself to help the Indians look for one of the parrots, which periodically got lost and had to be searched for.

Dulcie and her mother had turned a corner and disappeared and Eric went back to the bar to think about her. She's here by chance, he told himself, and so am I. I don't even know why I came to the bar so early today —I never do ordinarily. We never should have met at all. And yet—now that he had seen her—he felt as if he had been waiting for her. Nothing could have been more absurd.

He did not believe, and would not believe, that anything important could happen to you by chance. If it was significant you willed it yourself, planned it, and brought it about.

He was thinking hard about this and it startled him when the woman in the stiff white suit spoke close beside him. "That girl looks enough like you to be your twin sister. You were extraordinarily stunning together." She smiled and he smiled back, and for the first time felt pity and even sympathy for her. He glanced at her brother and found him looking at him too, smiling. Mephistopheles had come back and was leaning against the door, still noncommittal because of his beard, but softened, it seemed, around the eyes.

Eric realized that everyone who had seen them together those few moments had been pleased by the sight. Both of them were beautiful, and young, and vital; triumph was implicit in them. Together, they had undoubtedly conveyed an impression of inevitability, as if the past and future met for an instant, coalescing. The other three looked almost exhilarated.

Then the moment passed and they were self-conscious, did not want to talk about it any more, and wandered away.

The next morning, about ten o'clock, Eric asked Señorita Montero for directions and set out to find the house. He had no plan or intention or, rather, he intended to do nothing at all: only to walk by and look at it. Mrs. Parkman, he felt sure, would be annoyed if he came to pay a call so soon.

The way was along a narrow little dirt road, prodigally lovely with thick blooming bushes of poinsettias. Innumerable prints of bare Indian feet were set in the dry dust, the pattern of centuries, quietly woven. The houses hid behind whitewashed walls covered with purple-red bougainvillaea, and above them he could see coffee trees, loaded with green and scarlet berries. Occasionally he passed an Indian, dressed in dirty white pants with a gray checked blanket tied about his waist and an opennecked shirt. They passed silently, without glancing up, bent low under the weight of great wood or charcoal bundles carried on their backs. A cart went by, drawn by two pert, if tattered, little donkeys, and the driver smiled to Eric and nodded. There was a certain tenderness in the air in Guatemala, a softness and gentleness he found beguiling.

As he walked he watched for the place Señorita Montero had described and, when he approached it, was surprised to find his heart beating faster. It was the same as the others: a whitewashed wall covered with vines and, behind it, through the trees, he glimpsed the top of a small pink house.

The ornate iron gate was also massed with bougainvillaea, the blossoms crisp and transparent, as if they were butterflies which might rise any instant and swarm away. He gave a casual glance through as he walked by but only saw more flowers, red, yellow, purple, and he heard the harsh scolding voice of a parrot. He quickened his step and went on, continuing up the road and taking the next right turn.

An hour later he passed the house again, on his way back. This time, feeling bolder, he walked more slowly and, when he reached the gate, stopped, glanced quickly up and down the road, then stepped up close and peered through.

Suddenly a laugh spilled through the quiet air and he started as if someone had hit him, tried to find where it came from and then, glancing upward, saw her sitting on top of the wall, a few feet from him, still laughing.

"Are you looking for someone, Doctor?"

He stepped back and could feel his face burning. She sat facing him, arms clasped over her knees, her head tilted sideways. And he was astonished again at her bright pure fragile beauty. She wore a white cotton dress with many embroidered ruffles on the skirt; there was a black rebozo over her head and she was barefoot.

"I was—" he began, but could think of nothing further and stopped, agonizingly embarrassed.

"You've had a long walk," she said, and now her smile was tender, as if she regretted having caused him embarrassment. "You went by here more than an hour ago."

He went and stood beneath her. "Yes. I did. I was looking for you." He was puzzled. "How did you know I'm a doctor?"

"The lady at the hotel told me yesterday. She told me all about you." She was still smiling. "Won't you come in?"

He hesitated. "May I? You don't think I'm rude?"

She laughed again, turned quickly and disappeared from the wall. A moment later she unlocked the gate and he stepped in.

"Well," he said, looking down at her.

Then, in order to stop staring, he glanced around to see what his surroundings were. The house was set back some distance and a great jacaranda tree clouded most of it with purple bloom. The center of the patio was paved with flagstones, while around the walls flowers had been planted. Once, perhaps, they grew politely, but now they had become a lawless tangled swarming wilderness, a tumult and confusion of fertility, full of violent gorgeous color. The parrot, whose querulous voice he had heard earlier, teetered on his perch like an irresponsible drunk. A little monkey sat on a low branch of the tree, regarding Eric with bright black eyes. He had a collar about his neck and was fastened to the tree with a twenty-foot rope which, as he turned now and leapt to a higher branch, he carried with him over one arm, managing it like a woman with a long-trained evening gown. There were three or four wicker chairs, a glass-topped table with a basket of knitting on it and some books, and two large comfortable chaises.

"This is a little paradise," he said, feeling as if he had been allowed into something uncannily warm and comforting and full of incalculable promises. "Does it belong to your mother?"

"No. Daddy had some Guatemalan friends—we're staying here while they're away. My father is dead, you know." She said it as though he actually would know, and apparently took it for granted Señorita Montero had repeated to him everything she told her yesterday.

He lowered his eyes and watched a small lizard skitter across between them and disappear under a bush. "I know. I'm very sorry."

"Yes." She gave a soft sigh and turned away, tactfully, to let the difficult moment pass. Then she asked him if he would like something to eat or drink. "A glass of pineapple juice, perhaps? Or would you prefer something stronger?"

He smiled. "No, nothing stronger. That would be fine."

She turned and clapped her hands, with the air of a child playing at imperiousness. She whispered to him: "Isn't it incredible the way they do things here? See—" she said, pointing to a young Indian woman who came almost instantly out of the house. "It's like magic." She told the woman what they wanted and then asked him to sit down. She flung herself gracefully into one of the chaises, crossing her ankles, folding her arms behind her head.

"This is a *real* Indian dress," she said earnestly. "Don't you think it's pretty?"

"Very pretty." He sat down and lit a cigarette, after first offering one to her which she refused. He felt as baffled as if he had wakened in the midst of a dream and found the dream had become actuality. Everything about her bewildered and delighted him—she seemed some incredible combination of child and woman and something more which set an obscure alarm to ringing.

"Where is your mother?"

"Indoors. Writing letters. Why?"

"I was wondering. Won't she be a little—surprised—

to find me here? So soon, I mean? Maybe I shouldn't have come in."

"Of course you should. I asked you to. Mother knows I'm not a child."

"You're not much more. How old are you?"

"Seventeen. Almost eighteen," she added quickly. "How old are *you?*"

"I'm old—twenty-nine." He smiled at her.

"My!" she said, as if impressed. "Of course, you don't look it," she added comfortingly.

He laughed heartily at that, and began to feel more at ease. The Indian woman came back with glasses of cold pineapple juice. They sipped silently a moment or two. He drew a deep breath and realized that he had a sense of ease and contentment he had not felt in years, and perhaps had never felt so keenly before. He could not have explained why, for certainly her beauty alone could not do this to him.

"Where do you live?" he asked her.

"Kansas City. Have you ever been in Kansas City?"

"No. I can't say that I have."

"It's nice," she said, and nodded wisely. "Very nice. You'd like it. You must come and visit sometime."

"Thank you very much. I'd like to."

He was beginning to feel a little lightheaded and could not account for that, either. The sun was hot, but no hotter than it had been every day, and it had never troubled him before. Maybe she's a witch, he thought wryly, and has cast a spell over me. He glanced at her again, after that thought, and she looked, certainly, not in the least like a witch. Still, this strange peace and well-being must have treachery in it somewhere.

"You're from San Francisco, aren't you?" she asked him, going blithely ahead with the conversation, since he seemed to bog down repeatedly. She did not do it like a girl brought up to be carefully polite, but rather as though she had keen awareness of the feelings between people and, since he appearently needed help she gave it, unselfconsciously.

"Yes. And I am a doctor, as Señorita Montero told you. At least, I was one. Now I'm not so sure."

"What do you mean by that? Has anything bad happened?"

"No. Nothing bad. I'm just not sure I want to spend the rest of my life cutting people up. I'm a surgeon, you see." He sounded, to himself at least, very apologetic.

"But think of the good you can do!"

"I'm not so sure. Maybe I never should have become one. Three or four months ago I got drunk one night and convinced myself I could see everything much more clearly than when I was sober and that I didn't want to do what I was doing and never had. So I got on a plane and took off for Mexico City. Then I came here. I'll have to go back pretty soon, I guess."

"Oh—" She sounded genuinely disappointed. "Don't go back right away. We just got here."

He laughed. "All right. I won't—not right away."

He stood up and began to stroll about, hands in his pockets. He kept his back to her for two or three minutes as he pretended to examine the flowers and then, all at once, she was beside him. He turned and saw in her eyes, gazing up at him, that same innocent wonderment, almost adoration, which had been there yesterday. But there was no flirtatiousness, no invitation—it was as if, living behind her own beauty, she were aware only of his.

"Just think," she said softly. "Kansas City, and San Francisco. We never would have met."

The Indian woman came to pick up the empty glasses; they watched her go.

"I sent her out early this morning," she said, "to look for you and tell me when you came by."

He was shocked. "You did?" And something seemed to warn him: Time to get away from here. Something is beginning to happen you don't want to happen. He wondered now why he had come in the first place. There were so many pretty girls. Why had it seemed necessary to see this one again?

"Of course. I knew you'd come by." She smiled. "And I didn't want to miss you. I wanted to look at you again. You're like a cathedral—all the lines meeting and resolving—" Her hands traced delicately a pattern of perfect harmony. "It makes my eyes happy just to look at you." Then she frowned a little. "Is something wrong? Maybe I shouldn't have said that." She turned and went to stand beside the parrot, which began to move nervously up and down along his perch, yawping out loudly from time to time.

He followed her. "I'm sorry, Dulcie. I didn't mean to hurt your feelings. It's just that I'm—"

"I know. You're cautious. You have to be. Every compliment seems like a trap to you. You're afraid of women—"

He laughed. "I certainly never thought so. And I don't believe anyone else did, either." He found it very amusing she should have said that—about him, of all people. She was such a child.

Now she tilted her head to one side, studying him, and though her eyes were clear as sea water, he began to feel uncomfortable; they might also be as deep. "You've never been in love," she said.

"No. No, as a matter of fact, I guess I haven't. But how did you know that?"

She turned a little, laughing again, plucking a pink hibiscus blossom from the bush beside her and began fastening it in her hair, arms held high. Everything she did was easy, fluid, graceful, almost catlike. He wished he had not thought of that image—the only animal he detested.

"You think I can't know anything because I'm young. Women don't learn much more as they get older—they don't learn very much by experience, either." She smiled. And all at once she touched his arm, briefly, as if to reassure him. "Don't look so puzzled. Of course you're afraid of women—you've been running away from them all your life. Just because you made love to lots of them doesn't mean you weren't running away. You were trying to dominate them—and prove to yourself you had nothing to be afraid of. Weren't you?"

"Well—I—" He gave a hopeless shrug. "What else do you know about me?" He tried to look as if it were a joke, but he felt distinctly uncomfortable. He glanced around, wishing her mother would come out and put a stop to this conversation.

"Nothing. That's enough, isn't it?"

"I—uh—I think I'll be going along now."

"Why?"

He stood gazing down at her, caught by her merry pliant beauty. He felt a violent impulse to pull her against him and hold her there, making her aware of his physical strength—and set himself free. If he could make love to her, he knew he would never fear her again. He reached out to take her arm and, as he did so, an enormous cat came through the doorway, padded into the garden and approached them, smiling. He stared at it.

"My God!" He pointed. "What is that damned thing?"

The cat grew in size as it came toward them, becoming bigger with every step it took, until, now that it had reached them and was standing beside her, it was the size of a small leopard. And it was still smiling, looking directly at him and smiling. Slowly it ran its tongue across its mouth, as if savoring something it had just eaten or, perhaps, was about to eat.

He stood there, overcome with a terror and loathing greater than he had ever felt.

"What is it grinning at?" His voice sounded strange to him, far away, taut with fear.

She reached down and picked the cat up and, obediently, it became cat-sized again. She held it in her arms and stroked it—a pretty white kitten, with eyes the color of her own, seawater.

"You don't like cats?" she asked him.

He was soaked in sweat and he wiped one hand over his face with a kind of helpless desperation.

"No. Not very much," he said.

"Shall I take her indoors?"

"No, of course not. I'm sorry I acted like that. I don't know what came over me there for a minute. I thought—Well, never mind."

Still holding the kitten, caressing it, she went to stretch out on the chaise again. He felt an impulse to run, dash through the gate and set off down the road as fast as he could go, and he felt horribly ashamed of his cowardice. A man who had won medals in the War "for bravery in action, beyond the call of duty." Scared of a kitten and a girl. Unbelievable.

He sat down again and tried not to look at the kitten as it lay snuggled up close against her, curled into itself now, purring contentedly.

"What's its name?" he asked politely, impelled to make some conversation about it, if only to prove to himself the animal was of no concern to him. See? He could talk about it, inquire after its name and habits, as if it were a dog or—anything but a cat.

"Porphyria."

"Porphyria? Where in the hell did you get a name like that?"

"I don't remember. I suppose I read it some place or other, and it stayed in my mind." She looked down at the kitten a few moments, stroking it, and he watched her hands, fascinated, trying to imagine how they would feel on his body, pretending it was he she stroked, not the cat. The patio was much hotter now than when he had come and he felt very weak, almost the way he had when he was wounded, just before he passed out.

He told himself that he must get up and go, before something really terrible happened. Then he raised his eyes and saw her crouched there, staring at him—Dulcie had vanished and only the cat remained in the chair, as big as Dulcie, crouching, gazing steadily at him. He leaped up and rushed to the gate. He grabbed the gate handle, twisting and turning it frantically, feeling the cat close behind, knowing that it was about to pounce, knock him to the floor and fasten its teeth in his neck. He did not dare look back but kept struggling with the lock, panting, sweating, wild with rage and terror.

Suddenly the handle gave way and the gate swung open, almost as if it had been blown by a great wind, and he set off down the road, running as fast as he could. He ran on and on, back toward the Tzanjuyu. And, though he knew he was running faster than ever before, he kept forcing himself, harder and harder, until his lungs felt torn to shreds, the blood throbbed in his legs and arms, and there was a loud singing in his ears. He did not slacken his pace or once look back until he had reached the hotel grounds and gone several feet up the path.

Then he stopped and turned swiftly, to catch the animal and do battle with it. He stood in the middle of the road, half-crouching, his legs spread wide, his arms held out and his fingers curled. His eyes stared wildly about.

There was no cat, no person, within sight.

He looked around, searching carefully, in case it should be hidden somewhere, watching him and waiting. But he found nothing. And, at last, he walked on up the path to the hotel, around the front, and into his room where he sat down in a wicker chair and stared at the floor.

I'll leave tomorrow morning.

I'll pack tonight and tomorrow I'll get the hell out of here. I'll go back home. If it happened, I'd damn well better get out. And if it didn't, then I'm going crazy anyway and I'd better get back to where I can get some help if I need it.

He spent the rest of the afternoon putting through a call to Guatemala City, and the Spanish indifference to time made him so furious he all but forgot why he was in a hurry to leave. It was six o'clock before he had the arrangements completed and went into the bar for a drink.

The Mephistophelean one, in his dirty white sailor suit and dark-blue beret, looked up casually from his drink. "They tell me you're leaving, señor." They were standing side by side at the bar.

It was the first time Eric had heard him say that much and he glanced at him in surprise. "Tomorrow morning," said Eric. "Early," he added, in a voice he was surprised to hear sound so meaningful, as if anyone would understand quite well why he must leave as early as possible.

For a moment, he found himself and his present state of mind extremely comical, and could regard it with almost the same detachment he regarded a belly slit open by his scalpel—a belly which belonged to no one at all as he went to work on it.

"Isn't it soon?" the man asked him.

"Soon? What do you mean by that?" Again he was surprised, for he had interpreted the question as a subtle challenge, and his voice, now, was angry.

The man only looked at him, then shrugged his shoulders, finished his drink, and left. Eric scowled after him a moment and then suddenly banged down his glass and rushed out. The man was strolling along the pathway, followed by the stalking turkey. Eric ran after him.

"What did you mean by that? What is it *soon?*"

The man stopped and looked at him, amused and puzzled. "Why, nothing in particular, señor. I had thought you meant to stay longer. I should have thought—" He shrugged.

"You should have thought what?" Eric glared at him

belligerently, and could feel his fists clenched at his sides. Again he stood apart from himself and looked on, amazed at how funny he had become.

"Señor, I see I have offended you. I'm sorry. Señorita Montero had told me she expected you to be here some time longer. Certainly you are at liberty to go when you please."

"You're damned right I'm at liberty! I don't know where she got that idea anyway. I'm leaving tomorrow!"

"Very well, señor." Eric was peering at him but it was difficult to tell, with that black beard, whether he was smiling at him or not. "I wish you a good journey."

"Thanks!" snapped Eric, and turned on his heel. He went back to the bar. The big woman and her brother were there and he looked at them closely when he came in, to see if they would make any comment about his leaving. In fact, he got the distinct impression that they had been talking about him. One word, he thought to himself. Let them say one word.

He ordered another drink and stood with his back to the room, as he had been standing last night just before he saw her. He began, slowly, to let himself remember: He had been standing thinking about nothing in particular almost at peace with himself, almost a vegetable, in fact, aware only of the hot sun streaming onto his back, the big thick flies that buzzed through the room, the raw feel of bourbon in his throat—anticipating nothing. Then she had come through the doorway, laughing. And as he saw her again, almost as clearly as yesterday, he had a sensation of sweet piercing pain, which took him by surprise.

After his experience with her that afternoon he would not have believed he could feel such intense nostalgia and gratitude. For how could he *possibly* feel gratitude, considering what she had done to him? Then he remembered that very likely she had not done anything—his own imagination had done it. Even if she wanted to, after all, a woman could not change into a cat, though he had often thought how logical it would be.

Well, then, supposing it had been a hallucination—it was she who had alarmed him into producing it, and that was reason enough to distrust her. What kind of woman could be capable of giving a man a start like that? They had tried all kinds of tricks on him the past fifteen years or so, but this one was in a class by itself. No, there was no doubt about it. She was the one who must be held responsible.

He wondered vaguely if he had had enough presence of mind to make up any sort of excuse for his abrupt departure. But what possible difference did that make? When something extraordinary happened, it was absurd to expect oneself to behave with ordinary calm politeness. And he would never see her again, so it could scarcely matter if she considered him a boor.

Now he had begun to feel nervous and excited, as if his muscles were little snapping rubber bands; his breath was coming faster. He went back outdoors and began to walk, in the opposite direction from her house, and when he got back it was time for dinner.

Convinced that he would not be able to sleep, he took a pill and fell asleep promptly. A few hours later he wakened and sat up with a start, staring about the moonlit room, filled with panic and confusion. He felt that something terrible had been about to happen and that he had only saved himself by waking. But now, though he could not remember what had menaced him, he found a new terror:

He had no idea where he was.

He sprang out of bed and moved about the room, trying to discover whether he was in his own apartment, or in the house his family had lived in. He sought frantically for familiar chairs and objects but could find none and then, just when the terror had mounted to a pitch that seemed unbearable, he remembered.

Of course. The Tzanjuyu. Guatemala. He was leaving in a few hours. Or perhaps he had slept right on through the day and it was now night again—trapping him here for one more day. He switched on the light.

It was only three o'clock; he had plenty of time. He started to turn it off again but decided not to. The dark seemed too unfriendly, peopled with threatening figures he could neither find nor identify. He picked up a book and began to read. It was no longer possible to stand apart from himself and be amused. The terror, though its source was unknown, had become too great, too dangerous, too engrossing. He could not get free enough even to wonder at it, now.

About five he got dressed. I'll go out, he decided, and take a walk—work up an appetite for breakfast. The car that was to drive him back to Guatemala City was leaving at nine.

He set off down the road.

And presently, because the morning grew rapidly so bright, the air was so fresh and fragrant, he began to walk briskly and to feel the movement of his body and muscles again. He strode along with his hands in his pockets, smelling everything and seeing everything, and before he knew it he was glad to be alive again.

He decided to go by Dulcie's house. Just walk past and stop a moment and say good-by to her, without, of course, either seeing or speaking to her. Too bad, he thought, with what he believed was a certain ruefulness, that he would never see her again. She was so marvellously captivating. If they could have met somewhere else, at home, not down here in this strange land—and without her mother around. It would have been so much simpler if he had not had to meet her mother.

The sun got hotter and the day more brilliantly blue; clouds rolled foaming across the mountains. He passed an old Indian carrying a great bouquet of tiny wild orchids. Two women went by him, their eyes cast down, each balancing on her head a great basket stacked with bottles. He noticed again how the Indians had their own gait, a kind of skimming scuttle—and a profound silence that seemed to him both serene and mysterious. The buzzards hovered everywhere in Guatemala. They sailed in slow swooping curves through the sky, and perched on roof tops and in the trees; up close their stench was like a deserted battlefield.

He slowed down as he approached her house because he knew that once there he would pause, tell her good-by silently, return to the hotel and have his breakfast and leave. He enjoyed his loitering and the mildly poignant sorrow he now felt for something which might have been both beautiful and significant in his life but which was about to end—before it had quite begun. The gods must have been, in some way, against it. He smiled, vaguely pleased with these maudlin thoughts.

It would be a pleasant little episode to recall later as part of the dreamlike quality of this country where nothing had seemed real to him, where he felt not even responsible for himself, what he might do or say or have happened to him. That feeling had been a relief, after all the years when he had been insistently in charge of everything he did. Now it was over.

He stopped outside the gate and stood remembering how she had waited for him yesterday morning, sitting on top of the wall in her white dress and bare feet, looking down at him and laughing. Automatically he glanced that way. She was not there now. It was only six o'clock and all of them, her mother and the Indian maid and she, must be asleep. He would not have come by unless he had been sure of that. Then why should he feel this slight curious disappointment?

He pictured her sleeping, perfectly serene. She would have no bad dreams or wake up in panic, not knowing where she was. Then he saw himself lying beside her, waking to look at her and, after a moment, reaching out to wake her, too. Time to go, he decided, when his thoughts took that direction.

Absently he touched a shrub with a long drooping dark-red blossom, almost like an animal's tail. And, as touched it, he started back in sudden horror, for it was warm and moist, as if he held something of flesh in his hand. He looked at it with repugnant loathing and let it go.

The feel of it had made him a little sick and he turned to leave, forgetting to bid her good-by. He had again an urgent need to get away quickly and wished he had not come back here at all. He had only made himself feel a fool and a coward.

He took a step and, as he did so, the earth began to tremble, very very slightly. He thought for a moment he might have imagined it. But the quiver came again and he stopped, testing the earth with his feet, pressing down hard upon it. He knew that Guatemala had many earthquakes, and was neither alarmed nor frightened. There were no natural phenomena, he believed, which could scare him very much.

Why should they? He had spent his life studying and mastering them.

The tremor came again, and this time it was a rude hard jolting shake, as if the ground had moved sideways beneath him, like dogs tugging opposite ends of a tablecloth. He felt a sharp spasm of fear and the premonition that something altogether beyond his control was about to happen. Instantly the ground heaved beneath him and he staggered, trying to keep his footing, stumbling toward the wall. He heard a sudden high fanatic laugh—whether a woman's or an animal's he did not know—fierce and shrill and defiant. The ground rushed up again and he leaped high to avoid being sruck by it, his arms and legs flying out grotesquely, grasping at the vines, at the air, and he heard again the taunting laugh. There was a distant rumble, growing steadily louder, like the sound of mountains crashing; the world itself seemed to be breaking up. His ears were humming and the shapes and colors about him grew vaguer, then began to plunge at each other, blending and blurring like a madly spinning kaleidoscope. He staggered this way and that, battling hopelessly as the earth rolled beneath him in enormous swelling waves. His head felt as if it had detached itself from his body and whirled in the air above him. The waves rose higher and higher and he reared back, raising both arms to ward them off, when they struck him full force. He heard once more the laugh and, mingled through it like a high reed instrument, a woman's terrified scream, or perhaps the wail of an animal.

It's a coward's fate, he told himself, when he realized where he was—in some dark fathomless cave. If I had not been so much afraid of her I would not have made plans to leave and I would not have passed her house one last time and the earthquake would not have caught me, because the ground never opens in many places, only a few, and the chances are I would not have been in one of those places.

And then he realized that, since the earth had broken open and he had toppled in, he must be trapped someplace impossible to escape from, where he would be smothered, strangled to death by the lack of air or, even, by the earth itself.

These, then, must be his last few moments and it would presently happen: A cave-in, perhaps, crushing him; and he would have only air enough in his lungs for a minute or two at the most—probably not even that because the shock and fear would make him gasp automatically and then there would be no air in his lungs at all. The earth would fill his mouth and nostrils and he would have reached the last moment of his life.

He had watched so many people die: some who died quietly in their sleep, some who died screaming and fighting, some who died when they were old and sick and their lives used up; babies dying almost before life had begun, young men and women dying when they wanted and needed most to live. He had thought that he was used to death. Now, he realized that he might have become a surgeon to ward off his own great fears of death, to master them through helping others live. To control, himself, both life and death.

He had not succeeded. He found himself an abject craven coward. During the War he had been brave—but he had not believed then that he could die. Well—he had met himself face to face at last. This must be the ugliest sight in the world, he thought—your own self, when you finally confront it.

The place where he was seemed dark and perfectly hollow, airless. It might have been the lack of air which made him feel as if he were being crushed or it could have been motionless water, the exact temperature of his body. Still, if it were that, if he had fallen into some subterranean pool, he would not be breathing, and would obviously have drowned by now.

But I'm only lying here and waiting.

He was amazed to discover his own passivity—though it had probably lasted no more than a few seconds. I may not be buried very deep, I may be able to get out. He prepared inside himself to make the effort, intending that it should be great and final, that he would risk everything on it at once, break free and escape, or find that it was impossible. Whatever was going to happen, must be made to happen immediately.

He slowly gathered his strength, like a knot inside him, crouched in close upon himself, legs and arms doubled against his belly, and prepared to spring, like a vast steel coil. Whatever was in his way, whatever it was that enveloped him, would be burst and ripped and broken open by the immensity of strength he began to feel, and he would be free. He had as great a conviction of his impending freedom as he had had, a few moments earlier, of his impending death. Or perhaps it was the same conviction —for this effort he was about to make seemed so enormous it almost promised to set him free from life itself.

I'll yell at the same time, he thought, as if he believed that would give him added strength. And the next instant he heard the yell, his arms and legs burst wide, and he had leaped off the bed and was standing beside it, looking around him.

The room was deeply shadowed, though slits of sunlight came through the closed shutters. The floor was tile, set with a mosaic pattern he could see as he looked down at his bare feet. There was, in addition to the rumpled bed, a great chest, two chairs, and a small desk, all painted black, in the Spanish fashion; some tin candlesconces and frames holding mottled mirrors or religious paintings hung on the whitewashed wall. Dulcie stood beside him.

He saw her with no particular surprise. It was as though, once he found that he was not in a deep cave but in a room, that he was neither dead nor about to die, he had known she would be there.

"I think you should lie down again, Eric," she said, in her voice that was light as the dandelion puffs he had blown when he was small.

She wore a ruffled white blouse and a full black skirt. There was a red hibiscus in her hair, rows of silver circles on one arm, and her legs and feet were bare. She touched him and her hand felt neither warm nor cool, only soft and tender; she smelled of some faint fragrance that sent part of his mind off trying to find where he remembered it from, and why. She was looking up into his face with an eager little smile, though there was concern in her expression, too.

He did not want to lie down again and was, in fact, afraid of lying down since he had been in this bed, apparently, all the time he believed himself in a cave or pool, and he was not at all sure he could prevent himself from falling back again into one or the other if he did lie down. It seemed advisable to stay on his feet and in touch with reality.

"How can the house still be standing? I should have thought it would be completely destroyed. Or is this all that's left of it?"

"All that's left? No. Everything else is the same. How could it have been destroyed?"

He smiled at her for teasing him. "I've seen earthquakes," he said. "But never one like that." He shook his head at the end of the sentence and was unpleasantly surprised to find that it seemed to have nothing in it but one large iron ball which rolled slowly about, tilting his head by its shifting weight, first to one side and then to the other. "What in the hell," he muttered, and tried it again. The ball rolled back and forth.

Dulcie had come a little closer and he sensed that she might be expecting him to fall and was going to try to help him if he did. He spread his feet wider, looking down at them to make sure he did it right, moving the right one first, planting it solidly, and then the left. As he looked down he noticed that he was still wearing the gray slacks, but his shirt was off and he saw his wet brown hairy chest and arms. He raised his head slowly again, afraid that if he moved it quickly the ball would roll and his head might tip back so far his neck would be broken.

"There *was* an earthquake, wasn't there?"

"No, Eric. There was no earthquake. I don't know what happened, but I suppose you must have fainted."

He gave a start of horror. "Fainted? Me? My God, I never faint!"

"You were lying out there in the road. One of the Indians passing by saw you and called Marcia. He helped us bring you in here."

"*Who* brought me in?" he demanded, watching her cannily, for it had occurred to him that damned animal might have carried him in. The idea was so funny he burst into laughter, but a chill ran over his back and arms.

"The Indian, and Marcia—and Mother and I." She smiled and made a little gesture. "You were heavy. You must weigh at least a hundred and ninety."

"One eight-eight," he said, and scratched the back of his head. But, as he did so, tipping his head without remembering the iron ball inside it, it rolled suddenly forward and crashed against the front of his skull and he pitched over, feeling her body against him for a moment, just at the last.

He heard them talking about him, though they were whispering. But he was much too clever to move or open his eyes or by any sign let them know he could hear. He felt an intense curiosity about what they would say—two women talking about a man—as if he had sneaked in the back door of some forbidden temple and would now learn the eternal secrets. They stood beside the bed, Dulcie and her mother, looking down at him.

"It's getting late, Dulcie."

"It isn't midnight yet." Several more hours had slipped out of his life, then; there had been sunlight, the last he remembered. "Let me stay a little longer. He may wake up. I think he's sleeping now. A couple of hours ago he moved around and mumbled and I think that's when he changed from being unconscious to sleeping."

"I don't like to have you in here. He may have a fever, or any kind of sickness. I'm afraid you'll catch it."

"I've never caught anything, Mother. I want to be with him. And I'm not afraid. Anyway, I don't believe he's sick from fever—I think it's something else."

"What else could it be? He's been unconscious for most of seventeen hours. I still think we should have a doctor come out from Guatemala City."

"No, Mother. Please don't send for one yet. I'm sure it isn't that kind of sickness—I think he's had some kind of shock."

"It must have been quite a shock, to put him into this condition."

"Don't make fun of him. When he can't defend himself."

There was a long pause.

"I'm afraid you're in love with him, Dulcie."

"I know I am. Look at him. He's perfectly beautiful. How could anyone not love him?"

"You don't love people because they're beautiful."

"Lots of people loved me because I am. But it's not only the way he looks. It's everything else he is, too."

"You don't know him well enough to know what else he is."

"I can feel it, though."

There was another pause, probably while Mrs. Parkman shook her head. "You're so young—so helplessly young. I'm afraid for you."

"Don't be afraid, Mother. What is there to be afraid of?"

"So many many things. Well—stay a little longer, then, since you want to so much. Good night, darling."

"Good night, Mother. Mother—let me kiss you. I love you."

"I love you, Dulcie. Marcia will sit with him when you go to bed."

The door closed softly.

A few minutes after that he opened his eyes, moving restlessly first, as if he were just waking. He looked up and saw her sitting in a chair beside the bed, leaning forward with her hands clasped lightly in her lap, watching him with a wide intent gaze. He felt ashamed that he had listened and absolutely horrified by what he had heard. How *could* she have fallen in love with him? What had he done or said? He felt as if he had been implicitly accused of a crime, and tried to persuade himself that he was innocent—it was only because she was so young, at the age where a girl will fall in love with anyone because she is prepared for it and waiting.

He would do the only thing he could—and which he felt sure her mother was expecting: he would get up and get out of there immediately, go to Guatemala City, and fly home.

Still, he could not escape the obscure conviction that something terrible had happened to him. She had had no right to fall in love with him and he blamed her for it, as if she had tricked him unfairly. In a way, he was lucky nothing worse had happened to him, while he lay there unconscious and at her mercy.

He looked at her and she looked so soft, so helpless, as her mother had said, so beautiful and gentle, unguarded, willing to accept him without question or complaint— that he filled instantly with remorse and shame and had to look away.

"Eric— You're awake?"

"Yes. I'm awake."

"Are you feeling better?"

"Much better, thanks." He did not like the curt sound

of his voice, but that was the way it came out and there was nothing he could do.

"Can't I get you something to eat? There's some hot soup in the kitchen."

"No, thanks," he said. And then changed his mind. "Yes, I think I would like some. If it's not too much trouble."

She smiled eagerly, as if delighted to have a chance to do something for him, and ran out of the room. "I'll be right back."

He got up hastily, felt under the bed for his shoes but could not find them. He searched around for his shirt, opened a large chest and found it in there, jerked it off the hanger and slipped it on. Then, buttoning it as he went, not bothering any more about his shoes, he stole softly to the door, found the living room empty and hurried across it. He was still weak and dizzy and as soon as he was out on the road and had a place to hide, he would sit down again and rest.

He went on into the patio. There was a moon and he made his way across, hoping he would not disturb the parrot or monkey and set them to chattering. He reached the gate and was trying to open it when he heard her voice.

"Eric!"

He leaned back quickly, taking refuge in the shadows, and felt sweat break over his body. Dear God, don't let her find me, he prayed.

She came quickly through the doorway and walked straight toward him. He stayed in the shadows, even when she was standing in front of him, as if his own desire not to be seen could prevent her from seeing him.

"Eric—what are you doing out here?" She sounded genuinely puzzled.

"I'm leaving. Unlock the gate."

"Eric—"

"Unlock that gate!" He whispered the words harshly and, as she hesitated, grabbed her by the arm and jerked her roughly. She winced and gave a soft little moan; he let her go. His heart was pounding as if he had run a mile race and his chest heaved with the effort to breathe.

"Unlock it," he repeated, begging her now. "Please,

Dulcie, for the love of God, unlock it and let me out of here."

"But why? Why do you want to go? You mustn't go out there alone now. Wait until morning. I'm not trying to keep you a prisoner, Eric."

At that last, saying in soft-spoken reasonable words exactly what it was he feared, he had to laugh. "I know you're not. But I'm late. I had made plans to leave for Guatemala City. I'm flying back to the States. My plane has left already. I've missed it—don't you understand that?"

"There are others, Eric."

"But I had to get back!" His voice rose at first and he made a sudden hard gesture with one fist, then instantly subdued his tone again. The last thing he wanted was for her mother to hear them and come walking out, smiling as she had the other day. That disgusted him infinitely, to realize he had her mother confused with the giant smiling cat; he glanced toward the door, half expecting the animal. The door was empty, softly lighted from within.

"Come back," she said tenderly. "And have your soup. You haven't eaten anything all day." She took one of his hands in her own and he followed her, meek and docile.

Under one lamp, on a corner table, she had set a tin tray with a pottery bowl of thick soup, a blue linen napkin and, in a narrow silver vase, two lushly opened red roses. It was the sight of the flowers that made him ashamed of himself. They signified her innocent eagerness to please him and made his own urgent need to escape seem even more childish and absurd. He gave her an apologetic smile and picked up the spoon.

She sat on a nearby chair with her hands clasped over one knee and watched him. "Is it hot enough?"

"It's wonderful. I didn't know how hungry I was!"

She jumped up. "Let me get you something more." She started to run out, but halfway across the room she stopped and turned around, her head cocked to one side, smiling mischievously. "Can I trust you?"

He laughed. "You can trust me."

She went on and he finished the soup, enjoying it more, it seemed, than anything he had ever eaten. He was calm and easy now, too, no longer afraid; relaxed and perfectly content. He looked around the room and thought how pretty it was, with its red and black tiled floor, the small round fireplace, the Victorian couch and chairs covered with a hand-woven Guatemalan fabric, the carved Spanish chests and desk. There was a primitive religious painting on one wall, tin candlesconces and mirrors and Indian rugs on the others.

He had never been so comfortable.

The earlier part of the day, since the moment he had fallen unconscious in the road, seemed incredible. Nothing like that had happened to him before, and now he thought it wise to convince himself it had never happened. Certainly when you saw giant cats appear from nowhere and were knocked down by an earthquake no one else felt, the most sensible course afterward was to make up your mind that none of it had even been imagined— much less, had actually occurred. That nonsense is over and done with, he told himself firmly; he was convinced he had made a new start in life.

Everything seemed different to him now.

Dulcie, for example, coming through the door carrying another tray, walking quickly and silently in her bare feet, was merely the prettiest girl, he had seen in his life and, perhaps, the sweetest and simplest, as well.

She moved the soup bowl and set a plateful of ham and potato salad before him. She put down a cup of hot coffee, sugar and cream, and a dish of sliced pineapple. All the while he watched her, enjoying the serious absorbed expression on her face, the glint of her hair under the light, the smoothness of her bare arms reaching before him, the curve of her breasts.

There was only one thing wrong with Dulcie from his point of view: She should have been a little older than seventeen and she should not have been a virgin, which he knew with certainty that she was. He liked to think he was tough and calloused, but still, virgins gave him some qualms of conscience, not quite pleasant. He felt too responsible to their mothers.

"I'm sorry we didn't have something more," she said. "I hope that's enough."

"It's fine."

He began to eat and she picked up an orange and sat peeling it in her fingers, tossing the rinds into a bowl, separating the orange carefully and eating the sections one by one. Each move she made was delicate and dainty and so completely feminine it gave him a kind of exquisite pain to watch her.

"If only you didn't have to go away," she said wistfully.

"Maybe I don't," he replied, to his own surprise.

"Oh, Eric!" She clapped her hands together like a gleeful child. "I hope not!"

He glanced up from his plate and she was watching him with an artless intensity that made him ashamed of his cowardly plans to escape from her. "I won't," he said. "I can get out of it."

"Oh, Eric, I'm so glad! We'll have fun together—I know we will."

He smiled mysteriously. "I never doubted that for a minute."

He finished eating and lit a cigarette. Dulcie put the plates back on the tray and carried them to the kitchen while he sat, one leg cocked over the arm of his chair, feeling very lordly as he watched her waiting on him. When she came back she stood before him with her feet apart and arms clasped behind her, smiling.

"I'm sleepy," she said. "I'll go to bed now." He half expected her to come and kneel beside him and ask him to hear her prayers. "Will I see you in the morning?"

He got up, grinding out the cigarette. "Show me where my shoes are. I'll go back to the hotel. I'm okay now."

"But you don't have to go, Eric. It's so late, and no one uses that room anyway."

"You're sure it's all right? I'll leave early."

She laughed. "You don't have to leave early. Mother and I like you."

He was convinced by now that not only had he imagined the earthquake and the giant cats, but he had also imagined hearing her tell her mother she loved him. And, since these things were in his mind and had no relation to reality, he was free to initiate, himself, whatever was going to happen between them.

"Dulcie, before you go, I want to thank you. It was very kind of you to take me in like that. I can't account for it. I have no idea what happened—I'm not a guy who goes around keeling over. And I appreciate what you and your mother did—especially since you'd only seen me a couple of times."

"Why, Eric, we'd have done that—if we'd never seen you before at all."

"I know you would."

"Good night, Eric."

"Good night, Dulcie."

He watched her walk out, turning at the door to smile once more, and then went into his own room. With his clothes still on he lay down and tried to sleep. But he had slept so much during the day that it was impossible now. After an hour or so he got up and switched on the light, found his shoes, and sat down to write them a note. He thanked both Dulcie and her mother, said that he was going back to the Tzanjuyu and would return during the day. He left the note on the bed, switched off the light, and went out softly.

He opened and closed the patio gate very carefully, so the bells would not sound, and had walked nearly a quarter of a mile before he realized that she must have put the key in the lock for him, so that he could leave if he wanted to.

I could fall in love with a girl like that, he thought, grinning to himself.

But of course I won't.

He glanced around, to make sure he was not being followed, and the road was empty in the moonlight. He was back at the Tzanjuyu in twenty minutes and went promptly to sleep.

He made up a story to tell Señorita Montero—who, in turn, would tell the others—to account for his absence yesterday and explain his change of plans. The story was a good one, a little elaborate, but plausible and in keeping with his conviction that a lie should be impossible to check. Then, when he saw Dulcie and her mother, he told them about it so that neither they nor Marcia would mention his presence with them the day before. And they all laughed delightedly.

"Of course, Mrs. Parkman," he explained, "I'm not usually a liar. But I feel embarrassed about what happened yesterday and I'd like to keep it as quiet as possible."

"You can trust us, Doctor," Mrs. Parkman said, smiling.

The next two or three days he was not quite sure if he was ingratiating himself with Dulcie or with her mother. In any case, her mother no longer made him uneasy because he had decided that he would never make love to Dulcie, and that gave him such a good feeling of self-abnegation that he was more affectionate toward the two women, and himself as well.

Mrs. Parkman left them alone most of the time. Either she trusted him, or she trusted Dulcie; it pleased him to see a girl of Dulcie's beauty brought up to be her own guardian in life.

They sat in the sun in the patio hour after hour, talking, interrupted now and then by the parrot, watching the monkey and laughing at his mischievous tricks. They ate cool slices of fresh pineapple, and papaya with lime juice sprinkled over it, and drank many glasses of iced tea which Marcia brought whenever Dulcie clapped her hands. The walls enclosed them in brilliant light and heat, in violet shadows that formed like pools back in still corners, in the flowers spilling and climbing everywhere. Dulcie and her wonderful quiet garden had absorbed him. He could feel himself change each morning as he entered it, as if he had been waiting anxiously, not quite believing it would be there this time, and again, when he left her at night, and returned to his own untidy world at the Tzanjuyu. It was the first refuge and peace he had ever found, and he marvelled, three days later, that he had ever been such a fool as to have wanted to run away. All the rest of his life he would have this to remember, and he knew that someday he would need it badly.

He did not consider himself a man capable of or seeking premonitions. But the way things had been when he left, you did not have to be a seer to know that these few days would be a haven of serenity and content to which he would return many many times.

He did not even notice the absence of the white kitten at first and, when he did, did not mention it for fear she would have Marcia bring it out. He wanted nothing, however trivial, to spoil this treasure he was gathering to take back home with him.

He had discovered a quality in her which surprised

him: all at once he realized that she had not had very much to say, while he had been talking with more freedom and energy and initiative than ever before in his life. And he knew, furthermore, that she was always listening. She never cut off her interest, lost track of it, or diverted it to another subject. It was as if, by listening, she drew his thoughts and troubles into herself where, he did not doubt, she could better handle them than he.

He told her about his family and how he had grown up: very poor, his father an immigrant Danish laborer with great ambitions for his four sons. He told her about his brothers and himself; how hard his mother had had to work, taking care of them; about his years in college, playing football and working his way through school; his training and internship and the three years and a half in the Army. The story was simple and ordinary and he did not try to dramatize it but, nevertheless, for the first time it seemed to have more interest, more excitement, and more dignity than he had ever given himself credit for.

And, while he told her what had happened to him, he found that he was also telling her how he had felt about it, discovering much he had not known himself: more bitterness than he had suspected, and considerably more idealism.

"You're beginning to make me think I'm a hell of an interesting fella," he told her one day, when he suddenly turned self-conscious.

"You are, Eric."

"Nobody could be interesting enough for the amount of talk I've been doing about it. I don't know what got into me. It's as though I wanted to give myself away to you—get rid of myself, maybe. Leave myself here and go back home without me." He laughed, not very happily.

She was stretched out on the chaise beneath a manzanilla tree which had dropped a few of its yellow blossoms into her black skirt. She lay beautifully relaxed, watching him with a tender little smile. She was here now, so near he could touch her, though he had not, but sometime very soon their lives would separate and the separation would be permanent. It made him feel sick and scared and lost.

"Dulcie," he said, "when are you and your mother leaving?"

"I don't know. Whenever we get enough of being here."

"Where will you go next? Home?"

"I don't think so. Mother doesn't want to go home yet. There's still too much of Father left."

"You mean he's home—not here with you?"

"He's here, too, of course. But not as much. At home, he's more insistent. He's everywhere and in everything. We must wait for him to leave, at least part of the time."

"And will you be able to agree about when he's left?"

"Yes, I think so. Mother and I understand each other very well."

"I think you understand everyone. I've never met a girl—woman," he corrected hastily, "who seemed to understand so readily and easily."

"There probably isn't as much to understand as everyone pretends."

He sat quietly a moment. "There's always seemed so much to me. But maybe that's what happens when you learn quite a bit about any one thing—what's inside a human body, for instance. There's so goddamned much there and it's so intricate—it makes you think you haven't learned anything at all. That's when you start to get scared."

"Scared of what?"

"I—don't know. But I know that one day in the operating room I had somebody's belly open—I can't remember if it was a man or a woman—and all of a sudden I got so scared I wanted to turn and run as fast as I could. I finished the operation, of course, but later on I realized that I didn't know what the hell I'd done and I waited in agony for three days to find out if anything had gone wrong. She got well—the patient was a woman, I remember now. And I came down here."

He shook his head and could feel the sweat start. He gave a shivering spasm, though it was midafternoon and the heat folded round them like sheets of hot metal.

"Now I don't know what I'm going to do. I'm afraid I can't trust myself to operate again. I can't imagine what's ahead of me." He was sitting with his legs spread wide, elbows resting on his thighs, his fists clenched;

looking down he saw three or four drops of sweat fall onto the flagstone. He was almost as terrified as he had been that day in the operating room. He began to shake all over. And then her hand touched his shoulder.

"Eric—"

Her voice went into him so that he scarcely realized it had come as a sound. He turned and saw her face close to his, sea-water eyes and pink moist mouth, soft skin, hair light as spindrift. He caught the delicate scent of her breath, rousing a sudden desire to get drunk on it, drunker than he had ever been. And while he stared, entranced, he began to notice that all about them the flowers were growing—growing taller, reaching, spreading, swelling to vast yellow and red and purple and pink trumpets. The trees were growing too, multiplying, thickening; great vines trailed from them, twisting and writhing, moving closer, stretching greedily toward them. In another moment, obviously, they would be snatched up by this close terrible gorgeous jungle, seized and swallowed, and would disappear forever into its moiling chaos.

He sat helplessly, wondering in some dull way why she did not try to do anything about it, did not even take notice of what was going on all around them, only continued to gaze at him. Vaguely, he heard her say: "Don't be afraid, Eric. You mustn't be afraid of life or it will turn on you. I think I do understand you, as you said. But you can only understand people by loving them, you know—there really is no other way." Now the pupils in her eyes began to swell until the black almost engulfed the green, and her face changed—slowly, it seemed, but, almost, instantaneously—and she had become a perfectly sleek, extraordinarily beautiful black panther.

"I love you, Eric," she said.

He leaped up. "Dulcie!"

The words were repeated. "I love you." But they were no longer words—now, a soft hiss.

He looked around frantically. Everything was in motion—the flowers, bending, plunging, leaping ecstatically; the trees, still rooted, but their vines and branches swaying, swooping, jerking in tumultuous convulsion. Even the ground was pulsing and throbbing beneath his feet, as though it had come alive.

He looked desperately about him but could not even

see the house; the jungle must have eaten it first, and now was advancing on him. While there she sat at his feet with the mere tip of her tail, circling round behind her, moving in gentle sinister rhythm.

She watched him, and she was smiling, as if this trick of hers, having pretended first that she was human, was the most entertaining she had ever played. And why not—since he had undoubtedly been more thoroughly taken in by it than anyone she had ever played it on before?

He stood and looked at her, wondering if he dared to try to make a break. But, by sneaking his eyes surreptitiously around, he saw that not only had the house disappeared, but the walls and gate as well. There was nothing but the restless heaving jungle, and this animal at his feet, watching him and smiling faintly, amused, no doubt, at his alarm.

"I hope you're not hungry," he said.

This is the funniest one yet, he reflected. This is so goddamned funny that if it was anyone but me I'd die laughing.

"No," said the panther agreeably. "Not just now." Its voice was somewhat nasal, and he could not be sure if it miaowed or spoke in words, but whatever it did, he had no difficulty understanding.

"You wouldn't like me, anyway," he assured it eagerly. "Everyone's always said I'm indigestible as hell. They think they'll like me when they begin—but I don't go down so well."

"We'll see."

He coughed and cleared his throat and stretched his neck a little. He looked at the panther and it looked back at him, and apparently for the time being it had no special intentions of devouring him. The jungle had quieted down, too, though it was still as overgrown as before, a dishevelled anarchy of trees, flowers, vines and creepers, but there was less commotion.

A sly thought entered his mind that if the panther actually was not hungry it might be willing to let him escape, since it certainly could not be a very smart animal, capable of thinking ahead to when it *might* be hungry. Or could it?

It moved closer to him and his stomach gave a quick

sickening clench as he realized how big it was, reaching to his thighs, and how powerful the muscles were under that sleek gleaming and glossy black hide. But all it did was walk around him twice, surveying him as it did so, looking whimsically amused all the while, and then it leaned against the backs of his legs. The next thing he knew it was purring, a loud rumble that echoed through the length of its body, and which he could feel as it pressed itself against him with what seemed to be intense affection.

Was it possible the beast actually liked him?

He found himself a little flattered, as well as tremendously relieved. To charm a panther, even for a moment, was a quality he had never suspected might be among his potentialities. He experienced a moment's wondering pleasure and self-admiration; then quickly jerked himself back to reality.

This affection—since there seemed no other way to interpret its liquid and ardent behavior—was something of which he must take immediate advantage. It might be real or it might be another ruse, like the first one where the perfidious beast had played it was a beautiful girl— though that must have been at least a thousand years ago. But one way or another, he had better try to use its temporary good humor for improving his own predicament.

He reached down, along one leg, moving his sweating hand slowly and tentatively, feeling for the back of its neck, half expecting that at any moment it would fasten its teeth into his wrist. He bent slightly sideways, feeling behind him, and then his hand touched the top of its smooth head and his fingers began to stroke. The purr grew louder and now the animal glided around and stood gazing up at him with what he would have sworn was a look of fondness and pleading.

"I wish you wouldn't be so afraid of me," it said, in a most wheedling and reasonable tone. "I enjoy being petted."

"You do?" Every time the damned thing spoke he was surprised all over again. Or was he only imagining that it talked to him? Still, why not? If it could change from a woman to a panther, it would not be any great additional trick to talk as well. It could simply carry that ability along with it, from one life to the next, whenever it took the notion to change disguises.

He even had a sudden happy thought that before it decided to eat him it might change back to Dulcie again. But he knew it would be foolish to count on that. The safest procedure undoubtedly was to cajole it as much as possible right now and try to get it to let him escape.

He knelt before the animal and it stood facing him, gazing at him with those green and black eyes, thoughtful, speculative, humorous eyes, except for their disconcerting habit of never blinking as he stared into them and never looking away. While he stroked it, running his hand down along its shining back and flanks, he tested himself with it, but the animal won the test each time; it was always he who must look away.

And the while it kept up its steady rumbling purr.

"Look here," he said finally. "Don't you find things rather confining here?" He glanced around, indicating the dark discordant jungle, which had grown even more knotted and confused since the last time he looked.

"Not particularly. Why? Do you?"

"Yes, I do. I'm not accustomed to jungles and I can't even breathe very well in them." The air had become wet and torpid, and seemed almost a heavy weight. "For instance," he said, "I'd like to go for a walk."

The panther gazed steadily at him, but neither nodded its head nor spoke. Slowly he stood up. "Let's take a look around," he suggested. The animal blinked now, but only one eye, which startled him. However, it offered no objection and he began peering about, trying to remember which way the gate had been. Might as well just start off, he decided. It may be miles from here by now.

The jungle was all alike and there was no place where it looked easiest to begin——everywhere the same brawling network teeming with enormous flowers of every color, a living struggling labyrinth from which, he was sure, only a fool could even imagine the possibility of escape. The ground underfoot was soft and spongy, with starry green moss he sank into at every step. Nevertheless, he began to move slowly forward, pushing aside vines and branches, taking care they did not snap back in his face before he could move away from them. It was almost black in there and, though he had expected the panther to follow him, after a few minutes he turned and could not see it anywhere. He stopped where he was, puzzled, scratching his head. Was it possible it had lost interest in him already and was simply going to let him leave without further trouble?

Considering the nature of the beast, which he imagined he knew very well, that seemed most unlikely. Probably it was up to some cunning trick of its own and he might as well let it know that he was onto it. Making a soft clicking sound with his tongue against the roof of his mouth, he dropped to one knee and held out his hand, suggestively rubbing together his thumb and forefinger. "Here, kitty, kitty," he called softly. "Here, kitty, nice kitty. Kitty cat." That should bring it.

And, in fact, it did. The next moment he caught a diamond gleam and the animal padded up to him.

"Did you think I was lost?" it asked him blandly.

"No. Not at all. I just wanted to make sure where you were." So it was not going to let him get away. Well— He shrugged his shoulders and, after giving its head another reassuring stroke or two, asked it, "Shall we go on?"

"If you like. I'll be right behind you. Don't worry about me."

"I won't."

The cat chuckled a little at his tone and he wished it had better taste than to make fun of him, but probably it was too wrapped up in itself to realize how grim his predicament was. After all, his feelings could not be very important to a panther's way of thinking, since they merely dwelt in the same house with its next meal.

He continued forcing his way through the dark jungle, stepping over great roots that came looping up out of the earth and would have tripped him, avoiding the cables scalloped from tree to tree which might have caught him about the neck and strangled him. He would not have believed that anything natural could be so brutally disordered, so sinister and so cruel. There seemed no end to it and he began to fear that he was lost and would never find his way into the open. And, for all he knew, the panther was now amusing itself by letting him go ahead, pretending to be agreeable. If they ever reached the road, that was when it would be most likely to stop playing with him—that was when it would spring, fasten its great sharp teeth into his throat and lie upon his chest, drinking his blood, until he died.

Still, even if that was the animal's intention, it was following pacifically now and he must do what he could to save himself. He had heard that an animal could smell terror and certainly if that was true it knew quite well how scared he was. But he had also heard that terror angered them further, and it did not seem in the least angry. It had even offered a few encouraging words along the way.

He worked hard and furiously, struggling with the jungle, and hours seemed to go by without progress. He was getting weak with exhaustion and fear and rage. Finally, in reckless desperation, he turned. "Why don't *you* help me?"

The animal's voice replied, soft and reasonable. "How can I? I'm down here and you're up there. Unless you want to follow me and crawl on your belly. Anyway, you're almost out."

"I am? Thank God!" He rushed ahead, striking away the branches, one after another, increasing his speed until suddenly he burst into the open and stood once more on the road that led to the Tzanjuyu, past Dulcie's house. He stopped, sweating and tired; the panther sat beside him, waiting, perfectly still and placid. It curled its tail about its front paws and, after a moment, lifted one paw and began to wash it, carefully and delicately. He had a glimpse in the moonlight of its sharp narrow teeth and long pink tongue.

"Let's go," he said.

"Go where?"

"Home. Would you like to come along?"

"Thank you. I believe I will."

He began walking up the moonlit road and, when he turned once and glanced back, it did not surprise him very much to find there was no jungle back there. Only the bougainvillaea-covered walls, turned white by the moon.

I only hope to God, he thought, there's no one awake at the hotel. How in the hell could I ever explain coming in there with a black panther? The panther walked beside him, looking about with interest at the fields and trees and houses they passed, sniffing the night air with obvious enjoyment. Once, it glanced up at him and smiled. Every time that happened he felt a cold morbid chill.

"If only you wouldn't do that!" he said irritably. And the next instant was astonished at how quickly one begins to take things for granted. Imagine talking in that tone of voice to a panther. He must be out of his mind.

"Do what?"

"Smile like that. It isn't human!"

When they were in sight of the hotel he paused and looked down at his companion, hoping it would suggest that it leave now and go back to its jungle. But it did no such thing.

"Will you come in?" he asked it.

"Thank you, I will."

"They won't like it, you know. If they see us. So let's try to be quiet."

"Don't worry about me. I have no trouble being quiet."

It was making fun of him again. "That's right," he agreed. "You don't. All right, then, *I'll* be quiet." He slipped his shoes off and, holding them in one hand, continued on up the path to the hotel. "There's a side entrance. We'll be less likely to meet anyone that way. Follow me."

They crept softly up the stairway, across a sun porch, and down the hallway to his room. Eric's heart was pounding with the fear of discovery. He had not had time yet to worry about what would happen once they got to his room. And then they were there. He unlocked the door and went in, the animal sliding through beside him, caressing his legs.

"Let me lower the blinds before I turn on the light."

He pulled down the shades and switched on the single bulb that hung from a wire overhead. Then he turned around and he and the panther regarded each other. It's such a superb-looking creature, he thought. If only it had been a different kind of beast, neither predatory nor carnivorous, he might have become very fond of it, perhaps have enjoyed keeping it with him as a pet. But what kind of fool must he be to allow himself such a thought? He was amazed to find how easily it had lured him—simply by behaving with this gentle urbanity—into forgetting, even a moment, that he was its next meal. The panther would be going about its business, its muscles rippling and its black hide sleek and polished, with him inside it. He shuddered.

At least, he thought, God has given us one great blessing. When we are in mortal danger, we can never wholly comprehend it. If that were not so, I'd have gone raving mad by now. Or perhaps I have. But, since he could not be sure, he must try to avoid thinking about it. That effort in itself, if he actually applied himself to it, might be enough to tip him over the edge into insanity.

"What shall we do now?" he asked.

"I'd like to sleep," said the panther, and glanced toward his bed. "It's rather narrow, isn't it?"

"Oh, never mind that. I'll be glad to sleep on the floor," volunteered Eric quickly.

"I don't think that will be necessary. We can be quite comfortable together."

Well, then, there was nothing else to do. He must lie down in the same bed with the animal. If it sensed that he did not trust it, probably it would be that much more likely to kill him without wasting further time. For the present, it seemed content to divert itself with him.

Taking one fluid easy bound, the panther leaped onto the bed and spread itself along the side next the wall. It lay there, relaxed and elegant, watching him.

Eric unbuttoned his shirt and flung it away and, as he bared his chest and shoulders, he glanced at the animal and saw it run its tongue across its mouth. I don't even care very much, he thought. I'm so worn out it would almost be a relief not to wake up tomorrow morning.

Still, the thought of lying with his bare skin exposed to the beast's hide, roused a deep repugnance. He had not noticed any wild or obnoxious odor about it, but was certain its hide must give off oils and secretions which, if they once got onto his skin, would never again wash off no matter how he might scrub. He took up a light wool blanket, though the night was warm, and covered himself with it.

"I always sleep wrapped up like this," he explained and, without further delay, switched off the light and lay down, taking care to lie so that the animal was not touching him. They lay perfectly motionless, side by side, for several minutes. Neither of them spoke.

Well, thought Eric wryly, there can't be much doubt but that this is the damnedest tail *I've* ever slept with. And, almost immediately, he fell asleep. He did not actually expect that he would ever wake up again, but he had by now such a complete sense of unreality and detachment that whether or not he lived through the night seemed no concern of his.

He woke to the feeling of a rough moist caress across his cheek and the realization that it was day and the sun had heated the room intolerably. He opened his eyes and looked directly into those of the panther which lay beside him and had been licking his face. He gave a deep hopeless groan and turned his head away.

"You shouldn't have done it," he said wearily, shaking his head. He must have slept soundly, for he could remember nothing, but now he felt dismally tired.

"Done what?"

"You shouldn't have let me wake up to another day of anxiety. Don't you know there's a limit to what a human being can stand? No, I suppose you don't. How would you? You remember how to talk, but apparently you forget everything else."

The animal left the bed in a light bound and took to pacing about the room. "I want to get out of here. You don't like jungles and I don't like houses. Take me back."

"Take you *back?*" he repeated in horror.

"Yes. Take me back."

"I can't—" he began. But, as the animal paused in its pacing and turned to give him a steady gaze, he obediently sat up in bed, holding his head for a moment and staring down at the floor. He dragged up a sigh that seemed to break his heart, and then he stood, slipped his feet into the Indian moccasins, reached for his shirt and began buttoning it. He rinsed his face and brushed his teeth and combed his hair, marvelling at how he was still under the necessity of performing such useless activities, belonging to a different life altogether.

"Come on," he said. "We're sure to be seen this morning."

At the door he paused. "I have an idea. Suppose I

put a leash on you, some kind of rope. That will make it look a little better if anyone sees us together."

The panther smiled and shook its head. "Still worrying about what people will think. Do you imagine that if anyone does see us, they will try to stop us—or even come up close to look?"

"No. No, I guess you're right. They wouldn't do that. Not unless they were crazy."

"And certainly if I took it into my head to bolt, no leash *you* could hold would keep me back, would it?"

"No, it wouldn't. Let's go."

They went out the door and down the hall and, to his intense relief, though he kept looking sideways and backwards, they did not meet anyone. However, he did see Mephistopheles in his sailor suit, sitting on the stone bench staring toward the lake. He took the path behind the bench and walked swiftly, hoping to get by and down the road before he saw them. Three young Indian boys were flinging water from tin cans onto the dry earth. They gave no sign of seeing either Eric or the panther, but that did not surprise him very much since they appeared oblivious to almost everything.

They had passed Mephistopheles and gone several yards beyond when, as Eric had feared, his voice hailed them.

"Doctor!"

Eric turned despondently. The panther paused. "Good morning!" called Eric, cheerfully as he could.

"Good morning, Doctor!"

Eric waited. Mephistopheles said nothing else. Merely sat there and grinned, and waved his arm once. He did not jump up or give a start or even stare as if he saw anything unusual. Eric glanced down at the panther and found it watching the other man steadily. A terrible thought occurred to him: suppose those two were in some kind of league together! It seemed perfectly plausible, now that he considered it.

"Going for a walk this morning, Doctor?"

"Yes, just going for a walk."

He waved and went on, he and the panther, strolling along side by side. They passed two Indian men on the road and neither of them even glanced up but walked by, bending under their heavy burdens.

As they drew near Dulcie's house he had a dreadful

instant of wondering what would happen when she saw him standing there with a black panther at his side. But there was nothing else to do. He jangled the bell at the iron gate and waited. He heard a bustle inside and reached down to stroke the back of the animal's neck as the gate opened and Dulcie appeared. She gave a happy little cry.

"Porphyria!" She reached out and took the white kitten from him, cradling it against her, stroking it and talking to it. Then she looked at Eric. "I was so afraid she was lost! After you went yesterday I looked and I looked and I couldn't find her anywhere!"

Eric stared at her, nonplussed, and then, after a moment, something seemed to slide and resolve within him and it no longer seemed strange that Dulcie was holding the kitten against her cheek and smiling up at him. She touched his arm.

"Come in, Eric. Forgive me for being rude, but I was so afraid she was gone. I kept her locked up the last few days because I know you don't like cats, but Marcia forgot and left the door open yesterday afternoon and I guess she followed you when you left."

"Yes," lied Eric. "She did. I was walking home and glanced back and there the little rascal was. So I took her home with me." Dulcie seemed perfectly well satisfied by that explanation and, the way things had turned out, it might as well have been the truth as what he knew to have actually happened.

He and Dulcie strolled into the patio, the gate clanged shut behind them, and everything was exactly as it had been just before the trees and plants and flowers had begun their monstrous spreading and growing. Once again, the patio was filled with flowers and sunshine; the monkey moved about in the jacaranda tree, sweeping his rope behind him; the parrot hobbled up and down his perch and blurted out one of his numerous complaints from time to time. Dulcie kept the kitten close against her, first petting it, then holding it back in both hands to look at it, laughing and delighted to have her pet again.

"I'm so glad you came early today, Eric." He must have looked puzzled for she watched him a moment, smiling. "Don't you know what time it is? It's only seven-thirty. I just got up." She pursed her lips and touched his face with a quick delicate gesture, full of affection. "You must have been eager to get here."

Eric ran one hand through his blond hair. "Oh, I was."

"We can have breakfast together—won't that be fun? Let's eat out here. I love to eat out of doors, don't you?" She clapped her hands together and Marcia came immediately. "Will you bring breakfast out here for Dr. Thorsten and me, please?" The Indian girl nodded and smiled shyly. Each time they met she embarrassed Eric by the way she looked at him, not quite staring, but as if she were surprised to see a man who looked the way he did, blond and brown at the same time, and so much bigger than the men of her own country.

She turned to go but Dulcie ran toward her with the kitten. "You didn't even notice Porphyria!"

"Oh, she's come back! Oh, señorita, thank God she's back!"

"Take her in the kitchen with you, Marcia. And don't let her out of your sight again." Marcia held forth her hands.

Eric spoke up quickly. "Let's keep her here, Dulcie. To tell you the truth, I've gotten kind of fond of her." It had occurred to him that if he kept the kitten where he could watch it he might be able to prevent it from changing disguises on him the way it had done yesterday.

Dulcie smiled gratefully. "Oh, that's nice. I'm glad you like her better, Eric. She's such a pretty little thing—it does seem a shame to treat her like a pariah."

He stood with his hands in his pockets and his feet apart and drew a deep breath, enjoying thoroughly the feel of air drawn deep into his lungs and slowly released. The day was blue and brilliant and, within the walls, warm and consoling. He watched Dulcie move softly about, smelling a flower here, touching another there, graceful and happy and lively.

She was obviously aware of him watching her but she kept on with her role, pretending to be absorbed in the scents and colors and warmth, moving so that she showed him only her profile. Then all at once she turned. "It must have been a day like this when God finished the world, don't you think?"

As he watched her he felt a slow ache move through

his body, a yearning which became steadily more painful. "I'm sure it must have been."

She took two or three quick steps to bring her before him. "And you and I are Adam and Eve. Oh, Eric, I do love you—"

His eyebrows twisted and he stared down at her with bewildered incomprehension, as though what she had said was some abstruse mathematical formula. "You—" he began slowly.

"I love you, Eric. I've loved you from the moment I first looked at you. But I was afraid to tell you. And then, yesterday, when I did—you were so strange. Didn't it please you, Eric? I've never loved anyone before."

He reached out then and his big hands pressed the back of her shoulders, drawing her close up against him; she was so much smaller that the top of her head came only to his chin. And she let the kitten go, held it in one hand and let it spring to the flagstones. Her arms went eagerly about him and as she sighed he felt her warm breath fan his throat.

"Dulcie, darling, darling—" he murmured. He wanted to say more but something seemed to be strangling him —like the patients he had seen drown in their own blood. The image sickened him and he could not imagine why it should have appeared at this time, when he was happier than ever before in his life.

They heard a discreet little cough and he released her instantly, springing back a step, terrified that her mother had found them. But it was only Marcia, carrying a tray with their breakfast on it. Eric felt such intense relief it made him weak and he turned away, ashamed of his fear, hoping neither of the women had seen it. Dulcie had run to help Marcia clear the table and they were moving things about, arranging the plates and cups, setting down the basket of rolls, the silver coffee pot and bowl of fruit. Then Marcia, casting one more shy look at Eric—who had recovered enough to stand nearby watching them—was gone.

"Now," said Dulcie, happy as a child at a picnic, "isn't this delightful? I've never had so much fun. I always eat breakfast alone. I get up early and Mother sleeps late— because she reads so late at night." She lowered her voice. "She can't sleep well any more, you know." Her voice returned to its usual soft light tone. "Why don't you sit here, Eric, and I'll sit on the edge of the chaise. Here's your napkin. Shall I pour the coffee for you now? Imagine—" She finished pouring and straightened and stood looking down at him, her face glowing with a warm and winsome smile. "Imagine how lucky people are who always have someone to eat breakfast with." Then she sat down.

While they ate she continued chattering gaily and Eric listened, but more to the sound of her voice—which seemed almost like a merry splashing little waterfall cooling some arid place inside him—than to whatever words she said. The kitten played nearby, chasing a stray dry leaf, then dashing about trying to catch the end of the monkey's rope. The monkey entered into the game, too, but somewhat maliciously, Eric thought. For he dangled the rope before the kitten's nose and, when she swiped her paw at it, snatched it away and held it tantalizingly out of reach, snapping his teeth rapidly together and watching her with his wicked black eyes.

Then he lowered the rope again and Porphyria stood on her hind feet, reaching and jumping, dancing back and forth, while he kept it just beyond her. The contest went on for several minutes until all at once Porphyria caught the rope between her claws. Instantly the monkey snatched her off her feet and drew the rope back, to fling her across the garden. But Dulcie was too quick for him. She was there in a flash, plucked the kitten away and scolded the monkey, shaking her finger in his face and telling him he should be ashamed of himself. The monkey sat and watched her, not at all remorseful, and then turned its back and swung into the higher branches where he sat sullenly, peering down at them. Eric observed the performance with amusement and affection, wondering what there could be about such a simple series of events which made them seem meaningful to him.

"The kitten looks like you," he told Dulcie. "Pretty and graceful and delicate." And harmless, he added in his thoughts. But so did the panther look like her. In fact, when you got right down to it, the panther was her. For hadn't Dulcie disappeared at the very instant the panther appeared? There could be no other explanation.

She must be both of them: white kitten and black panther. It was something he should take care not to think about.

Dulcie lay back on the chaise again, sipping her coffee and smiling at Eric, who kept her under his intent gaze. He felt progressively more helpless. I could spend the rest of my life this way, he thought, and was amused by his own resentment at being happy. I don't know how, but she creates some aura of wonderful excitement and absolute contentment. And she takes everything away from me—initiative and independence and everything I've ever guarded and held in respect. She could destroy me—if I let her.

Perhaps it was the garden, so warm and full of perfume and somnolence; so dangerously sensual and evocative. He stood up, making a considerable effort, for he had no wish to move at all.

"Let's go for a walk," he said. "I'll take you visiting."

"Wonderful! Where will you take me?" Apparently she was not afraid that her spell could be cast only in the garden; she must believe it went with her wherever she chose. And perhaps it did. But he might as well know for sure.

"There's a rich Indian down the road I visited once. Let's ask him to show us his collection of masks."

"Yes, let's." She looked as pleased as if he had just offered her the most enchanting gift. She clapped her hands and told Marcia they were going for a walk and gave Porphyria to her, with instructions about how and where she must be kept in their absence. "Tell Mother we'll be back—" She paused and glanced up at Eric, questioningly; then laughed and shrugged her shoulders. "Later."

She turned and walked to the gate and he opened it for her. She went through and he closed it behind them; she slipped her hand into his and they set out together.

For several minutes they were quiet, walking along, breathing deeply the smells of the heat and the dust and the flowers, feeling the nearness of the mountains and lake. From time to time she looked up at him, smiling, and he returned her smile.

"Aren't you happy?" she asked him finally, and her voice had such intensity of joy, it was clear she had asked because she wanted to know that he was sharing it with her.

"Yes," said Eric soberly. "I am happy. I'm so happy I'm—scared."

"Scared? But how can you be scared at being happy?" She had stopped in the middle of the road and now she took hold of his arms.

"You're so young, Dulcie." he shook his head. "If you only weren't so young."

"What difference does that make? I'm old enough."

"Old enough for what?"

"Anything," she said practically. "Anything you can think of."

He laughed. "I suppose you are. I suppose you really are."

"Of course I am. Eric, don't be afraid of anything. Be happy. Be as happy as you can, whenever you can. It may not last so very long, you know."

At those words he felt a shock that made his skin crawl. He grabbed her shoulders and gave her a sudden hard shake. "Why did you say that? What did you mean?"

She looked so small and so pathetically bewildered that he was ashamed of himself. His hands dropped and he took a handkerchief out of his hip pocket and wiped his face. "It's so damned hot," he said apologetically.

She sighed gently. "You're always at war, Eric. With the weather or Porphyria or happiness or time—or me." She plucked a pink hibiscus blossom and held it in her hands, turning it slowly and studying it carefully. "I think you should declare peace, with all of us." She swept one hand out in a gesture which took in the world and herself as well. She was smiling again.

He looked at her, feeling as if all his strength and energy were thrusting from his eyeballs, shoving hard behind them, trying to reach her through them. It did not seem possible she could be as guileless as she appeared. And yet, she had never been anything else. He had watched her carefully, more carefully than he had ever watched anything in his life, for the signs of treachery, the smallest slightest change of tone or expression, some clue that she was wily and perfidious and waiting to find her advantage over him. But her sea-water eyes were so clear, there was no doubt he could see into the depths of them to the very bottom, where the powdery sand moved softly and little fish swam silently back and forth. There was nothing else hidden in their depths; no monsters, no dangerous unknown creature waiting for him to betray himself.

I can trust her, he thought. I know I can. And I must. Perhaps she can save me. But the next thought was the old one: And what if she doesn't? What if I trust her and give her myself and she only wants to make me a captive for her amusement, like that monkey she keeps on a rope in the patio to play with when things seem dull? If she did that to me—I'd kill her.

That thought, slipping out of its leash so easily and confronting him, was a greater shock than what she had said and made him completely forget whatever it was she had done to alarm him. He could not look at her any more and he wiped his face again. She had looked away, too, as if something had hurt or threatened her; and then she turned and walked slowly ahead of him, her head bent.

He watched her, full of anguish, despising himself. It seemed incredible he had grown so rotten that he no longer believed in the possibility of goodness and kindness. He went after her and took her arm, turning her gently.

"Dulcie," he said in a low voice. "Dulcie, forgive me." He could not say what it was she must forgive him for, and hoped that she did not know.

"Yes, Eric. Of course." She lifted one hand and her fingers touched his hair, delicately, with infinite love and trust. "Let's go see the rich Indian," she said, measuring out the words slowly and carefully, like a child learning to talk and taking care with its pronunciation. "Shall we?"

He had a sudden overwhelming impulse to drop to his knees before her, tell her everything he had ever been afraid of or ashamed of, and clean himself out for the rest of his life. He bent and his mouth touched her forehead, and then they walked on, hand in hand.

So this is what it is, he thought. This what it is I've run away from and denied could even exist. And yet it does. He felt almost stunned by the discovery, though he still preferred to think the day was extraordinarily hot.

The rich Indian's house was made of whitewashed adobe, with living quarters opening off two sides of the courtyard and a barn off the third. The family was gathered in the courtyard paved with hard dirt, surrounded by their animals. Three cows stood in the barn, several pigs wandered about, two dogs slept in the shade. The wife was busy weaving cloth and two little girls helped her, while the eldest daughter stood in the sun and combed her long black hair. Except for the occasional sounds of the animals, there was almost perfect silence. Eric and Dulcie entered into the conspiracy of silence and were very quiet, talking softly to the Indian, who showed them his collection of costumes and masks, worth, he said, five thousand American dollars, which he rented at festival times.

Most of the masks represented blond men and the oldest girl looked at Eric and pointed at one of the masks, smiling, while the two younger ones giggled; the father frowned at them to stop their rudeness and they turned away soberly and obediently, but the older girl continued to stand, combing her hair and staring at the visitors.

Eric talked to the Indian at length about the old traditions and festivals, asking many questions, and seemed to wish to prolong their visit. Dulcie showed no impatience. She listened, asked a question now and then herself, wandered curiously about the courtyard and peeked into the barn, and seemed as happy and content as if she had been waiting all her life for just such a moment at this one. She apprently had no wish to get him away and alone with herself again; and when he became convinced of that he suggested that they leave. She smiled and agreed readily. She gave the impression in that as in everything else that she waited for him to decide and that his decision was always pleasurable to her.

The old Indian looked at Eric as they shook hands and spoke to him softly in Spanish. "If she is your wife, you are a fortunate man." Eric blushed and glanced nervously at Dulcie, hoping she had not heard or did not understand Spanish, and they left, waving good-by to everyone. The last time they turned around the eldest daughter was leaning against the wall, watching them, and still combing her long black hair.

On the way back he made up his mind to be rash: He would ask her and not be afraid, either that she would take some advantage of his asking, or that the mere fact of asking—and thus betraying his anxiety—would cause him to hear an unfavorable answer.

"Have you and your mother decided yet when you will go back home?"

"No. We're still waiting for Father."

"How long do you suppose you'll wait?"

"Until it seems safe. He's here now, more and more. If he spends enough time here, we might even be able to get back before he does and keep him out." Then she shook her head. "That's a terrible way to talk about the death of someone you love, isn't it? But we do it all the time," she added, with the air of a little girl confessing that she did all sorts of naughty things and kept right on doing them, too.

"I don't think there's anything terrible about it. You both love him—and he certainly can't ask anything more than that."

"No. I suppose it's the best we can do. I hope there'll be someone to love me, when I'm dead."

"Dulcie!" The sound of his voice was a frightening moan. She turned in alarm.

"Eric! What is it?"

"How can you say such an awful thing? How could you possibly say it?"

She shook her head, gently smiling. "Poor Eric. You're at war with death, too."

"Of course I am!" he said fiercely, angry with her for the first time. "I've spent my life at war with death! How could I be a surgeon otherwise?"

"You told me you'd begun to doubt that you wanted to be a surgeon. You said—perhaps it had been a mistake."

He shook his head, and the heat seemed worse than ever. The sweat was pouring off him, and she looked so cool and fresh and agonizingly lovely. He was suddenly more afraid of her than ever before. He felt sick and feared that he might be going to faint again. He felt as if he might begin to vomit and was sure that if he did all his guts would spill out onto the dirt road and he would die where he was.

He stood there and closed his eyes and clenched his teeth and could feel himself swaying perilously to and fro. He was, he knew, in greater danger than ever before in his life, though he did not know why. Then he felt her lips touch his, surprisingly cool, considering the day's heat, and there was a scent to her breath like every perfume he had ever longed to trace to its ultimate source and take into himself. Her arms went about him and suddenly he grabbed her hard, as if he believed she could anchor him to earth, clenching the back of her hair with one hand, pressing her against the length of his body, trying to press her into him. But, when his mouth began forcing her lips apart, he let her go. It would have been some invasion of her self which he had no right to. It might have made him reckless, and he was as terrified of hurting her as he was that she might hurt him.

She stepped back and looked up at him, smiling a little, and then she gave a quick crooning sound and laid her palm against his cheek. "Eric—that was the most wonderful thing." She was watching him and seemed to be waiting and he stared at her, tortured by desire and some unknown fear.

"I love you," she said. "I love you, and I'll always love you."

He took her arm roughly. "Come on. We can't stand here like this. Someone will see us. Your mother will hear about it. I'll take you home."

"I don't want to go home, Eric. You're my home."

"Dulcie, for God's sake, watch what you're saying!"

She was walking beside him, looking at her feet, and as he said that she glanced curiously sideways at him, and then was quiet once more. They did not speak until they reached her gate.

"I'm not coming in," he said.

"Why?" Then she gave a sudden delighted little laugh. "You're afraid of my mother!" She laughed again and took hold of his hand. "I won't even tell her you kissed me."

He had to laugh himself at that. "Thanks. I think we'll all be happier if you don't."

"Even though I always tell her everything," she added.

"Everything?" he repeated, gently mocking. "In all your long and checkered career?"

"Well, of course there's never been anything like that. But if you'll feel better, I won't tell her. Come on."

Abruptly, in fact rudely, he jerked his hand away. "No. I've got to put in a call. I'm going. Good-by." He had taken several steps when he heard her run after him.

"Can I go with you? I won't listen to the call. And then you can come back here and we'll have lunch together."

He looked down at her, feeling himself completely overwhelmed by her beauty and yielding innocence. there was no possible way to explain how he could need so frantically to get away from her and, at the same time, want to stay with her more than he had ever wanted anything. But the need to escape was greater. Everything inside him seemed to be quivering and pounding and his head was swelling enormously. He must have begun to look grotesque already and, in another moment, she would notice it. He turned, without another word, and set off, walking with long rapid strides. He did not turn once and, though he wanted to run and had the strongest conviction that he was followed by something unbelievably horrible, he refused to give way to his fears. He forced himself to walk. But the strain was so great that when he reached the Tzanjuyu he went to his room and fell on the bed, completely exhausted.

There's probably never been another goddamned fool like me, since time began.

He thought of how amused his friends would be to see him so terrified of a girl like Dulcie. They would not have believed it. And the women who held him responsible, because of his extraordinary looks, for having broken their hearts. He could hear them laugh.

I can explain it all easily enough, he assured them. It's because she's so young. She's so young that I have to be careful not to hurt her—she's more vulnerable because of that and I can't let myself do it. And also, just to be perfectly honest, she's so young I can't trust her. She thinks she loves me, but she's too young to know what the hell she's doing. His friends and the women nodded and smiled and he wiped them out with one brush of his hand, turned over onto his stomach and fell asleep.

He had forgotten to open the windows and woke up soaked in sweat, hanging onto the edge of a troublesome dream, pushing at something which leaned insistently against him. Outdoors was a pale green twilight and bars of fading red low in the sky. He turned over and found the panther lying beside him, though with its back turned, daintily cleaning its fur. He sprang up.

"How did you get in here?" he demanded. He would have been willing to swear it could never happen again.

The animal rolled over in one graceful flowing movement, and lay regarding him. "What difference does it make how I got in here? It's plain enough I'm here, isn't it?"

The damned beast had a kind of infuriating logic—infuriating, no doubt, because he would never have accepted it as logic at all, if it had been less dangerous to him. Such logic was nothing but the power of its jaws and teeth and muscles and the half-sheathed claws which lay upon the rumpled spread.

"She sent you here, didn't she?" said Eric, his tone both accusing and annoyed. He was not trying at all to be placatory.

"*She?*" repeated the panther with a delicate inflection, smiling amusedly.

"Don't pretend you don't know who I mean! Why should we act as though we don't understand each other? I know what's going on and so do you." He went to the washbasin and rinsed his face and neck and then stood before the panther again, drying himself. "I may as well tell you one thing."

"Yes?" said the panther politely.

"Everything's changed since yesterday. I'm not afraid of you any more. I don't care what you do to me. Eat me up if you like."

The panther smiled and eased down once more to lie on its side; its eyes glowed large and fiery in the dim room. It was undoubtedly the most splendid and imposing creature he had ever seen, and there was, in addition to its beauty, something of refinement, a kind of suave civility which, beyond any doubt, made it that much more insidious.

Then he wondered, watching it lie there on his bed, if any of its smell had got off onto him, since, not expecting it, he had not taken the precaution of covering himself. Swiftly he stripped off his shirt and, still somewhat afraid of offending it, whipped it quickly past his nose and drew a deep breath, hoping he had been subtle enough so the beast could not tell what he was about. It was not fear that made him surreptitious, he told himself; only common courtesy. There was no odor he could detect, but nevertheless he threw the shirt into a heap in the corner, then unbuttoned his pants and shorts and flung them on top of it. The panther continued to watch him with courteous interest.

He had taken his clothes off almost before he realized what he was doing and suddenly felt horribly exposed and vulnerable, as if something about his nakedness might rouse the beast's malice or appetite. He turned his back and went to a chest of drawers where his clean linen was kept, took out a pair of shorts and stepped into them quickly, buttoned them, and jerked some slacks off a wall hook. Then he turned around once more, surprised that the absence of clothes could have made such a difference in his feeling of safety. In a way, it was funny—almost as though he thought the animal was a connoisseur, fond of particular delicacies. That idea made him shudder, but he pretended it was only a chill and slapped his arms a couple of times, as if to warm them.

Since he had started off so bravely today, he might as well keep it up. There was nothing to lose, and it had begun to seem even possible that he might, if he were clever enough, dominate this creature, make it his pet, and so deliver himself of it forever.

"I wonder if you expected to find me in bed with someone else," he said, smiling. "Perhaps that's why she sent you."

"You keep talking as if I have no volition of my own. Why do you insist on believing I was 'sent'? Why can't I simply have come myself—to see you again?"

"You took such a fancy to me yesterday, of course."

"Why not?"

"Why not! If you had any idea how foolish you sound—to people, that is."

"You're only willing to accept your own way of looking at things. Perhaps, if you had a little more imagination—" The animal spoke affably enough, but there was also something of amusement and contempt in its tone.

Eric turned away and lit a cigarette. I'll be damned if I'll get into a philosophical argument with that fool cat. I've done a lot of silly things in my life, but that isn't going to be one of them. He sat down in a wicker chair and faced her. As the room grew darker she blurred, her outline became vague and shadowy, and only her eyes continued to glow, constantly gazing toward him, as if she had all the time and all the patience in the world.

"Look here," he said, beginning on a very positive tone, though he was not at all sure what he was going to say. "I think the time has come for us to have an understanding."

"An understanding?" repeated the panther, with an archly humorous look. "That seems unlikely. But tell me what you have in mind."

Eric got up and began to pace the room. Somewhere in the hotel one of the Indians played a marimba and he noticed again how their music, while always plaintive, was never sensual. It sounded particularly strange to him in his present wild company—that sad, austere little melody, meandering haplessly about the halls.

"I want you to tell me exactly what it is you have in mind." His hands were in his pockets and he was wandering up and down, like a man consulting over a business deal or some not very important personal problem. "In regard to me, that is," he added, pausing and looking at the panther, as though he were stipulating one more clause to be included in the contract they were drawing. "Am I likely to wake up any time and find you here? Are you going to follow me and turn up at odd moments, constantly threatening me just by the fact of your presence? Are you going to eat me someday when you get tired of playing this game? Tell me what you're going to do with me."

The panther seemed almost to shrug, then began to lick one of its soft heavy paws, turning it over idly and cleaning the fleshy part. After a few moments, while Eric waited with more irritation than anxiety, it looked up at him. By then he was standing beside it, watching it perform its toilet.

"I'll be truthful. I don't know."

"You don't *know?* But that's incredible! You must have something in mind, and I'll bet you know exactly what it is, too."

"I don't plan my life," said the panther pridefully. "I let things happen."

"That's all very well for you to say, since if they start to go in a direction you don't like, you can always change them back again to suit yourself. Am I mistaken, or are you smaller than you were yesterday?"

"I don't know how I looked to you yesterday."

"Much worse, believe me," said Eric, and turned around and stared out the window. Then he pulled the shades and switched on the light, for he did not like being in the dark with her, even though she could obviously do him as much harm in the light.

"I want to talk to you about a friend of yours," he said.

"Who's that?"

"Dulcie."

"What makes you think we're friends?"

"I met you at her house, didn't I?" he demanded sharply. And then his situation suddenly seemed to him so absolutely absurd that he was convinced he had actually and finally lost his mind. He was talking to a panther as casually as if it were anyone he had happened to meet in a railway station. And, what was even more alarming, he now was speaking to it exactly as he would to a woman who had begun to get on his nerves. Nothing could be more fantastic. And, in addition, he had ceased even to wonder if it was real or imaginary. There was his proof: He had gone insane, just as he had feared might happen when he performed that last operation. Well, at least he need not worry about that any more.

The panther left the couch, pouring itself off, as it seemed. "To tell the truth," she said, "your way of questioning me and looking at things has begun to get tiresome. Don't try to impose your plans and personality on me. Live in the cage you've made yourself, if you like, but don't try to get me into it with you. I've been quite patient so far," the beast added significantly. "And now—I'm leaving you.'"

"You're leaving? You're going away without even being asked?"

"Yes," she said. "I'm going away."

"You don't want me to take you back to your jungle?"

The animal turned its head and smiled at him, as much as to say that he really was a fool. "No thank you." She walked toward the door and Eric moved swiftly to open it for her, but before he got there she had gone on through, disappearing like quicksilver. He unlocked the door with frantic haste and flung it open.

"Will you be back?" he yelled.

He looked up and down the corridor. She was nowhere to be seen and as he stood, staring first this way and then that, Mephistopheles strolled by in his dirty sailor suit.

"Good evening, Doctor."

"Good evening. Did you see a—" Then suddenly he stopped, realizing what he had been about to say.

Mephistopheles was standing before him, waiting politely, and seemed to be smiling. "Did I see *whom?*"

"Not who you think!" snarled Eric, and slammed the door. He washed again and combed his hair, put on a clean shirt and a pair of moccasins and went out. Resolutely he set off down the road toward Dulcie's house. He walked swiftly and was there within fifteen minutes. He jangled the bells and Marcia opened the gate.

"May I see the señorita?" His voice was urgent and he was moving forward already.

Marcia did not answer but bowed her head in the meek submissive way she always had with him, as if he were no human being but one of the stone idols her people worshipped, when they had left their Christian services. She stepped back and he went in.

Dulcie and her mother were seated at a table in the patio, having dinner. Dulcie had turned—apparently at the sound of the bells—an eager expectant look on her face, and now was getting up. For an instant the entire scene stopped still, as if he recorded it, freezing it into something he would remember always:

The table was littered with flowers, red and pink and white hibiscus, bougainvillaea, roses and lilies; among the flowers burned several tall yellow candles. There was no other light but the moon and he seemed to have come upon an enchanted garden. Dulcie was wearing an evening gown which looked like a ballet dancer's costume, with many skirts drifted together in layers, misty gray tulle upon deep red. The bodice outlined her delicate breasts and left her shoulders bare. Three or four bright blue butterflies were strewn across the skirt and one more perched at the edge of her naked shoulder. She was so exquisite that he stood and stared, temporarily lost.

Then the scene went into action again as, with a little cry of delight, she rushed toward him. "Eric, you've come! We'd almost given up hope! Here, sit down. Marcia, bring Dr. Thorsten his soup. Your place is all set. Oh, Eric, wouldn't it have been a shame if you didn't come— I got all dressed up for you!" She raised her arms above her head, fingertips touching, and spun quickly before him.

"It's lovely," he mumbled, and turned to her mother. "I'm sorry if I'm late, Mrs. Parkman."

Mrs. Parkman smiled pleasantly though, it seemed to him, coolly. "It's quite all right, Eric. Won't you sit down?"

He did not want to explain to Mrs. Parkman that he had not known he was expected, since Dulcie must have told her he was coming and then simply trusted that he would. Well— He looked at her. Why not? She should be able to trust the world for almost anything, and never be disappointed.

And, of course, there was the possibility that she had asked him to come to dinner, and even the further possibility that he had told her he would be there at a given hour. Now that he had taken to living in two worlds, one with humans and the other with an assortment of giant cats, it could scarcely be strange if he now and then mixed his dinner engagements.

He took his place and began to spoon up the soup Marcia had set before him. "I had to make some calls to the States. It took a long time," he said, feeling that he must explain to Mrs. Parkman why he was late.

During dinner the three of them talked softly and pleasantly and as Eric looked at Dulcie and her mother, at the table with its litter of flowers and candles, around the patio to the parrot drowsing on his perch, the monkey sitting up a few branches in the tree holding onto his rope and watching them, Porphyria curled in a white ball at Dulcie's feet (the thought passed through his mind that she had hurried home and changed disguises with remarkable speed), at the black outline drawings on one wall, the red and gilt chest beside the door, the carved and painted statue of the Virgin Mary back in one corner—he felt overwhelmed with gratitude.

If this were the end of my life, he thought, I couldn't be happier. I couldn't want anything more than this moment. He looked again at Dulcie and she was watching him tenderly. As their eyes met she leaned slightly toward him and pressed his hand briefly.

"Isn't it wonderful?" she said. "The three of us so happy together." She looked across then at her mother, and they smiled to each other, with what seemed to Eric some profound understanding. Dulcie would create just such smiles and understanding with whomever she met, wherever she went to her life. It was not her beauty alone, but her self, which seemed a perfect tranquil and harmonious whole.

And, as that realization came to him, he felt himself completely desolate, as if an empty future had shown itself to him, beckoning. He shook his head, warning it away. Why should he fear it? She loved him. She had said, only a few hours ago, that now he was her home. He sneaked a glance at her to see if she had changed since then.

Her head was bowed as she ate, the pale blond waves of her hair swinging forward so that he could see only the edge of her profile, the pretty nose and long lashes and curving mouth. No, she had not changed. But he was eager for her mother to leave them so that he could ask her; the mere thought that she might have, had set up an extraordinary clamor which demanded to be resolved.

They drank their coffee together and then Mrs. Parkman stood up. "Will you excuse me? I'm going to write some letters." She extended her hand. "I'm very happy to have known you, Eric. Good-by."

Eric was so glad to get rid of her that he did not, for a

moment, realize what she had said. Then, while Marcia was still clearing the table, he turned to Dulcie.

"Did your mother just tell me good-by?"

Dulcie, who was standing close beside him, nodded her head slowly. "Yes. She did. We're leaving tomorrow."

Eric felt a tight hot band close around his skull and begin to draw tighter. "You're leaving?"

"Yes." She smiled consolingly. "I'm sorry, too."

"You didn't tell me anything about it this afternoon." He spoke tensely, his voice almost inaudible, nervously watching Marcia to see when she would leave for the last time. He would have been glad to pick her up and hurl her across the patio to get rid of her, smash her like a bug against the wall, and he felt almost strong enough to do it.

"I didn't know this afternoon, Eric. We decided later on. Mother says that Father is here too much, so we're going away. Moving about helps her lose him for a little while, at least. Perhaps you don't know what it's like, Eric, but it's very difficult to live with someone who's dead but who won't leave you alone."

"Then you knew you might," he said.

"We might have left any day at all."

"Where are you going?"

"We're never sure. Eric—" She sat down beside him on the chaise. "You look as though you're angry. Are you?"

"I'm—knocked out, I guess. I thought—Dulcie, you said you loved me." He turned to her with honest pleading. "You did say it, didn't you? Or did I imagine that you did?"

She smiled and leaned toward him; one hand stroked lightly across the top of his head. "Of course I said I loved you, Eric. I do."

"Is that why you're leaving? Your mother wants to get you away from me? You've told her?"

"I told her long ago," said Dulcie, infinitely gentle, as if she knew he must be encouraged and protected. "A week ago or more—whenever it was you were sick."

"Then that's why she's leaving. I knew it. But she can't take you, Dulcie. I can't let you go away from me—I love you. It was true what you told me that first day—I never was in love before. But I am now. Completely."

"And you're twenty-nine," she said solemnly, wonderingly. "Such a lot of your life to live without love." She shook her head and sighed softly. "Poor Eric."

"Don't pity me, for God's sake. I've been happy enough. I've been— Oh, the hell with what I've been. That doesn't matter to you and it doesn't matter to me any more, either. But I love you—and I won't lose you."

She said nothing at all for a few moments and then she got up and moved away from him. He sat still and watched her as she stood there, one arm at her side, the other raised with the forefinger touching her lips, looking downward, like a little girl in school who has been asked too difficult a question. And as he watched her, seeing that she had within herself everything on earth he wanted, he felt an agony more intense than he had believed possible. He yearned to possess her, but not as he had possessed other women, or only partly in that sense; he wanted to fold her to himself, keep her with him, love her and protect her for the rest of their lives. It no longer even seemed strange he could be capable of such a wish —it had become absolutely natural, the truest need he had ever had.

They both waited silently for two or three minutes, and then he got up and went to her and took her into his arms, gently. She tipped back her head and looked up at him.

"You do love me, don't you?" she said softly. "And you hadn't thought you could."

"I guess I hadn't thought I could love anyone. I wasn't looking for love."

She smiled sweetly. "You weren't looking, but aren't you glad you found it anyway? Or that it found you? It's a lovely thing to have."

His hands stroked her hair, carefully, and he bent and put his mouth against her throat. He was amazed to find such a capacity for reverence. It's as if I never knew who I was before, he thought.

"You're a lovely thing to have. You're the only thing I know about love, or ever will know. You're all I want to know about it."

He lifted his head and she rested her smooth warm cheek against his, easily relaxed in his arms, her hands lightly balanced upon his shoulders. "But when you can feel love for one person," she said reflectively, "you can feel it for others, too."

He held her closer, profoundly content, filled with gratitude. "I don't want to feel it for anyone else," he said stubbornly.

"But you will, Eric. You'll never be the way you were, again. You won't want to be any more." And very gently, scarcely seeming to move at all, she disengaged herself from him, and stood apart.

He looked at her, studying her carefully, trying to be sure what it was she had meant but refusing, at the same time, to let himself know. Then he decided that since he had come this far, there was no use being a coward. In fact, he could not be a coward now; by recognizing his love for her and admitting it to both of them, he had made it impossible to back into the cave where his life had so far been spent.

"Dulcie—aren't you going to marry me?"

"Marry you?" she repeated, genuine surprise in her voice.

"Of course. You say you love me. I've told you that I love you. Well— What else would we do but get married?" He watched her and his eyes narrowed with suspicion. She had been playing with him, and now she was preparing to abandon him. Don't jump to conclusions, he warned himself. You may have misunderstood.

She turned partly away. "I hadn't thought of that, Eric."

He grabbed her arms roughly and swung her back to face him. "What do you mean—you hadn't thought of that?" His voice was hard with fury, and had grown louder. She raised one cautioning finger to her lips, and glanced toward the house.

"I hadn't thought of getting married."

His fingers pressed into the soft flesh of her arms, and his teeth were clenched. He felt a rage beginning inside him and wished he could warn her, for he knew it was dangerous to both of them.

"Then think about it now," he said, his voice so low it seemed to have been buried inside him. "Think about it now and tell me what you're going to do."

Her face was still turned up to his, and though he felt ashamed and knew that he was hurting her, he would have snapped the bones in her arms if his strength had been great enough. He had begun to feel a terrifying sickness and hatred; her face had blurred, as though he were trying to see her through dense fog.

But she did not complain, seeming to understand that she must let him hurt her, to ease his own pain. "I don't think we should be married just now, Eric."

He let her go, flinging her back with contempt and disgust. "I know what's happened! The most ridiculous thing in the world—your mother has made you promise not to marry me—*just now*." He was sneering and felt that he had become hideously ugly, and hoped that he had. "She wants you to go away with her for awhile and try to forget me and she's sure you will because you're too young to remember anyone for more than a couple of weeks and maybe not that long, because you'll have some other goddamned fool in love with you before then."

Now there were tears in her eyes which spilled slowly out, tracing down her cheeks. She raised one hand and brushed them away, but they kept coming and she did not make the gesture again. When she spoke, though, he realized that she was not crying out of pity for herself.

"My mother didn't make me promise anything, Eric. She hasn't said she doesn't want me to marry you. But I can't leave her just now—not for a few more months, at least. You wouldn't want me to, would you? And Eric —I don't believe it's wise to trust too far the things that happen in another country. Being away from home changes everything too much. But I do love you—and I always will love you. We may be married someday—if you still want to."

"What do you mean by someday?"

"I don't know. How can I tell you exactly? It depends on so many things. On you, as well as on me. And on what happens to us both before we meet again. Eric—" She reached to touch his arm, but he jerked away, as horrified as if he knew her touch would rot him. "Why are you angry? Why does this seem such a terrible thing to you? Why do you look as if you hate me now?"

He made a sound of disgust and turned and walked toward the gate. There he stopped, staring down at the flagstones for several moments, and seemed to feel himself dissolve. I must be dying, he thought, neither alarmed nor sorrowful. And then, after awhile, he saw her again, looking up into his face.

"I should have left the first day," he said. "I must have known then what was going to happen. I wanted to leave and I should have done it."

"But you couldn't, Eric, don't you remember? Something kept you from going. Why won't you accept what you have?"

He looked at her for a long while and then suddenly, to his great surprise, he laughed. He laughed until his insides began to ache.

"This is so goddamned funny! It's the funniest thing I ever heard of in my life! Of course it had to happen. If I was ever going to fall in love at all—it had to be with someone like you. A baby. A pretty little girl," he said savagely, "too young to know what she was doing."

Dulcie sighed and shook her head. "I wish I could help you, Eric."

"Help me!" He laughed again. "Haven't you helped me enough? Good-by, Dulcie." He opened the gate and the bells jangled. He walked through, not bothering to close it, and started down the road. He had gone only a few feet when her voice called him again, pleading and soft.

"Eric—Eric, don't go like this." She ran up to him. "I love you, Eric. You know I love you. I wasn't lying and I'm not too young to know what I'm doing. If you want us to meet again we will. We may only be apart a little while."

Her voice, though still soft, was so intense and urgent that he knew she meant every word she was saying. At least, she meant it that moment. Her eyes looked up at him with submissiveness and adoration, like Marcia's when she pretended he was the idol she worshipped. For that one instant she was as completely his as she could ever be, if they lived a lifetime together.

But she would leave tomorrow, and though she said they might only be apart a little while, he knew that was too far to trust her. The moment she stopped looking at him exactly as she was now, he would have lost her. And he did not believe he would ever find her again.

He stood and stared at her, as if he could absorb her through his eyes, take her into himself and keep her there so that she could never escape him. But as he stared, she changed subtly and slowly and in another instant the eyes gazing back at him were no longer soft and trustful but glowed fierce and fiery, treacherous, cruel, relentless. It was the panther which confronted him now.

A groan began in his belly and came out a hard grunt and his hands reached to fasten the animal by its throat. The game was over between them, the playfulness and visits; this time it had come with lust for his blood. His fingers closed slowly, experimentally, about its throat. He was very very careful as he touched it for he knew that any sudden move on his part would be counteracted by the panther, which could kill him in an instant. But he had taken its throat so gradually and easily that it did not seem to realize what he was about to do and his fingers began to close slowly, his thumbs pressing up under its jaws; he found a strength in his hands he had not known was there. Deeper and deeper his fingers dug into the panther's throat and he felt the life ebb from it slowly, without a struggle. Then, at the last, he gave one sudden swift vicious jerk, and heard the crack as its neck was broken. It grew limp and became heavier, harder and harder for him to hold up. It had died almost with gratitude, he thought, and was surprised to feel as though he had participated in something miraculous.

His arms went about it, tenderly, holding it against him, for he did not want it to slip down into the dirt of the road. He felt he must protect it from that, not soil its black burnished hide, even now. Quite lovingly, he leaned his head against its head and, supporting it with one arm, his fingers stroked across Dulcie's blond hair, which he saw again, as he found that she lay in his arms.

He picked her up and carried her into the garden where he laid her on the chaise. He went back and closed the gate, softly, so the bells would not jangle, and then he knelt beside her. She was as lovely as she had ever been.

I don't think I hurt her, he thought. She doesn't look as if she died in pain. I hope it was easy for her. I wouldn't have wanted to hurt you, Dulcie—you know that, don't you? He felt they understood each other still.

Perhaps, in a sense, their understanding was even more perfect, being final, incapable of any change. And he sat, watching her. Once he reached out, very carefully, and spread her skirt, to make it fall more gracefully. She had put it on to please him. The night was silent.

A door slammed in the house.

He turned his head swiftly, feeling a quick clenching panic, as a sudden howl rose, winding and twisting, like the sound of a monstrous cat in agony. He caught the glimpse of a gigantic tiger just as it sprang, claws extended, saw the great opened mouth and glistening teeth, the enormous crushing body hurtling through the air and then he fell beneath its weight; its claws fastened high into his back and ripped him open. He sprawled beneath it, aware of some vague relief, and felt almost glad it had ended this way. Then he heard, or perhaps imagined that he heard, one final long-drawn yowl: *"You killed my Dulcie . . ."*

THE END

Have You Read These Bestsellers from SIGNET?

☐ **THE CRAZY LADIES by Joyce Elbert.** New York now . . . and the girls who love there. That's what this sexy novel, a candid closeup of the pill-age girls, is all about.
(#Y4122—$1.25)

☐ **THE PRETENDERS by Gwen Davis.** The exciting bestseller about the jet-setters is a masterful portrait of their loves, lives and fears. (#Y4260—$1.25)

☐ **RELATIONS by Johannes Allen.** A successful Danish businessman becomes involved with a tumultuous sixteen year old girl. The book follows the man through the affair to his destruction and gradual rehabilitation. The Danish movie RELATIONS will open in the U.S. this Spring. (#T4215—75¢)

☐ **BITTER FRUIT by Roy B. Sparkia.** A scorching, fast-paced novel of sex in the raw, bound to titillate from the first page to the last. (#T4340—75¢)

THE NEW AMERICAN LIBRARY, INC.,
P.O. Box 999, Bergenfield, New Jersey 07621

Please send me the SIGNET BOOKS I have checked above. I am enclosing $_____(check or money order—no currency or C.O.D.'s). Please include the list price plus 15¢ a copy to cover mailing costs.

Name_____

Address_____

City_____State_____Zip Code_____

Allow at least 3 weeks for delivery

Have You Read These Current Bestsellers from SIGNET?

☐ **THE FRENCH LIEUTENANT'S WOMAN by John Fowles.** By the author of **The Collector** and **The Magus**, a haunting love story of the Victorian era. Over one year on the N.Y. Times Bestseller List and an international bestseller. "Filled with enchanting mysteries, charged with erotic possibilities . . ."—Christopher Lehmann-Haupt, N.Y. Times (#W4479—$1.50)

☐ **LOVE STORY by Erich Segal.** The story of love fought for, love won, and love lost. It is America's Romeo and Juliet. And it is one of the most touching, poignant stories ever written. A major motion picture starring Ali MacGraw and Ryan O'Neal. (#Q4414—95¢)

☐ **JENNIE, The Life of Lady Randolph Churchill by Ralph G. Martin.** In JENNIE, Ralph G. Martin creates a vivid picture of an exciting woman, Lady Randolph Churchill who was the mother of perhaps the greatest statesman of this century, Winston Churchill, and in her own right, one of the most colorful and fascinating women of the Victorian era. (#W4213—$1.50)

☐ **THE AFFAIR by Morton Hunt.** Explores one of the most engrossing and profoundly troubling of contemporary concerns. Morton Hunt allows the reader to enter this secret underground world through the actual words and experiences of eight unfaithful men and women.
(#Y4548—$1.25)

THE NEW AMERICAN LIBRARY, INC.,
P.O. Box 999, Bergenfield, New Jersey 07621

Please send me the SIGNET BOOKS I have checked above. I am enclosing $_____(check or money order—no currency or C.O.D.'s). Please include the list price plus 15¢ a copy to cover mailing costs.

Name_____

Address_____

City_____State_____Zip Code_____

Allow at least 3 weeks for delivery